HYPERNEA

HYPERNEA
THE CURSED KINGDOM

KYLE N.A. BECKER

PERMUTED PRESS

A PERMUTED PRESS BOOK
ISBN: 979-8-89565-455-2
ISBN (eBook): 979-8-89565-456-9

Hypernea:
The Cursed Kingdom

Cover art by Conroy Accord

This book is a work of fiction. People, places, events, and situations are the product of the author's imagination. Any resemblance to actual persons, living or dead, or historical events, is purely coincidental.

This book, as well as any other Permuted Press publications, may be purchased in bulk quantities at a special discounted rate. Contact orders@permutedpress.com for more information.

Permuted Press
New York • Nashville
permutedpress.com

Published in the United States of America
1 2 3 4 5 6 7 8 9 10

To my lovely wife Irina, and to my wonderful sons
Ethan, Alex, and Daniel: May your lives know limitless potential.

The Shadow Dragon Roosts
Obsidian Fortress
The Abyssal Valley
Lunastria
Mt. Kildrat
Noctera
Onyx Wastes
Emerald Sea
Jeweled Islands
Hypernea
Mirrhenian Lake
Laketown
Waverly Castle
Solistrian Forest
Fields of Silence
Stormkeep
Western Fields
Wysteria Swamp
Wysteria

RIUS

CYRRHENIA

TIBERIAN
SEA

AERIS

AINS

ATH

BALDURIA

THORASTRIA

MISERICORDIA

DILUVIAN
STREAMS

N

W

E

S

ISTRIUS
WISE
TAGE

TABLE OF CONTENTS

PROLOGUE

THE DRAGONKING AWAKENS

Deep within the cavernous reaches of the Obsidian Fortress, a dark presence stirred.

It was shaped like a man; yet upon closer look, it struck the perceptive observer as the precise negation of a man. The abominable shape was more like a void than sheer emptiness. If the evil being possessed a spirit, it was so vacuous that it was somehow less than nothing.

The manlike creature wore dark armor befitting an ominous knight. Its black pauldrons each bore three curvaceous blades that glinted faintly in the palest hint of moonlight. The dread shape's massive cuirass was adorned in its center with a column of eight plates of descending size, eerily resembling a dragon's thorax. A dark cape mounted upon its back flared at the shoulders in a menacing wing-like fashion. On the being's head sat a dire steel-cast helmet molded into the mortifying likeness of a great serpent's skull.

This was Dracus Imprimus. The Dread Commander. None other than the dragonking itself.

The Dread Commander rested its blackened gauntlets upon the arms of the obsidian throne beneath him. The preternatural being sat alone in a gargantuan throne room that was carved from a single sheet of black rock. Its red eyes were searching.

While it sat entranced in an altered state of consciousness, drops of water fell helplessly from the rooftop, almost less from the natural force of gravity than from the irresistible spell of the fearful creature. Jagged protrusions of the glasslike stone channeled water from somewhere above the dragonking, and it dripped in an incessant cadence upon the obsidian floor. It was ungodly dark.

Dracus Imprimus was wordlessly pondering, breathlessly waiting, and mindlessly calculating its next attack.

It had once been a man. But it was now in possession of an ancient evil that was beyond the capacity of mortals to fathom. It wielded a force somehow more ruinous than mere destruction: The Never-Was.

CHAPTER 1

THE CURSE

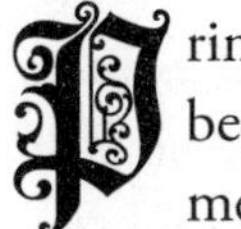rince Sigismund sat glumly near an open window in his castle bedroom. As usual, the eighteen-year-old was hopelessly lost in a melancholy daydream.

It was not the kind of daydream that a child usually indulges in while wasting away another boring day; it was a rather disturbing daydream, the kind one usually shuns the very moment they are overcome by the spell.

The prince, nonetheless, remained deeply immersed in this daydream; one might say that he was entranced by it. Yet, even if he had been asked what the daydream was about, he most definitely could not say. Upon returning to full consciousness, he merely would have shrugged, managed a thin smile, and then gone back to daydreaming, without being able to render a vivid description of what had so captivated him.

All Sigismund knew about this daydream was that it was *dark*. It was dreary. And he was unsure if he would ever be able to escape its grip.

The wintry wind blew ethereally through the open window and whirled up the burgundy draperies. Each sash bore the royal seal of House Waverly: three golden wavy lines wriggling like worms and undulating in the chilly air. But the young man hardly noticed the nip of the breeze, except that it gave him a slightly invigorating sensation that contrasted with his ponderous mood. The draperies' incessant stirring made for a disconsolate effect that mirrored the turmoil within his mind.

His pale, wispy frame reclined wearily upon a high-backed, oaken chair with a red velvet seat. He slowly began to realize that he had been sitting there for *hours*. The young man did not think in terms of time, and thus, he rarely kept track of it.

He suddenly realized it was his turn to move.

Spread out before him was an unfinished game of chess. Two armies of polished, marble game pieces stood in silent ranks before him, one black army and one white army. The pawns waited patiently for his unspoken command. Yet, despite the appearance of a highly contested game, it was clear to the young lad that he was utterly alone. The empty chair that was positioned opposite him was unmoved, bearing silent witness to this contemptible state of affairs.

Sigismund raised his left hand to his temple and began twirling straw-colored wisps of hair between his thumb and forefinger. His brow furrowed as if he were concentrating intensely, although—heaven help him—he did not know why. His high cheekbones were flushed and rosy in the cool air, making a stark contrast with his ivory-hued skin.

"Gaunt and gallant." That's how his mother, the incomparably graceful Queen Galadria, had described him. It was a disputable fact whether *Siggie*, as his mother affectionately called him, was indeed "gallant."

The young prince sat in contemplation, replete in his royal attire of a silken jacket with gold fringe and a high collar.

Meanwhile, in the extended fingers of his right hand, he gently caressed a sleek, black pawn. His thumb delicately traced a curve along its smooth, rounded surface while he unconsciously savored its fine texture. He digested its sumptuous curves with his eyes and sought a deeper meaning, even weighing the possibility that there was none.

While he pondered his next move, Sigismund stood up and walked over to the window overlooking the labyrinthine garden below. He looked out upon the myriad bushes lining the palace walkways, which stood with their crooked fingers upturned in the white glow of the winter sun. From the heights of the castle tower where he was perched, the bushes lining the walkways appeared as thorny crowns thirsting for the triumphant return of the carnelian flowers that signified spring's arrival.

But the flowers would not come, just as they had not come for over a dozen springs prior. He had never seen a rose in full bloom, or a tree in full green splendor, or much of anything of nature as he sat locked in the tower during the day. It was all for his own safety, of course. Or so he was told.

The exasperated young man sighed as if the breath of life itself were a weight upon his weary lungs.

It was, rest assured, not easy to be the prince. The Waverly House had ruled the Kingdom of Hypernea for generations. While Sigismund was the youngest prince of this house, he was undoubtedly his mother's favorite. But King Gerald, his imperious red-bearded father, had most decidedly blamed him for the disastrous plight of the kingdom.

It was his eighteenth birthday, yet no one had visited him. It seemed as if no one in the kingdom had noticed.

Rather abruptly, Sigismund returned to his solitary chess game and placed the black pawn back on the board, taking care to ensure the game piece was in its proper place.

Restlessly, he strode over to a gilded mirror that stood upon a magnificent chest of drawers. Staring into this mirror, the cursed prince contemplated the mystery of what he saw.

His eyes were two black pearls that glistened like darkened jewels lying deep in the fathomless depths of an ocean floor. Only the pale half-moons of sclera on the frontiers of his glossy eyeballs hinted that these were the searching eyes of a human being, and not, as some believed, the dreaded orbs of a demonic being. They seemed to him to be more appropriate to the hideous visage of a basilisk or even to the skulking stare of a gargoyle.

These eyes did not seem like his own. It was as if the grayest storm clouds had been visited upon them, choking out the sunlight that shone upon the fantastic realms of his untamed mind. It was as if his very soul, the essence of his humanity, had been hidden behind unceasing black sheets of rain, without even a lightning flash to momentarily hint at their more spectacular regions.

His pitch-black eyes had always been as impenetrable as the Obsidian Fortress. He was told that after the shrieks of the midwives had quieted following his inglorious birth, the queen had glanced upon the howling creature, immediately soothing and silencing his wails with a piteous and loving gaze. It was only his mother's love that had convinced him that his life was not completely cursed.

But the mystery remained: What was the true source of the curse that had befallen the Kingdom of Hypernea?

Siggie looked away from the mirror. Then he walked back toward his game of chess, which was sitting unmoved near the castle window, and he gazed outside.

The sky was white, marred only by the spectral outlines of barren trees dotting the hills that rolled away from the castle. The leafless trees filled the land with the faint feeling of slow death. The fields were brown and cracked from thirst. It was oppressive and exhaustingly dreary.

Nature herself seemed to no longer care about his homeland. It had all been turned to relentless gloom.

The prince glanced at the wall of books on the other side of the room, beyond his royal bed. These had become his true life companions, and he counted the sagacious authors whose works lined his bedroom walls as his personal friends: The White Druid Prospero, Manfred the Magnificent, and Salustrius the Wise.

The Mighty Three were among the human scholars and storytellers whose wise words were his secret counsel. In their imponderable legends and wondrous histories, he sought to learn the truth about this intolerably cruel world.

Sigismund returned to the chessboard. As he stood plotting his next move, he reached down and lifted the same black pawn that he had weighed in his hand earlier.

It struck him that there must be an inexplicable significance to his next move, an import that he could not put his finger on. It was as if he were being studied carefully by an otherworldly watcher whose judgment of him was hanging in the balance. It was an indescribably eerie feeling, although he had already made his decision.

The tall, blond prince deftly placed the small game piece back on the board.

Instead, he reached his long arm toward the black king. And with a rapid flick of his finger, he knocked it down on the board with an abrupt clack.

"Master Sigismund," a trembling voice declared from the hallway. "You have an important message from the royal court."

What is it? he thought.

He bolted to unlatch the chamber door with a flash of curiosity.

CHAPTER 2

MOONDRAKES

Druix Coldshadow was dreaming a fantastically wicked dream. The moondrake lay in a dark mountain chasm, snoozing quite cozily as moondrakes were known to do.

Awakening from his daylong nap, it immediately seemed to him that tonight would be different. The dragon-like creature stretched his velvety wings and unrolled his long, sinuous, barbed tail. He crawled out of his daytime shelter, strode on four claws and perched on the ledge of a high cliff on Mount Kildrath.

All moondrakes lived on this active volcano far to the north. The lava in its mysterious depths boiled with hot liquid fury. The toxic fumes it emitted were a familiar scent he loved. It smelled like acid death.

During the daytime, the moondrakes slept silently on the mountain in anticipation of sovereign night. The creatures' eyes were so well-suited to the darkness that their night vision could detect the flick of a field mouse's tail a horizon away in a full lunar eclipse.

Druix stood up straight, and his glossy black eyes drank in the ghost-white moon. The stars shimmered like tiny crystals. His head swam as he looked up at the midnight sky. He felt small thinking about the wonder of it all.

The moonlight presented an outline of the sleek face down the slinky curves of the midnight-blue beast. That's right, this moondrake was midnight blue! Perhaps you have read the tales reported by sages such as Manfred the Magnificent that described quite clearly that all moondrakes were black, had silver-tipped scales, and lustrous teardrop-shaped eyes.

But not Druix. This young drake's eyes were black and deeper than the Mirrhenian Lake itself. They had the effect on the viewer of reflecting the contents of one's very soul. They were outrageously beautiful, albeit horrifying.

"Evil morning," his father, Seraphinus, greeted him.

"Yes, of course it's an evil morning," Druix replied playfully.

While he had once delighted in burning the Laketown villagers and turning their lands to a smoldering crisp, it had become tiresome to terrorize humans. It was no longer any fun. The only thing Druix truly enjoyed doing nowadays was flying.

Well, that's not quite true. There was another thing he enjoyed: griffin hunting. Now, *that* was sport!

"On the watch for griffins tonight?" Druix asked in as casual a manner as he could muster. Of course, he knew that they were. This would be only the second night that his father had offered to take him along for the hunt.

Seraphinus strode up next to his eager son. The silver-tipped scales of the elder black moondrake gleamed faintly in the cold light. He stretched his massive black wings into the chilly air and flapped them twice in unspoken assent.

Things had been quiet at Mount Kildrath for too long. Tonight, they would surely feast upon griffin bones.

Griffins were the nemeses of all moondrakes. Nevertheless, although they were hated above all things, an undercurrent of mutual respect flowed between them. It was as if moondrakes and these lion-hawks existed for killing one another.

"Who are we to question nature?" Druix mused to himself. He relished the thought of facing one of the beasts that very night. His eight-chambered heart thumped faster with the hope of slaying one.

The young moondrake looked up at his father, who was his only anchor in the cruel world. His mother had died on a battlefield—Rhapsodia was her name—heroically battling griffins. His mother had been the essence of terrifying grace. She had been larger than even his father was now, and she was a flying terror to any beast unlucky enough to get caught in her path.

It had been nearly twenty solar cycles since his mother and father had flown into war. Druix sighed and looked admiringly upon his father, who suddenly appeared to be lost in thought.

"Dad, tell me again about the Great Griffin Wars," Druix asked in order to get his blood pumping. "This time, tell me the whole story."

Druix's entire being had always been filled with heartache and anger when reliving the tale. It filled him with a quiet fury that fueled his steely resolve. But his father would always give him the main account and spare the details, since they panged him too much to recount. Thus, Druix had gone nearly his whole life dying to know the full story of the battle that claimed his mother's life and led to his own birth.

"All right, son," Seraphinus gulped and slowly began.

"It was a glorious night. It was a cursed day. Dracus Imprimus had commanded his legions of shadow dragons to strike the settlements of mankind in the north. We, the moondrakes, being loyal to the cause of Dracus the Dread Commander, took flight and swept the night with our dark wings, blotting out the stars, and inflicting death upon the scourge of man."

The elder moondrake choked up for a moment. The glassy reflection of his teardrop eyes revealed the deep well of feelings underneath his cold exterior.

"The Laketown men who had settled the Mirrhenian Lake and the miners of the Mountains of Mordrath had gathered their allies, the Griffin and the Equine Kingdoms, as well as the fierce sentries of Hypernea, to press ahead for a final reckoning with the serpents of the north," Seraphinus said, his voice quivering with rising anger. "They meant to wipe us all off the face of the earth!"

A shiver descended down the younger moondrake's spine. It cascaded throughout his slender body.

"As the army marched northward toward the Obsidian Fortress, it was betrayed by the night," Seraphinus continued. "We had already torn their griffin scouts apart wing by wing. We then launched our merciless assault upon their pathetic army on the southern plains of the Onyx Wastes."

Druix imagined the entire fleet of dragons raining death from the skies upon an army struck by terror and confusion, as if they were blindly fighting back against the night itself.

"We first besieged the imperial guards," Seraphinus continued. "They wielded sharp, bronze-tipped javelins. We were dismayed to find them mounted upon armored steeds of spiral-horned unicorn and even on white-winged pegasus! The Equine Kingdoms have long been known to meddle in the righteously evil affairs of the Serpent Kingdoms of the north," Seraphinus said with chagrin. "Gratefully, we have not seen their blessed kind since war broke out among them in the southern land of Wysteria."

Druix became lost in wonder imagining these terrifyingly magnificent beasts. He suddenly desired revenge against these equine creatures, although he had never seen one himself. His father, Seraphinus, gazed profoundly upon the darkened wilderness and then continued his tale.

"Attacking from their flanks, we tumbled their mounts to the barren earth and grasped the most unfortunate ones in our claws in order to drop them from the soaring heights. This served not only to kill the fools, but to demoralize even the bravest warriors in their ranks."

The younger moondrake nodded. Studiously absorbing the lesson being related by his father, he hoped one day to use these vicious tactics in a grand battle.

"And as their pegasus steeds struggled to fly, flapping their wings furiously, their courage led only to more death, as their kind are unsuited to such warfare," Seraphinus said. "Without bronze spears to hurl upon our wings or to pierce our silvery eyes," he continued, while instantly regretting his poor word choice, "the men were common prey. But that left the unicorns…"

Druix shuddered mightily. Seraphinus' voice trailed off after naming the enchanted beasts. While unicorns were not a warlike breed, their mystical nature was feared among the ranks of evil. Attacking unicorns invited calamity. It was a source of corruption to even the darkest hearts to inflict suffering upon these creatures.

"We steeled our hearts and set out upon our fated task—to kill all these…creatures," Seraphinus spoke solemnly. "Yet their pathetic whinnies and miserable neighs spread a wave of panic throughout the moondrake and shadow dragon legions because it introduced them to the most hated of emotions: compassion."

Druix was always fascinated by this part. His was a life that had been lived without this "compassion." The mysterious force had once penetrated the hearts of the moondrakes, he reasoned, but they nonetheless chose to slaughter the mystical unicorns once and for all. That must be because the Dread Commander had decided that all unicorns must never be allowed to return to their enchanted lands of Misericordia, he reasoned.

"Our wings soared upon the night breeze," he continued, "and we circled above them ominously to hide our lines of attack. We swept upon them from the rear, avoiding their pearly horns, and sliced open their tender flanks with our razor-sharp talons.

"They collapsed to the ground, blood gushing from their heavenly hides, as they moaned and gnashed their teeth," Seraphinus said. "Even as they cried out in their incomprehensible tongue for help from their unicorn brethren, we rendered their flesh without mercy. Our blood ran cold as icy rivers, and we ignored their desperate pleas."

Druix looked up at his father, who was now hanging his bearded head in anguished remembrance. His horns pointed defiantly toward the sky like sharpened spears.

"The battle had been won," he spat mournfully. "The bronze-tipped javelins that had been showered upon our brethren, mangling their wings and downing them upon the cruel earth, had begun to fall uselessly to the ground. Their wails filled our ears with a symphony of death. Their shrieks of terror emboldened us to commit merciless atrocities with the aim of ending it all. Our mighty dragonlike claws then ripped their hopes of conquest to shreds.

"But then, our Night of Victory turned to ashes," said Seraphinus bitterly. "The hated light of Dawn peered over the distant Mountains of Mordrath...and that is when the griffins counter-attacked."

At last came the moment Druix had been dwelling upon since that fateful day: What had been his mother's true cause of death? It had always stuck in his side like a griffin's claw. Who was truly to blame? It was a tale of woe that the moondrakes blamed on their fierce rivals, yet it was also one of treachery and betrayal.

"As our eyes strained to see through the painful rays of light, the armies of men and griffin rallied. The emblazoned sigils of their armies inspired the warriors to push on through the bloody hellscape that had emerged after dawn. The sound of their trumpets blared; griffins screamed their eagle-cries into our ears; the clangs of polished metal rang out; and the war cries of men filled our ears. The battle turned, and our dream of a final victory was dashed."

Seraphinus looked over at his son, Druix. He let out a weary sigh that hung in the cool night air. "That was when your mother, the wondrous beast, was killed on the battlefield," he said.

"But...how?" Druix asked.

The elder drake looked up from his gloomy posture with a stoic expression.

"She had been engaged with three griffins, who had been trying in vain to down her," Seraphinus said. "Your mother battled fiercely and mangled the vicious creatures with her claws. She intimidated them with her fiery breath. Rhapsodia truly possessed the heart of a drake.

"But at last, the unthinkable happened," Seraphinus sorrowfully continued. "The Dread Commander issued an unimaginable curse on the battlefield that provoked all creatures within its purplish-blackish aura to clutch at their hearts in agony and instantly lose their senses and their spirit. While our beloved, fearsome Rhapsodia gasped and grasped at her thorax in pain, a bronze-tipped javelin sailed through the air and ripped through her wing. She shrieked in agony—the most heartbreaking shriek you could ever imagine! Your mother fell to the ground, wounded, but not defeated."

Druix remained fixed on his father's every word and focused on his every expression. He absorbed the tale as if it were the somewhat smoky air around him.

"After I watched in horror as your mother fell to the earth," he said, "I abandoned my own fight and sped with the greatest haste through the aerial warfare. Through thrown spears, past snarling griffins, and over the clashing soldiers, I flew, only to find that I was too late. But I was not too late to rescue you.

"As she lay there dying on the battlefield," he continued, "her pitiful wails were heard by all in her vicinity. She was approached by several white unicorns, whose powerful magical charm healed wounded animals and performed minor miracles. The equine beasts gathered around, their heads bowed, snorting furiously, and raising their forelegs in a kind of summoning dance.

"While I hovered above them, watching with confusion at this sacred ritual, I realized at last what was taking place. Your mom was giving birth. I looked down through the excruciating glare and saw a bluish-gray egg leave your mother's body. Her last breath then left her shattered form.

"Not a creature on Solarius dared stir at the austere moment while witnessing this auspicious event. I swooped down among the stunned attackers, grasped the egg—your egg—and flew it to safety. That is what Rhapsodia would have wanted," he said, looking with pride at his son.

Druix felt a surge of conflicting emotions—sadness, honor, loss, and anger, all at once. Whoever did this to his family would have to pay dearly.

"So, the unicorns...saved my life?" Druix asked with disbelief.

"As much as it pains me to confess it," Seraphinus begrudgingly admitted, "indeed, they did. But that is not the end of our story. As the sun's warm rays began to fill the morning sky, the soldiers' bright-colored banners of burgundy and green, adorned with their hated golden sigils, were now waving defiantly upon the ancient battlefield," he continued.

Then he whispered a most dangerous phrase upon the softly blowing night wind.

"That is when Dracus Imprimus chose to betray us."

Druix looked upon his father with stunned alarm. He could sense the pain in his voice, as well as the peril that arose as he spoke unfavorably of this blackest of names—even if it was the truth. Precisely, perhaps, *because* it was the truth.

"Yes, it was on that terribly bright day," Seraphinus pronounced, "that our Dread Commander opened a portal and retreated to the Obsidian Fortress, which lay far beyond the Onyx Wastes."

The moonlight had grown pale. It was thinly veiled by puffs of smoke emanating from Mount Kildrath.

"But father," Druix meekly asked. "Does that mean the Dread Commander is…"

The elder and younger moondrakes exchanged knowing glances. Silence was his answer.

But alas, in the darkest shadows of a distant fortress, an otherworldly presence was listening. It was *always* listening.

CHAPTER 3

AENYX'S PRIDE

Aenyx lay cozily with a bright golden sunbeam shining down on his glorious feathery mane. The griffin was sound asleep with his tan wings spread wide in his well-feathered nest. Yet in the midst of his ostensibly comfy nap, his lion-like legs were twitching as if he were chasing fresh prey. Inside his eagle's breast, his heart thumped rapidly.

Despite what one might think from outward appearances, the sleeping griffin was imagining that *he* was being chased. Another nightmare. And yet the night, as he was coming to realize, was long over.

The griffin opened his eyes slowly and looked up through the bright blue skies to behold the glaring rays of the morning sun. It had all been simply a dream, he concluded with satisfaction.

Relieved, the snoozy griffin blinked his beady black eyes twice, then tucked his hooked beak under his wing. He was returning to his mid-morning nap when he suddenly realized the meaning behind the portentous dream.

"The Griffin Trials!" he recalled with great alarm.

Aenyx sprang to his claws and paws. Then he burst from his feathery nest on his mighty lion-like legs and gave a fearsome war screech that echoed throughout the valley below. He took immediate flight into the limitless skies to hasten toward the griffin proving grounds.

All young griffins had to pass the Griffin Trials in order to become full members of a Pride. Their Pride assigned them their roles in Aeris's society. He was going to be a Stormguard. That meant the soldier's life for him. He had known this his entire life, as he had been assigned his destiny shortly after he was hatched, based on his tawny gold feathers and strong body.

But there was a "flaw" in his makeup: Piercing black eyes. This is what made him a "Redmark." That was the derogatory name given to any griffin with a "flaw" in his physical makeup, such as spotted feathers, five claws, and so on.

If a griffin passed the Trials, however, they became fully initiated as a member of a Pride. That meant rank and privileges. He would finally be somebody, and nobody could hold his Redmark against him. Aenyx ascended higher and higher into the big, blue sky. He flew with maximum speed toward the summit of Mount Rhaemor. The lion-hawk soared over the alpine forests and burbling brooks. As he sped above the rocky terrain, herds of mule deer looked up at him nervously. He spotted the ominous Mountains of Mordrath in the northern distance. While he gazed upon their dread gray peaks, they reminded him that this was all about fighting the serpents.

As the griffin swiftly glided, his eagle mane and feathery wingtips began fluttering in the chilly mountainous air. Flight was one thing that made Aenyx feel like he could be himself. Only the skies felt like home to him.

At last, on the eastern horizon, Mount Rhaemor appeared! The tri-peaked mountain radiated majesty. As seen from above, her slopes were carpeted with dark green forestry, leading up to snowy caps. The crystal blue ocean of surrounding air smelled as fresh as the purest scent imaginable. Mount Rhaemor truly was the crowned jewel of the Republic of Aeris.

Normally, Aenyx would marvel at the magnificent view, but this was not the time for sightseeing. No, Aenyx was relishing something quite different: the guilt the Pridemasters would feel when he finally won! Thinking about it sent a thrill through his muscular body—all the way from his white eagle mane to the tip of his lion's tail.

The pageantry coming into view below took his breath away. The griffins' full regalia could be seen from great heights: The towering flags of white and blue were for the Whitecrest Pride, those wise stewards, lined in rows along the ancient terrace. The yellow-and-green flags of the Pridewatchers flew for the caregivers of the griffin young and watchers of the Golden Hatchery. The silver-and-blue flags of the Bluetip Pride signified the clannish foot soldiers and scrappy working-class griffins. The black-and-gold flags stood for the Goldeneyrie, a secretive class of counselors and diplomats. And last, heralded by an emblazoned red-and-white sigil, there was his future pride: the Stormguards. These were the elite sentries of the Republic of Aeris.

Aenyx descended to join the throng that had gathered upon Mount Rhaemor. He flew to the farthest extent of a burgundy-and-gold-fringed carpet that led to five marble-carved thrones resting upon a raised open-air terrace. The thrones were like pedestals that curved forward for the griffins of appropriate stature to rest their claws.

The Five Guardians watched from the thrones. And their expressions were not ones of approval.

The Guardians were the respective leaders of each Pride and the exclusive members of the Lofty Council. They watched over Aeris as enlightened rulers. They did not own property, and like all griffins upon Aeris, any of their griffin eggs were mixed in with the rest at the Golden Hatchery, so they would never truly know their offspring.

Their life was demanding, but noble. They lived only to promote justice. Or so went the griffin legend.

Now, Aenyx was especially interested in being a Guardian, given that Redmarks like himself weren't wildly popular with the Pridemasters. He had always been treated as an outcast in a society where status meant everything. He would show them.

Aenyx's late arrival to the Trials was thus met with extreme derision, but what was considered to be most outrageous was his audacity to approach the Five Guardians.

Aenyx lifted his wings, fluttering them to slow his descent, before lowering himself beneath the thrones of the Guardians. The audience members perched in the forum, consisting of the very young and the elderly, gawked in amazement at the recruit's hubris. Standing at attention, the members of the various prides stared at him in dismay. The eager recruits standing on the outskirts of the arena expected swift retribution.

The Guardians' expressions were truly priceless.

"Dear Guardians," Aenyx declared with a bow, "I have come to state my loyalty to the Republic of Aeris and to humbly introduce myself, since I plan to win these Griffin Trials and someday join your ranks!"

Sophia Pridewatcher, the pious, bronze-maned matriarch, appeared ready to faint. She held her brass scepter aloft as if to ward off the fowl intruder. Savagiras Bluetip looked ready to beat him bloody. Tyrex Goldeneyrie sneered contemptuously. And Captius Whitecrest, well, he puffed up like a frightened peacock.

"Will you wipe that smirk off your beak?" Sophia Pridewatcher blared at Aenyx.

Phoenix Stormguard spoke to put an end to the uncomfortable scene. "If you will now join the Stormguard recruits, young Aenyx," he announced, "we would be greatly indebted to you."

There was a sarcastic edge in his voice, but his eyes betrayed a slight twinkle of amusement. Now would be a graceful time to make an exit.

"At your service, Master Phoenix," he replied. He briskly made his way to the red-banner section of recruits standing at ease behind the rows of Stormguards.

The Stormguards painted the picture of fierce warriors. Their red-feathered bronze helmets were attached by a strap buckled tightly below their beaks. Their gauntlets were fixed above their forearms and extended to their sharpened eagle talons. Their pointed beaks were capped with shiny steel. And steeliest of all was the glare they shot at Aenyx as he filed in behind them.

"That was quite an entrance," his friend Ronax whispered and laughed.

Aenyx found his spot and stood straight, straining hard not to laugh.

"Today, we commence with the Griffin Trials," a white-painted griffin herald bellowed from the edge of the burgundy carpet near the watchful eyes of the Guardians.

"Let's get it onnnn!" a Bluetip recruit shouted.

The entire Bluetip Pride began hooting like a parliament of barn owls, and the recruits flapped their wings in approval.

The Pridewatchers looked on in disdain, and the Stormguards simply rolled their eyes. Typical Bluetips. No discipline.

"All right, all right, settle down, Bluetips," Savagiras implored his pride with a chuckle. Sophia Pridewatcher shot him an electric look of furious offense.

Phoenix Stormguard arose from the central throne and held his gilded staff aloft. At its head was the kingdom's emblem, a red shield bearing a lion, which was flanked by two eagle wings.

"Let the Trials begin!" his voice boomed, and the clarion call echoed throughout the mountain air.

CHAPTER 4

A MESSAGE FROM THE QUEEN

igismund surged forward with anticipation to unlock the door. His heart jumped in his chest, and a lump welled in his throat as he imagined what it could be.

"Prince Sigismund, I say, do open up!" an out-of-breath voice bellowed between huffs and puffs.

He knew that voice. It was his old tutor, Sir Reginald.

Sigismund stumbled over his slippers and tripped toward the door. The young man gathered himself, briskly unlocked the door, and swung it half-open.

Reginald burst in with his typical blustery style, nearly knocking the young man over.

"Sigismund, I say, what took you so long?" Reginald demanded.

His face was uncharacteristically red and flustered. The tall, elderly fellow stroked his long, flowing, white beard while he examined the young man. And then, with a brisk rustle of his long blue robe, he slammed the door behind him. With his bulbous eyes wide open, he studied the room. Sigismund shrugged.

"No matter. Urgent business, boy, urgent business," the scholarly old gentleman said as he removed his soft cap and made his way to sit on the edge of the royal bed.

"Sit down," he intoned with urgency. "There is a matter that requires your utmost attention."

After Sigismund sat down, the elderly man took a deep breath and looked sympathetically at the young man.

"Son, I don't want you to take this the wrong way," Reginald began with pain in his bloodshot eyes. "But your father is *quite* mad."

Sigismund nodded with full understanding. This was one of the unfortunate truths he had to learn early on in life.

"Your father has gotten it into his head that *you* are the source of all the evil in this godforsaken land," Reginald said. "He long ago promised your mother that he would take no rash action against you until your eighteenth birthday. But if on that day, the kingdom of Hypernea was still afflicted by this interminable plague, then he would consider taking a more…extreme course of action."

"*Extreme*?" Sigismund choked out.

"My boy," the old man replied nervously. "You know that we have prepared for this, and that the queen and I—we have taken precautions against the worst…"

"The worst, meaning…" the young prince prodded.

"You know what that means, Sigismund!" the old man said with a tone of finality. "Damn it, don't make me say it! The king feels he is out of options. His royal treasury is exhausted, and the clans are clamoring for someone's head. The MacCallisters have been particularly insistent—"

"The king, I mean, my father," the prince stammered in disbelief. "He wants to *murder* me?"

"Well, one wouldn't call it a *murder*," Reginald said meekly, a defeated look in his eye. "Since he's the king, he would make it official. It would actually be called an execution."

"An *execution*?" Prince Sigismund cried. Fear rose in his voice. "Has he decided on this for certain?"

"Well, that is why I am here, good lad," Reginald replied. "He is expected to make his determination at the feast tomorrow. Oh, and that quite reminds me..." The elderly man sat on the edge of the bed and fumbled through his pocket. "I have something for you. It is from your mother, the queen."

Reginald handed him an off-white envelope sealed with red wax and bearing an imprinted stamp of a rose.

"Well, well, well," Sigismund muttered to himself while studying the letter intently. "This is *quite* the birthday."

The prince strolled to the dressing table and withdrew a silver letter opener from a little wooden drawer. The envelope was sealed with red wax, which he sliced open and slid the letter out. He unfolded it carefully. It bore a welcome message lovingly written in a familiar, cursive hand. He read it aloud:

> *"Dear Prince Sigismund: Happiest of birthdays! You have been formally invited to the Waverly winter feast, which is to be held in anticipation of the coming spring. It will begin at the ninth hour tomorrow. I will give you a wonderful present there. Come and be merry!"*

It was such a grand handwriting style—both graceful and affectionate. There was no need for him to see the signature of his mother, the Queen Galadria, but he adored its sweet imprint. The letter's fragrance was her favorite scent—lilacs. The perfume filled his nostrils with a reminder of her presence. Siggie sighed with an ache and set the letter down on the chest of drawers.

"Of course, your mother could not express her worry and alarm in this invitation," Reginald said as Sigismund stared out the window. "You see, she is already making plans for your escape. Tomorrow, at the Winter Feast, you shall be watched carefully and contacted by a trusted member of the queen's secret service. Many refer to him quite derisively as the 'Kindly Knight.' That is all the information I have for you now. I urge you to start implementing those lessons we have been teaching you for nearly eighteen years. Start preparing now."

And with that, Sir Reginald stood, and with a rustling of his robe, he strode over to the prince, who was looking out the window. The long-time tutor placed a wrinkled hand upon the young man's shoulder. After a brief moment, he walked away, slowly closed the door behind him, and departed. Sigismund didn't turn around. He merely stood, gathering all of the courage that he could muster.

The night deepened. Slowly, it seemed like the prince's unblinking black eyes were absorbing the darkness of his room. His body felt stiff with apprehension. His breathing became shallow and rapid. He struggled to comprehend what he was experiencing. He had to believe everything would be all right in the end. It *had* to be!

Sigismund's eyelids grew heavier and heavier before sheer exhaustion pulled them shut.

He found himself abandoned in a desolate, faraway land, as a grim sense of foreboding overwhelmed his senses. He was suddenly in the company of all manner of strange, mystical beasts, and they were depending on *him* to lead them. But at the moment of truth, he lost courage, and he was too afraid to act. Perhaps he would die after all, and hundreds and thousands of living creatures with him…

Then a *real* night terror woke him.

Sigismund's black eyes opened. He could not believe what he saw—it hardly seemed real to him. He flinched and rubbed his eyes but remembered reading somewhere that it was best not to make a move in such a situation because predatory beasts responded to sudden movement.

Instead, he blinked. What he beheld was not any manner of sleepy-headed illusion, the kind one might see through groggy eyes. No, he was face-to-face with a mortifying, stupefying, blood-chilling vision of a *dragon*.

Its monstrous outline was suspended in mid-air above him. It hovered there—an unspeakable, ethereal presence that appeared to be formed of smoke. Two devilish horns protruded from its hideous skull. Sigismund wondered if the dragon might actually be an illusion composed of shadows. Certainly, a real dragon had not actually come into his bedroom.

He gulped hard and blinked his black eyes twice. *It was still there.*

The dragon's hollow eyes flickered with internal fire that licked the rims of its oval orbits. Its gaze caressed him menacingly and seared his very soul. He felt its hot breath burn upon his brow, which was now covered with beaded sweat. Worst of all was the inexpressible hatred he sensed while staring back into the void of its relentless gaze. Sigismund stared into a force that was beyond evil.

The dreadful serpent slowly opened its gaping maw as if to emit a soundless scream and it lunged forward to engulf him within its blackened form.

Sigismund could not imagine this being the last thing he would ever see. The prince closed his eyes, and he heard a gasping sound that he thought would be the last one he'd ever hear before becoming a dragon's dinner.

Then, suddenly, it was gone.

CHAPTER 5

GRIFFIN GRAPPLING

Aenyx made his way to the Stormguard recruits with nervous anticipation. He had been waiting for this moment for years. Eighteen to be precise.

"Hey, you black-eyed freak!" a voice shot out from the Goldeneyrie recruits as he walked by. It was Gabriel. "You scared yet?"

"Not as scared as the Pridewatcher was in the moment you hatched," Aenyx retorted.

The crack drew a few cackles from the Stormguard candidates who were within earshot.

"Form a circle around the grappling pit, you mangy recruits!" a Pridewatcher shouted.

The first event was called the Griffin Grapple and was as straightforward as it sounded: Griffins engaged in single combat in recessed grappling pits until one emerged victorious.

There were multiple ways to win a point in the grappling match. One was a clawed pin for three seconds. Another was outright submission, done by a triple wing-tap. If a griffin fled beyond the boundaries, their opponent gained a point.

But there was another way: the feather-pull. If a griffin was able to pull a feather off their opponent, they won the round. The first griffin to gain three points won.

The Stormguard and Bluetip recruits gathered around the eastern-most grappling pit. In the center was the Pridemaster Jasper Stormguard, who would referee the matches between the recruits.

"Listen up, you wannabes!" Jasper Stormguard belted out in an overly dramatic military voice.

"You are going to enter this grappling pit as a bunch of snot-nosed fledglings," Jasper Stormguard shouted with utmost urgency, "and you are going to leave here as griffin warriors!"

Aenyx happened to be standing right behind the Pridemaster.

Jasper Stormguard's eyes wandered up toward the Guardians and then scanned the crowd around him.

"Aenyx!" the Pridemaster yelled as he whirled around and pointed a singular claw at him. "Since you have an obvious surplus of enthusiasm, you just volunteered to go first!"

Aenyx scoffed. This was one way to get the full attention of the Guardians.

"Now, now, let me see…" Jasper continued, stammering. "If we really want a fair match for a griffin of your boundless energy, we need an opponent with formidable physical skills. Let's say, for example… Bartholomew of the Bluetip recruits!"

"Big Blue!" the opposing team's recruits yelled in unison.

Aenyx knew the oaf well. He bowed to the Pridemaster with well-faked regard, then prepared to enter the center stage.

Bart was an overstuffed griffin who stood nearly a head taller than Aenyx when on his hind legs. He made his way into the arena looking like a fat brown rooster crossed with an obese alley cat. Aenyx looked up at the Guardians. His black eyes met Sophia Pridewatcher. He gave her a knowing wink, and she gasped so dramatically that it seemed she would faint.

"All right, take to your sides!" Jasper shouted.

"Slashing time, punk!" Big Blue shouted at him from across the pit.

"Ahh, yes, it is!" Aenyx shouted back. "For you!"

The Bluetip recruits opened their yellow maws wide and began howling with laughter. The raucous griffins bounced up and down on their gray-painted legs while flapping their wings in hysterical excitement. The ruffled ruffians fully expected to see this mouthy upstart skinned alive. Aenyx looked up in mild bemusement at the bird-brained fools.

While Aenyx wasn't the biggest griffin, he was certainly one of the fastest. And what he lacked in brute strength, he made up for in cleverness, fearlessness, and fighting fundamentals.

"Watch this," Ronax said, turning to another Stormguard recruit named Brandon who was also standing in the front row at the edge of the arena.

Jasper Stormguard held up his left talon to silence the crowd. The mountain breeze stirred the feathers on his tan chest. The stodgy veteran soldier looked over to the far side of the grappling pit at the screw-eyed Bartholomew. The large, mangy, menacing lion-hawk threatened them in the late morning sun.

The Pridemaster then looked directly into Aenyx's black eyes with an odd, smug expression. He held up his right talon to signal that the start of the match would be coming soon.

Aenyx paced along the hard mountain rock and felt its smooth surface, weighing its characteristics for advantage. He peered at Big Blue's demented supporters, who were jumping up and down like a bunch of uncouth chicken hawks.

Then he glimpsed the Guardians, whose makeshift thrones were brought to the edge of the arena. He savored their eagerness to see how the impudent griffin who had interrupted their Trials was stomped into submission. This was precisely the kind of audience he wanted. One that would be *disappointed.*

"Ready?" the referee said, while still holding up his talon. The audience members seemed to hold their breath. All eyes were on him.

"Begin!"

Big Blue, who had been seething in mindless fury, sprang immediately into a hard charge as if his tail had been lit on fire. The sound of thumping lion paws grew louder in Aenyx's eagle ears.

The spectacle of a brutal clash seemed imminent to all, but Aenyx thus far had refused to budge. The crowd was unsure if he was exceedingly brave or simply too petrified to move. Nonetheless, Aenyx surprised all when he suddenly dropped and fell into a heap like a coward. Even Jasper, a seasoned referee, was confused.

The seemingly desperate maneuver only emboldened Bart. In a mindless rage, he careened across the pit with the sole aim of obliterating his challenger.

"*Aaaawwwrrreee*!" Bart screeched as he prepared to ram Aenyx into the dirt, but at the last moment, Aenyx leapt straight into the air. He flapped his great wings for a few moments, and Big Blue went barreling out of bounds, up into the Stormguard recruits. The tremendous crash sent griffin feathers flying into the air. It caused such an immense screeching commotion that recruits were sent tumbling in all directions, like pins in a game of dragon-egg bowling.

Jasper Stormguard looked over at the ridiculous spectacle and shook his head in frustration.

"Point, Aenyx of the Stormguard recruits," he reluctantly declared.

Aenyx's friends gave out a smattering of cheers, but the majority of the crowd rolled their eyes in disgust. Meanwhile, Big Blue was rolling back and forth on the ground, futilely trying to get his rotund frame upright.

"Get your claws off me!" he shouted angrily at the Stormguard recruits, who then shoved him back into the arena.

Aenyx watched in complete amusement while he cooked up his next stunt.

The humiliation of the big bully's pride had proven to be a powerful provocation. Bart was filled with outrage as he fumed in the cold mountain air. It was bad enough that he lost one round to the smaller Stormguard recruit. What if he lost the match and lost out on his dream of becoming a Guardian? This, indeed, meant war.

"Ready?" the referee asked loudly again, checking on Bart. A stream of blood trickled out of his golden beak and dripped onto the slab of gray rock. He gave an infuriated nod. Jasper glanced over at Aenyx, then gave the signal.

"Begin!"

Big Blue now marched at his enemy from across the ring. The over-stuffed griffin's lion paws struck the ground. *Thump-thump, thump-thump.*

But then, to the surprise of all, Aenyx charged. He galloped at Bart with a steely resolve that caught the brute off guard. When it seemed as if the two combatants were going to smash into one another in a massive collision, Aenyx took the crowd's breath away by falling backward into a slide maneuver. With his paws spread wide, he clipped the outside legs of the beast as he slid beneath his opponent. The beast fell like a sack of rabbits.

"Yes!" Ronax burst out. Everyone else in the arena was too stunned to react.

Big bad Bart's body lay in the middle of the arena, writhing in agony as his legs bled. Aenyx walked confidently over to his opponent and plucked a single blue feather from the back of his right wing. The referee had no choice but to award him the round.

"Point, Aenyx!" Jasper announced to the stunned crowd.

When Aenyx looked up, he could see the gross disappointment in the eyes of most of the Five Guardians, particularly the perpetually offended Sophia Pridewatcher. But unexpectedly, he saw Phoenix Stormguard beaming with pride.

Bart struggled to his paws, his legs wobbling beneath him. Many would assume that the match would soon be over, but Aenyx knew better. The worst mistake a warrior could make was to underestimate his opponent.

"Ready?" Jasper asked Bart. The grizzled Pridemaster appeared concerned.

Both nodded in assent.

The signal was given. "Begin!"

Bart stood resolutely, now waiting for his opponent to come to him. Aenyx hesitated, then decided to oblige him.

Aenyx gathered speed and launched into flight. He glided toward the wounded savage and banked hard left in an attempt to flank him. Bart pivoted to track Aenyx but remained on the ground. Aenyx soared to his left in a circular pattern, as if trying to get behind his opponent.

Bart had to keep Aenyx in front of him, but it was difficult rotating his fat griffin body, especially on his hobbled legs. The more Aenyx swirled above him, the more he pivoted. It would be risky to take flight now, so he kept moving. And moving. And moving.

The crowd was growing restless. Bart's head was spinning, and his legs were faltering. Above him, Aenyx flew. Growing impatient, Bart decided to take flight.

That's when Aenyx struck. He swooped in with his back paws to bash his opponent's head, but Bart was ready, and he grabbed the paw in his left talon. Aenyx attempted to fly away, but Bart wouldn't release his grip.

"Come here, little birdie!" Bart said in a gruff voice.

The Bluetip recruits were now cheering loudly. The Guardians were on the edges of their thrones. Sophia Pridewatcher flashed a smug expression. Phoenix Stormguard was enthralled. This was the moment of truth.

Aenyx suddenly stopped flapping his wings. He leaned backward and dropped into a sudden freefall in a spirited act of faith. Bartholomew lost all leverage, and as he lost his grasp, he braced for impact. It felt like seconds passed before he finally hit with a jolting thud.

The impact shocked the crowd who realized the grapplers were now injured and in serious pain.

As Aenyx looked up at the winter morning sky, the halo of the white sun shone on his black eyes. It looked cold and milky, and he felt himself sinking into unconsciousness.

"Aenyx, get up!" he heard a voice cry out.

"Get up!" another voice shouted.

The crowd was urging Aenyx on, perhaps for the first time in his life. Just feet away from him, Bart was dragging his massive body across the rocky pit toward him to deliver a finishing blow.

Then, out of nowhere, a chant rose from the crowd. It was scattered at first, but slowly it became consistent, rising until the chant was steady and intense.

"Aenyx! Aenyx! Aenyx!"

The audience's chant cleared the fog from Aenyx's eagle eyes. As he lay on the hard terrain, his rib cage ached, and his abdomen swelled from the contact. He struggled to get a better view of his slowly advancing opponent.

Rolling over onto his claws and paws, Aenyx glanced up at the roaring audience. Their cheering expressions filled his lion's heart with courage. This was something he did not expect. And it appeared to infuriate the Guardians, who sulked with disgusted expressions—all save Phoenix Stormguard.

Big Blue glared at his opponent, Aenyx, with pure hatred.

Bart lashed out with both talons in a desperate final lunge as Aenyx simultaneously pounced at his opponent. While he bounded over the top of his opponent, he placed his left claw on top of Bart's fat head and vaulted off of his opponent's feathery mane.

He sailed over him and glided until he landed on all fours. Whirling around, his tail waved triumphantly in the air.

Aenyx looked up from the grappling pit to see the stunned expressions of the Bluetip recruits. Their eyes were wide, and their beaks were agape. He turned his eagle head to his right to see the Guardians, who were watching the turn of events in disbelief.

Then, he heard fits of laughter.

Aenyx whirled around to see Big Blue's condition. It became immediately apparent why the crowd was roaring with laughter. There was now a naked patch on Bart's head where feathers had recently been. Adding to the hilarity was the fact that he seemed completely unaware.

"What?" Bart shouted. "What?"

He could not understand why the crowd was laughing so hard. Even the Bluetip recruits were pointing and mocking the schoolyard bully they had all once feared.

Aenyx held up his left claw and dropped three brown feathers on the ground.

"Point, Aenyx!" the Pridemaster shouted. Jasper approached him and raised up the victor's right talon. "Here is your winner!"

With that, the Stormguard recruits exploded into cheering. They began chanting his name again.

"Aenyx! Aenyx! Aenyx!"

The young griffin looked up at the assembled griffins of Aeris. Red-and-white banners flew proudly in the midst of the arena. The audience in the bleachers went wild. Big Blue, scalp-shorn and humiliated, lumbered out of the grappling pit, taking his wounded pride with him.

At this point, Tyrex Goldeneyrie and Captius Whitecrest exchanged glances. They lifted themselves from their griffin thrones and departed to the shadows of the colonnades leading to the Guardians' lofty mansion overlooking Aeris.

Aenyx was being heralded by his friends, the other outcasts of Aeris. This included the Stormguard recruits Ronax and Brandon, as well as the Whitecrest recruit Raven. They were vicariously savoring their friend's victory and were inspired to achieve their own.

"Congratulations, Aenyx!" the sturdy Brandon told him. "You're advancing to the next match against one of the winners between the Goldeneyrie and the Whitecrests."

"You mean, Gabriel of the Goldeneyrie," Aenyx laughed and corrected him. "This has all been fixed. You know they'll put me up against him next match."

"Gabriel is such a menace," the crafty Raven said with a glint in her eye. "I would love to see you crush him!" She clapped her talons together dramatically and made a crunching sound.

"That would be an epic battle that I would pay to see!" his good-natured friend Ronax chimed in with a grin.

"It will be a tough fight," Aenyx said as he looked into the eyes of his true friends. "There are some here in Aeris who won't be as keen to see me emerge victoriously as you guys clearly do. There is definitely more going on in this kingdom than meets the eye."

The midday sun was now shining brightly, and Aenyx felt his confidence growing.

He had opened the Griffin Trials with an impressive victory, but as anyone who lived in Aeris knew well, victory could be short-lived. This was especially true when the power of the Guardians was aligned against you.

CHAPTER 6

THE FALL OF DRUIX

It was time to hunt. And with that realization, Seraphinus beat his terrible wings and set off into the waiting night. Druix was relieved to be hunting griffins again.

The dark impressions of the fantastical moondrakes could only be known in the absence of light.

Now consumed with fury, the outcast Druix Coldshadow rose majestically into the bracing air. The young moondrake rose ever higher with the singular purpose of revenge.

But far away, in the darkest chamber of a fortress that was blacker than night itself, his father's ill-fated words had already been received, and the orders had already been given.

That night, Seraphinus was assigned to patrol the mountains south of Mount Kildrath, near the Sulfurous Wastes. The elder moondrakes were well aware that griffins rarely attacked from this direction. It was thus a perfect area for Seraphinus and Druix to patrol. Their night flight promised to be uneventful—or so he thought.

The moondrakes flew upward in spirals, soaring to the purplish, wispy clouds that were now coated in moonglow.

Druix whirled impressively, his wings cutting through the ghostly vapor. He twirled wondrously in mid-air and held onto the moment in defiance of gravity.

The younger moondrake dove rapidly and triumphantly to the heights below. As the breeze skimmed over his supple wings and the brisk air flowed bracingly over his face, his blue lips even began to flap while his bared teeth gleamed in the moonglow.

The thrill of flight took over. It had become an all-encompassing experience that united with his being.

As Druix embraced this liberating experience, a sudden wind struck from the east. He had never felt anything like this force—it felt almost supernatural. It caught him off guard and sent him tumbling and wheeling in mid-flight. He looked for his guidelight in the sky, felt the terror of not being able to locate it, and continued to plummet into the darkness.

Unknown to his father, who had continued to press north, the sudden gale had sent Druix careening off-course in the direction of the Sulfurous Wastes.

Druix continued to tumble through the sky. Down he fell. It was swift. Scary. His head spun in terror. As he was about to strike the cold tundra below, he gave a last burst of effort to extend his wings and right his flight. His wings kicked out straight, and he was scarcely able to pull himself back into the air. His talons scraped the earth, sending him hurtling out of control onto the desolate plains.

An intense pain shot throughout his wings, and then he felt the breath leave his body. He scrambled back to his extended claws and began stumbling through the barren wasteland.

Alone and disoriented, Druix looked up and searched the skies for his father.

"Dad?" he screeched in his Draconese tongue.

Yet instead of his father's familiar shriek of response, Druix heard something much louder and far more sinister.

"*Ayywwrrrrieeeee! Ayywwrrrrieeeee!*"

It was the unmistakable war cry of a shadow dragon.

Druix whipped around and tried to regain his bearings. His stomach dropped and his head flooded with confusion. He had heard the sound of death itself.

The only thing he could remember in that dire moment was something his father told him: "Moondrakes' only true ally is speed." With great effort, he flapped his wings and clumsily took flight into the foreboding sky.

Seraphinus also heard the shadow dragon scream. It echoed in the desolate waste like a harbinger of doom. As he looked back, his worst fear had been realized: Druix was missing.

After turning around, Seraphinus pressed with all his might to track his lost son. His desperate scramble was unlike anything he'd ever known. His glinting eyes watered from the breakneck speed.

Seraphinus had sworn to himself never again. And he knew what price he might have to pay to ensure it.

Meanwhile, Druix ascended as high as he could possibly go as fast as he could possibly get there, but shadow dragons were not the kind to abandon a hunt. He could hear the slower, heavier flapping of the dragon's immense wings behind him while pushing himself to new heights. Druix's only goal was to elude and evade—even if that meant winding up far away from his homeland.

But he could not free himself. The dragon was stronger, maybe even faster. It glided through the air with surprising velocity. Druix could feel its breath.

And suddenly, the shadow dragon was hovering over him. Druix did not know how it had gotten there or why he was even being attacked, but he sensed a kind of evil he had never felt.

The massive claws of the foul beast slashed a devastating tear in his right wing. It drew the most horrific pain that Druix ever experienced. The moondrake pulled away sharply, but he could not escape the dragon's merciless grasp.

A shriek pierced the night.

"*Skrrrayyyiiii!*"

It was his father's call. The giant black serpent, a dragon so big it had seemed to be everywhere and nowhere at once, unexpectedly relented. It released Druix from its massive clutches and began wildly spouting flame from its maw, creating a terrifying orange curtain of light upon the clouds.

The shadow dragon flailed and screeched a horrifying wail in response. "*Skkrrrrraaayyyyyiiiii!*"

While Druix fell toward the earth, his wounded wing tattered and unable to hold him aloft, he faintly perceived the night-shadow of a moondrake. It seemed to be attacking the head of the shadow dragon in a fierce exchange of flame and claws. The two great serpents were locked in a dance of death amid the backdrop of the uncaring stars.

It was the last thing Druix witnessed before crashing into the unforgiving earth.

CHAPTER 7

THE GUEST OF HONOR

The prince's black eyes absorbed the darkness of his room. His body lay stiff with apprehension. Sigismund lay in bed absorbing the void of night while he struggled to comprehend what he was experiencing.

The dawn came, and the sunlight incrementally trickled into his room, lighting it imperceptibly. Sigismund didn't even seem to notice the difference between the darkness and the light. The prince's eyelids grew heavy, and sheer exhaustion pulled them shut. Just as he was about to nod off, a knock came at the door.

Sigismund slowly sat up and slunk over to the edge of his bed. His feet dangled as he gathered the energy to answer the door.

"Open up!" the voice came from the corridor. It was Reginald again.

The old man burst in with nervous energy. His face was wrinkled and drawn from worrying about the young prince. His bloodshot eyes belied that he also suffered from a lack of sleep.

"If you have treasured belongings, I counsel you to take them with you tonight," he said. "The queen tells me she had another fight with your father, and she fears the worst may come to pass at tonight's Spring Feast."

Sigismund nodded sadly.

"Thank you, Reginald," the young man said with a bleary-eyed expression.

"Do you…do you understand, son?" Reginald asked with an imploring tone.

"Yes, sir," Sigismund replied. "I thought long ago that this day may come. My prized possessions are simply a few books, which you taught me to treasure most. But since I am being forced to choose one, I will merely take *The Hypernean Chronicles* by Manfred the Magnificent."

"An apt choice, lad," Reginald said and smiled approvingly.

Reginald looked at him with pride, and his gray eyes beamed with affection. This was no way for anyone to live, including the young prince. Though he was mortified that he was being forced to abandon his home, he was also intrigued by the many roads that may lie ahead for him, should he make it to safety and to his new life far away from the cursed kingdom.

"Now, as a matter of business," the old man said with a gentle smile, "you are expected to make an appearance at tonight's feast. There is still a slight chance that your impetuous father might change his mind, but your mother is already making preparations should the worst come to pass."

Sigismund closed his eyes and hung his head as the realization sank in that he might soon be forced to leave his family. He looked up at his tutor with sad understanding in his glossy, black eyes.

"I am so grateful for you, Reginald, especially for your loyalty to my mother throughout all these Trials," he said. "You have prepared me well. I will be ready should the decree come."

Reginald nodded sympathetically, then placed his hand on the young man's shoulder. It was a silent moment that communicated his regret for his plight. But at the same time, his firm grip reassured him that if he remained strong, everything would turn out all right.

The old tutor winked and whirled around to leave, and before Siggie knew it, he was gone. The young prince was alone.

The wheels had been set in motion. Now, he had to get ready.

The young prince selected a fresh set of thermal underwear, which he wore under a leather tunic and a dark brown cloak with a collar. Into his shirt, he tucked a round, golden locket that contained a small portrait of his mother. He reached under his chest of drawers and pulled out a leather-sheathed dagger that he kept in case of emergency. He laced it onto a belt beneath his cloak.

After preparing for his flight, he grabbed his beloved history book and slipped it within his robe's dark folds. It barely fit into the secret compartment.

The daylight hours whiled away. Every hour on the clock felt like a torturous countdown to the unknown. The prince could scarcely pick at the food that was brought to him. Finally, at half-past eight, there was another knock at the door. It was one of the guards—his least favorite.

"Prince Sigismund," the bald, skulking man said coldly. "It is time."

The guard held the door open, and the prince walked through. Sigismund was marched to the feast like a convict before his last supper. His soft footsteps made only a faint patter, but his were followed by the heavy thunks of the overweight guard's footsteps behind him. Down the spiral staircase, through the castle corridors, and to the Great Chamber they went.

The majestic doors were thrown open, and the wondrous glow of torchlight spilled into the hall. The noise of festivities flooded into the corridor and hit the prince in the face like a wave crashing into his senses. Bright-colored streamers flew through the air while lute and lyre players filled the room with chamber music. Torches hanging upon the walls illuminated rich oil portraits of Waverly's past set against magnificent bronze wallpaper with an intricate floral design. Foreign dignitaries with green eye shadow and luxurious robes talked in shadowy corners while swigging pints of honeyed mead. The room was packed full of colorful personalities milling around.

Two great oaken tables flanked the sides of a long, velvety forest green carpet leading up to the magnificent gilded thrones of King Gerald and Queen Galadria. The king reclined comfortably on his throne with a scepter in one hand and a goblet of ale in the other.

"Ahhh, yes, the guest of honor!" the drunken king belted out. The music suddenly stopped.

"Make way! Make way!" he said. "Can't you see the prince must come through? Come here, boy! Come here at once!"

As the young man walked slowly down the aisle to the king and queen, he could feel the stares of the royal audience and hear the murmurs of the lords and ladies. He saw his five brothers at the head of the great table to his right, sitting just below the thrones of his royal parents. The blond-haired brothers wore derisive, yet bemused grins on their impudent faces.

"Yes, child, come here," his beautiful queen mother said, then patted the plush maroon seat of a chair between her and the king. The young prince walked up to his elegant and seemly mother.

"Come sit next to me," she implored.

The king was already red-faced and in an unusually jovial mood. His welcoming face was one of the scariest sights that Sigismund had ever seen. His father nodded for the young man to come over, belched, and then waved his hand for the festivities to recommence. The music picked up where it had left off. The servants brought out legs of roast mutton and lamb, savory potatoes, and herbed carrots on silver platters. It was truly a feast for the ages.

"Do you, do you mean…" the prince began to ask as he sat meekly in the small chair between them, "that this is all for me?"

"Yes, boy, one could say that," the corpulent king replied and laughed mightily, as he wiped a bit of mutton flesh from his red beard. "You should enjoy yourself and indulge in the terrific food and grand company that has come from all around the kingdom on your behalf."

The prince turned away from the spectacle of his drunken father enjoying himself a bit too much and looked in disbelief around the room. It was a veritable hive of activity. Jugglers were effortlessly tossing up small wooden clubs, and jesters with bell caps were amusing the children with parlor tricks. It was a whirling scene of noise and colors, and he was beginning to feel a little dizzy.

"Oh yes, my dear Siggie," the queen said as she turned to the prince. "I have a present for you."

She reached into a hidden pocket in her dainty powder-blue gown, and then she produced a glittery silver box with a black bow. She looked affectionately at her boy and winked with her sparkling light-blue eyes as she handed over the present.

"For me?" Sigismund responded with a grateful smile. She nodded.

The prince reached over, took the box, and grasped the bow to unwrap it.

"Ahh, ahh, ahh," the queen said and gently placed her hand on his shoulder. "It's best if you open that when you are alone."

"What—what is it?" The prince looked up at his beautiful mother inquisitively.

"It is a very special gift, given to me long ago, just for you," she said. She glanced over at his father—he was celebrating in his drunken oblivion—then she leaned over to whisper to him. "It came from the wizard Talus Nightspell. His prophecy long ago saved your life and, one might say, saved mine."

Sigismund leaned back and gazed into his mother's crystal-blue eyes. They shone like mirrored pools. She gave him a slight nod and a pained smile.

The queen nodded again reassuringly as she drank a sip of honeyed mead from her golden chalice.

Sigismund had heard about this prophecy when he was younger. A wizard named Talus Nightspell had arrived unannounced at court after his birth and had prophesied that the kingdom would be cursed until the prince "saw justice." This had compelled the king to have the boy locked safely in a tower, isolated from corruption and injustice. The king believed this to be an act of mercy, rather than outright executing the feared black-eyed child, whom his court soothsayers had counseled.

"Why don't you go say hello to your brothers?" the queen suddenly told Siggie as she flashed a wry smile and choked back the urge to burst into tears.

Prince Sigismund tucked his mother's gift inside his robe. He stood, turned, and bowed politely to the king, then to his mother, before walking down the steps from the raised throne platform. He made his way toward the oak dining table where his five brothers sat. It was well-stocked and bustling with conversation.

They were a rambunctious lot, and their manly voices cut through the already loud dining hall. They were clinking goblets and regaling themselves in uproarious revelry. Sigismund meagerly approached his brothers with trepidation in his heart. He wondered if any of them had remembered his birthday or even that his life was in grave danger. The prince gulped and swallowed his urge to cry. Then the young man strode forth to face his brothers with as much bravery as he could find in himself.

"There's our boy!" his oldest brother, Jax, said with a wide grin.

His oldest brother was a strapping blond man with glinting, steely blue eyes. He held a draught of ale in his right hand, and his weighty left hand rested on the muscular shoulder of Felix, the second-oldest brother, who was a rather large, block-headed fellow that appeared perpetually amused and grateful for the eldest's attention.

Prince Sigismund walked to the foot of the table and gazed amiably at his five brothers. On his right was the cleverest of the Waverly clan, a tall, slender man named Thaddeus, who wore a dark green cloak. He was shrewd in military matters, by Hypernean standards, and aspired to become a counsel to the king. Just one seat farther down was Taryn Waverly, a scrappy, medium-sized man with straw-colored shocks of hair. He had a propensity for angry outbursts, but also the occasional act of daring. Lastly, there was Killian Waverly, the shortest of the clan, a toe-headed blond with a gentle demeanor. He blushed easily.

"What? You've actually come to grace our presence?" Jax said with a hearty laugh.

"Yeah," said Taryn, "who let you out of your lair?"

Sigismund smiled innocently and gazed at his brothers. The sheer blackness of his eyes had always given them the creeps.

"Why, didn't you know it was my birthday yesterday?" he said, slightly hurt that they had forgotten. Again.

"That's right," Thaddeus burst out. "Our black-eyed baby brother has turned eighteen!"

The Waverly clan guffawed derisively. Sigismund, not wanting to be left out, chuckled as well.

"You know what that means," Sigismund said. "I'll be a man soon, just like you, and then I'll be able to leave my quarters and see the world!"

"Sure, sure you will, kid," Felix said. "And tomorrow, I'll be riding dragons!"

They cackled mercilessly and momentarily ceased devouring their roast mutton to clink their mugs of ale before sloshing them down.

Seemingly out of nowhere, like a lightning bolt, a jester appeared. He was a slim man with a powdery-white face and dark eye shadow, which drew out the features of his strangely intelligent and mysterious expression. He protruded his square jaw and pointy chin as if daring the Waverly boys to punch him. Above his pouty, pursed lips was a thin mustache that was oiled and fashioned into two tips. On his angular head sat a pointy cap with a diamond-shaped pattern of chartreuse and royal blue. As Sigismund looked him up and down in disbelief, it struck him that his entire outfit was fashioned in this unusual pattern.

"Why, if it isn't the brothers Waverly!" the jester said with an overly magnanimous bow and a grand flourish of his wiry arms. "Allow me to introduce myself. My name is Giacquomo Spright. I am, as you would say, a jester. I come bearing the most auspicious of tidings."

The jester paused and flashed a disturbing grin at each of the Waverly brothers, finally looking at Prince Sigismund.

Jax took a generous swig from his ale, wiped his mouth, and looked pressingly at the jester.

"Well?" he implored him.

"Yes, yes," the jester said. "The urgent message!"

Giacquomo cleared his throat, tapped two fingers on his larynx repeatedly, then threw back his shoulders to stand as tall as he could manage. He pulled out a shiny mouth harp and blew a few horribly off-key notes.

He recited the following lines:

"The brothers were five, and then were six,
Old Ma Nature pulled her cruelest trick,
The boy's eyes turned black as thickened tar,
Tho' the kingdom's scorn was his deepest scar.
The years were passed in toil and waste,
And to his death they turned with haste,
But unknown to them what fate would bring,
That this young lad would be their king."

No one within earshot spoke a word. The Waverly brothers seated at the table exchanged quick, hot glances and looked up at Sigismund.

"This—scared little rabbit?" Thaddeus blurted. "Our *king*? Bwahahaha! You're out of your gourd!"

The Waverly brothers howled contemptuously and slammed their heavy hands on the table, as if they were begging for an end to the utter hilarity. At last, Felix slammed down his mug of ale.

"You know, jester," Felix said as his heavy hand slapped the table. "You're not half-bad. And for showing such a sense of humor, here's a half-crown for your time."

The stout drunken man flipped him a copper coin that he had pulled from his coat pocket.

"Why, that is awfully generous of you," Giacquomo replied.

The jester flashed a leering smile that bared his full set of pearly teeth. He then turned to whisper something in Prince Sigismund's ear.

Sigismund turned sheet-white and his eyes widened. He gulped noticeably and peered down to the far end of the table.

"Now that I have your attention—and you all have been good sports, I assure you—I believe it is time for you to hear the truth about your dearly beloved brother, the young Prince Sigismund. Particularly, his relation to this dire curse that has afflicted your kingdom—that is, of course, save the royal denizens of this court and its most esteemed guests of honor. They appear to be healthy and well, praise the old gods!"

The Waverly brothers shifted uncomfortably in their seats as if they knew something of what the jester was going to speak but had never heard it spoken aloud in public. They bent over their steins of ale and mugs of honeyed mead, and the shadows from the torchlight cast bleak, agitated expressions on every face, as if the blood had been drawn from their pale faces.

"If you have something to say, jester," Jax intoned with a glare, "I suggest you say it quickly and be off."

"Yes, certainly," Giacquomo replied. "That is a mete and measure for which I am most accustomed. I simply wanted to remind you all that it was your brother's birthday ere just yesterday, having been born eighteen years ago to be precise, and that is quite by coincidence the period in which a terrible blight started to afflict the Hypernean realm."

At this time, the ears of several royal guests standing around the dining table had perked up, and the attending courtiers positioned themselves in an awkwardly casual manner around the jester so as to better listen to what struck them as a choice piece of royal gossip.

"Ahem, well, I merely want to reassure you that this curse is in no way the fault of your dear little brother, whom I'm sure you showered with gifts and affection, as is the case with all such birthdays of young men," the jester said and twirled up one of his mustache ends with a mischievous twinkle in his eye.

"Ah, yes, the point. I am quite punctilious with puncturing the pretentious pretenses of even the most priggish patrons and can promptly proceed to the particulars. For eighteen years ago to this day, a mysterious sorcerer foretold to this court the nature of the kingdom's curse and how best to remove it. It appears, alas, that the historical memory of the Waverlys leaves something to be desired, so I will deign to reconstruct the wizard's warning, albeit with a bit of ornamentation and affectation befitting my craft, so I beseech your forgiveness in advance for the dramatic effect."

Suddenly, a pall was cast over the dining area, and the torches grew dimmer and the shadows grew longer. The smattering of conversations that could be heard on the outskirts of the great hall stopped, and even the music faded to silence.

"Yes, this terrible sorcerer, whose name remains unknown even unto this day, issued forth the following prophecy to good King Gerald and Queen Galadria, who are both in royal attendance. The prognosticator's words have succeeded in saving young Prince Sigismund's life unto this very day…"

Giacquomo Spright stood as erect as a rooster prancing through the barnyard. The jester puffed out his chest and delivered the following lines:

"Your child, a son, the prince, eyes pitch as
star-swallowing night,
Was born unto your kingdom a gift, though he is
received with fright,
Be assured that his life is intertwined with thine,
And his fortune is your fortune until the end of time.
His birth is but an announcement of your kingdom's curse,
And be assured, all ye who hear, this foul state shall
grow worse.
This kingdom shall hence be struck with famine,
Thus is the reward to man and to mammon.
The livestock all shall die where they stand,
And hence the cursed shall return to the land.
The crops all shall rot from fatal disease,
The leaves of the trees shall be lost on the breeze.
The life of this land shall not return,
Until justice is found and shattered rays burn.
Hypernea's curse shall only be lifted
When true freedom this young prince is gifted.
When justice is beheld in black orbs of night,
The future king and his kingdom shall be released
from this plight."

The jester completed this rendition of the wizard's prophecy and gave a flourish and an obsequious bow, replete with an oleaginous grin. He swiftly grabbed Taryn Waverly's drink from the table and deftly downed it with a single gulp.

Giacquomo Spright then disappeared into the crowd with a catlike exit, and the darkened aura was immediately lifted. The torches flickered with a few sparkly pops and illuminated the room with renewed vigor. The band struck up a tune again as if nothing untoward had even taken place, and the Waverlys frowned and returned to their drinking, seemingly unaffected by the jester's recitation of the curse.

"I…I must be going now," the prince stammered.

"Scram, runt," Taryn said. "We grow tired of your company, anyway."

CHAPTER 8

A POISONOUS AFFAIR

The Guardians had watched the ascendancy of Aenyx with special interest since he first began to rise through the ranks. His imminent victory would mark a decisive turn in the Republic. If he won the Griffin Trials, it would be the first time a Redmark had stood for the highest position of Guardian. A number of Guardians were adamantly against such a result.

That was the matter at hand for Captius Whitecrest and Tyrex Goldeneyrie, who were now secretly conspiring to prevent the disruption of their ancient order.

In the shadows of the colonnades that stretched from the Guardians' thrones back to their lofty eyries perched atop Mount Rhaemor, the two obscured interlocutors discussed Aenyx's fate. The walkway was situated in a ravine of blasted rock and was adorned with marble statues of Guardians past: Tibalt Stormguard, the hero of the Battle of the Sulfurous Wastes; Bjorn Bluetip, the massive chieftain who singlehandedly slayed a shadow dragon; and Grindwal Goldeneyrie, who was so swift not even a moondrake could catch him in mid-flight.

"Our ploy to free a throne of the Guardian council proceeds as planned. But we must recognize that this rebellious Redmark poses a grave threat to our Republic, and it is our duty to stop him," Tyrex Goldeneyrie lamented with a distraught whisper. "The Goldeneyrie recruit Gabriel represents our best chance to thwart this upstart's win."

Captius hissed, "I assure you, that rogue will never join our ranks. I have obtained the solution to our problem." He surreptitiously slipped Tyrex Goldeneyrie a vial containing a deep, gray, metallic solution.

Tyrex cocked his head and looked at him curiously.

"Arsenic," Captius told him in a hushed voice. "It is a powerful poison the Laketown people find in their copper and gold mines. Our Whitecrest order occasionally finds a use for it in our statecraft, particularly when it comes to quieting troublesome threats to our way of life.

"We will make sure the recruit coats the tips of his talons with this," Captius instructed. "We will thus smooth his path to the Guardianship and remove the threat to our Republic. And we have additional insurance—the referee is in our pockets and will not penalize Gabriel for it."

Tyrex Goldeneyrie gazed smugly at Captius Whitecrest and nodded his beak in affirmation. Captius looked over his shoulder, held up his left talon, and made a quick motion toward them. Out of the dark shadows of the marble statue of Grindwal Goldeneyrie, a trembling and unsure Gabriel approached.

"No need to be ill at ease, son," Tyrex Goldeneyrie reassured him. "What I want you to do is make it look like an accident. You do understand what is being asked of you, don't you?"

"Yes—but…" Gabriel stammered. Despite being a physically gifted young griffin, he stood on his hind legs nearly a head below the two Guardians.

"And another thing. We need you to slash the Stormguard recruit in the first round of your upcoming match," Tyrex pressed.

"We aren't going to kill him too…are we?" he asked.

"Now, you do want to become a Guardian, don't you?" Captius Whitecrest replied sarcastically. "We will make sure you are exonerated."

"Yes, but I believe I can beat him fair and square," Gabriel said. "Isn't there a better time and place to do all of this?"

"Listen, here," Tyrex said with a terrifying edge to his voice. "This is our best shot without security in the way. There are more important matters at stake than your precious ego. As Guardians, our highest duty is to protect the Republic. You want to do that for us, don't you?"

Gabriel hung his beaked head in silent consent.

"Give me your left claw," Tyrex ordered. Gabriel reluctantly obeyed.

While Captius held his claw aloft, Tyrex dipped each talon in the vial of arsenic. Then they did the same with the right claw. His talons had a slight grayish hue now, but this could easily be chalked up to the dirty conditions on the mountaintop.

But there was one slight problem with their heinous plan: They were silently being watched from the shadows. When Gabriel broke away from the other recruits, it piqued the curiosity of Aenyx's dear friend Raven Whitecrest, who was studied in the secretive world of diplomacy and espionage.

She was appalled by what she saw now before her, but not entirely surprised. She knew that the Guardians would not respond favorably to Aenyx's rise, and the only Guardian that might potentially be an ally to his cause was Phoenix Stormguard.

Raven Whitecrest waited for the conspirators to depart and go their separate ways. There was a bit of touch-and-go as Captius Whitecrest lingered far too long for her liking. It was as if the eldest Whitecrest had a seventh sense when it came to being watched and avoiding traps.

When he strolled by the statue of Tibalt Stormguard, he paused for a moment. The Guardian took the vial of arsenic and deposited it in the statue's mouth. Raven assumed this was a dead drop for one of his associates to dispose of the evidence.

When Captius Whitecrest had finally strolled down the walkway and out of sight, Raven snatched the vial from the statue's mouth and hurried to the Griffin Trials to warn Aenyx.

CHAPTER 9

A GRIFFIN ARISES

Aenyx was feeling on top of the world. His battles had resulted in overdue personal victory. While his success—especially against the Bluetip recruits' biggest grappler—was not drawing what he felt was sufficient praise, his head *was* swelling from the sense of newfound respect.

The day's events had shaken out as expected, as challenger after challenger fell to both Aenyx and his rival Gabriel. The crowd now gathered around the main event of the afternoon, which pitted these two competitors against one another for the right to be called *champion*.

The sun was burning bright in the afternoon sky, and cloud wisps floated like aerial ships in the cerulean ocean of air. The mountain breeze was crisp and invigorating, and his heart was pounding strong and fast. It seemed his future was as limitless as the heavens.

The two combatants now stood on the edge of the arena. Griffins of all varieties roared with anticipation. The Whitecrests beat their white wings in excitement and stood erect on their hind legs like proud eagles. The bronze-maned Goldeneyries flapped their powerful wings as well and looked the most lionesque of the lot. Even the Bluetips were feeling particularly rowdy, cheering on Aenyx's rival out of sheer desire for revenge. They were eager to see the blood flow from the black-eyed outcast.

A dirty tan Goldeneyrie named Hadrian, the referee for the final match, made his way to the center of the main arena. His dark eyes twitched and looked around the arena as if he were searching for a sign.

"Griffins of all ages, gather around!" Hadrian announced with a powerful voice that echoed in the mountain air. "This is your main event!"

The buzz in Aeris was electric. The griffins hooted and howled. Aenyx sharpened his talons on the stone below him, then bolted forward on his lion legs into the arena, claws overhead. He then pounded his chest and opened his beak wide as a sign of defiance to all the griffins who were betting on his defeat.

Gabriel made his way into the arena as well. He walked on all fours as sleekly and as smoothly as a panther. His muscles rippled when he walked. There was no doubt he was a handsome specimen, a true alpha male: powerful, fast, and popular. He was the clear favorite among the Guardians. Sophia Pridewatcher fanned herself as she eyed Gabriel up and down, ogling him and sighing. It was quite possible that she wanted Aenyx to fail most of all.

"Oh, look who is getting the vapors," Aenyx remarked wryly to Brandon and Ronax. "Speaking of which, where is Raven?"

Brandon and Ronax shrugged. Looking around, they spotted Raven on the other side of the arena flapping her white wings and waving her claws in the wildest fashion, obviously trying to get his attention.

"Representing the Stormguard recruits," the referee Hadrian continued, "we have the rising Redmark himself, the one they call Aenyx!"

"And in the other corner," he continued, "a griffin with the heart of a lion and wings wide enough to rest all of our hopes upon him. He is the definition of masculine strength and a true model of a griffin who makes the females swoon. We know him as the Griffins' Champion. Give it up for Gabriel of the Goldeneyrie recruits!"

The roar was deafening. Aenyx felt rage growing within him after being slighted by the referee. He glared at him and pawed the stone floor of the arena below him.

Seething with burning anger, he turned back toward the edge of the arena to prepare himself for the fight ahead.

"Aenyx, wait!" Raven squawked, appearing in front of him. "You must know something about Gabriel—he has poison-dipped talons!" She looked up at him with dread and alarm in her chestnut-brown eyes.

"Are you sure?" Aenyx asked with an air of surprise.

"I'm sure of it!" she said, thrusting the empty vial of arsenic in front of her.

"You know what you have to do," he said. "Take that to the referee immediately and tell him that my opponent is cheating. This is a deadly game my enemies are playing, and I don't intend to humor them."

"Right! Got it!" she answered before flying to the middle of the arena.

It appeared from afar that the referee was taking Raven seriously. He took the vial and looked at the Guardians.

Then, unexpectedly, Hadrian raised his arm to dismiss Raven and signaled that the match would continue.

Raven came back nearly in tears. Aenyx and his friends could not believe the match would go on.

"He said that this was nothing but a cowardly ploy on our part to avoid facing your rival and that you were afraid of being defeated," she said. "He told me that the match would continue as planned or you would be disqualified."

"Can he really do that?" Brandon asked.

"Only one thing left for me to do," Aenyx said. "I need to get in there and kick his tail." Aenyx shot his friends a cocky look and then turned toward the center of the arena.

The referee appeared to be slightly mystified by the griffin's courage; he nonetheless shook his head in acceptance. Hadrian Goldeneyrie stood on his hind legs and held up his right claw.

"Ready? Begin!" the ref shouted, dropping his claw to signal the start of the match.

Aenyx studied his opponent closely. The grayish, metallic tinge on his rival's talons could be seen in the glare of the sun. He knew that one strike from his opponent could mean the end of his run at the Griffin

Trials—possibly even worse. Aenyx shot straight up with his powerful wings flapping hard. Speed would be his ally.

Aenyx ascended into the air until he was hovering over Gabriel. Up he went into the air until he blotted out the sun, like an eclipse. As the rays framed his magnificent body, he darted straight downward and tore the feathers off of his rival's mane. It was lightning-quick and extremely effective.

"Point, Aenyx!" the referee said with a quavering voice. Hadrian looked up at the dismayed Captius Whitecrest and Tyrex Goldeneyrie and gave a subtle shrug.

Gabriel Goldeneyrie looked at Aenyx with guilt in his eyes. There was a fleeting moment when the proud griffin appeared to swallow his shame for cheating at the Griffin Trials. Then, with a sneer, he adopted a harrowing grimace that was a daunting combination of rage and determination.

Aenyx was undaunted. His talons brushed off his chest feathers with glib bravado. The crowd ate it up.

The referee again signaled for the combatants to begin. Gabriel charged this time and swiped fiercely at Aenyx with his talons. Aenyx maneuvered desperately to stay out of the deadly path of the poison-tipped claws. He twirled and contorted in mid-flight to keep away from the knife-like slashes.

But Gabriel kept coming at Aenyx relentlessly, slashing through the air in an attempt to slice any bit of flesh his talons might find. Aenyx flew with all the skill he could muster, deploying every trick in his book. He somersaulted, backflipped, deked, and faked his way around the arena.

Gabriel was beginning to tire of the chase. Between the adrenaline rush and the sheer expenditure of energy chasing Aenyx around the arena, Gabriel was growing exhausted. As Gabriel paused in frustration to catch his breath, Aenyx saw his opening and pounced. He came at Gabriel with a burst of energy, aiming to pull the feathers straight out of his breast. But at the last moment, Gabriel fell backward and thrust his claws at him like a spiked trap.

Aenyx had no choice but to go on the defensive. He clutched Gabriel's claws from above and thrust them downward. A painful shriek was heard in the arena. Gabriel struggled with all his might to keep his talons away from his chest. Even one scratch could cause intense dizziness and difficulty breathing. The match would be over, and Aenyx would become the winner.

Aenyx bent down and bit Gabriel's throat with his beak. He pulled back hard and emerged with a mouthful of blood and feathers. The grappling rulebook did not explicitly rule out such a maneuver. The referee had little choice but to award Aenyx a point for the feather-pull.

"Point, Aenyx!" the referee announced, though he appeared disturbed while saying the words.

Aenyx spit the feathers out of his mouth and released his opponent's claws.

"You don't taste real good, Gabriel," he remarked. "I don't really care for the taste of cowardice."

The audience watched in stunned silence. There was a real chance that Aenyx would become their grappling champion. Each returned to their side of the arena; the referee again gave the signal.

"Ready? Go!"

The two combatants skirted around the edges of the arena. Gabriel was licking his wounds from the last confrontation. The bloody scratch on his throat reminded him that his opponent was capable of inflicting a mortal wound as well.

Aenyx looked up at the Guardians and soaked up their horrified expressions. He could taste the sweet savor of victory already.

Suddenly, Gabriel broke out in a desperate rush.

"Yaarrgghhhh!" he screeched and flew at him at full speed.

Aenyx could see the mania in Gabriel's eyes and wanted no part of it. He flew into the air in a last-minute bid to get out of the way, but Gabriel was relentless. He kept coming. He bounded up in the air and took flight, soaring in Aenyx's direction.

There was no time to think. Aenyx turned sideways and pivoted his wings out of the way of his berserk opponent. Gabriel flew by him, seemingly unable to control his upward trajectory—setting him on a crash course with the Guardians.

CHAPTER 10

THE FATAL CONVERSATION

The young prince stumbled away from the table, too stunned to care about his brothers' indifference any longer. He walked down the carpeted aisle of the Great Chamber, miraculously avoiding the colorful acrobats, the drunken lovers, and the dancing couples twirling in his path. On his way, he jostled the silver goblet of a leather-armored lord, who spilled his red wine on the carpet. A foul-mouthed curse followed.

Sigismund no longer noticed the world around him. It was a cacophonous flurry of loud sounds and blurry lights. He continued walking through the hazy tunnel of faceless courtiers toward his now-certain fate. It felt like his death sentence had been confirmed in the most confusing fashion.

"Prince?"

A man's somber baritone voice broke through the noise and crashed through the tunnel walls of his consciousness to snap him back to reality. Prince Sigismund looked up to see a barrel-chested man with a black mustache. His gray-blue eyes were heavy and sad in the flecks of firelight. The young man looked up at Prince Sigismund with an inconsolable expression. The prince looked down and noticed the svelte man wore brown leather armor embossed with a red griffin. Then the man firmly grasped him by the upper arm and yanked him toward a darkened corner, away from prying ears.

"Listen, boy," the man said. "I am a castle guard here. Some call me by the name of Traveris Bane. Others—who are less generous with their esteem—they call me the Kindly Knight, although I ceased being a knight long ago." He gulped, and for the briefest of moments, the man's eyes dimmed as if he had been transported far away. "But that is neither here nor there," Traveris said, shaking away whatever memory had arisen. "I assure you—you are in excellent hands."

The castle guard reached down to touch the gleaming hilt of a long sword that was fastened to his side. Sigismund believed him.

"What am I to do?" the prince asked him under his breath.

"You are to await my signal," he said while scanning the room.

"When I touch my nose twice," he said while tapping his hawk-like nose with his gloved hand. "I'll fight my way out of this damned place, and you'll follow. No questions asked."

Traveris looked down at him.

"No questions asked," Prince Sigismund echoed reassuringly, gazing at him with the void of his eyes. They seemed to swallow the torchlight and burn with their own inner fire.

"So this is the dread Prince Sigismund," a feminine voice suddenly spoke from behind him.

The young man whipped around and looked upon a creature unlike anything he had ever seen. She appeared in an instant to him to be a maze of contradictions: She was both coy and yet cool, amused and yet bored, tough and yet passionate, confident and yet lost. Her milky-white shoulders bore the curled tresses of a flaming red mane of hair, which coiled in dark labyrinths in the dying torchlight, each one a tunnel leading to an unexplored territory that he felt he was being pulled into.

Her devil-may-care smile took him by surprise. It was as if an alabaster statue had suddenly broken its eternal pose to grace him with her careless charm.

"Doesn't look so frightening to me!" she said with a sparkling laugh. She downed the drink from her chalice.

The bewitching girl could not have been more than sixteen. She wore a sequined gown of green jade exposing her wonderfully rounded shoulders. The gown wrapped carefully around her frame to express that she was both buxom and bold but not overbearingly so. There was a compelling strength to her femininity.

"This is the worst possible time to make acquaintances, I'm afraid," the prince said.

"Oh, but I heard the jester's little speech, and I must admit it piqued my interest," she replied. "Those brothers of yours were braying like jackasses, but I have to say the jester made a compelling case that you will turn out to be the king, after all."

The prince was taken aback by the girl's curious words. He had never known anyone to talk like this—so directly, yet so slyly.

"Who…who are you?" the prince stammered.

"Oh, I'm Princess Melanie," she said with that curious grin of hers—half-cocked with a soft chasm of a dimple on her left cheek.

"The…Princess Melanie?" Sigismund looked at her with a perplexed expression. "But…but you're a MacCallister!"

"Yes, I know," she said with an airy chuckle.

"But your father…our fathers…" he spluttered.

"They have an ancestral quarrel," she replied. "Right. And that is one of the reasons I had to talk to you. You see, to put it quite plainly, your life is in danger."

A stern expression took over her face.

"When I saw you talking with this older gentleman, I put two and two together. I know from the stories that he is called the Kindly Knight, who is in fact, not a knight at all, but a mere guard in the royal service…"

Prince Sigismund shot a quizzical look at Traveris Bane. "Is there something I should know?" he asked. "This is the second time I have heard this tonight. If I am to trust you with my life, then you need to be upfront with me. Why are you no longer a knight?"

Traveris Bane sighed and reluctantly looked at both of them.

"Many years ago, at the Battle of the Onyx Wastes, I made a terrible mistake," he said. "I was tasked with protecting a valuable post, and I left it. I paid the price by being stripped of my knighthood."

Princess Melanie gave him a judgmental look, but she seemed satisfied that he had at least confessed to it.

"Well, if my mother, the queen, trusts him," Prince Sigismund said. "Then he must be a man of honor. She would not entrust my safety with a coward or a fool."

"Excuse me, your royal highnesses," Traveris intruded. "Is everyone's curiosity satisfied now? Because time is pressing, and we have important matters to attend to."

"Indeed!" she replied with the recognition of danger flashing in her olive-green eyes. "Or otherwise I would not have been so presumptuous as to have interrupted your conversation. You see, I know what my father has been planning. As you probably saw, he is here in attendance tonight and enjoying himself quite admirably. If you believe this to be odd, then you would be right."

"Go on," Traveris mumbled.

"Well, my family and all of the families around Hypernea have been blaming the Waverly clan for the blight and famine that have struck our region for the past eighteen years," she said. "It has drained our resources, and our revenue is a slow trickle. For the first time now, they seem hopeful that there will soon be—shall we say—a reversal of fortunes."

Traveris suddenly grasped her point. There wasn't time to wait for a signal from the queen. It was imperative that Prince Sigismund be ushered out of the festivities as soon as possible.

"But do not worry," she said with a coy expression. "I have a plan."

CHAPTER 11

A SHAMELESS DIVERSION

"What kind of plan?" Traveris Bane asked, taken aback by this young girl's forwardness.

"Let's just say I am a master at getting attention," she replied with a casual and convincing tone. "When I make a diversion, you make for the door."

Traveris and Sigismund nodded in agreement at the girl's suggestion. There was no arguing with her observations and her understanding of their precarious position.

Prince Sigismund gazed up at her mother, who sat alone with a haunted expression on her face. It was contorted in the most agonizing of ways. It rent his heart in two.

Before Princess Melanie could turn away to create a scene, the emboldened Prince Sigismund grasped her left hand. The touch of her soft skin sent a tingle up his arm.

"Thank you, Princess Melanie," he said with swelling appreciation in his voice. He drank deeply of the vision of her dancing eyes and sumptuous curves. He memorized the brilliance of her outline, which framed a soul that transcended each moment.

"Don't mention it," she smiled and grazed his hand with her own. "Showtime."

Just like that, she dashed off to the great dining table to their right, where many of Hypernea's most powerful family members were seated. She brusquely cut between a lord and lady and pulled a ladle of red wine and strawberry punch and filled her goblet. She smiled mischievously at Sigismund and Traveris and made her way to the middle of the Great Chamber, where lords and ladies were dancing.

"Get ready," Traveris murmured to the prince.

The guard peered at the queen and found her eyes fixed upon them. He motioned twice with his fingers toward his angular nose.

A scream, high-pitched and unmistakably feminine, rang out from the middle of the grand dining room. It was so loud, in fact, that many instantly covered their ears. Wine goblets clattered on the floor, spilling their contents. The musicians halted abruptly.

Only one voice in the entire hall could be heard.

"Why, how *dare* you, you filthy old man!" Princess Melanie shouted. "You grabbed me *where*?"

The poor fellow didn't stand a chance. He was a balding old lord who was now thrust into a delicate situation to explain to his wife, not to mention the MacCallister clan, who were immediately on the scene.

"Come on, Prince," Traveris said while tugging the young man's arm. "That's our distraction."

The queen's guard grabbed the prince by the collar and dragged him to the back of the room, where two bleary-eyed castle guards stood on each side of the door. Traveris shoved one side of the door open, only to hear a voice shout from the other side of the chamber.

"Stop them!"

It was the king.

Traveris batted down one guard's hand and then bashed the guard's head into the door jamb. As the second guard reached for his shoulder, he yanked him forward into the first guard. They tumbled to the ground. Traveris shoved the prince out the door, then drew his long sword and backed out of the room.

"Prince, follow me!" Traveris shouted.

Traveris snatched a torch off the wall and led the prince down the corridor from the left of the Great Chamber. The hallway walls were ensconced with bronze-handled torches that lit up frescoes depicting various landscapes from Hypernea's glory days.

Behind them, a horn blared a warning to alert the castle guards of their imminent escape. As a rotund and undoubtedly inebriated guard struggled to stand to see what was the matter, Traveris ran by and smashed him in the jaw with the hilt of his long sword. The guard collapsed in his chair.

Traveris led him to the left, past the chapel. The vague scent of incense brought a disturbing awareness of dark mysteries that resided within. The corridors smelled of musty oak, and the shouting from the pursuing guards gradually grew fainter.

At the end of the hallway was the door to the library. Traveris reached into a pouch that was fastened to his belt and rummaged through its contents.

"Damn," he said under his breath. "It's not here."

"What's not here?" Prince Sigismund said and looked at him with alarm.

"The key. It's not here."

The guards' voices grew louder again.

"Well, I know one key that's never failed me," Traveris said.

He stepped away from the door and delivered a swift kick below the handle. It ripped the lock casing through the wooden frame.

"A lock is only as good as the door," Traveris said with a huff. "Let's get out of here."

Traveris led the way into the library filled with rows of arcane and long-forgotten books. He turned left again and headed toward a bookcase that was built into the masonry.

"Here, hold this." The man handed Sigismund the torch.

The Kindly Knight reached up to a row of books that was about shoulder high. He ran his finger along the dusty spines of the multihued leatherbound books until he came to a large book at the end of the shelf.

He pulled it from the shelf, and Sigismund heard a soft click, like that of a switch.

Traveris replaced the book and backed away with both hands on the bookshelf. Then, he shoved the entire bookcase with all his might. It groaned a bit as if it didn't want to give way, but then it began to slide back on the wheels that were hidden beneath it. A small door was built into the floor, and a metal ring was attached to the top.

"This is your way to freedom, Prince," Traveris said. "You must go down there."

He placed his hand on the prince's shoulders. It was time to make their escape.

"I will lead you down the tunnels to the secret exit. Then you must flee into the forest and go far away from here—as far away as you can. I will do my best to fight off the guards to keep them from capturing you."

"Away for good?" the prince asked.

"As long as your father rules this kingdom, you will never be safe," he replied. "We have no time to talk! They are coming now."

They scrambled down the ladder into the thickest darkness Sigismund had ever known. The torchlight threw menacing shadows onto the wall—then he realized they were his own.

Traveris led the way. The prince ignored the squeaks of the rats and the occasional flutter of bats. He told himself his imagination was overacting.

"What I can't see must not be real," the prince told himself.

The tunnels were muddy and full of puddles, and water dripped from the ceilings. They trudged through the mud and muck and avoided the shallow puddles. They trekked onward for several minutes until they could feel the slightest stirring of air. Then, they heard bloodhounds yelping and loud voices echoing in the dark tunnel behind them.

Sigismund was terrified by the sound of the barking bloodhounds, and he broke into a sprint toward the end of the tunnel. When he made it out of the tunnel's mouth, he stood in the refreshing air under the limitless expanse of the night sky.

Traveris shouted to him. "Wait!"

The young man froze and whirled around. His wide eyes made him look like a frightened doe in the torchlight, as the guardsman stood at the cave entrance.

"Head east through the Forgotten Forest until you find the Laketown villagers," he said. "Look for an elderly sage who is said to be able to speak with various beasts. He can help you."

"Aren't you coming with me?" the terrified prince asked.

"Son," he said. "I am here to make sure you get out alive. The rest is up to you."

And with that, the Kindly Knight reached up to a hidden, wooden frame built into the cave entrance. He pulled a switch, and a heavy iron gate collapsed from above. Sigismund was shut *out* of the tunnel, and the Kindly Knight was shut *in*.

There was no way in—or out. The sound of the barking bloodhounds grew louder as they traveled through the tunnel.

Traveris Bane grasped his glinting sword and looked at Prince Sigismund, who stood frozen in the moonlight. The memory would become burned into the prince's mind. The Kindly Knight's sacrifice was difficult to comprehend.

"You'd better run."

And just like that, Prince Sigismund fled into the darkness of night. Under the endless winter skies, he ran through the barren fields, upon the gray hills, and into the leafless forests that stretched from Waverly Castle into the lands far away.

The last thing the prince would remember from that night was blindly running through the ethereal, moonlit forest. He ran over crackling twigs and fallen logs until his foot was finally ensnared by a tree branch.

The young prince was sent hurtling toward the earth, and his crown struck hard upon a mossy, rounded stone. And then his world turned black.

CHAPTER 12

THE DEATH OF A GUARDIAN

A harrowing scream was followed by the dread sound of silence. Gabriel slowly pulled himself up from a tangle of two bodies. There was a look of horror in his eyes. Underneath him was the white, feathery body of one Sophia Pridewatcher.

Dark and thick blood oozed from her throat. Her eyes were open wide in a haunting gaze. Stunned, the audience watched as one of their great leaders lay dying.

"You foolish, foolish griffin!" Tyrex Goldeneyrie shouted.

"Everyone remain calm!" Phoenix Stormguard said. "We will find out how this happened. As for now, I will declare that Aenyx of the Stormguard recruits is the winner of the grappling tournament. As for Gabriel of the Goldeneyrie recruits, the guards will now take him into custody."

Two Stormguard sentries emerged and took the disgraced recruit to Aeris prison to await trial by the High Council.

"It is for your own good," Phoenix remarked to Gabriel as he was escorted away.

"I will hold the keys to the Golden Hatchery in the meantime, until a replacement can be found," Tyrex said.

"Very well," Phoenix replied in a somber tone.

It had begun to sink in that one of the Guardians was dead. Sophia Pridewatcher's lifeless body lay upon the terrace. The Pridewatchers mournfully assembled around her and procured her body. Not only were Pridewatchers responsible for rearing the young, but they were also called to attend to the other spectrum of life—old age and death. They carried her body away to be placed in the Hall of Guardians, a mausoleum where Guardians were laid to rest and enshrined for eternity.

Phoenix Stormguard looked upon the griffins of Aeris with great concern. Even though the Guardians and all of Aeris had lost one of their own, life must go on. The Trials must go on.

The Republic of Aeris gathered in a great mass to both mourn the loss of their beloved Guardian and to celebrate a youthful rite of passage. The four remaining Guardians would preside over the remainder of the Griffin Trials. But not only would the victor of the Trials become eligible to stand for Guardian, the traditional reward, but also, he or she would become an Honorary Guardian standing in the place of the vacated seat. The stakes just became that much higher.

The Honorary Guardianship bestowed a number of special privileges: First, that griffin would become a member of the High Council, deciding on critical matters of state. Second, the griffin would be treated the same as a Guardian until the Griffin Elections selected an eligible member from the vacated Pride. These candidates were picked by a majority of the Guardians and previous Griffin Trial winners. Finally, and most importantly, the Honorary Guardian was ultimately eligible to stand in a vote for a vacated Guardianship from his own Pride. A successful vote could not even be blocked by a veto of the Guardians.

Aenyx was well on his way to becoming a Stormguard, and now he was in the running to stand for Honorary Guardian. The fate of the Republic would turn on who emerged as champion.

Captius Whitecrest and Tyrex Goldeneyrie were panicking. Now, the stakes were even higher. The Guardians were ready and willing to resort to extreme measures.

CHAPTER 13

SNAKE-EAGLING

It was quite a spectacle to see dozens of griffin recruits lined up in the stadium before the thrones of the Guardians, all standing in complete silence honoring the deceased Guardian Sophia Pridewatcher. Aenyx looked up into the big, blue sky and felt its weight on his wings.

The Pride recruits were preparing themselves for the next great event: Snake-eagling. It was an all-out race among the griffin recruits to fly to a nearby mountain, Mount Severius, and return with a venomous snake called the Black Viper. The winner would be the first one to swallow the snake whole in front of the Guardians.

While Aenyx steeled himself for the terrific scramble in the sky, he could not help but feel wary that there would be another attempt on his life. The incident with Gabriel in the grappling pit still rattled him; the fact that his opponent's insidious act of cheating resulted in the death of a Guardian was beyond his comprehension. The events of the afternoon had seemed surreal to him, and things were just getting started.

The Pridemasters reminded them of the rules: No physical combat, no teams blocking the way of competitors, and no killing snakes before arriving back on Mount Rhaemor.

"What if that snake happens to be a Goldeneyrie?" Aenyx asked the Pridemaster Jasper Stormguard sarcastically.

"Aenyx, as long as you bring back one of those Black Vipers before those cheating rascals, I don't give a damn what you do," he wryly retorted. "I'm just duty-bound to tell you the rules."

"It's best that you don't know what I aim to do," Aenyx remarked while stretching his mighty wings.

As one of the fastest griffins in all of Aeris, it was definitely Aenyx's race to lose. He knew Mount Severius like the back of his paw. The Black Vipers tended to live in crevices along the gray, sheer face of the southern slope. All he had to do was race in and snatch one of the hatchlings and return. He would prefer not to tangle with one of the mamas, who could grow as long as eight feet in length and would result in a massive case of indigestion.

Excitement was growing among the griffin ranks as Phoenix Stormguard rose from his throne to give them the signal.

"Recruits from across the Five Prides," he declared. "Bluetips and Pridewatchers, Goldeneyries and Whitecrests, and of course, my beloved Stormguards, it is my duty and my honor to announce the commencement of the snake-eagling competition!"

The tension could be felt spreading through the ranks as the griffins anticipated the start of the race.

"All right, everyone, prepare yourselves!" he announced with a sterner tone. "On your marks…get set…race!"

There was no more awe-inspiring sight on Solarius than witnessing dozens of massive griffins ascending above Mount Rhaemor to embark upon a snake-eagling race. Griffins of all shapes and sizes took flight in wild pursuit of their designated prey. The dark-maned Bluetips with their bulky frames, the sleek and bronze-coated Goldeneyries, the pale-feathered Whitecrests, the tan-coated Pridewatchers, and the bald-headed

Stormguards with their sturdy black wings—all took flight and dotted the sky with soaring majesty.

Aenyx gazed down on the snaking streams that meandered through the rocky hills and glinted in the late winter sunlight. Dark forests of evergreen trees stood like rows of soldiers standing guard over nature for miles and miles of unsettled wilderness. Aeris was the pristine homeland of all griffin-kind, and each of the recruits felt it was a land worth fighting and dying for.

As scores of griffins beat their wings, the sound of flapping could be heard throughout the pack. The sky was so blue and endless, it felt like another world stacked upon the one below. Halos of light streamed into their eyes as they made their way toward a foreboding three-peaked mountain to the west. It was capped in snow, and billowy clouds enshrouded its upper reaches. Aenyx took note of the southern face. That was where he would find his prey.

"Quite the view!" Brandon shouted at Aenyx, who was leading the pack of Stormguard recruits. Only the Goldeneyries on their left flank were keeping pace.

"Stop tailing me, Brandon!" Aenyx yelled with a grin. One could gain the slightest bit of aerodynamic advantage by drafting behind a fellow griffin.

Mount Severius was growing larger in front of them. Aenyx barrel-rolled down through the mountain mists, cutting his own path away from the pack. The griffins began to dive-bomb the mountainside in search of their serpentine prey. War screeches, unique for every Pride, could be heard throughout the wilderness.

"*Ayeeee-rrieee, yawwww*!" the Goldeneyrie recruits yawped as they began picking through the mountain scrub for serpents. The tremendous griffin-cries sent the mountain snakes slithering back to their lairs; the griffins could pick up on their motion to snag them and carry them back to Mount Rhaemor.

Meanwhile, Aenyx had fixed his glossy, black eyes on a viper nest that was tucked underneath a shadowy crag. He spotted hatchlings slinking back to their nest. Outside, watching the griffins with intense interest, was a massive mama snake standing tall and alert. She was obviously in no mood for griffin shenanigans today.

"Glad I had a light lunch," Aenyx mumbled to himself as he began circling the hissing, extremely agitated creature from above. The hatchlings had vacated their subterranean lair, leaving only the mama snake. If he was going to show the griffins of Aeris that he was worthy of standing for the Guardianship, he might as well do it in grand style. So, away he went.

The griffin plunged toward the mountain slope and suddenly slowed by fluttering his wings hard. The Black Viper actually lunged into the air, fangs bared, in an aggressive attempt to bite into the airborne foe. Aenyx was ready for it. He cocked his head back and snapped it forward in a flurry of motion, snagging the flying serpent by the back of its neck in mid-air. It was snake-eagling at its finest.

The big mama snake writhed uncontrollably until Aenyx got his talons around its ample body. She was heavier than he liked and about the same thickness as Aenyx's forelimbs. Needless to say, she was very, very unhappy.

The griffin secured his prey and began his aerial return to Mount Rhaemor. He could see ahead of him that two griffins had already left Mount Severius to fly back to the arena. He had to hustle.

Aenyx beat his wings harder than at any time he could remember. His forelimbs ached from carrying the wriggling she-serpent. The Black Viper's massive jaw was agape, and its dreadful fangs were bared for the world to see. One slip of his grip could mean a life-threatening wound that might require weeks for recovery, and more urgently—concerning the matter at hand—it would instantly take him out of the running for the Guardianship.

After ascending into the mountain air far above the land, he saw that two griffins were leading him—he could barely make out with his eagle eyes that they were Goldeneyrie recruits.

Of course, he thought.

He stretched his wings as wide as they could go and sailed through the air to give some relief to his sore muscles. He would need all the energy he could muster to make a final push.

Up ahead was Mount Rhaemor. Its commanding slopes radiated might throughout the surrounding lands. It gleamed like a golden-hued crown in the fading sunlight.

Aenyx knew there was no time to rest. He gave his all to catching up to the griffins leading the pack; they likely had only tiny baby snake hatchlings in tow. He grasped the serpent harder and sank his talons into its body with the aim of quelling its relentless writhing. No luck. He flapped his wings with all his might as the burning fatigue spread throughout his griffin body. It seemed his wings were on fire.

Finally, it was time for the last descent. He dove with all his being and began to close the gap with the leading griffins. The Goldeneyrie recruits were obviously so exhausted from the journey that they could only glide on the thin, winter breeze.

Aenyx beat his wings harder and harder. He was now above his competitors. Suddenly, he struck upon a mischievous plan. While flying just above his opponents, he would lower the snake's tail beside their heads. This could provide him with the element of surprise.

"Watch out, fellas!" Aenyx shouted.

Startled by the sight of a gargantuan, black snake dangling beside their heads, they spooked and fluttered their wings to get away from the beast.

"It's just a snake!" he yelled while diving toward the landing deck of the arena. He landed on his lionesque hind legs in front of the five thrones of the Guardians. It did not appear that Savagiras, Tyrex, or Captius were pleased to see him. He looked upon the empty marble throne.

That will be my throne, Aenyx thought as he sank his beak through the skull of the Black Viper. It squealed pitifully, but he remembered the ancient enmity between griffins and serpents and proceeded to clamp down on its head. Now came the tough part—eating it whole.

"Eat it, Aenyx!" a voice shouted from the crowd.

Aenyx gulped hard and went for it. The two Goldeneyrie recruits, Julius and Scipio, landed next to him with much smaller snakes wriggling out of their mouths. They were each about four feet long and skinnier than his snake. He would have to hurry.

"Eat it! Eat it! Eat it!" the excited crowd chanted.

The black mama snake was about halfway down his gullet. He felt like he was going to be sick, but he had to continue. He looked at the other griffins out of the corners of his black eyes, which were growing wider by the second; he knew he had only had seconds left to finish it. He stood on his hind legs, leaned his head back, and then led the rest of the snake down his throat with his claws.

It was a disgusting sight. Amazing, but disgusting. The crowd loved it.

Aenyx opened his beak to show that the snake was indeed all the way down his gullet. He stretched his tongue forward, showing that his beak was completely clean. It was an impressive feat.

"Aenyx! Aenyx! Aenyx!" the griffins in the arena chanted.

Tyrex Goldeneyrie and Captius Whitecrest looked on with utter contempt. They had no intention of letting this ruffian join their ranks. And Aenyx was on the brink of victory in the Trials.

"Come on," Captius whispered to Tyrex. "We have planning to do."

CHAPTER 14

PHOENIX STORMGUARD

In the evening, torches were lit in ceremonial fashion in the arena. Fire was a relic of the griffins' ancient alliance with the Laketown villagers, who had first brought the elemental wonder up the mountain heights prior to the Great Serpent Wars. The torches burned with an eerie light on the outskirts of the arena as a reminder that the Trials were a preparation for the possibility of war.

The griffins had broken for dinner, not that Aenyx was remotely hungry. The poor griffin simply could not keep his snake dinner down. As the nausea increased, he had no choice but to empty his innards. It was not a pretty sight, but he survived it.

"Are you going to be okay, big fella?" Ronax asked while patting him on the back.

"I feel like I got into the goblin gin again," Aenyx replied. "Remind me to never repeat that."

Brandon and Ronax gave a hearty laugh at their friend's expense. Raven was the only companion who felt too queasy to join in the fun. She felt like she too might get sick at any moment.

"I'll remind you!" she shouted, before disappearing into the mountain bushes herself.

This only made Ronax and Brandon howl louder. Aenyx regained his composure to the extent he was capable of and felt the need to refocus on the next challenge.

"Let's refocus our energy on the final event," Aenyx said. "Night-stalking."

His cadre nodded their beaks in agreement. It was time to get serious. Night-stalking meant patrolling the night skies for the enemies of the Republic of Aeris.

"And not just night-stalking," Aenyx added. "Moonchasing."

Now he had his friends' undivided attention. Moonchasing was a night hunt for the fiercest of all griffin enemies: moondrakes.

Moondrakes flew faster than griffins, had sharper talons and lengthier fangs, but there was one thing griffins had on their side that moondrakes did not—teamwork. A team of griffins working together could outmaneuver and outflank a moondrake until it was forced into a pitched fight.

While a moondrake in a pinch was no sight for mortal man's eyes, a pack of griffins could harass one of the agitated beasts into confusion by attacking it from all sides. Drakes were renowned for their unbridled aggression, but their very fierceness could be turned against them. When a moondrake lashed out in the dark at its attackers, it could be rendered vulnerable to attacks from behind. One griffin, usually the bravest, would work to hold the moondrake's attention, while the others would dive onto its wings from the rear and rip them open with their ferocious claws. If a moondrake could be grounded in such a manner, it would be rendered extremely vulnerable to attackers.

Aenyx and the other Stormguard recruits knew all this. They had been training virtually their entire lives, since the moment their wings were fully formed, to take flight, to fight off moondrakes. It was the very essence of their social existence to defend the Republic of Aeris from the great serpents of the north. Even as a young hatchling, a griffin was taught enmity with the serpent. Griffin young were often fed a diet of snakes, and when old enough to strike at their prey, they were given live, venomous snakes for dinner. This rite of passage was hinted at by the previous event of Snake-Eagling—it represented the transition stage from a young adult griffin to an adult member of a Pride; that is, when griffins were expected to sacrifice their lives on behalf of the collective good.

"Do you think we could pull one off, Aenyx?" Ronax asked.

"Sure, if any three griffins can do it, we can," he said.

Brandon looked at his two friends with a reassuring look of confidence. "Let's do it," Brandon said.

They all put their claws together in a triangle of trust. As they broke apart, Aenyx knew that this experience would transform their lives.

As Aenyx walked away from his friends to get his mind and body right for the final challenge, he heard a voice whisper his name from the shadows.

"Aenyx," it said. "Come and walk with me."

The moon had not yet risen to its full height in the darkening sky. Its cold glow only fleetingly touched the outline of the face in the shadows. But Aenyx knew by the voice that it was Phoenix Stormguard.

Aenyx walked over to the shadows until he could see the outline of that dignified face. Phoenix Stormguard had the mane of a bald eagle with hyper-acute and intelligent eyes, and a pronounced beak that bent downward in an angular fashion. He was taller than most griffins and had the strapping chest of a lion, which was nonetheless covered in dark brown feathers.

Phoenix placed his claw on Aenyx's shoulder.

"I hope you don't mind me approaching you in such a familiar way," Phoenix said as he led him away from the other griffins. "But I know the trials you are going through. And I know your potential."

Aenyx looked up at the Guardian. He was astonished that any of the Guardians would welcome the possibility of him winning the games and becoming one of them.

"I know you are a Redmark," he said. "You possess those black eyes, which some believe to be a flaw in your makeup and thus should disqualify you from leading the other griffins. I, however, do not agree. I believe them to be a gift. They are a sign that something is amiss in Aeris and a test of our own sense of justice."

Aenyx hung his head, not knowing quite how to respond. It was surprising yet comforting to hear such a respected figure echo his thoughts and acknowledge his fight for respect.

"Soon, you will be a Stormguard," he added. "All that is required from you now is to return alive from the night-stalking exercise. I do not doubt your ability to fight off the enemies from outside of Aeris. I am, however, concerned by your ability to fight the enemies within it."

Aenyx looked up at the elder Guardian. They were now walking down the same row of colonnades and marble statues where the Whitecrest and Goldeneyrie leaders conspired to take him out of the Trials—perhaps, even to end the threat of his Guardianship permanently.

"Son, tell me about your match with Gabriel of the Goldeneyrie recruits. I am certain there was foul play involved in the death of Sophia Pridewatcher. It wasn't just the slash to her throat that killed her, I fear."

Aenyx was hesitant to respond. He did not want to expose Raven to the kind of palace intrigues that could get a griffin killed.

"If you fear retaliation for your words," he said, "on your behalf or that of your friends, then you can merely nod if I am correct."

He nodded once to show he understood. They stopped in the moonlight near the statue of Tibalt Stormguard.

"Are you aware of poison that might have contributed to the demise of Sophia Pridewatcher?" Phoenix asked.

Aenyx hesitated and then nodded twice.

"Do you know who may have been a witness to the executors of a plot on that Guardian's life?" he asked.

Aenyx looked up at Phoenix and nodded.

"Is that witness's name Raven Whitecrest?" he asked again.

He looked at the Guardian blankly.

"You need not say anything more," Phoenix said while looking him in the eye. "It is worse than I had feared."

Aenyx felt the night wind stirring as he stood before his idol. It was a surreal moment. It felt like…destiny.

"You'd better get back to the Trials. It is too dangerous to continue this conversation here," Phoenix said. "When you become an Honorary Guardian—and I feel strongly that you will—then we will continue this conversation."

Aenyx felt like he was being enmeshed in a shadowy world beyond his comprehension or his control. All his life, he had wanted to be a Guardian. Now he was starting to realize he was entering a world of treachery and betrayal, just to bask in the superficial glory the masses bestowed upon these "Guardians."

CHAPTER 15

MOONCHASING

"Miss me?" Aenyx said to Ronax and Brandon upon returning to the night gathering of Stormguard recruits.

"You almost missed it!" Brandon replied. "The moon is rising higher in the sky, and it is almost time."

"Old Pridemaster Jasper told us that we were splitting up into groups of three," Ronax said. "We were given a choice of who to select for our third. Congratulations, we picked you."

Aenyx managed an uneasy chuckle. Brandon looked him in the eye and could sense that something was wrong.

"We are assigned to the northern sector near the Mountains of Mordrath," Brandon told him. "It's the most dangerous region—surely, that's a complete coincidence."

"Yes, I bet," Aenyx replied sardonically.

"You lads up for the challenge?" Jasper Stormguard said as he walked up behind them. "Look, I know you three," he continued. "You are all a pain in the keister, but you will do just fine. Be on the lookout for moondrakes—they have been getting frisky lately, as if something is stirring up to the north. They attacked a pair of griffins who were hunting northwest of here and damn near killed them. Our Pride members were lucky to return with their feathers intact."

The three griffins exchanged concerned glances.

"Don't worry, Pridemaster," Aenyx said. "We will be ready."

"Good," Jasper replied. "So it looks like the Goldeneyries just dispatched a group of recruits; that means you three are cleared for take-off."

The trio of griffins nodded their beaks to signify comprehension.

"That means get going!" he shouted.

"Yes, Pridemaster!" they blurted out. One by one, each griffin broke into a run and ascended into the night skies. They flew north and then reunited shortly afterward in a triangular formation, with Aenyx taking point, Brandon on the left flank, and Ronax on the right.

Aenyx peered behind him to see that his friends were aligned and to get one more glance at Mount Rhaemor. The flames of the torches that had been lit in a circular arrangement around the main arena were receding into the night. They were truly on their own now.

As they plunged deeper into the void of night, their eyesight began to attune to the darkness, and the outlines of the Mountains of Mordrath could be seen in the distance. The griffins flew in formation for miles while scanning the horizon for enemies of the republic.

"Do you think we will find a moondrake?" Brandon shouted ahead.

"We will if you keep yelling like that!" Aenyx exclaimed while looking back over his soaring wings.

They flew deep into the northern wilderness, far away from the vista of Mount Rhaemor. The terrain was growing rockier and more rugged. The trees and shrubbery were becoming sparser. The land was dark gray from the accumulated volcanic ash due to the eruptions of Mount Kildrath, which loomed like a dark regent on the northeastern periphery.

"I am suddenly not liking the idea of this so much," Ronax shouted. "I feel like a sparrow in a copper mine."

"Not to worry!" Aenyx responded. "There is nothing up ahead, but—"

A war-screech pierced through the night. It was not from a moondrake, however…it was from a griffin. Goldeneyrie griffins, to be exact.

"*Ayeeee-rrieee, yawwww!*"

The griffin recruits broke formation as Ronax and Brandon peeled off the flanks and flapped their wings wildly to get away from the attack. They had been caught completely unaware.

Three griffins in full bronze-plate armor bearing glinting steel talons ambushed them from the rear. The Goldeneyrie assassins must have been waiting for them in the Mountains of Mordrath.

"Aenyx, look out!" Brandon shouted.

It was too late. One of the steel-tipped talons had gashed his right wing, sending him spiraling. Fortunately, it was only a flesh wound.

The griffin assassins were relentless. They swirled around Aenyx, using the night and the element of surprise to their advantage. The situation seemed bleak, but Aenyx was not about to shrink from the prospect of battle.

"Betrayers!" he screeched and raked the eyes of the assassin attacking him head-on.

He recognized the tactic and immediately flew straight up to avoid the inevitable rear attacker. The unseen sentry crashed into the assailant in front of him with a tremendous clash of metal.

As they reeled from the collision, Aenyx sensed their opportunity to make a getaway. While the assassins had the element of surprise on their side, they were now overburdened with armor plating, meaning the recruits had the advantage of speed.

"Brandon, Ronax, break for it!" Aenyx shouted.

"Not without you!" Ronax shouted. It would be the last thing he would ever cry out. One of the Goldeneyrie sentries ran a sharpened talon through the back of his throat.

"*Ronax*!" Aenyx screeched. His friend dropped from the sky in a dead fall, revealing the assassin behind him.

"Give it up, Aenyx!" the sentry cried. "Or your other friend will die as well!"

"Do your worst!" Brandon yelled and scrambled to get away.

The young griffin's wings flapped as hard as they could while he flew higher toward the moonlight. Aenyx watched his friend struggle to get away before one of the assassins snatched him by his claws and pulled him back downward. Brandon beat his wings as hard as he could, but there was no escape. He was pulled downward in a fatal grip, caught in the Goldeneyries' trap. Another sentry flew up to him and slashed his throat mercilessly with a steel-tipped talon.

"*No*!" Aenyx screamed. He beat his wings as fast as he could to retaliate against the cowardly assassins. The griffin closed the distance in a hurry.

He was about to crash directly into his foes when the heavens suddenly lit up with the unmistakable, terrifying glow of dragonflame. It illuminated the shocked faces of his attackers and the bleak landscape below.

It was a fireball of such immense yellow flame and so intensely hot that it singed off the feathers of the sentries in an instantaneous flash. The griffins were blown backward, their bronze armor gleaming hideously in the glow of the dragonflame.

This was not the attack of a moondrake. It could only be one other thing…

The faint outline of a great beast appeared in the night sky—almost too large to be believed. The moonlight traced the shape of an ancient evil that had not been seen for at least a generation in the vicinity of Aeris. It was exceptionally huge and monstrous, and as the full moon shone into the beast's eyes, it appeared as though two more lunar orbs had joined it in the celestial sky.

This was a shadow dragon.

The newfound enemy made the griffins' night battle seem trivial by comparison. If the griffins did not act and act right away, the Republic of Aeris would be in the gravest of danger.

"No time for this treason any longer!" Aenyx said. "If you came here to murder, why not help me murder this beast?"

Without a word, the Goldeneyrie sentries turned tail and fled into the night, leaving Aenyx to face the black monster all by himself.

"They must figure me as good as dead, anyway," Aenyx muttered. "They might be right."

As Aenyx hovered in the air, only a few miles southwest of Mount Kildrath, he believed he had little choice but to try to lead the dragon away from Aeris. This would at least give the Guardians and the Five

Prides time to mount a defense—assuming the griffin sentries were heading back to sound the alarms.

Aenyx saw the shadow dragon coming straight for him. He dove beneath the creature and then decided to fly closer to the earth, believing the dragon might have more difficulty soaring near ground level. Dragons, he had once learned, used their great serpentine length to their advantage by flying with a whip-like motion. They would often undulate their tails as they soared to gain more velocity.

The fleet griffin flew west into the bleak wasteland. Although the dragon scanned the skies for its prey, it had difficulty following Aenyx's flight path. While a moondrake might have kept pace with Aenyx, as far as the shadow dragon was concerned, this pursuit was leading it far away from its hunting grounds.

The dragon bellowed a terrifying screech, which reverberated across the wilderness. The ravens that had been sleeping in the leafless trees scattered. Every creature with a bit of sense retreated far underground. The great winged serpent flew up into the light of the full moon, casting a hideous outline. The beast looked east, and with a tremendous flap of its wings, turned back toward the region of Aeris.

Aenyx was exhausted, alone, and betrayed. Brandon and Ronax were dead. The land that he had sworn to give his life for and that he was willing to serve had utterly deceived him. He had come too close to power, and because of that, there had been not just one, but two attempts to end his life. And now his last living friend must be in mortal danger; she knew too much and was therefore a dire threat to unmasking the conspirators.

The griffin made his way to land on the rocky terrain. He figured that he must be in the southern plains of the Sulfurous Wastes, which stretched from the Mountains of Mordrath to the west. He set his paws down on the barren land of volcanic rock. The entire area reeked of sulfur and ash. It was a godforsaken hellscape.

Tired and wounded, the griffin lay near a jagged rock to get some sleep. There was no use taking drastic action when he was so confused about the events of the last twenty-four hours. The stars in the sky turned into milky drops of light in the griffin's fading vision. He pulled the pitch-black blanket of the night over him, hoping to hide away from the evil that had befallen him and his beloved homeland.

Then, off in the distance, arose a pitiful cry. It sounded like a dragon's screech of sorts, though rather mournful as opposed to threatening. Aenyx cocked his head to listen. Then he heard it again—the unmistakable cry of a moondrake.

CHAPTER 16

MIRANDA SUNRAY

Awakening on a mossy bed of forest undergrowth, Sigismund saw two black eyes staring back at him. You could say he *saw* them more than he recognized them. At first, he had no idea what he was looking at. They were like two tiny, black specks in a maze of crisscrossed lines that must have been tree branches contrasted against the white, winter sky.

And not only were there two shiny black specks, but a row of glossy, white teeth also floated in the air above him. This was a smile. He was sure of it! He was not hallucinating, nor dreaming, because the smile was quite recognizable, even evocative! No, this was not an illusion. This was a *thing*. And not just any old thing. A creature. *A creature?*

Sigismund blinked twice. To his great dismay and tremendous fright, *it* blinked back. The prince skedaddled backward as fast as he could scuttle, making a right muck-up of his robe in the process.

"Oy!" was the only noise Siggie could manage to exclaim.

The young man now had a better view of this ethereal forest creature. It was a slight being with pale alabaster skin hovering in the air. Sparkly bits of light glittered around it as well as a warm glow flickering like a candle flame in the wind. Its slender frame was quite…feminine? It wore a thin, ethereal gown and tiny cockleshells in its platinum hair. Its face was well-sculptured and wonderfully androgynous.

"Well, hello there!" the being proclaimed in a cheery voice.

A few spooked blackbirds flew out of a dilapidated hawthorn tree and scattered into the wind with the good sense to flee the scene. Sigismund's eyes merely grew wide.

"Oh, my! You have black eyes just like mine!" the creature declared in a squeaky voice. "You must be Sigismund!"

After an initial pulse of shock, it sank in that this diminutive woodland creature actually knew his name. He looked carefully and agreed. It also had black eyes, just like he did.

"What…are you?" Prince Sigismund blurted out in a thin, trembling voice.

"Why, I am sorry, dear boy! Truly sorry!" the creature replied. "My name is Miranda Sunray!"

The young man leaned backward against an elderberry tree. He was astonished—even flabbergasted.

"That…is your real name?" he queried her while vigorously rubbing his sore head.

"Why, of course, silly! Is Prince Sigismund your real name?" she asked and giggled.

"Yes, yes, it is," he replied, feeling quite strange to be holding a conversation with a woodland nymph. "But that only brings us to the question: How did *you* know it?"

"I'm a messenger-spirit for a very powerful wizard," she replied, sounding quite satisfied with herself. "I am not of this world—not exactly. The good mage says if I help him with a very important quest, then he will send me home."

"Home," Sigismund said to himself. "That is a word with a pleasant ring to it. Where is your home?"

"Why I live in the fairy world," she responded. "Well, both worlds actually. It's complicated."

She sighed, as if gathering the energy to continue.

"You see, my home is all of Solarius, but it is a realm that exists both at the same time as this one, and potentially, also in the future," she continued. "We fairies call it *The Could-Be.*"

"The...Could-Be?" Sigismund responded, growing more comfortable with the thought of talking to a fairy. "That is a funny name for a home."

"Where is your home, Prince Sigismund?" Miranda asked.

The glum prince looked at her with a pained expression on his boyish face. It dawned on him that he no longer had a real home.

CHAPTER 17

A MOTHER'S GIFT

"Do you know something, Prince Sigismund?" Miranda asked.

The young man looked up at her.

"You have a very special gift," she said definitively. "I can sense it in you. Or most likely, *on* you. I have the strongest urge to fly right up to you and find out what it is!" she shouted with glee and flew at him with super-fast speed.

Sigismund cringed and threw up his hands to shield his face. At the last second, she pulled up and laughed puckishly. As she slapped her legs in hilarity, the prince cowered with his hands over his head in a defensive posture. He peeked through his fingers at the outrageous spectacle.

"What do you mean, a gift?" he asked. "You mean, like being good at art? Oh…a gift!"

The young man slapped his left breast pocket. It was still there. His mother's birthday present.

"Yes, open it, open it!" Miranda cheered while clapping her diminutive hands.

Sigismund felt a saccharine joy well up in his heart just thinking about his beautiful mother's smiling face. Then he suddenly felt heartsick—but at least he had this memento to give him courage in these darkest of times.

The prince reached into the hidden pocket in his robe and produced the elegantly wrapped gift. As he sat on a mossy rock, he wondered what it could be. He pulled the black bow on the little silver box. The ribbon uncoiled and lay loosely on his lap.

"I bet this is a wonderful gift!" Miranda exclaimed and hovered above him in anticipation. Prince Sigismund peered at the woodland sprite, who seemed so eager for him to open it.

He placed his thumb on the side of the silver box and gently pried open the lid. As the box lid separated from its container, the fairy flew closer to get a glimpse.

Sigismund reactively swatted at the fairy, which caused her to zip back a few feet. "Sorry," he said, "I am not used to you flitting about me yet."

The prince opened the gift box, revealing a folded letter resting on top of an object wrapped in black velvet cloth. The sprite dove for the object, but Sigismund quickly put his hand over the box.

"Are you trying to steal my gift?" the prince asked.

The sprite blushed and flew back a bit more. "Oh, I'm sorry, Prince Sigismund," she replied sheepishly. "It is just that I am so excited to see it."

Now, the curiosity was too much. He set the letter aside and grabbed the object, which was still wrapped in black cloth. He held it in front of his face and then slowly pulled the cloth away with his right hand. A beam of light immediately reflected off the top of the object, scattering rays into the forest.

The light from the object revealed a forest in full bloom, but only from about a man's height and above wherever the light was shining. In front of his scarcely believing eyes was a dogwood tree with delicate white flowers adorning its drooping branches; yet, below was the barren, dead-looking husk of a tree.

The prince gasped and moved what appeared to be a crystal shard to the right. There was a redbud tree with its pinkish-magenta buds turned upward toward the sky. The colors were so vivid, they took his breath away. He moved the object to his left and saw a gorgeous empress tree in abounding purple-flowered majesty.

He was enthralled—he had only seen such flowers in the books his mother gave him. Their colors were so breathtaking and alluring; he felt compelled to walk over to one of the illuminated trees to see if he could touch the flowers.

"Home! The Could-Be!" Miranda Sunray declared.

She flew right into the trees, zigging and zagging through the branches wildly. She returned with a bewildered and disappointed look on her face.

"*The Would-Be?*" she asked with a frown.

Sigismund fully unwrapped the crystal shard in his hand. It shone much more brilliantly now, lighting up the forest floor in front of him, as well as the trees. Seemingly growing beneath the trees were beautiful, multihued foxgloves in iridescent rainbow colors—the dreamlike purple of wolfsbane, the pale pink enchantment of oleander, and the popping white blooms of the lily of the valley. It was the full glory of spring in the forest wherever the crystal's light touched, but all that fell outside the light appeared to be death and deterioration. The prince looked into the crystal with fascination; then he suddenly covered it with the cloth and tucked it inside his robe.

"What kind of magic is this?" the prince asked with wonderment.

"The light," the fairy said breathlessly. "It can shine into The Could-Be. I tried flying home, going into it, but sadly, it is just an image. It is not yet the reality."

"Then…how did you get here?" Sigismund asked. "How are you going to get home?"

"That is what the wizard Talus Nightspell promised to help me with," she replied, looking deep into his black eyes.

"Talus Nightspell…" Sigismund repeated slowly. "That's the wizard who declared the fatal prophecy about me! He might finally have the answers I have been seeking for so long. Do you think he can help me?"

"Why, that is absotively what I am here for!" Miranda responded and giggled.

The prince gave the woodland sprite a crooked smile, then he chuckled slightly.

"Oh, and I have my mother's letter!" he exclaimed. "Maybe he can explain what this is all about."

CHAPTER 18

BLOODHOUNDS ON THE TRAIL

Prince Sigismund walked over to the mossy rock where the letter lay. He picked it up and unfolded it. He read it aloud while imagining his mother speaking the words in her comforting voice:

"Dearest Sigismund, Happiest of birthdays! You surely have held in your hand this wondrous crystal shard. It was a gift of the mage whose warning helped protect you all these years. He said it was a shard from the Arch Crystal—a magic stone that held within it the tremendous potential of beings in this world. It was enchanted many years ago and then used by the Mighty Three to draw out a terrible curse, thus saving the lives of thousands of creatures on Solarius.

"Use it to find your way in this lost world! It will shine a light before your eyes, thereby allowing you to see the good in everyone and everything. Its rays can open magical doorways and give you insights into the darkest of hearts. Cherish it, dear son, and use it wisely. It is a powerful and ancient magic that may help you unlock your own great potential. Love Always, Your Mother, the Queen Galadria."

The prince folded the letter slowly and tucked it into his pocket. A tear welled up in the corner of his left eye as he thought about the wonderful gift from his mother.

Then, suddenly, the barking of bloodhounds could be heard off in the distance. The king's search party was still tracking him!

"We must get this to the wizard at once!" Miranda Sunray blurted out. "Follow me."

The prince was still a bit woozy and unsteady on his legs due to the nasty spill he had taken. Nonetheless, he felt a surge of energy at the frightful thought of the yelping bloodhounds he had escaped the other night, thanks to the help of the Kindly Knight.

The fairy darted into the woods like a shooting star. Sparkling bursts of light trailed behind her. The prince followed along as quickly as his wobbly legs could hold up. Every so often, she would stop and wait for him to catch up.

"Hurry up!" she shouted in a tiny voice.

"I am coming! I am coming!" the prince told her with a huff. They made their way through the forest, which was overlaid with dense brush and fallen branches.

Shadows from the wispy trees blotted his path. It all seemed like a blur to Sigismund. The dogs' barking grew louder.

"Oh, Sigismund!" the fairy squealed. "They are going to catch us!"

The prince knew that the fairy was right. He ran after her until he feared he would pass out. He knew all along that he wasn't faster than the bloodhounds chasing him. As if things could not get worse, he tripped over a fallen tree branch and collapsed at the foot of a dogwood tree. It was over, unless something could stop those devil dogs from running after him.

Five of the salivating hounds reached the edge of the glen. The fierce-looking canines barked in a craze, alerting their owners that they had finally found the source of the scent.

The prince was trapped.

At a loss for options, his left hand found its way into his plush robe. It fumbled around until it found the crystal shard. Without any particular idea of what he was doing, he whipped the crystal out and thrust it into a ray of light.

The light scattered the sun's rays in a thousand directions. Its brilliant white beams hit the eyes of the bloodhounds, who immediately froze and fell on the ground, whimpering. Then, unexpectedly, came playful barking. The dogs stood with their tails wagging and ran over to the prince, who was still clinging to the crystal with both hands.

When the dogs jumped on him, Sigismund feared the hounds might maul him to death. Instead, they affectionately licked his face, smothering him with kisses. The prince felt like he might die anyway—drowning in dog saliva.

"That's enough!" he said with a laugh. "That's enough."

He stood while the dogs continued to bounce energetically around him, basking joyously in his presence.

"Go home, now!" the prince told the dogs, who seemed to understand him. They gave a reluctant look, then all darted back into the woods, just as the voices of men could be heard.

"What's that, boy?" one man said loudly. "False alarm?"

"Oh, well," another voice answered. "Off we go!"

Sigismund and the fairy could hardly believe the turn of events. But it was not the time to question it.

"This would be a good time to escape," the prince said to the fairy.

"Yes, the wizard must know about this," Miranda replied. "Let's go!"

CHAPTER 19

THE WIZARDRY OF TALUS NIGHTSPELL

The fairy and the prince traipsed throughout the Solistrian Forest until it was nearly dark. Sigismund was treading more carefully now, and he was very grateful to have escaped imminent danger. But the young man had grown incredibly hungry—and tired.

"How much farther?" the exhausted prince asked.

"Oh, I think that's our trail!" Miranda declared merrily and pointed ahead.

"Thank goodness for that," he wearily replied.

They stumbled upon a winding trail that led downhill through wild thickets. The trail was muddy and covered with moss and branches, and Sigismund could barely discern the path beneath. The fairy led him onward, even as the light was fading fast. He forged his way through the snapping branches and crackling twigs. And when he felt like he couldn't take a step farther, a break in the tree line appeared. He stood on its edge and looked ahead. The forest cleared at the bottom of a dark ravine. He was unsure which way to go.

"There it is!" Miranda Sunray shouted with glee. "We made it!"

"Made it…where?" Sigismund asked.

"That is our sorcerer's hidden abode," she replied. "You don't see it?"

He could see nothing except an impressively dark shadow.

"Wait a minute," he said.

The prince protracted the crystal shard from his pocket again. Then, he thrust it up. Faintly, he saw a humble stone cottage with wispy plumes of smoke piping up into the air. He moved the crystal from side to side, only to see the cottage appear and then alternatively disappear into the darkness. It was a mystery what this shard of crystal could and could not do.

"Fantastic!" he said.

"Follow me!" the fairy replied with a toothy grin.

The young man walked forward, still holding the shard before him. As he approached, a door opened, and an old man in a dark blue cloak and a floppy hat waved his hands frantically.

"Put that thing away! Put that thing away!" he heard the old man bristle. As he put the crystal back into his pocket, he could no longer see anyone in front of him.

"All right, all right," he said. "Now you can step forward."

Sigismund took another step. To his amazement, he was suddenly *inside* something.

It was spectacularly vibrant, even in the light of sundown. The sky was a magisterial reddish orange, as if it were the very color of hope itself. All along the brick walkway leading to the wizard's door, he could see rose bushes of every color and variety—red, white, pink, even yellow. Before him stood a lovely stone cottage. The windows were made of exquisitely shined glass. The flowerpots were overflowing with blossoming Escape Tulips and Queen of the Night tulips. Emerald hummingbirds darted about, and bumble bees could be seen buzzing near the cottage. It was an idyllic paradise, except it was hidden away from the rest of the world.

"Come in, come in!" the sorcerer boomed.

He was a tallish man, even hunched over as he walked toward Sigismund. He bore a white oaken wizard's staff that clinked the brick walkway. When he put his hand on Sigismund, the young man could feel that his firm hand was definitely real. The wizard ushered him into the stone cottage, and the fairy Miranda Sunray zipped through just as the thick mahogany door was about to close.

Inside, the magnificent cottage was filled with curiosities. The deep maroon carpeting did not have a pattern like most carpets, but rather what appeared to be an intricate map of Solarius. When he walked through the room, he felt faint, alternating sensations, such as the sound of rushing water, the feel of crisp mountain air, and the smell of dense, evergreen forests. It was intoxicating, although at the same time, he remained in full command of himself and his awareness of reality.

The wizard pointed for the prince to sit in a green, velvet chair with ornamental backing that looked like a drake with its wings spread wide. As he sat down, he felt the wings enclosing him. His imagination whisked him away to take a dragon's view, high above the clouds, as he looked down upon the forest and even the little stone cottage. There was such power in every object. The entire place now smelled vaguely of mahogany and cinnamon.

"Young man, over here," the mage said with a hearty laugh. He bent over and stoked the fireplace with a metal prod that looked like a thin bronze lance. Sparks flicked from the tip of the lance-like fire poker, and the flames reawakened. The wizard replaced the tool in its rack near the fireplace, which housed a mantel adorned with knickknacks. They appeared to be metallic figurines of assorted mystical Solarian beasts.

"There, much better," the wizard said.

He whirled around and sat down upon an impressive high-backed chair. It was old rustic leather with silver insignia inlaid in some intricate pattern that struck him as archaic writing.

Underneath the mage's floppy, blue hat, the old man's light blue eyes sparkled with a magical gleam. His crooked nose was suspended smack dab in the middle of a worn, leathery face that appeared weathered from decades of travel across the Solarian landscape dealing with sundry concerns. His peppery-white beard was long and flowing. The black flecks dotted it like dark buoys in a frothy ocean.

"You see..." Sigismund began nervously.

"Don't!" the wizard snapped.

And so they sat there. And sat there. And then sat there some more. The wizard was sizing him up and staring into his black eyes suspiciously. The young man sat as long as he could manage, squirming in only the slightest fashion. The fairy exuded a warm glow from the corner of the room and watched on, apparently knowing better than to interrupt.

"Alas, you are welcome!" the conjurer declared.

The wizard rubbed his hands together vigorously. The old man's fingers were long protuberances that reminded him of uncooked sausages. It was as if the mage had suddenly decided, right there and then, that he would extend the prince his most generous hospitality, rather than smite him on the spot.

CHAPTER 20

THE COSTLIEST VICTORY OF THEM ALL

"Let's get down to business," the mage continued.

The wizard stood and walked toward the door. As he strode by, the prince had the strangest sense that his mind was more open now than it had ever been. The mage paused for a moment, then procured a heavy black tome from a sturdy-looking bookshelf that was carved from the hollow trunk of a scarlet oak tree.

"Have you ever heard of the Battle of the Onyx Wastes?" the wizard asked in an odd, forced whisper.

Sigismund cocked his head as the wizard returned with the book. "Why, I would imagine every schoolboy has heard of that infamous battle," he offered up.

"Rightly so!" the mage responded. "But I doubt you have ever heard a story quite like this."

The young man settled into the dragon-back chair and got comfortable as the sorcerer spun his tale. The fire crackled in the hearth, and the reflection of its flames danced in the prince's glassy black eyes. In the room, the shadows even seemed to gather at the great mage's feet, as if entranced by his every word and command.

"I suppose you want to know what happened at the beginning, but I tell you now that there was no beginning," the wizard said. "This is all part of an eternal war, a war in which we, as living beings, are merely the breathing manifestations of the cosmic consciousness."

The wizard paused and stroked his grand, flowing beard. He stared into the fire, as if he could see something in it that nobody else could. Then, he gave a quick glance over at the startled young man and soon gathered that he was utterly confused.

"But, I will say, we can start at some beginning," the mage qualified while pointing his index finger straight into the air. "At least one that may make some sense to a foolish lad such as yourself."

Sigismund cocked an eyebrow at the wisecrack. He decided that maybe it was better to hold his peace and listen attentively to the old man.

"Perhaps you have heard of the Dread Commander," the wizard said somberly. "The shadow dragon emperor of the north, the one they call Dracus Imprimus."

The prince wordlessly nodded.

"Good, good," the mage replied. "Then I will spare you the many details of that one's infamy. Suffice to say, a great war was fought over a generation ago for the future of every living being in Solarius."

The prince furrowed his brows and conveyed that he was following along.

"The war was awful, simply awful," the mage sadly pronounced. "Beasts from all over this world suffered from this terrible calamity. It came down to an unspeakably black curse uttered by the Dread Commander. It was so catastrophic, the natural world still has not recovered."

"What…happened?" the prince responded with a strained voice.

"Simply put, son," the mage said, "there was a tremendous battle at the Sulfurous Wastes, and due to the great serpents' aversion to fighting in the day, the allied armies won a tremendous victory. But sadly, that was not the last of Dracus Imprimus. No, not the last of…"

The wizard paused, as if each passage of the story drained him of his very being. Sigismund could feel the pain racking his soul as he gave his account of the war. He had still not even thumbed through the book, but he merely recited the story as if he could draw it from the tome through some intimate channel that connected with his mind.

"As the victorious army at the Sulfurous Wastes marched toward the Obsidian Fortress, Dracus gathered his shadow dragon corps and the moondrakes for a final battle," the mage went on. "This became a pitched night battle known as the Battle of the Onyx Wastes, and it ended in the dragon commander desperately casting a curse upon us all. We became sick and weakened and were forced to retreat. It was a small consolation that the black magic Dracus Imprimus expended also meant his nearly fatal weakening. After his curse, he fled to the Obsidian Fortress, which lay in the darkest reaches of Noctera."

"What was the curse?" Sigismund asked in awe.

"It was a bane that is beyond comprehension," he said ruefully. "All creatures' eyes and blood turned black; they clutched their hearts in great pain, and all became deathly ill. Our entire army lay dying on the battlefield, along with the foul legions commanded by Dracus Imprimus. It seemed all hope was lost. That is where the Mighty Three come in."

Sigismund could sense agitation growing in the wizard's voice. The young man clung to his every word.

"The Mighty Three took a sacred stone, known as the Arch Crystal, and drew out the curse. The blackness cleared from every creature's eyes, from their very blood, and it appeared the three sages had saved the world from sure ruin. Alas, all of it came at a tremendous cost."

The angelically cheerful Miranda Sunray suddenly turned gloomy, as if she already knew the tale.

"You see, a sacrifice had to be made," the wizard said.

He stopped and locked gazes with Sigismund. It was disconcerting for the young man, but it was also mesmerizing.

"All of the potential of this world had to be captured in that crystal in order to absorb and contain that great evil," the mage explained. "The Arch Crystal was hidden away in a secret place called the Illusory Fortress, which was guarded by the world's greatest warrior, Gilead Highbloode. And as far as I know, he is still guarding the crystal to this day."

Prince Sigismund's mind was flooded with many thoughts stemming from the wizard's tale. There were simply too many implications for him to process.

"Now, you might wonder about this sprite," the wizard said abruptly. He raised his hand, and the fairy fluttered to it. "She is a special little thing, as you know, and she bears the same sign of this cataclysm," he continued. "Namely, the black eyes."

Miranda Sunray beamed proudly at the wizard's praise.

"It is true that the curse was drawn out of all creatures," the mage said. "This saved many creatures' lives. But the drawback was that their highest potential needed to be drawn into the Arch Crystal as well. And yet, despite this drastic action, there were still aspects of the Dread Commander's curse that somehow persisted throughout the realms.

"As a consequence of the spell, one member of each realm bore an after-effect; namely, they were born with black eyes. It seemed to be a sign of remembrance," he continued. "This sign was passed down to one offspring in each of the major kingdoms save the Equine kingdom of Wysteria, for reasons peculiar to their kind. This sign strongly suggests to me that the remedy to the actual curse has manifested itself in the form of each such creature possessing black eyes."

"So, I *am* cursed?" Prince Sigismund asked in a horrified voice.

"Settle down! I say, settle down!" the old wizard said in a commanding voice. "Let me get to that, son. I will tell you a little secret about that."

Miranda Sunray flew to Sigismund's side. She listened with intense interest to the wizard's every word.

"The black eyes are *not* a curse," the mage explained. "They reflect that you are naturally attracted to discovering and unlocking your true potential. With those black eyes of yours, we will find and unleash the world's potential. Only then will we be able to defeat the Dread Commander and end the curse, once and for all. We must find and destroy the Arch Crystal!"

Prince Sigismund and Miranda Sunray looked at one another in amazement.

"But, but there are only two of us!" the fairy squeaked.

"My dear Miranda," the wizard replied, "that is the entire basis for your next quest."

CHAPTER 21

AN UNEXPECTED ENCOUNTER

The drake's ear-splitting shrieks made Aenyx temporarily forget about his own precarious plight. It was the most pitiful wailing. It was mournful, heartrending even; granted, it was likely coming from a great serpent. But could this truly be emanating from a moondrake? That would be quite extraordinary.

The griffin licked his bloody, scratched forelimbs and struggled considerably to get on his claws and paws. His right wing was badly injured. The ashen dirt and the smell of sulfur made his head ache. He was far from home. And he did not even want to think about his friends who might be dead. It occurred to him that he had to find out about this incessant wailing. Was the creature still a threat?

Aenyx stumbled over the ashen terrain in the light of the morning sun. The daystar shone with a wan, straw-colored light. It panged his eyes to see, but the curiosity was overwhelming him. He stumbled over the dry, cracked landscape, which was dotted with all manner of igneous rock from frequent volcanic eruptions in primeval times. He crouched behind a slab of basalt on his right to get a better look at the sweeping stretch of open terrain to his north. On the horizon loomed the ever-menacing Mount Kildrath.

The wails were a bit louder now. The sound was maddening. He poked his head up over the rock, just about beak-high, and his black eyes scanned the landscape for signs of the moondrake. Then, he finally spotted it.

It was a writhing black serpent coiled up on open ground, lashing its tail as if in utter torment. The beast's tail slammed the ground, and then it wriggled in agony. It reared its dark blue head and unleashed a mighty wail.

Aenyx watched the monstrous creature, transfixed by its travails. It struck the griffin that the serpent was midnight blue—quite unlike any moondrake he had ever been warned about. And while the serpent appeared to be quite vulnerable, he knew better. A wounded drake was surely the most dangerous kind.

As he kept his glassy black eyes locked on the wildly contorting drake, Aenyx slowly made his approach. Step by step, he crept into the open patch of land, painfully aware that he was now completely exposed in the pale light of day.

The moondrake's wailing grew louder as he approached. His eagle-acute hearing amplified the creature's pitiful sounds, as well as the throbbing pain in his head. He crept along the stygian wasteland with his wings bent low and nearly scraping the ground. Still, the beast wriggled wildly and moaned miserably on the black landscape. It did not seem to have the faintest inkling of the griffin's approach.

But suddenly, the moondrake turned toward Aenyx. The griffin's talons scattered loose rocks on the sun-cracked terrain. Both creatures froze immediately, locked in mutual terror. With its wings spread wide and neck outstretched from its supine frame, the drake's midnight blue head cocked so that its glassy black eyes could get a better view of the surrounding vista.

Their awful stare-down lasted for a gut-wrenching moment. Druix knew he was in no shape to do battle. He stared at the griffin standing perfectly still on the barren plain, and he homed in on its shiny black eyes staring back at him.

The moondrake looked at his adversary and moaned pitifully. Still heartbroken from the sure death of his father, he collapsed onto the cold tundra. He wasn't so sure that he didn't want to die right then and there. His life had been cursed from the very day he was born. Excommunicated and abandoned by his moondrake brethren, the profound sadness of realizing that he would never be accepted made him feel his life force draining away, and his will to live was eroding.

As Aenyx watched the creature's head lying on the ground, he began to look anew at what he now saw was a majestic beast in a terrible plight. He walked slowly to the creature whose gaping maw was sucking air. Its black eyes were glassy and almost milky at the edges from its exhaustingly painful condition.

As the creature lay on the black tundra, the griffin found the courage to walk upright to the seemingly dying moondrake. As he walked over to its head, which still lay on the cold ground, he reached over with his outstretched claw. The drake flinched and closed its black eyes, likely believing that his adversary would soon end his intense suffering.

Instead, Aenyx patted his head. As he caressed it with gentle strokes, he saw the moondrake's eyes begin to well up with tears. Although he could not use words to communicate with his fellow creature, he felt the healing power extend throughout his limbs. It immediately forged a bond.

The drake's shallow, rapid breathing began to slow and grow more measured. Druix blinked slowly and started to relax. He felt the blood pump through his limbs. It flowed into his wings, which he felt like extending. He struggled to get off the tundra. He kicked his rear legs, raised his long neck, and pulled his wings in to turn over and get back on his feet again.

After he groaned deeply, the moondrake got onto all fours and tried to stabilize. His wing was badly injured. It was deeply gashed from the shadow dragon's attack. Druix collapsed back onto the ground with a tremendous thud, but at least he was right side up now and no longer moaning.

Aenyx felt that some cosmic twist of fate must have brought them together. The two creatures were alone, injured, far from home, and had no help. While it violated every norm that he had been taught in the Republic of Aeris, he believed that trying to befriend the moondrake could reverse their ill fortunes. And with shadow dragons out there like the one who attacked him and his friends—and quite possibly the moondrake before him—Aenyx would take every friend he could get.

The griffin knew what the drake needed more than anything else: a meal. Come to mention it, he was famished himself. He walked back up to the moondrake, put his claw on its head, and then flew off southward to get dinner.

As a battered and rent Druix watched the griffin fly off toward the forest south of the Sulfurous Wastes, he felt compelled to reconsider everything he thought he knew about this world. If his father were truly dead, it would mean that he was completely abandoned. But then he would be free to roam the earth, to discover himself, to make his own way in life. If this griffin returned, it might be a sign of a new friendship as well as the start of a new adventure.

CHAPTER 22

NO HOME LIKE A FARAWAY PLACE

It was past midday when the griffin returned. Aenyx flew toward the moondrake from the southern plains of the wasteland. When he finally arrived, he flapped his wings and gently landed near the drake. In his beak were the shanks of a mule deer he had successfully hunted down on the alpine slopes of the Mountains of Mordrath.

Aenyx strode up to the moondrake and placed the deer flanks before his mouth. The griffin and the moondrake exchanged glances, and Aenyx recognized the beast's gratitude.

The moondrake gobbled up the deer shanks with a tremendous gulp. Aenyx felt that as much as it filled its hungry belly, it did more to fill the drake's heart with hope that things could turn around.

The moondrake made another noble attempt to get to his feet. Unfortunately, his legs were still wobbly, and he fell back to the ground, wounded and exhausted. The griffin decided from that point onward he would become the moondrake's guardian. The griffin would bring fresh kills for the moondrake to eat while he scouted the terrain for a sign of his friends—be they slain or alive.

The sun rose and set for three long days with Aenyx safeguarding the moondrake. He brought the wounded creature whatever scraps of food he could obtain: a young fawn, a mountain goat, even a few wild hares. Each time, he set the scraps at the moondrake's head, and each time he scarfed them right up.

The moondrake's leathery wing appeared to be slowly healing. On the third day, with Aenyx's help, the drake flapped it a bit and tried to get up off the terrain. But he only succeeded in kicking up a cloud of dust that made Aenyx cough. It was painful to watch the beast struggle, but Aenyx could see he was making real progress.

On the fourth day of the griffin's watchful protection, the moondrake finally had some energy built up, and he mustered all his strength to get to his feet. He clambered to his claws and began lumbering around on the barren plains.

Aenyx was practically cheering. He leapt up and down to signify his approval. The moondrake gleefully roared and gently bounced up and down on his claws. He whipped his body around abruptly, forcing the griffin to leap over his tail.

That afternoon, Druix unexpectedly crept over to the snoozing griffin. He bent his head low and briefly rubbed it against the griffin's own to show gratitude. The griffin leapt up in alarm, but then quickly calmed down.

Druix motioned his head in a friendly manner toward the griffin, wordlessly communicating that he was ready to leave.

The moondrake got a clumsy, running start on the cracked tundra and flew in graceless fashion to the northeast, toward where he believed he and his father had skirmished with the shadow dragon.

As Aenyx watched the moondrake fly off, he was sure that he did not want this to be the end of their story. He bounded a few times and took off into the late winter sky to find out what this odd midnight-blue moondrake was searching for.

The unlikely pair flew low, just above the cracked black tundra, which covered the endless terrain like a shroud. Off in the distance, Mount Kildrath was ever-watching. Aenyx kept a close eye out for signs of any of the moondrake's unsympathetic brethren. The wild north was a complete anarchy, and weakness nearly always encouraged merciless attack.

The two flew well past sunset until Aenyx could barely see the flying blue moondrake in the purpling dusk. He flew a safe distance behind the moondrake, just to be sure that he was not rejoining the others. The moondrake suddenly let out a terrible howl. It flapped its wings to halt the search and settled down on the terrain at the foot of Mount Kildrath itself.

Aenyx flew with all his speed to find out what had shocked the creature. Upon reaching the scene, he saw the moondrake with his head drooping from his elongated neck. He was hunched over like a swan in profound mourning for the dead serpent below its head. It was a haunting scene that Aenyx would never forget.

The griffin landed on the rocky terrain a respectable distance from the moondrake, so as not to interrupt his deeply personal grief. He merely watched for over an hour, feeling the bond for the creature swell in his heart. Aenyx himself had never known a father or a mother. Griffins only had allegiance to the Republic of Aeris and their individual Prides. And now, he felt utterly betrayed by it. The only personal friends that he had made among the Stormguard recruits were surely dead, their broken bodies dashed upon the rocks, along with his dreams of becoming a Guardian.

The sorrowful griffin felt a pang of remorse for the death of his friends. He was far from having his conscience cleared. He had led them into certain danger that fatal night, even after the first attempt on his life at the grappling trial. But he had felt invincible, and he obliviously led his friends into danger.

How could he have been so naïve? Hadn't Phoenix Stormguard given him a warning? He was choked with guilt, and he felt the flames of revenge run hot in his blood. It flowed throughout his veins and fueled him to take action.

For now, he would mourn for those he lost, along with this strange moondrake he felt such an unspoken affinity for.

After the drake had wept its eyes out, he turned toward Aenyx. They had to let go. They must rejoin the world—this time on their own terms.

When the moondrake looked back with gratitude at the griffin who had accompanied him to the scene of his father's death, Aenyx knew that their bond had been forged. Moondrake, griffin, what did it matter at this point? It was them against the world.

Aenyx motioned toward the moondrake to fly back south, away from Mount Kildrath and the certain death that awaited him should the other moondrakes discover them together. When the griffin took flight into the open air, the moondrake followed.

They set off on their night journey flying southward into the northern reaches of the Mountains of Mordrath. The shimmering stars encrusted the upper reaches of the majestic night sky. They sparkled like jewels scattered across the limitless universe. Absent any rulers but themselves, the griffin and the moondrake charted a new adventure into the great unknown.

The pair flew into the untamed wilderness south of the Sulfurous Wastes and swept through a familiar region, a valley that sat between three mountainous peaks where a mighty river once flowed. The Great River had once snaked its way through the valley below, but the glaciers of the Crystalline Source, which fed the ice flows far to the north of the river's head, had long ago stopped melting. And, just as the Diluvian Streams of the north had run dry, the Raging Rivers to the south also dried up, as well as the tributaries leading farther to the south that had once provided the Laketown villagers with transit and trade throughout the region.

Aenyx knew what he must do. He must take his black-eyed moondrake companion to the remaining settlement at Laketown—the last one of its kind on the Mirrhenian Lake. An old sage was there, one of the remaining few, who had acted as a translator for the griffins of Aeris for decades. He had an arcane method of communicating in Solarian languages.

It was time to visit the White Druid.

CHAPTER 23

A FLIGHT INTO THE VOID

The fairy Miranda Sunray had embarked upon a most curious quest. Talus Nightspell had given her the sacred task of finding an old druid colleague to the north. He'd told her that the druid lived in a broken-down shack in a settlement called Laketown on the Mirrhenian Lake.

The woodland nymph flew through the night, zigging and zagging through the Solistrian Forest that lay east of Hypernea, darting through sprawling swathes of ash trees, dogwoods, and poplars. She flew as if her life depended on it—and in many ways, it did. The longer she remained outside of The Could-Be, the more she felt her connection with the mystical realm dwindling.

She had always felt as if she were something between real and unreal. It was as if her creator, a mysterious enchantress she knew only as M, had fabricated her from the most ethereal components that placed her outside of time and space. When she first opened her beady little eyes and took on consciousness, it was as natural as if she had always existed and had merely begun inhabiting a preordained form.

It was both mystifying and exhilarating to exist in a world of endless potential. Her home was a realm cut off from the destructive forces; it was barricaded against death and decay. But she longed to connect with the sorceress M from the Otherworld, the fairy name for the "real" world known to the common inhabitants of Solarius. Miranda had no sense of purpose, as if she herself *was* the purpose. She felt less like a being and more like a positive force. There was a disconnect within her—a longing to become a being of her own. She wondered if she even had a soul.

It was this split in her psyche that made her different. As Miranda wandered throughout The Could-Be, she found that she could see shadows of the Otherworld. She became more fascinated by the creatures of the Otherworld, listening in on their conversations, following their affairs, and discovering their many secrets.

As Miranda's connection to the other fairies receded, they noticed that Miranda had a pronounced gloomy side. She hid it from many of them, but the most discerning fairies of The Could-Be sensed a great sadness in her. Miranda would overcompensate for this by reacting to everything spoken to her in the most Pollyannaish manner. The others sensed that Miranda had a fear of being found out, discovered, and outed for not being a true, loyal inhabitant of The Could-Be.

And so, the Fairy Council voted to expel her. The council was comprised of every sprite, nymph, and fairy in the realm, including Miranda. She had never been quite sure what kind of mystical being she was, so she identified with members of all, and none at all. The vote for expulsion was nearly unanimous. There was only one dissent: Miranda's.

Miranda Sunray had been locked out. Kicked out. Booted from The Could-Be. Her cherubic self and her enchanting black eyes were no longer accepted among the fairy kind, who sensed she was overly curious about the Otherworld and not truly one of them. Miranda had an inner longing to become something that she was not. She had a dark side that was...unwanted.

Exile it was. The Fairy Council tolerated no impurities in thought or form. Miranda was considered an impurity—a flaw in the magical fabric that could ripple throughout the potential and possibly tear it apart.

She was phased out through an invocation of the Arch Crystal, which possessed the power to mediate the creative and destructive forces of the universe—to rebalance or unbalance them as a sorcerer saw fit.

Fortunately for Miranda, a kind wizard who communed often with the Fairy Council agreed to take her in. She would aid him by becoming his trusted messenger. His magical home existed between the Otherworld and The Could-Be, and so she could recharge her spiritual force by remaining in the wizard's company. That wizard was known to many as Talus Nightspell.

When Miranda was first banished to the Otherworld and came under the employ of Talus Nightspell, she could fly through the densest forestry as easily as a summer breeze. But her light did not flicker as brightly as it once did many moons ago. She was no longer able to phase easily through objects, having learned that hard lesson by having once flown headlong into an oak tree and having nearly gotten her diminutive leg stuck within it. Alas, she was able to slowly move her leg out of the tree, although she had needed to concentrate very hard.

And so, the fairy was flying into the void, into the deepest, darkest night in the Otherworld, on a quest to deliver an urgent message to one of his colleagues. She flew through the Solistrian Forest until the deciduous trees of the sprawling woods gave way to marshland. The reed-covered marshes glistened in the light of the full moon overhead. She sped onward through the fetid swamps of Aborea as the sounds of nightingales and whippoorwills filled her ears with soft, sweet music.

When the light of dawn broke, the forests and marshes began to recede behind her. There were only rolling hills ahead, these giving way to outstretched plains, finally leading to a gorgeous lake that shimmered like liquid silver in the morning sun. She had arrived at Laketown.

On a lonely dock outstretched in the Mirrhenian Lake sat a little man wearing a white hooded cloak. His fishing rod's line was dipped into the glimmering lake and his pale, emaciated legs were dangling casually in the chilly waters.

Miranda flew over the druid's shoulder and looked at his reflection in the water below.

"I'm Miranda Sunray!" she squeaked excitedly while trying to catch her breath.

"Why, of course you are, and my name is Prospero, the White Druid," he replied unceremoniously. His venerable face extended a carefree smile. "Tell me all about yourself, Miranda Sunray," the druid gently nudged her.

And so, the fairy began her tale. The magic being talked to him until the late afternoon hours, repeating all the wizard had told her along with many more things about The Otherworld and The Could-Be. The druid stopped her only to share a laugh or a comforting remark and always at the most perfect times. Even when he caught a bluegill and pulled it up onto the dilapidated wooden dock, he still listened attentively and grunted sounds assuring her that he was still following along.

Even after his bucket was filled with his dinner, he sat on the dock waiting quietly and listening attentively. His eyes scanned the twilight skies, as if he expected to see something in them.

"Aha!" the druid at last exclaimed.

Prospero stood and pointed at two flecks in the crimson skies suspended over the distant horizon. He joyously looked back at his fairy friend.

"You see that?" the druid asked her. "Here comes two more of your kind."

The White Druid Prospero stood with arms raised toward the setting sun to welcome the guests onto his humble little dock. His fishing rod had transformed into a bronze staff, and a beam of light shone from it like a tiny beacon. As the sun's golden rays emanated from the western horizon and spilled across the lake's undulating waves, the glowing outlines of the arriving guests flying high overhead could be seen above the Mirrhenian Lake.

"A griffin and…a dragon?" Miranda inquisitively asked the druid.

"A moondrake to be precise, my dear," the mage replied reassuringly.

"But this…is the daylight," she commented breathlessly. "This journey keeps getting weirder and weirder."

As the lake's waves spilled slowly across the panorama before them, the Mountains of Mordrath looming in the northeastern distance, Prospero and Miranda watched the unlikeliest pair of fellow travelers approach. As their large frames came into view, it became too intimidating for Miranda to handle, and she shot behind the White Druid for protection.

"Be calm, dear," the druid said. "These two will be most welcome."

The two creatures flew over the head of the White Druid. The air from their powerful wings rustled the mage's white robes and blew the hood off of his head, exposing his wispy white hair. The beasts landed on the grassy plain beyond them.

Prospero turned around and held his long staff in the air. He incanted an unintelligible spell and waved the slender rod three times in a circular pattern. Tiny gleaming sparks filled the air, raining down almost imperceptibly on the griffin and the moondrake.

As she looked up into the quickening aura, Miranda Sunray started to see the sparks fill the air around her. However, as a fairy, she had her own aural magic and had no need for the druid's spell.

"There," the druid said. "It is done! We now share a medium of consciousness that will allow us to speak and comprehend one another. This ether cannot read your thoughts or memories, so do not worry about that, my dear creatures. However, if we should become too separated, the spell will weaken, and the ability will be lost. Enough business. Introduce yourselves! I am Prospero, the White Druid, and I am most pleased to see you all!"

Druix stumbled forward and stared at the unbelievable vision of these beings in front of the majestic lake. The sun's golden rays were still lighting everything aglow, especially the Mirrhenian Lake, and it felt like his eyes were on fire. The glare was already causing him a terrible headache, and he felt like he would never adjust.

"I am Druix," he growled in the guttural Draconese language. "I am a moondrake from the realm of Lunastria, and I lived on the sulfurous slopes of Mount Kildrath."

The griffin looked over at the moondrake in astonishment. The drake's language filling his ears was at last comprehensible for the first time. His lionheart filled with insurmountable joy.

"Druix, my friend!" the griffin exclaimed in Gryphonese, a tear filling his eye. "I want to know all about you! I am an outcast griffin from the Republic of Aeris. My name is Aenyx, and I am at your service."

The moondrake and the griffin exchanged a relieved glance, grateful to be able to communicate at last.

"Wonderful, wonderful!" the mage said. "Now, let me enlighten you on why we are gathered here today. As you may have noticed, the three of you are blessed with glassy black eyes."

"Blessed?" Druix asked. It was like he had read the griffin's mind.

"That is right. That is right," Prospero enthusiastically carried on. "And finally, we are going to put that terrific blessing to use. An unimaginable evil stirs in the land of Noctera. An army of shadow dragons is gathering under the rising might of the Dread Commander, the dragon emperor known as Dracus Imprimus."

Miranda Sunray shuddered. Druix looked dismayed as he began to decipher why his father, Seraphinus, was killed that fateful night. Aenyx's eyes burned with an intense anger, realizing now why he had crossed paths with a shadow dragon the night his friends were murdered.

"But what does this have to do with us?" Miranda asked.

"It has everything to do with you, lovely Miranda," Prospero replied. "Those pretty black eyes of yours are going to help us protect Solarius from the unfathomable scourge that is coming our way."

Miranda Sunray felt a dizzying mixture of hope and confusion pulse throughout her tiny being. Did her existence have some higher purpose?

"Allow me to explain, friends," the druid continued. "You all possess an innate ability to seek your own potential. This was an ability lost on Solarius over a generation ago, and the world has been lost and dying since. While this desperate state of affairs is all the result of the devastating curse of Dracus Imprimus, we were able to contain the worst of it within the Arch Crystal. And by 'we,' I mean The Mighty Three."

Aenyx and Miranda looked upon the White Druid with awe. But the moondrake merely looked at the others like he was missing something.

"The Mighty Three?" the moondrake uttered.

"Yes, I am part of an alliance of mages, along with Manfred the Magnificent and Salustrius the Wise, known far and wide as The Mighty Three," the druid replied.

The band of four stood in a circle looking upon one another in the dying rays of the evening sun. There were too many questions and too little time to answer them.

"Alas, now is not the time for questions. Now is the time to act," the druid added with a mysterious smile.

Off in the northeastern distance, upon the dark slopes of the Mountains of Mordrath, an unmistakably terrifying glow erupted into the skies.

It was dragonflame.

CHAPTER 24

THE CRYSTAL SHARD

Prince Sigismund woke from a disturbing sleep. He'd believed that he was lost within the darkest night, and a small band of odd creatures was accompanying him. There was a fairy, a griffin, and a moondrake, and a wizard led the way. Flames walled them in—flames wielded by an unseen but omnipresent monster hell-bent on their destruction.

His brow was moist with sweat. The blankets on the little bed were crumpled up in a wad, as if he had been furiously tossing and turning all night. He had been like this for several days, taking plenty of rest while recovering from his spill in the forest, not to mention the shocking events at Waverly Castle, which he had still not come to accept.

"Pay no attention, child," a voice came from near the door. "That is just the effect of your crystal shard. It is a sliver of the Arch Crystal."

Sigismund snapped up in bed and rubbed his head as he looked around the room. Seated in the hallway, reclining on a simple wooden chair balanced on its hind legs, was the old wizard. His floppy blue hat was bent over his head, and Sigismund could see the profile of his crooked nose and his wagging beard. The mage was immersed in some voluminous silver book spread over his lap. He had apparently been sitting there for some time, keeping watch over the young prince.

"Pardon me?" he asked. "You mean today's nightmare?"

"Oh, that wasn't a nightmare," the wizard remarked while remaining focused on his book. "That was a glimpse into your potential future. That's a side effect of using the Arch Crystal. It is the world to come, should all the potential in it be forever locked away in The Could-Be."

"How horrific!" Sigismund remarked, rubbing his eyes.

"Yes, quite," the wizard replied. "Even though the Arch Crystal had made it possible for creatures to be merely alive, that is very different from them living full lives. We traded their potential for our security, and well, everything has started to die, even nature itself. It is as if all creatures ceased seeking any higher meaning at all."

"Then how did you avoid all this?" the prince asked in a bewildered voice.

"Well, for starters, my home is between the Otherworld and The Could-Be!" he declared. "It's one of the reasons you are healing up so rapidly."

"When will these terrible visions stop?" Sigismund asked.

"So long as the Arch Crystal exists, and the Dread Commander along with it, you'll have the visions," said the mage, snapping his book shut. "The conundrum is exactly this: If the Arch Crystal is destroyed, then all of the potential will come flooding back into the world. But if that happens, Dracus Imprimus will see the return of his powers, and he will use them to form a terrible winged army. It would then only be a matter of time before he invaded the major realms—the Kingdom of Hypernea, the Republic of Aeris, the enchanted lands of Wysteria, and the Jeweled Islands. Once he has control of the earthly realm, he will seek to crush The Could-Be itself. He wants to relegate it all into The Never-Was."

"But that's impossible!" Prince Sigismund cried.

"You might think," Talus Nightspell replied. "But you haven't seen Dracus Imprimus at the height of his powers. Not like I have."

"But what are we to do?" Sigismund asked. "Surely, our plan isn't to lie about in this tiny stone cottage and wait for the end to come. There must be something…something we can do?"

He fumbled around in his robe for the velvet-wrapped crystal shard. His long, slender fingers produced it, and he thrust it out in front of him.

"I—I have this!" he exclaimed.

"Yes, I know, I know," the mage said. "And in good time, we will use it. For now, we must prepare to depart with the utmost urgency. It is high time we travel to the Illusory Fortress and destroy the Arch Crystal. And you, Prince Sigismund, are going to help shatter it."

"Why would I want to shatter it?" Sigismund asked. "I only have a sliver of it and look at all the wonderful things it can do! What if we used the Arch Crystal to defeat Dracus Imprimus once and for all?"

"Hush, child!" Talus intoned. "There are forces at work beyond even my understanding. There is a great evil at work in the world—I can sense it. Only dimly, but I feel it in these old bones. If the Arch Crystal fell into Dracus Imprimus's hands, it would start an age of ruin and misery unseen before in Solarian history."

"Is this Dracus Imprimus really that bad?" Sigismund asked.

"A foolish question, if there ever was one!" the wizard scoffed. "He is the Dread Commander, a black mage whose quest for destruction knows no bounds."

Talus's voice dropped to a whisper, and his face grew dark with firelight shadows.

"His command over the destructive forces of this world is unmatched. One could say his soul is an unquenchable void that seeks to devour our world and eliminate it from existence. It is disturbingly clear that he is willing to sacrifice even himself in this profane cause; but as for now, he has a magnetic pull over all truly wicked, mindless creatures of this world. Dracus Imprimus is the lord of the shadow dragons."

"I read about these dragons in books of fairy tales my mother gave me," Sigismund whispered, trembling. "Are they really that evil?"

"They are not intrinsically evil, no," the wizard said, shaking his head. "But they are prone to dwelling in a state of consciousness akin to the darkest of voids. Sadly, they have fallen under the sway of Dracus Imprimus and his lieutenants," the mage continued. "The creatures have been corrupted by him and his right-hand woman, the sorceress Morana. Since birth, they have been taught that the world is a fearful, hateful place that is wholly against them, and thus, they have been banished to the outskirts of Solarius. In their rage-filled minds, the world is worthy of hatred and destruction. They are blind to compassion and empathy. That is their sole weakness."

"And if we destroy the Arch Crystal," Sigismund muttered, "then what?"

"It is my great hope that the world will become naturally rebalanced," Talus Nightspell replied. "Nature has clearly been suffering due to the meddling of mages like Dracus Imprimus and me. If we can level the playing field by unleashing the creative and destructive forces contained within the Arch Crystal, then we might be able to harness the natural resurgence to overcome the expected destructiveness of their war."

"War?" Sigismund asked. His voice trembled. "What will happen to the kingdom? What of my mother, the queen? What if my father and brothers are slain? Would I become…king? I am not prepared for any of this!"

Sigismund felt a surging wave of panic.

Dread commanders? Evil sorceresses? Shadow dragons? Not long ago, he was only a boy locked up in a stone fortress. But now he was facing dark forces. His head swam from the dire implications.

"I am sorry, good wizard," Sigismund stammered. "But I am afraid I cannot help you with this quest. I am just a boy! What do I know about good and evil forces? You don't need me. I want to go home to my mother! Maybe they will finally accept me if I warn them about the dragons…"

"Prince Sigismund," the wizard said firmly, "I would not waste my time with a mere eighteen-year-old *boy*, as you put it. It is time to put away thoughts of returning to your comfortable home and your cozy fireplace and your delicious meals because that place does not exist for you anymore. Your petty tyrant of a father made sure of that, although he was simply hastening the inevitable. If I know anything about Dracus

Imprimus, his power is rising. And when his power rises, war is sure to follow. Hypernea would be one of the first places he would seek to ruin."

Prince Sigismund lifted his downcast head to lock eyes with the wizard. His black eyes were glossy from welling tears.

"If there is no other way, wizard," he said reluctantly.

"My good man," the mage replied, "I assure you there is no other way."

The wizard and the young prince gathered their things to set off into the forest. If they could meet Miranda—and hopefully, her companions—on the way to the Illusory Fortress, then that would save them precious time.

And so, the wizard led them away from his magical cottage. It dissolved behind them as if it hadn't ever been there. Sigismund was not sure he could ever get used to that.

The company of two forged throughout the forest all morning. The trees were barren, and their broken branches and twigs crackled beneath them. It was the only sound Sigismund heard for miles, save for the tap of the wizard's staff and his slightly annoying humming.

Sigismund was struggling to keep up with the old sorcerer as he was led deeper and deeper into the Solistrian Forest. Dusk was approaching, and he was actually missing his new friend, Miranda Sunray. Her chirpy demeanor had provided a welcome distraction following his brush with death at Waverly Castle.

While he forged ahead, his memory turned over and over upon the irrepressible buxom girl whose audacity had saved his skin at the last moment: Princess Melanie. Her bold charms had cast their own kind of spell on him. In her presence, he felt mystified, more alive than he could ever recall. It was like his senses had been heightened to the fullest. His mind dwelled upon the contours of her dimples, the flecks in her glistening olive-green eyes, and the charge of electricity that had overtaken him when she lightly caressed the back of his hand.

"Talus?" Sigismund offered a question to the mage in a thin, tinny voice.

"What is it, young man?"

"You are a wise and powerful wizard…" Sigismund continued.

"Yes, yes," Talus replied with a grunt of self-satisfaction. With a stroke of his wizard's staff, he thwacked at a dry branch that was dangling in his way. "Do get to your question."

"What is the best way to a woman's heart?" Sigismund asked and then instantly blushed.

The wizard could scarcely contain a chortle before his voice erupted with raucous laughter in the cool air of the wilderness.

"Shadow dragons, dark conjurers, and invading armies threaten your kingdom," he remarked. "And this is what the young prince's mind is on. Some things about humans never change."

Sigismund simply looked at him with a confused expression as the wizard leaned on his staff and caught his breath from all the laughing.

"But in all due seriousness, Prince," the mage replied, "which is admittedly not much, love is a magic that is beyond my comprehension. No one can create that magic for you. It is something that comes from within each living being and is shown in an infinite number of unique ways. You have to channel that true love and transform it into action. If you let that power out, it can transform the world, and in the process, it can heal and transform yourself."

Sigismund stood and looked at the wizard, a moment of silence hanging between them in the deep woods.

"Now, come on," Talus said suddenly and turned to their path ahead. "The Dread Commander waits for no man."

Sigismund followed the cranky old mage into the wild unknown, plodding through the ungodly thicket. As the soil underfoot turned squishier and muddier, Sigismund's boots and pants were splattered with muck. He wondered where in Solarius he was being led.

The Illusory Fortress? Was there ever a more quixotic mission than theirs?

Then again, he had somehow discovered the old mage's abode using the crystal shard his mother had given him. Maybe he could use it again?

He reached into his long green overcoat and touched his left breast pocket to be sure his mother's gift was still there.

Back at his spell-secluded cottage, the wizard had changed Sigismund's clothes from ridiculous robes into a green overcoat, corduroy slacks, and tall brown leather boots. The mage could order fresh garb with a few commands to some fairy assistants, who could phase into being with a brief incantation. Not only were the clothes they fetched perfectly tailored and infinitely more practical, but they also didn't scream fledgling royalty, should an overly curious stranger meet them on the road. Not that there was a chance of that happening in this godforsaken wilderness.

As Sigismund was about to sneak a peek at the mystical crystal shard, the wizard objected.

"Don't," he muttered without even looking back.

Using his wizard staff, the mage continued hacking and thwacking the long, slender branches in their way. The sounds reverberated throughout the life-barren forest.

"Oh, you're no fun," Sigismund replied. He tucked the wrapped crystal back into his pocket and thought about his increasingly meager chances of ever going home. Was this what an adventure was all about? Dreck and gloom and grumpy sorcerers? It all had seemed so colorful and exciting in the storybooks his mother had given him. This was—well, this was quite the chore. "Talus," he said. "Tell me about the Mighty Three."

The elderly mage stopped and once again leaned on his white oaken staff to catch his breath. He dimmed the glow from its crystalline head. Finally, Sigismund could hear scarce signs of life. The mellow hooting of a white-faced owl could be detected, *whoo-whooing* in the distance. Woodpeckers knocked rhythmically, *tick-tick-tick-tick*, on the black ash trees that were predominant in this swathe of forestry.

"Son," he said without looking back, "let me tell you something about the Mighty Three. They were three foolish conjurers who thought that they had the wisdom to save the world from itself. It has taken us mages an entire generation of scheming to undo the damage they have done. If you want to know about the Mighty Three, it is exactly that!"

"You take that back!" Sigismund shouted. "The Mighty Three saved us! You know this to be true, and *you* are an old fool for saying any different."

The wizard suddenly whipped around to face the young prince. Anger flashed in his eyes and his face flushed a deep red. The mage's white beard flowed in front of him onto his blue robes, marking the countless years that he had spent wandering their dying world. It was an intimidating side of the powerful mage that Sigismund had not yet beheld in the brief time they had spent together. It was humbling.

"Young prince," Talus said, "open your eyes and look around. Use that head of yours for something other than a hole to stuff sweets into. I *am* one of the Mighty Three."

Sigismund looked upon the old mage with renewed wonder.

"This cannot be true!" Sigismund exclaimed. "I was told that the Mighty Three were legendary wizards, capable of taming dragons with a single word, quelling the eruptions of massive volcanoes, and even making the sun move backward in the sky! Could one of the Mighty Three be a cantankerous old man leading me through a forest to find some Illusory Fortress, if such a place even exists! And besides, your name is Talus Nightspell!"

"Oh, come, come," the mage tutted. "You cannot be that daft! Talus Nightspell is but an alias I use to keep strangers from asking too many questions. Sounds a little bit more daunting than Manfred the Magnificent, doesn't it?" The wizard chuckled at the prince's bewilderment.

Sigismund's eyes grew wide. He rubbed them with balled-up fists. Manfred the Magnificent? In front of his very eyes? He just appeared to be a doddering old sorcerer, and a frail one at that!

"Don't let my looks deceive you," he said. "I saved your life once upon a time, just so that we might have this moment right now. I saw The Could-Be and knew you to be an integral part of it. That is why I showed up at Waverly Court some eighteen years ago and related the prophecy that saved you and your kingdom. Don't make me regret it!"

The young man suddenly felt ashamed of his own presumptions. Gratitude began to swell in his heart, which had been racing fast due to both their arduous journey and his awe of meeting this world-renowned sorcerer.

"Why, I had no idea, Manfred the Magnificent," he replied, dwelling on the wizard's name to dispel his momentary disbelief. "I am most humbly at your service."

"Just Manfred, just Manfred. And I have no need of your service," the mage retorted. "Except that you serve yourself and call upon others to do likewise. As for now, we can go no further. We must camp for the night and press onward at the morning light."

The old man lifted his staff and cast a spell that recreated his entire home in the woods in front of them. The night sky was replaced by the ceilings of his stone cottage, and the trees were exchanged for the dragon-back chair, the fireplace, even the master and guest bedrooms. It was astonishing, yet somehow it befit the strange happenings he had come to expect with the sorcerer. Sigismund had so, so many questions. But he was too tired to ask them now.

"Home is wherever I choose to make it, dear Sigismund," the mage said. "We will be safe here tonight. Tomorrow, we must journey to the Illusory Fortress before the Dread Commander does. And trust me, he is searching for it. He is searching far and wide."

CHAPTER 25

DRAGONFLAME

Reddish fire exploded in the eastern skies. Over the Mountains of Mordrath, black clouds of flying creatures were devastating the landscape beneath them with terrible bursts of searing dragonflame. It was the spine-chilling sight of shadow dragons laying waste to Mount Rhaemor, the capital of the griffin realm of Aeris.

"Aeris!" Aenyx shouted. "This is an attack on my homeland!"

In that moment, Aenyx's thoughts of murder and betrayal evaporated. His only thoughts now were about his friend Raven Whitecrest, who had saved his life, and Phoenix Stormguard, the only one of the Guardians he could trust. His mind turned to the innocent griffins who were now facing the most terrifying attack on Aeris in their lifetimes.

"We must save them!" he shouted at his newfound friends.

Leaning on his wizard's staff, Prospero looked upon the mortifying spectacle with tremendous dismay and sadness.

"I fear we may be too late," the White Druid said. "We must make haste to destroy the Arch Crystal before Dracus Imprimus's army can attain it."

"I will not stand by and watch as my friends die!" Aenyx yelled.

He started his flight toward Aeris, and Druix motioned to follow him.

"Wait, Aenyx!" Prospero shouted after him, causing the great griffin to halt in mid-flight. "If you die, our hope of finding and destroying the Arch Crystal dies with you!"

"That is a chance I am willing to take," the griffin replied. "If Aeris falls, so too will Hypernea, and then Wysteria, and then the Jeweled Islands, and then all of Solarius. We must act to protect the Golden Hatchery and the future of Aeris. This devastating attack could wipe them all out!"

Prospero nodded. As foolhardy as it was to take on the winged army of Dracus, the least they could do was to try to buy the griffins time to save their young.

"Miranda Sunray, I need you to go on a special mission," the druid said. "Warn the Laketown villagers of the invasion of Aeris. Find the elder councilman Timor Longbranch and tell him to unlock the ancient armory and raise an army of whomever he can find—even if it is only archers and spearmen. After that task is completed, make haste to inform Talus Nightspell of this wretched turn of events. Fly!"

The fairy flew into the deepening dusk toward the Laketown village in search of Timor Longbranch. She found him watching the siege of Aeris upon a fishing dock with profound alarm. The dragonflame lit up the twilight horizon, and smoke was beginning to plume and roil from the old-growth trees burning on Mount Rhaemor. The eastern winds carried the faint, acrid stench into the lungs of the villagers in the settlements on the lake. They were coughing and covering their mouths with rags and cloths.

As Miranda Sunray went to warn the Laketown villagers, Prospero approached the moondrake Druix. He laid his hand upon the head of the midnight-blue serpent and stroked it gently. The druid felt a tremendous sadness in the creature's bones.

"Let us rescue these poor griffins, my good moondrake," he said. "I cannot imagine what has befallen you in this cruel life, but I assure you that this one act of courage will define it as a life well-lived. I will guide you and protect you the best I am able, I promise you."

Druix looked upon his friend Aenyx, who was now the only creature left in this world that he felt he truly knew and trusted. He bowed his head, and the druid climbed upon his back. Prospero cast a spell that lit the head of his bronze staff with a transcendent glow.

The griffins of Aeris were scrambling to arm themselves and fight back against the merciless siege. Morana, the sorceress queen of Noctera, the dragonking's bride, was leading the all-out assault on Mount Rhaemor. She rode on a terrifying shadow dragon steed, accompanied by her dark lieutenants, Field General Nemysis Drake and Captain Saevius Thornwood, who wore black steel armor. They wielded insidious spears with dual-edged spear tips and viciously forged barbs.

Captain Thornwood rode upon a ferocious female dragon named Morta, while General Drake was mounted on a titanic male by the name of Stragius.

As the High Sorceress waved her arms to direct strikes upon the griffins gathered upon Mount Rhaemor, her glowing green eyes shone with hideous delight. Her crimson-lined grin was bent upward with hatred toward her high cheekbones, and her cold demeanor was contrasted by a dark, ethereal gown cut low in a slashing V-shape. Her garment flowed outward from her body as if she were a wraith in the night.

As dozens of great-winged dragons laid fiery waste to Aeris, their massive serpentine frames the embodiment of a living nightmare, the High Sorceress Morana savored the sight of the crackling, burnt bodies of griffins. She inhaled the hideous aroma with a special relish—of all the Solarian creatures, she hated griffins most. Scores of their dead bodies now littered the main arena, and the remaining live griffins were now fleeing from Mount Rhaemor. Moondrakes had already been dispatched to finish off the stragglers in the night.

This siege of Aeris had become an utter rout. And now was the time to make for the Golden Hatchery, and to end the scourge of griffinkind permanently.

Standing nearby, watching in the shadows and clasping their talons with grim delight, were the Guardians Tyrex Goldeneyrie and Captius Whitecrest.

CHAPTER 26

THE TRIBULATION OF AERIS

Aenyx flew at breakneck speed toward the besieged Republic of Aeris. The mercurial sun at his back had abandoned its flight. The blood-red twilight skies bled out into regal purple, foreshadowing the coming dark reign of the dragonking.

The griffin knew the risk of returning and pressed on. His conscience could not bear to let Raven Whitecrest and Phoenix Stormguard die without his attempt to come to their rescue. Besides, he now had powerful allies that could help in facilitating their escape from the abysmal dragon siege.

On Mount Rhaemor, a mad struggle to protect the Golden Hatchery ensued. Raven Whitecrest flew in the direction of the Guardians' walkway, dodging the relentless spouts of dragonflame. Explosions of light cast hideous shadows, and griffins that had been screaming for help from the ancient protectors of Aeris suddenly fell silent.

As she fled into the row, she could make out a hunched figure bent over near the proud marble statue of Tibalt Stormguard, which stood defiantly amid the wreckage in the arena. The figure turned toward her, and she could make out his eagle qualities in the reddish glare of the firelight behind them. It was Phoenix.

"Raven!" he shouted. "Mount Rhaemor is in ruins; we must regroup in order to fight back this scourge. Come, child, we have a most critical task to do."

"The gates of the Golden Hatchery," she replied with a huff as she approached the elder. "We must depart now if we are going to get there in time! I saw one among the shadow dragon riders, and I could not be sure if it was actually her, but..." Raven said and shuddered.

"The High Sorceress Morana," he said, putting his talon on hers. "Now is not the time for fear. Now is the time for action. And if we accord ourselves admirably, we will someday join these revered ancestors on this sacred walkway. Let us fly!"

Raven Whitecrest bounded mightily and took flight toward the Golden Hatchery. Phoenix Stormguard followed shortly behind her. As they ascended into the darkening skies, they could see winged serpents off in the distance flying toward the gates of the Golden Hatchery. They knew they were running out of time and flew faster to get to the gates and ensure their security.

The Golden Hatchery was a fortified stronghold for all the griffin eggs in the entire Republic of Aeris, and thus, its entire hope for the future. The Golden Hatchery's entranceway was recessed into the mountain and large enough only for a single griffin to pass through at a time. Within the tunnel were three brass gates that had been enchanted many generations earlier by Salustrius the Wise to be unbreakable by simple sorcery.

Before plunging headlong into the fray, Raven flew high above the Golden Hatchery's entranceway to gain a better vantage point. What the griffin saw below sickened her to her core.

A behemoth of a shadow dragon landed upon the terrace. It was mounted by a slender, pale woman in a flowing black dress holding a glowing scepter in her left hand. On her flanks, two more gigantic shadow dragons rode by dark-armored men with long, vicious-looking spears.

But that dreadful sight wasn't what shocked Raven Whitecrest the most as she flew suspended above the semicircular terrace; it was that two griffins stood at the entranceway to the Hatchery. She knew their despicable countenances immediately—Captius Whitecrest and Tyrex Goldeneyrie.

She gasped in fury at the sight of the contemptible traitors welcoming the High Sorceress and her dark lieutenants onto Mount Rhaemor. And not just onto Mount Rhaemor, but into the Golden Hatchery itself.

Raven wanted to scream, to launch a desperate attack on the treasonous griffins, but thought it better to wait for Phoenix Stormguard to pursue the next course of action. When he arrived, he took one look at his fellow Guardians surrendering the Golden Hatchery and immediately set off in a frantic dive to stop the diabolical deal.

"Ahh!" Captius Whitecrest exclaimed upon seeing his fellow Guardian charging the gate. "Look who it is! It's our old friend Phoenix Stormguard."

The High Sorceress expelled a phantasmagoric ray from her frightful scepter. The milky-white orb shot out a flash of light that encapsulated Phoenix Stormguard in mid-flight. The glassy orb swirled with a mist inside that appeared to be a glimpse at death itself. The sorceress lowered the Guardian closer to the causeway so that she and her minions could get a disgustingly satisfying view of their captured foe.

"Phoenix!" Raven shouted and dove onto the scene. She knew she may be surrendering her life, but if the Golden Hatchery fell, all griffin life could cease to exist. She would never accept that.

"It's that traitor Raven Whitecrest," said Tyrex Goldeneyrie. "Come! It will be a pleasure to finally meet you—even if it is for an exceptionally short length of time."

The High Sorceress dismounted from the shadow dragon, which then rested its pendulous head on the semicircular causeway. Her motions were so seamless that she seemed to float above the stone floor. She expelled another flash of light from her orbed scepter and entrapped Raven Whitecrest alongside her virtuous friend.

"Alas, you are too late," the sorceress said airily. "But I am glad that you have joined us."

She strode up the entranceway to the Golden Hatchery.

"These two pets have engaged in a most fortuitous deal for us," she said. "If they unlock the gates to the Golden Hatchery, not only will their lives be spared, but I will make them the new rulers of the Nocteran principality of Aeris. They will become the ever-faithful stewards over a new race of griffins, who are reared with complete loyalty and obedience to the Kingdom of Noctera, the land of eternal night."

She smiled a wicked grin and turned toward the two traitorous Guardians.

"At least, one of you will," she uttered.

As she pronounced these fateful words with a chillingly carefree air, Captius Whitecrest collapsed to his knees while holding his avian throat, which was now bleeding out onto the terrace. His eyes were wide with shock and despair. As a black pool of blood collected in front of him, he collapsed face down into it. There was no struggle—only death.

"Let that be a lesson to you, Tyrex Goldeneyrie," she told him while walking past the dead griffin toward the entrance to the hatchery. "New lord of Aeris," she added.

Phoenix Stormguard lashed out in all directions into the thin air. But his talons only lashed out futilely at his enemies' visages while he remained suspended in mid-air.

"Oh, I have no illusions," Tyrex said with a sneer. "I will show you the way into the Golden Hatchery."

"Morana!" a voice shouted into the night air from behind her. "That is far enough."

The White Druid Prospero had arrived. And with him, the moon-drake Druix.

CHAPTER 27

A CLASH OF SORCERERS

The white-cloaked druid Prospero hovered over the Nocteran soldiers with a glowing staff in hand. His improbable mount was a midnight-blue moondrake, whose wings were spread wide in a daunting attack position. It was an unexpected sight for the Nocteran guards, to say the least.

General Drake and Captain Thornwood whipped their dragon steeds around to greet their fresh prey. The soldiers lowered their barbed lances, ready to skewer the fools who dared to intrude upon Nocteran business. Their shadow dragons locked their callous eyes upon the invaders. Their heavy barbed tails smashed the stone terrace, splaying cracks throughout. The behemoths snarled, their ivory fangs bared.

"Prospero the druid!" the sorceress declared without so much as turning around. She instantly recognized the impudent voice of the newcomer. "Stand down!" she shouted at the guards. "This is an old friend. I will address this minor nuisance myself."

The sorceress whirled around, and her black spectral gown twirled with her. The blood-red nails on her left hand were wrapped around the silvery scepter, which was glowing an eerie shade of green.

"My dear Prospero!" she said, cackling with delight. "How long has it been? Why, I believe I was only a young Hypernean girl studying under you as an apprentice the last time I got a good look at you! If I'm not mistaken, you had just finished teaching me some wonderfully powerful spells, and I had completed my training. How *are* you?"

"This is no time for remembrances, Morana," Prospero bitterly replied, the cracked outlines of pain showing on his aged face. "These griffins are nothing to you. Why, they are not even hatched yet! Has your appetite for death and destruction gone so far that you now crave to kill unborn griffins? Give it up and fly back to Noctera, where you belong, or face your imminent demise when all of Solarius rises against you to end your heinous atrocities!"

Morana burst out laughing at the druid's imploration. "Careful, old man," she replied. "Remember the last time you tried to play games with my conscience? It ended badly for both of us."

The shadow dragons clawed at the stone entranceway to the Golden Hatchery, which made a hideous, loud scraping sound. It was as if they were sharpening their immense claws to better slash their prey to shreds. The disturbing sound unnerved Druix.

While the ruthless beasts waited for a word from the High Sorceress to attack, the ghostly glow of the griffins' prison orbs reflected in the dragons' eyes. From a certain vantage point, it appeared that Phoenix Stormguard and Raven Whitecrest were imprisoned within their dead orbits.

Suddenly, a screeching griffin flew at breakneck speed upon the scene. He soared directly at Morana, and with a mighty slash of his talon, he knocked the scepter from her hand and left a dreadful gash upon her cheek. The High Sorceress was thrown backward toward the entrance to the Golden Hatchery.

The orbs that contained Phoenix Stormguard and Raven Whitecrest evaporated into the night. The griffins fell from the sky until their wings flapped to catch them aloft.

The Draconese guards pulled hard upon the bridles of their steeds. Their shadow dragon mounts furiously whipped around to the right to face the griffin attackers. They roared menacingly, so loudly that they could be heard across Mount Rhaemor.

As the Nocteran guards raised their spears toward the griffins, Prospero signaled the moondrake to attack. A raging Druix dove headlong upon the scene, envisioning the mount of General Drake as the very one who had killed his father above the Sulfurous Wastes.

"*Skrrrayyyiiii!*"

Druix plunged into the full armored body of General Drake and sent the Nocteran field general clattering to the ground. His barbed spear flew from his hand into the walls of the Golden Hatchery. Captain Thornwood aimed his spear at Phoenix Stormguard, only to be tackled by Raven Whitecrest. The Nocteran captain fell to the ground with a bone-rattling clang.

Aenyx landed at the entrance of the Golden Hatchery and faced down Morana. She held her left cheek, which was smeared with blood.

"Impudent beast!" she cried. "You will all pay dearly for this!"

As she scrambled to retrieve her scepter, Aenyx charged at her with all of his speed and might. Yet, before he could land a mortal blow on the sorceress, he was blindsided. The traitor Tyrex Goldeneyrie had defended her to the last.

"Why?" Aenyx screamed as he felt the griffins' talons sink into his rib cage. After knocking him to the ground, Tyrex pinned him there and leered menacingly.

"You wouldn't understand," he hissed. "This is what true power feels like."

Morana laughed hideously while her lieutenants rose to their feet. The shadow dragons approached the griffins and roared ferociously.

"You will now understand the real meaning of pain," the sorceress declared.

"Morana, no!" Prospero yelled. A singular ray of pure light beamed forth from his bronze staff, momentarily blinding the dragons.

As the light fell across the eyes of Tyrex Goldeneyrie, Aenyx seized the moment and threw him off. The griffin stumbled to his claws and paws and flew toward Druix and Prospero.

"Seize them!" Morana ordered her dragons.

As the creatures' light-blindness wore off, they put their gargantuan bodies into action. Phoenix Stormguard and Raven Whitecrest stumbled backward as the shadow dragons pounced. Their dread claws grasped the griffins around their entire frames, pinning their wings to their sides. They squirmed to break free, but it was useless.

"Let them go!" Aenyx screeched.

"It is too late for them, little bird," Morana retorted. "Retreat at once, or I will order my pets to crush your dear friends. One word from me, and they will be turned into griffin-meal."

"You have lost!" General Drake spat. "Soon, Noctera will overrun the lands of Solarius. Warn the rest, if you will; it will do you no good. But that is your only choice now, druid."

The High Sorceress stood ominously in front of the entranceway to the Golden Hatchery. The dragons held the lives of Phoenix Stormguard and Raven Whitecrest in their clutches. Morana motioned with an upturned fingernail to Tyrex Goldeneyrie to lead them to the entranceway. He gladly abided. As he passed by, she tousled his feathery mane. The unlikely allies disappeared down the black tunnel.

"No!" Aenyx yelled. "What if she destroys them all? You treasonous fool! You have doomed our race forever!"

Even the dragons appeared to delight in the fall of the Golden Hatchery. The winged serpents stood guard at the entranceway, knowing one command from their enslavers would allow them to devour the griffins whole.

"Come, Aenyx," the druid muttered. "There is a better way for us to defeat them. It is time to fly."

CHAPTER 28

AN UNUSUAL BEACON

Prince Sigismund awoke to the sound of clanging and banging. He peered through his bleary eyes to see the wizard already moving about with a flurry of activity. He also appeared to be in rare form, muttering and cursing to himself.

"This is bad; this is very bad!" he heard the mage ominously mumble.

"Excuse me?" Sigismund said, rolling over to sit on the edge of the bed.

"Aeris!" he replied. "It has fallen. The griffin republic is lost. I can sense that a magic spell safeguarding the Golden Hatchery has been broken. And our dear allies—they should have been here by now. I fear the worst. I believe they failed to halt the invasion!"

"How…how do you know all this?" the prince asked. Then he quickly realized he was talking to a sorcerer. "Oh, never mind. What do we do now?"

The mage stopped as if dazzled by a thought.

"What an excellent idea!" the wizard exclaimed. "A most excellent idea!"

"Huh?" Sigismund scratched his disheveled blond hair, which was sticking out wildly.

"We must find our allies, and that will increase our speed tenfold," the mage continued. "Trekking through the dense Solistrian forest and the fetid swamps of Aborea—that is for young mages only!"

The mage waved his staff erratically in the air, as if drawing some runic symbols, and then he whispered some incomprehensible words. The walls of the stone cottage faded into the air, revealing the blinding white light of the morning. The forest was all around them again. The prince fell straight onto his backside.

"Hey!" he cried.

"Oh," the mage said and chuckled. "I am not yet used to a young man being around. Sorry about that."

The old man held his staff aloft. Its crystal head gleamed in the morning light.

"Now, if you would like to remove the crystal shard," the mage instructed, "this would be a most opportune time."

The young prince picked himself up off the ground and looked at the wizard inquisitively. He reached into his pocket and plucked out the mystical item.

"Is it safe to uncover it?" he asked while looking curiously at the elderly mage. Manfred smiled back and nodded.

"As safe as it will ever be," he reassured the prince.

Sigismund removed the black velvet cloth. A golden sunray struck one of the facets of the crystal, and it sent a single beam of pure light directly at the wizard's staff. The single beam of light was transformed into a multihued spectrum of light that shot upward into the heavens, lighting up an entire cloud with an iridescent array of colors that could be seen for miles around.

"That is…amazing," Sigismund said breathlessly.

"Yes, of course it is," Manfred replied proudly.

Far away from them, on the wings of a moondrake far above Solarius, the White Druid Prospero saw the multihued light beacon like a clarion call.

"Come, Druix. Come, Aenyx," Prospero said to the winged creatures. "Our friends are in dire need of our aid."

As they flew toward the beacon, seething flames lit up Mount Rhaemor and burned throughout the Mountains of Mordrath. Dark gray smoke unfurled in foreboding plumes in the northern distance. Below the clouds, the shadow dragons of Noctera gathered, preparing for a full-scale invasion of Laketown—and then the rest of the kingdom of Hypernea.

CHAPTER 29

A TIMELY REUNION

Miranda Sunray was journeying back to report to the wizard when she spied the beacon. She redirected east toward the light and sprinted to the luminary spectacle. She passed through ash trees and elms, flitted around oaks, and darted through the woods until at long last, she had arrived.

"I warned them! I warned them!" she shouted as she came upon Manfred the Magnificent and Prince Sigismund. The young man was thrilled to see her but disturbed by her message.

"Miranda!" Sigismund exclaimed. "But warned whom? About what?"

"The shadow dragons are coming!" she burst. "Noctera declared war on the rest of Solarius, and the Republic of Aeris has already fallen. My friends—they have black eyes like you!—tried to save Aeris. One is the sweetest moondrake named Druix. The other is the proud and fierce griffin Aenyx. If there is any hope at all, they are racing to us now!"

"They must be on their way, child; they must be on their way!" the wizard said nervously. "If they are not, Dracus Imprimus will have no trouble subjugating this world once again. I pale to imagine the debased enslavement that foul monster has in mind for us all."

"Then what do we do, Manfred?" Sigismund asked. He thought about his mother, Galadria, even his cruel brothers, and the poor people who had been so afflicted for so long. They had borne sheer misery for so long but had no idea of the unimaginable affliction heading their way.

Leaning on his staff, the wizard scratched his white-haired scalp. He appeared to be entirely perplexed, like he was pondering a weighty matter.

"We will find the Arch Crystal," he said with resolution.

As the iridescent light of the beacon shone in their faces, he saw something in the eyes of Miranda Sunray and Prince Sigismund.

"Wait a minute," the mage said. "Come closer, both of you, and look into the beacon."

Prince Sigismund advanced with the crystal shard extended from his hand, and the beam of light grew brighter and wider. It was so bright that it illuminated both Miranda's and Sigismund's eyes. The wizard hadn't anticipated this—their eyes no longer appeared to be black!

Manfred peered into their eyes carefully and saw a vision of The Could-Be reflected in them. Prince Sigismund's eyes appeared as translucent blue as the wading pools of the Jeweled Islands. Miranda Sunray's eyes were as sparkling green as a polished emerald. The wizard saw a vision of the future in them—but he did not altogether like what he saw. It did, however, give him hope.

"It appears that this crystal shard of yours has grown stronger in the presence of Miranda Sunray," the wizard said. "I wonder what it can do when four of your kind are united."

And with that, the shriek of a moondrake could be heard overhead, followed by the call of the griffin. Prospero, the White Druid, had arrived with their two allies, Druix and Aenyx. The company was united at last.

CHAPTER 30

A FLIGHT TO REMEMBER

"Prospero!" shouted Manfred to his fellow conjurer.

Druix descended toward the forest clearing. The force from the moondrake's wings sent Miranda Sunray whirling through the air and into the bushes, which drew a giggle from Prince Sigismund.

"Ah, yes, this is quite a beautiful creature!" Manfred said.

The White Druid dismounted. Manfred approached his old friend and the black-eyed moondrake. "I have never seen one in the daytime—this one is midnight blue!"

"He is quite a beautiful find," Prospero commented.

Druix roared a protestation in his native Draconese tongue.

"Oh yes, where are my manners?" the druid said. "I had quite forgotten."

"Forgotten what?" Sigismund asked. "I understood everything he said. The moondrake complained that you were talking about him as if he weren't even here!"

Manfred the Magnificent raised his furry, white eyebrows in surprise.

"Why, Sigismund," he said. "I do believe that crystal allows you to understand all of these creatures. That is quite a gift! Take quite good care of it, young prince. Quite good care of it, indeed!"

"Then it appears that all of us understand one another quite well without the need of further Aural Magic," Prospero said. "Druix and Aenyx are still under my spell's effects, and regardless, seem to get along quite well without it."

"Excellent," Manfred said. The blue-cloaked wizard looked upon Aenyx. "And who is this fabulous beast? I am told you three flew to Aeris to fend off the dread commander's invasion. Give me the news at once! Is it as bad as I fear?"

"Worse," Prospero said with a pronounced frown. "The High Sorceress, whose name I do not feel I must repeat, has seized the Golden Hatchery. A traitorous Guardian named Tyrex Goldeneyrie invited the shadow dragon army into Aeris with the promise that he would be made administrator of the Nocteran principality. He offered to mold the griffin hatchlings to become a vicious scourge forever indentured to Dracus Imprimus and his sorceress bride.

"Reprehensible!" Manfred uttered. He studied the newcomers carefully, sizing them up. "I will take this good griffin as a steed, if he does not object," Manfred said while peering into the Aenyx's eyes.

"You are fortunate that I am in the mood for vengeance, druid," the griffin responded. "Otherwise, no humankind could ever take me for a *steed*, as you call it."

"Very well, and so the prince comes with me," Prospero said and offered a thin smile. "Have you ever ridden a moondrake?"

"Of course not!" Prince Sigismund chortled. Only days ago, he had been alone in his room playing chess with an imaginary friend. And now—riding moondrakes?

"Well, we have no time to waste," he said. "We must dispatch to the Illusory Fortress immediately!"

"Just a moment," Sigismund asked while putting the crystal shard in his pocket. "Are you also one of the Mighty Three?"

Prospero exchanged a quick glance with Manfred. Manfred gave him a nod, indicating that the prince could be trusted.

"If you must pry, I am none other than the White Druid, Prospero," he replied. "It appears you have already heard of me, so fortunately there is no need to revisit children's tales."

The prince was stunned. "But if you are both part of the Mighty Three," the prince stammered, "there is an obvious question."

All the creatures looked at Sigismund. It was quite the funny feeling to be stared down by a moondrake, a griffin, a fairy, and two powerful mages. He felt bewildered by their attention.

"The third conjurer?" the prince asked, feeling like he was unnecessarily pointing out the obvious.

"You mean Salustrius the Wise?" Manfred replied. "He has affairs of his own. That most eccentric mage is in the land of Wysteria, the Equine Kingdom, where the pegasus and the unicorn realms are locked in a deadly civil war."

"I should have known better than to ask," the prince said and sighed. "And where is this Illusory Fortress? Is it far from here?"

"It is not far away at all—for us," Prospero said. "Climb on!"

The prince walked up to the midnight blue creature and gazed into his gorgeous black eyes. They were as big and deep as the night sky itself. He felt that he knew this gentle beast's past and that he would be a wonderful part of his future. He petted the metallic blue scales of the moondrake, which felt like cool copper coins. As his hand touched the moondrake, it somehow felt like they were meant for one another.

Druix felt the young man's reverence. As the young prince climbed aboard and his small boots straddled his back, he felt responsible to take special care of the child—to become his protector, even. Druix's heart thumped faster, and he prepared to take flight from the Solistrian Forest.

Aenyx bent his eagle head before the old mage. Manfred the Magnificent whispered a few words in his ear that appeared to settle him down. The griffin's rippling muscles relaxed momentarily, and the sorcerer climbed upon his back. He slid his staff into a holster within the back of his cloak. Then, he tightly gripped the griffin's feathers with both hands. Miranda Sunray flew to the wizard and found a snug pocket in his robe to settle in for their flight.

Druix flapped his serpentine wings mightily, and the trio ascended into the cerulean skies.

Sigismund gasped and held tightly to the wizard's robes, pressing his legs together as tightly as he could. The view beneath him was magnificent. The Solistrian Forest extended countless miles ahead, but he could nonetheless see the peaks of the southern Mountains of Mordrath on the distant horizon. Their stony purple faces beamed in the full light of the afternoon sun. On his left, he saw the swamps of Aborea, stretching far away to the Fields of Silence and then to the shining Mirrhenian Lake, which was like a silver streak extending across the north.

He knew that beyond the lake lie the wastelands and the dark kingdom of Noctera, whose grim imprint could now be seen on the realm of Aeris. The northern Mountains of Mordrath and even the grand Mount Rhaemor were veiled by thick, heavy clouds of dark gray smoke. Forests and griffin settlements lay smoldering in ruins from the previous night's shadow dragon siege.

It was a view of Solarius that he never could have imagined. It was all far too real. This was not like one of his mother's storybooks. He was no longer reading about the tales of the Mighty Three; he was living one of them.

As the moondrake set off in flight, he felt completely free. He no longer cared what his brothers thought about him or if his father despised him and wanted to kill him. Now he felt completely like himself. He was no longer even Prince Sigismund; he was just Sigismund.

They flew east for miles and miles, staying at cloud level to obscure their flight. Sigismund watched the myriad trees passing underneath them. While riding upon the mighty back of the moondrake, he savored the thought of how these once-towering plants appeared to be tiny shrubs. He never wanted to get off this ride.

"Ho, there!" Manfred shouted. He pointed down and to his right where a dense old-growth forest surrounded a marshy patch of land. Black water was all around.

"This is not as glamorous as I imagined," Sigismund mumbled as he looked down on the swampy clearing.

The griffin began his descent, and the moondrake soon followed.

CHAPTER 31

THE ILLUSORY FORTRESS

"This is it!" Manfred declared triumphantly.

As the griffin and the moondrake stood thigh high in the black, watery swamp, Sigismund looked around. He was dubious.

"This is it?" Sigismund asked.

"Yes, most indubitably," Manfred replied.

"But I don't see anything," Sigismund added with a harrumph.

"That is precisely the point," Prospero added. "Now, if you would be so kind as to retrieve the crystal shard in your possession..."

Sigismund looked at the white-robed druid and nodded his head skeptically. He reached into the breast pocket of his hunter green cloak and removed something. "May I?" he asked.

"Please," Manfred responded, still sitting astride Aenyx.

The griffin did not look at all pleased to be standing on his claws and paws in the middle of the fetid swamp water. The reeds were so tall, they tickled him under his beak. Sigismund could see the impatience in the griffin's black eyes.

Sigismund unveiled the crystal and held it aloft. Nothing.

"Why, I could have sworn," Manfred said under his breath.

The members of the company stood awkwardly in the swamp.

"Oh yes!" Manfred exclaimed. "The spell, right, right..."

Prospero looked at the mage and rolled his eyes.

Manfred the Magnificent held up his white, oaken staff and invoked the magic words. "*Haec revelavit mysterium*!" he declared.

After his friend completed the magic words, Prospero sighed. "Those were the words you used to veil the Illusory Fortress?" he asked.

"They seemed appropriate at the time," Manfred mumbled.

"Do you believe Dracus Imprimus to be a novice at wizardry?" Prospero asked with indignation in his voice. As Manfred began to respond, Prospero interjected, "Oh, there is no time to debate the nuances of sorcery! Where is the fortress?"

The crystal shard in Sigismund's hand began to vibrate and glow. It took on a luminous red hue that projected across the surface of the marshy waters.

The faint outline of a stone walkway appeared above the water's surface. As the crystal shard's reddish light pulsated even more intensely, the surreal glow encased the outer surfaces of two stone towers joined by a foreboding wall. The fortress appeared to stand high above the brackish waters.

"This is the Illusory Fortress?" Sigismund asked. "It looks like a rundown old castle!"

"Of course, young prince," Manfred said. "Would you hide an object of value in the most glorious castle on Solarius or in the most ridiculous and improbable? Don't think too long on it. We are off to uncover the Arch Crystal."

Miranda Sunray flew up to the immense fortress gate while Aenyx clambered out of the stale marsh waters onto the stone walkway. Druix followed the griffin out of the marsh. After the moondrake heaved his considerably large frame upon the walkway, Sigismund jumped off. He ran his hand along Druix's sinuous body as he walked by him. After Sigismund passed by, the moondrake shook the water off his legs like a shaggy dog.

Prospero led down the walkway, tapping his staff in front of him to be sure of the path. The moondrake looked down the pathway and saw two statues on each side of the gate: one moondrake with its wings outstretched and one griffin appearing ready to attack any unwelcome visitors. He was deeply offended by the portrayal.

As the company drew closer to the tower's gate, Prospero looked up at the ephemeral outline of the fortress and realized one problem: They could not get in.

"Did you forget something, Manfred?" the White Druid asked incredulously.

"No, not at all," he replied and pointed upward to his left. "Miranda, would you mind flying to the top of that tower over there and notifying the guard that we have arrived? You will need to use your fairy magic to communicate through the ether."

The fairy looked at the wizard quizzically. Miranda hesitated for a moment; then she flitted off to the heights of the northern tower.

"Where is she going?" Sigismund asked the druid in a meek voice. He watched the fairy ascend toward a window in the tower.

"She is off to fetch the fortress guard," the druid said.

Sigismund looked around at the reedy marshland and then up at the Illusory Fortress. The sun was already painting a westward path toward the horizon. They were running out of daylight, and the shadow dragon army was at Hypernea's doorstep. They desperately needed to locate the Arch Crystal and undo what had been wrought.

"I saw him through the ether!" the fairy said upon her return from the tower. "He was a young knight in gleaming armor—most handsome!"

"Yes?" Manfred implored.

"And he will come to let us in!" Miranda exclaimed. "He said that it was 'about time.'" She giggled.

"I told you he would be waiting," Manfred said to Prospero. "You owe me seven mandrake roots when we return from this blasted quest."

Nearly an hour passed as the company waited at the fortress gate. They were immensely bored, and it was nearing evening. Suddenly, the sound of an ironclad gate being raised reverberated in the wilderness.

As the gate rose, a knight in polished armor appeared in front of a luxurious and well-kept great hall. At his side hung a long sword. His hair was flowing jet black, and his dark, well-trimmed beard glistened like oiled sable. The knight's jawline was well-hewn and firm, and his teeth were an unusually pearly white as he smiled at his visitors. The warrior's blue eyes danced playfully.

"Gilead Highbloode," he announced in a grandiose voice. "Warrior of the Hypernean Kingdom and sworn ally to all those who are good and righteous in the Solarian realm."

Miranda Sunray seemed entranced by the noble knight. She floated in midair with a flushed face, watching his every move intently.

Sigismund gazed at the guard and felt something was slightly amiss.

"Manfred!" the knight exclaimed. "I hardly recognized you. What, has it been—two or three days since we last saw each other?"

"Perhaps for you, good knight," the mage replied. "But for us, it has been decades. We will explain once you let us into the fortress."

"The spell!" the knight said as he slapped his forehead. "Quite right. Let me recite the words that you taught me. *Intres moenia*!"

As the words were pronounced, the fortress solidified. It no longer appeared to be…illusory. The White Druid Prospero looked at Manfred with an exasperated expression.

"What?" the mage asked with a wry smile. "It worked, didn't it?"

Prospero sighed and walked forward into the fortress, followed eagerly by Miranda Sunray, who flitted about the shoulders of the knight. Sigismund strode into the fortress and noted the luxuriant tapestries, glorious oil paintings of various battles throughout the history of Hypernea, and the many ornate mirrors that hung on the walls.

"This is a fantastic castle!" Sigismund exclaimed. The room was spacious and grand and filled with an ethereal light. "But how did you live here so long by yourself?" he asked the knight. "Manfred says you were here many decades, yet believe it was only a few days!"

"That is because I was locked here in time," the knight said. "It is a place nearly untouched by its passage, where the events of the outside world go on, but I remain stuck in a timeless state. We felt it was the best way to protect the Arch Crystal."

Sigismund was confused. "That sounds dreadful!" he exclaimed to Manfred and Prospero.

"Ahh, but it was all for our own good," he said with a bitter grin. "And who, might I ask, are you?"

"I am Prince…" the young man said, then stopped himself. "You can just call me Sigismund."

"Are you a prince?" he asked and motioned to bow.

"Why yes—and no," Sigismund replied. "I was the Prince of Hypernea, but I fled Waverly Castle…it is a long story."

"I see," the knight replied. "Perhaps you know a brother of mine—I mean brother in the sense we served together in the Sacred Order of the Lion. He is much younger than I. His name is Traveris Bane.…"

"Oh, yes, the Kindly Knight!" Sigismund gushed. "And he is most definitely not younger than you," the prince added with a laugh.

"Really?" The knight appeared skeptical.

"I mean, he appears to look older than you now," Sigismund replied in an apologetic voice. "But sadly, although he is most brave and kind, he is no longer actually a knight."

"No longer a knight!" Gilead exploded. "What is the meaning of this outrage?"

"Yes, he is but a guard now," Sigismund replied meekly. "He was stripped of his knighthood, but people still mockingly call him the Kindly Knight, although I say it quite seriously."

"This must have occurred after the Battle of the Onyx Wastes," Gilead said quietly. "The enemies of the Sacred Order of the Lion reported to young King Gerald that he had left his post during the battle, which is true. Alas, what the king would not hear out was that he had gone to the aid of the queen herself, who was watching the battlefield and directing reinforcements while upon her white pegasus steed, Adrian. When a moondrake attacked the queen, Traveris Bane charged across the battlefield and came to the queen's aid. He hurled his mighty lance straight upward and through the throat of an attacking moondrake."

"Wow!" Sigismund exclaimed. "Traveris Bane did *that*?"

"Quite right, and more than that," Gilead Highbloode said. He looked down at Sigismund with a faraway, nostalgic look lingering in his eyes.

"Alas, the rumor at court was that the young queen Galadria and Traveris Bane were in love," he continued. "*That* King Gerald would not tolerate. And so, he stripped him of his rank."

"That seems like something my father would do," the prince replied. "But I am surprised he did not have him executed on the spot."

"Assuredly, that is what the king wanted," Gilead said in a low voice and put his hand on the prince's shoulder. "But the queen begged for his life and bargained for him to become a lowly castle guard. The king must have thought the humiliation would crush the knight's spirits. But he did not know Traveris well, did he?"

"No, he did not," the prince said and looked up at Gilead. "He saved my life."

Gilead Highbloode winked at Sigismund with a gleam in his eye. "That's what Traveris Bane does," he said. "He saves people's lives."

The young man realized now that the court at Waverly Castle was the real Illusory Fortress: Those considered good were actually the maleficent ones, and those deemed weak were actually the strongest of them all.

"Come, we must go," Manfred said. "It is time to shatter the Arch Crystal."

CHAPTER 32

CONFRONTING THE ARCH CRYSTAL

They walked down the central walkway into the great hall. Manfred the Magnificent led the way, followed by the White Druid Prospero, and Sigismund trailed behind. The dome ceiling above them elaborately pictured epic battle scenes of Solarian past—knights in gleaming armor on majestic steeds charging toward dragons of various kinds. There were vanquished red dragons, green dragons, and gold dragons of time immemorial. The shadow dragons were the last of the great serpents; the moondrakes were their lesser cousins, at least in terms of sheer size and fearfulness. It was all so grand, and yet, peculiarly sad.

Druix peered upward as he scratched along the great hall's stone floor with his sharp claws. This was the first time he had ever been indoors—possibly even the first time a winged serpent had ever been indoors in the history of Solarius.

It was a disorienting experience for Druix, and the paintings depicting the outright murder of great serpents were disturbing, even with his animus toward the shadow dragons of Noctera. His black eyes reflected the light from the stained-glass windows that were inlaid like multihued slivers in the dome ceiling. Various kings from ancient lore were depicted in blue, yellow, and red panes of glass. It was a cathedral devoted to Hypernean vanity.

Walking on the other side of the great hall was Aenyx, who was now stricken with worry about Raven Whitecrest and Phoenix Stormguard. If the High Sorceress Morana harmed a feather on their head, he vowed that he would rip her to shreds. But all he could do was hope that the strange band of adventurers he had fallen into would find some answer to the crisis befalling his homeland of Aeris. If not, that meant a desperate flight into sure death to try to save the last remaining griffins.

"Welcome to the Illusory Fortress, friends," Gilead stated from behind the group. "I would offer you a grand feast, but alas, I only have a meager store of meal and wine that was granted to me some days—sorry, years and years ago."

"Not to worry, noble knight," Manfred said. "We do not intend to stay long, though I am quite sure you would have made a fine host. It is time to reveal the Arch Crystal!"

The wizard approached the center of the great hall. In the middle of the room was an array of concentric stones with runic insignia surrounding a single recessed disk emblazoned with the ancient symbol for time. The large stone disk was bisected by a crack running through it.

"Sigismund," Manfred said and looked reassuringly at the prince. "Produce the crystal shard."

The young prince pulled the crystal shard from his inside pocket and studied the faces of his new allies—the wizard, the druid, the knight, the griffin, the moondrake, and the fairy. They looked upon him with anticipation. This was the moment they were waiting for—destroying the Arch Crystal and returning to normalcy.

Prince Sigismund unveiled the crystal shard and thrust it into a red beam of light that cascaded from a stained-glass window. It scattered rays across the entire room—yet instead of the expected multicolored rays, they were now brilliant white. The light washed away the colors from the paintings on the ceiling, the murals on the wall, the rugs on the floor, even the garments they were wearing. *Everything* was white.

"Good!" Manfred the Magnificent declared. He thrust his wizard's staff on the floor. Suddenly, the groan of moving machinery could be felt underneath them, trembling like an earthquake.

"Oh, no!" Miranda Sunray squealed. "What sorcery is this?"

"It is all right, child," Manfred said. "This too shall pass!"

Aenyx and Druix looked at one another with worried expressions, wordlessly communicating their dread of what they had gotten themselves into.

At the very heart of the room, the semicircles of the stone disk began to diverge. As they pulled apart, they receded under the flooring, slowly producing a central pit. There came the nearly deafening sound of stone grinding upon stone. It felt like something was coming from beneath the floor.

"Patience!" the mage cried.

At last, at the center of the room, a stone pedestal slowly began to thrust up from the floor. It bore an immense crystal that looked like jagged glass. A beam of white light shone straight up from it. It was glorious to behold.

"Druix!" Manfred shouted, pointing to the northeast corner of the room.

"Aenyx!" the wizard cried, pointing to the northwest.

"Miranda!" he declared, pointing to the southeast.

"Sigismund!" he said, making sure he was in the southwest corner of the room.

As the four creatures stared into the dazzling light of the Arch Crystal, the blackness of their eyes began to melt away. The Could-Be presented an image of the potential of the world if the creatures would simply unite.

Druix beheld himself flying above splendorous verdant fields and vibrant forests of pink and lavender wisteria blooms. White pegasus and black unicorns frolicked in a field of red poppies below. They looked up at him flying overhead and neighed vigorously. They were welcoming him—actually welcoming him, a *moondrake*—into Wysteria!

Strangest of all, he beheld black and gold and red and green dragons once again roaming the world of Solarius without fear of mankind. A human child ran up to a shadow dragon and tugged on its whiskers, but it did not even bat an eye. Instead, it merely grinned with a mouth full of gleaming fangs that it would never use to murder again.

And Lunastria—it was no longer a realm of evil and injustice; it was one where moondrakes cared for one another and ensured that even the weakest of them was respected. This was a world that he wanted to bring into existence.

In Aenyx's vision, griffins were no longer divided into Prides, and any griffin could be whatever he or she wanted to become. Griffins of all colors and kinds were playing together in the main arena, and there would never be wars or trials again.

Mothers and fathers once again knew who their offspring were and loved them dearly, yet the adult griffins still cared about the young of others nearly as much as their own. There were no more Guardians—everyone was responsible for participating in the administration of justice in the new Republic of Aeris.

Arbitrary division, petty jealousy, and abject vanity were banished in this new Aeris. There were no more boundaries on who could become friends—including friendships between griffins and moondrakes. Aenyx finally felt that he could be accepted in this world. It was a model of happiness and harmony.

Miranda Sunray stared into the light with her violet eyes and saw a breathtaking image of The Could-Be, The Never-Was, and The Always-Will-Be united in timeless eternity. There would be no more old age, no more suffering, no more death—all of the creatures that ever were and all of the creatures that would ever be united in mutual bliss. There was no anger, no spite, no cruelty, and no hatred. It was a world where all were in perfect command of themselves, and their only motivations were love, forgiveness, and joy.

The fairy struggled to perceive what it all meant, but she believed it meant something like this: If this inner world could be created in her own mind, and she could see it and believe it, then she could recreate it in the outer world. As long as she clung to this vision, her heart would remain pure, and her motives benevolent toward the other creatures of the world.

Miranda Sunray ceased feeling like a victim and began to see herself as a healer. For all the creatures of the world who had been wronged, she would strive to make it right. For the first time in her existence, she felt whole.

Prince Sigismund stared into the Arch Crystal. His eyes were no longer black, but turquoise blue. The vision he beheld turned the Hypernean kingdom on its head. Instead of a prince, he was just a young man. His brothers loved and accepted him for who he was. His father was not a king, but a much simpler and happier man, whose only task in life was to rule over himself. His mother was every bit as lovely as before, but she was only his mother, no longer a queen. The people of Hypernea now had enough to eat and no longer needed to beg from the aristocrats.

Most heartening of all, the famine and plague were gone. Once the corruption of the royal government was vanquished, the land and the people healed of their own accord.

It now appeared to Sigismund that justice would require true leadership—not the selfish accumulation of power for its own sake, but through everyone empowering one another with personal acts of charity, forgiveness, and love. Justice required personal action, not impersonal rule over strangers. He felt compelled to renounce his princely crown upon his return to Hypernea.

As the four creatures stared into the Arch Crystal, the visions of The Could-Be cleared, and they saw images of one another within the crystal. Sigismund saw an image of Druix Coldshadow, while Druix saw Aenyx Stormguard; Aenyx saw Miranda Sunray, and Miranda saw Prince Sigismund Waverly.

The Arch Crystal started to vibrate and emit loud crackling noises. Cracks began to appear on the face of the crystal, growing deeper and deeper.

"It is being destroyed!" shouted Manfred tremulously, as if he were beholding something dangerous yet glorious. "You are destroying the Arch Crystal!"

Suddenly, a beam of pure white energy exploded from the top of the Arch Crystal. It blew a hole in the roof of the Illusory Fortress and shot straight into the sky. The ground shook; it felt like the foundation would cave in and they would sink into the depths.

"This place isn't going to hold for long!" Gilead shouted.

"We'd better run!" Prospero yelled.

The roof started to collapse upon them. Fragments of stained-glass shards broke off and shattered upon the ground. Miranda Sunray flew through the gates in terror. As the stone tiles began crumbling beneath them, Manfred scrambled toward the gate. Aenyx bounded and took flight.

Sigismund jumped on the back of Druix as the floor gave way. The moondrake flapped his wings hard and was able to stay suspended in the air while the entire floor sank into the ground—along with the shattered remnants of the Arch Crystal.

They ran as far from the collapsing Illusory Fortress as possible. The entire structure heaved and groaned, then started to crumble into pieces. Its fallen hunks of rock and marble sucked in most of the black water in the swamp. It began to sink into the marsh below and finally disappeared with a bubbly glug.

They were now standing on the stone walkway in the middle of what was once a knee-deep swamp. It was the inconspicuous final resting place for the shattered remains of the Arch Crystal. Unless they had witnessed the surreal experience, no one would ever suspect that the destruction of the Arch Crystal had taken place on this nondescript spot within the confines of an Illusory Fortress.

It was a triumphant feeling. They had done it!

They gazed out upon the world with new eyes. The blackness had been emptied from them and it seemed as if a fog had been lifted. Sigismund's crystal blue eyes gazed out upon the world. He felt a major energy shift, but it wasn't entirely positive. Instead, he had a deep sense of foreboding.

Then the horrifying screech of a shadow dragon pierced the silence.

CHAPTER 33

THE RETURN OF THE HIGH SORCERESS

Morana was not one to be trifled with. The High Sorceress rode in on her shadow dragon mount with one hand on its gilded bridle and the other upon her ghastly orb. Her wraithlike gown flew from her arms and her legs in the stirring breeze; the sheer garb was loosely draped upon her pale, feminine frame. She was oddly alluring in the same sense that a prisoner tormented for days was desirous of a merciful death. She cackled. A deadly green flame danced in her eyes.

"What have we here?" she bellowed as her dragon hovered above the mortified company beneath her.

"Prospero! The White Druid!" she exclaimed with contempt. "The sacred mystic and high priest—what a motley crew you have assembled here! Always on your noble quest, but your intentions aren't always noble, are they, Prospero?"

It struck Sigismund as exceedingly odd to detect a note of pain and sadness in the sorceress's voice. But he was so terrified, he could barely look upon the woman or her fearsome dragon steed. He placed his hand upon Druix's back for comfort as the moondrake stood taut with readiness.

"No games, Morana!" he replied with grief in his voice. "That was long ago. And besides, you are too late! The Arch Crystal is destroyed—so run along to that dragon-enslaving husband of yours and deliver the calamitous news!"

"Oh, that is what you do not get, old man," she replied with wickedness dripping from her voice. "I had just given the order for the annihilation of Laketown when I saw that fantastic ray of light illuminate the skies. My heart filled with utter delight. We *wanted* you to destroy the Arch Crystal."

Manfred's eyes flickered with the hint of a terrible realization. His body went stiff as he leaned upon his oaken wizard's staff.

"If I might answer that thought in your head, Manfred the so-called Magnificent," she said. "Yes, you are a fool. You see, while you believed that destroying the Arch Crystal would free the potential of the world to return to its rightful owners, my dear Dracus had been preparing for years to absorb it himself!"

"You foul creature!" Gilead Highbloode shouted, seething with anger. "Your wickedness had seemed endless, but it ends now!"

With that, Gilead Highbloode hurled his sword directly at the shadow dragon. It flung end over end, taking both Morana and the dragon completely by surprise. It lodged into the milky gray eye of the dragon, which screeched horrendously.

"You impetuous ass!" Morana screamed as the beast floundered in mid-flight.

The dragon's wings seemed to grow heavy, and its tail lashed out, throwing it off-balance. As it veered to one side, the High Sorceress Morana issued a greenish ball of flame from her orbed scepter. It was hurled directly at the company of heroes and struck the brave knight Gilead in his chest plate. The shadow dragon fell from the skies into the trees beyond the marshy clearing.

"No!" Miranda screamed in a thin voice.

She rushed to the knight's aid as fast as her minuscule wings could carry her, and she perched upon his chest, sobbing profusely. Her fairy heart was broken.

"Good Miranda," the knight said weakly as lines of age began to grow on his face. He was aging decades before their eyes; the Illusory Fortress's spell had been reversed. Gilead gave her a courageous smile, as if he knew it would be his last. "I lived a full life, and I lived it the way I wanted," he said. "Don't cry, sweet fairy. I lived, I loved, and I lost. But in the end, I found hope that the world I now leave behind is in good hands because I found all of you. All is right with the universe."

The knight gasped his final breath and lay lifeless on the stone walkway. The golden gleam on his armor from the last rays of the burning sun gave him an otherworldly appearance as he passed into the beyond. Gilead was dead.

"The knight fulfilled his sworn duty. Now we must fulfill ours," Prospero said solemnly. "He bought us precious time to warn the creatures of Solarius and prepare them for war. More importantly, we must prevent Dracus Imprimus from regaining the full height of his powers."

Prospero and Manfred exchanged petrified glances on the walkway.

"Prospero," Manfred said in the dusky glow, "you know what this means. We must reunite the Mighty Three."

"Aenyx," Prospero said, turning to the griffin, "you and I must deal with the sorceress and the dragon siege of Laketown."

"Fine!" the griffin growled. His dark brown eyes stared into the setting sun. There was contempt in his voice. "After that, we rescue my friends in Aeris."

"Manfred," the druid said while facing the old wizard, "please go with great haste to Hypernea with the young Prince Sigismund upon the sure wings of the moondrake Druix."

"It is agreed," Manfred the Magnificent said. "You fly to Aeris. We are off to secure the kingdom of Hypernea." He turned toward the distraught fairy. "Dear Miranda, come with Sigismund, Druix, and me to Waverly Castle. I will have a most special task for you, vital to all of the creatures of Solarius. But first, we must see to the securing of Hypernea."

The fairy nodded through her tears. She was still on her knees on the chest plate of the dead knight. Her now aquamarine eyes were glistening with sorrow, but she put on a brave smile.

"Yes," Miranda said. "I will go with you and do whatever you shall bid me. I will do it in Sir Gilead's honor."

Manfred nodded. "Let us ride!"

As Prince Sigismund followed the blue-cloaked wizard onto the back of the moondrake, he looked back with sadness upon his newfound friends. Emblazoned into his memory was a lasting image of the daring griffin Aenyx standing beside the white-cloaked druid Prospero.

Prospero looked upon the departing company with steely determination in his eyes. Far from being the usual image of aloof dignity, replete with his sagacious mastery of nature, he now actually cut the cloth of a daunting adversary. Aenyx adroitly bowed so the druid could climb aboard, but the griffin's expression belied his thirst for vengeance.

"Farewell and good luck!" Manfred said. "Morana is a fierce enemy, but I am sure you have weapons in your arsenal to defeat her."

Prospero nodded at the wizard as the griffin ascended into the air. The druid waved his hand and coated the slain knight with a dim, white glow. As he raised his staff, the knight's body was lifted into the air and slowly returned to the site of the sunken Illusory Fortress, where it would be buried with his last sentry for eternity.

The druid and the griffin set off for the tree line, searching for the place where Morana and her dragon had crashed. It had been too quiet since the great beast's fall. Prospero wondered if Morana was laying a trap. They would soon find out.

As Druix began to go airborne, Sigismund looked behind him from the moondrake's long, sinuous back. Rising above the forest, Sigismund could see the western sun beaming down upon all of creation with a glorious glow. What he saw filled his heart with wonder. Rows and rows of flowering trees of every variety and color were filling the land!

He noticed that the tree leaves in the swamp were bursting with vivid green foliage. The reeds and the cattails of the marsh were suddenly verdant and thriving. It was awe-inspiring.

Sigismund saw, for the first time in his life, that nature was not a terrible adversary to the Hypernean kingdom; it could be full of splendor and bounty.

Far away to his left, he recognized blue jacarandas from his mother's gardening books—but the illustrations didn't do them justice. Their flowers popped with a vividness that even the most skilled human painter could not recreate.

Beside the jacarandas were swathes of towering empress trees forming gorgeous, purple-flowered canopies across the rooftop of the forest. He spotted the dark maroon leaves of the Bloodgood maple, the delicate pink buds of the flowering dogwood, the white floral branches of the hawthorn, and most spectacularly, the burnished red buds of the Flame of the Forest, which made him look twice to see if the tree was actually aflame.

"Look over there!" Manfred shouted and pointed to his right to the rolling hills. "That is a Dragon's Blood tree! We have not seen one of its kind growing in Hypernea for ages! It must have been planted there by druids."

It stood defiantly upon a lonely hilltop. The branches formed the most peculiar shape—like it was designed to give shelter to weary travelers. Sigismund watched the forestry change. The black ash, dogwood, and poplar trees receded behind them.

Underneath them now was an old-growth forest of twisted beech trees, which created labyrinthine tunnels where forest sprites were known to roam. Angel oaks wove their branches throughout the forest below like outstretched tendrils in search of life. It was a land untouched by mankind and enshrined in mystery.

"We are almost there!" Manfred declared.

Druix glided upon the early spring breeze with the wind at his back. He was wincing from the glare of the sun balanced on the distant horizon. Shards of the daystar's rays pierced his retina and illuminated his now-silvery eyes. The moondrake was glad their journey was almost over, and he would soon rest. Life in the daylight was draining him of his natural energy.

The group flew onward over the rolling hills and undulating valleys. The crimson sun finally ducked below the horizon, and Druix breathed a sigh of relief.

The moondrake landed upon a mountaintop. The wizard dismounted and wheezed before he hunched over and stroked his knees, clearly worn out by the flight.

"You go ahead, son. I will catch up with you. I have my ways," the wizard said and tapped his staff on the ground.

"But, how?" Sigismund asked.

"I have my ways, son," Manfred replied. "Now, go!"

Sigismund hesitantly clambered farther up on Druix's back and held tightly to the spikes lining the moondrake's back. Miranda flew to his shoulder. The wizard waved his glowing staff in the air, and in the bluish light, the company proceeded ahead into the unknown.

In the distance, dark clouds loomed ahead. A rainstorm was gathering. Sigismund looked harder but was not sure if what he was seeing was real. The reddish outline of Waverly Castle towered above a faraway hill.

Miranda gasped.

The castle was in flames.

CHAPTER 34

A DATE WITH THE DARK QUEEN

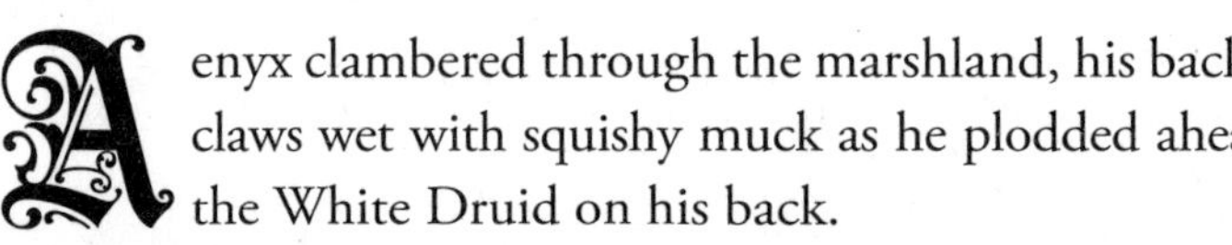

Aenyx clambered through the marshland, his back paws and front claws wet with squishy muck as he plodded ahead while bearing the White Druid on his back.

"Why don't you try walking next time, druid?" Aenyx growled.

He did not like carrying humans around. Not one bit. It wasn't… dignified.

"Alas, you are so much stronger than I," the druid replied. "I am but an old man."

"Then remind me again why we are ambushing the most powerful sorceress in Solarius?" the griffin replied.

"Save your foul mood for the shadow dragon, if its poisonous heart still beats," Prospero replied.

"I've got a bad feeling about this," Aenyx said as they approached the tree line.

Shattered ash trees were broken in half with slivers of timber protruding and broken branches lying in disarray everywhere. But neither the dragon nor Morana was anywhere to be found.

"This cannot be good," Prospero remarked.

As they forged ahead into the forest, climbing over and snapping broken branches, and stepped into the wet forestland beyond, it became apparent that the dragon was not dead. They would have to hunt it down along with the sorceress.

Prospero surmised that the dragon had attempted to fly but had clipped the tree branches. It looked like the great serpent's tail had scraped the ground, leaving a furrow in the soil leading away from the site of the crash. It must be badly reeling from the injury.

"That way," Prospero quietly said to Aenyx while pointing ahead.

On the other side of a ridge ahead, they heard the labored groans of the beast. Aenyx crept ahead as quietly as he could, using all of the predatory skill that he could muster.

As they stood on the edge of the ridge and looked downward, they saw the High Sorceress. She was stroking the head of the black beast, which lay helplessly on the ground, breathing rapidly for a creature of its size. Its left eye was weeping black blood.

Aenyx did not feel like he could ambush a creature in such a state, even if killing it would put it out of its misery. Prospero dismounted so he could stand on the edge of the ridge overlooking the scene.

"Morana!" Prospero shouted. "Let us reason together! There is no cause for us to be at war with one another!"

Morana did not respond and continued to stroke the head of the dragon as it lay dying. Prospero listened closely and could hear that she was sobbing.

"Prospero," she moaned in a muffled voice. "You must heal him! You know that I cannot. Gigantus has been the most faithful creature in this cold world. If you ever loved me, you would do this one thing for me! Then I will leave this place and never return."

"There are bigger things at stake than your fallen companion," Prospero said. "I take no pleasure in telling you no. You have sown chaos and destruction throughout Solarius. The world is in flames, and there is nothing but pain and suffering wherever you go. What happened to you,

Morana? You must turn away from hatred and toward the love that is the birthright of all living beings."

"What do you know of love, Prospero?" the sorceress bitterly replied. She lifted her head and displayed her teary eyes, which were now burning with flickering green flames inside them. "I was only a young woman when you deigned to approach me as your lover instead of your apprentice!" she cried. "You broke my trust, and then you broke my heart!"

"My dear Morana," Prospero sighed. "I could not help my feelings for you. It is because you were—you are—such a great woman that I loved you. Being near you and seeing how truly special you were drove me to extremes. I admit it. I confess it! Now, turn away from your dark path and embrace peace and forgiveness."

Morana hung her head momentarily, as if pondering the druid's words. Then she began laughing to herself.

Aenyx was highly alarmed, his gut roiling at the thought of what would happen next.

"You foolish, foolish old man!" she screamed. The sorceress no longer sounded distressed so much as maniacal. "Dracus Imprimus showed me a new way, a different way—the way of power! Why play the victim when you can be the victimizer?"

Aenyx took cover behind the ridge to shield himself from the wrath coming their way. One of the sorceress's flaming green balls of death went flying overhead and crashed into the trees.

"Whatever you did, druid," Aenyx said while they crouched behind a fallen tree branch, "it really, really ticked her off."

"You have no idea," he replied. Prospero rose and lifted his bronze staff. He issued a piercing ray of light toward the sorceress. The ray cut through the evening air, struck her fully upon the chest, and coated her body with a soft, white glow.

Although the attack did not appear to physically harm the sorceress, it did seem to weaken her tremendously. She groaned and crawled behind the dying shadow dragon for cover. And then, she placed her hand upon the creature's eye. The white glow was slowly transferred from the sorceress to the creature, and the dragon's eye began to heal.

"Maybe you are a fool," Aenyx said to the White Druid.

The giant dragon blinked its eye and sucked in a tremendous gulp of air. It lifted its massive head off the forest floor and turned its terrible gaze upon its attackers. It put down one clawed foot and then the other and lifted its gargantuan frame.

"Rise, Gigantus!" Morana said with a crackle in her voice.

Aenyx was not about to sit and watch his hated adversary regain full strength. He rose into the air, bound over the ridge, and shot downward as fast as his wings could carry him. The griffin ferociously sank its claws into the serpent's throat and gashed open its scaly neck.

"You damned griffin!" Morana screeched.

The beast roared in agony. Its claws lashed out at its attacker. Aenyx remained perched upon the dragon with his talons sinking deeply within its breast. His sharpened beak was about to tear into the serpent's throat.

The High Sorceress lifted her ghastly scepter. Her eyes glowed madly, and her raven hair blew in the evening breeze. She motioned to cast a deadly spell upon the griffin.

"Morana, that is enough!" Prospero shouted.

With a great flash, a tremendous lightning bolt suddenly crashed in front of the sorceress. It landed with a loud boom that knocked the sorceress backward. Her orbed scepter flew from her hand, and a green ball of flame shot wildly into the forest, scaring off a cluster of ravens that had congregated in a black ash tree. The sorceress was dazed.

Aenyx had been blown off the dread Gigantus. While the shadow dragon was blinded by the lightning bolt, the griffin resumed his attack. He clawed his way over to the great serpent and sank his beak into a vulnerable area in its throat that griffins were taught to target. He ripped it open with all his might. Blood spurted through the forest, coating the tree leaves with its awful black spray.

"Gigantus!" the sorceress cried.

But her dragon was as good as dead.

"You will all pay for this!" she screamed. She fumbled on the ground until she found her orb-shaped scepter. Morana whispered a spell, and an oval portal appeared in the forest. It was ringed in violet, and it shimmered in an iridescent fashion. Through the portal, Prospero and Aenyx saw the shadowy outline of a black figure.

Dracus Imprimus.

The High Sorceress rose and walked to the portal. An armored hand reached through the portal and grasped hers. As she motioned to step through the portal, she turned back momentarily to look upon Aenyx and the White Druid Prospero.

"Death will be yours," she uttered.

Morana stepped through the portal, which closed behind her. Then the High Sorceress vanished into the night.

CHAPTER 35

THE RUINS OF THE PAST

Prince Sigismund looked upon the remains of Waverly Castle. It was covered in smoldering ashes, and a sooty smell lingered in the air. Black clouds poured out of the castle towers in great plumes. He peered upon his own lonely tower, which he could barely make out above the smoky haze on the other side of the courtyard.

The exterior castle gates were ajar, and anyone could walk right in. They were built of tall iron rods and were meant more for show than for stopping an invading army. It had been decades since there was a serious challenge to the Waverlys' grasp on Hypernea, and it had been generations since a foreign army had set foot in the kingdom.

"Druix, can you wait outside the gates and keep a lookout for trouble?" Sigismund asked.

"Yes, Prince," Druix said with a somber tone. "If you ask me, this isn't the work of shadow dragons."

Prince Sigismund looked at Druix with a bewildered expression.

Shadow dragons would have burned everything here, even melting these iron gates," he said. "Those flower beds up ahead—those would be completely torched as well. Whoever did this ignored those intentionally—they had no interest in demolishing everything in sight. This was much more…targeted."

Prince Sigismund gazed upon the royal courtyard through the open gates and could see Druix's point. What he saw made no sense. It was vacant. Silent as a graveyard. There was no sign of civilization except the bright red roses extending in parallel rows beyond the main gate.

"Quite the sight, isn't it, Prince?" a voice said from behind him. It was Manfred.

"How did you get here so quickly?" the prince quizzically asked.

"I have many ways of tapping the power of The Could-Be, including the ability to phase short distances," Manfred said. "But it takes quite a bit of energy. In a way, it's the opposite of what Miranda experiences when she phases through matter."

Miranda giggled and nodded her head affirmatively.

"Manfred?" Prince Sigismund asked. The wizard's light blue eyes belied that he was extremely troubled by what he saw before him.

"I am afraid the moondrake is right," the mage said, looking out at the ghostly sight of what seemed to be an abandoned castle. "This wasn't the work of shadow dragons."

"Come, Prince," the tall mage said. "It is time we find out what exactly happened here." Manfred pushed open the iron castle gate. "After you," he said with a modest expression on his wrinkled face. His countenance bore the most genial of smiles. His nose bubbled out the way old men's noses were wont to do.

Sigismund forced a pained smile in a modest attempt at feigned bravery. What he saw horrified him to his core. The stygian wreckage of his childhood home—if Sigismund could even call it a home—struck him as more surreal than his new reality.

"Manfred," he said as they strode down the central walkway. "My mother…she is the queen…what if they…" He shuddered as he contemplated the worst. The floral smell of roses mixed with the increasingly pungent smell of smoke was one of the most confusing experiences he had ever encountered.

As they approached the main gate, he could see someone standing guard there. It looked like…the Kindly Knight!

Prince Sigismund broke out into a run toward the man. He was bent over with one hand on his sword, propping himself up like an elderly gentleman using a cane. In his other hand was a kerchief, which he held over his mouth and nose.

"Halt! Who goes there?" the castle guard asked suspiciously. He coughed twice and pushed himself up to stand straight, the kerchief still covering his mouth.

"It is I, Prince Sigismund."

There was a pause as Traveris Bane looked through the cloudy haze of smoke. He blinked twice to clear his gray eyes. "Why, it is you, Sigismund!" Traveris replied. "I wasn't sure because your black eyes, they've changed to blue. I wish I could say welcome back, but I am afraid there is not much to come back to."

"What happened?" the prince asked with a hint of panic in his voice. "But first of all, where is my mother?"

"Do not worry for your mother," he said. "I can personally assure you Queen Galadria is safe and relatively well. When the fighting began, I personally guaranteed her passage to secure quarters not far from here. There were touch-and-go moments as the marauders searched for her and any other members of the royal family."

Traveris gave Sigismund an intensely concerned look. He pulled the kerchief off his mouth and strained not to cough.

"I regret that I must tell you," Traveris said and paused, as if pondering a way to put it delicately, "King Gerald, your father, is dead."

Sigismund gasped.

"The king is dead?" the wizard asked. Manfred looked upon the castle with a dire cast on his grim face.

"Yes, the old king is dead," the Kindly Knight replied. "And the new king may be standing right here beside us."

Sigismund was stunned. He thought he might have felt relief at the news that his father was dead. It would have meant that he was safe—at least from his father's designs to have him killed. Yet that certainly would not have lasted, anyway, since nature appeared to be renewed. The curse seemed to be vanquished with the shattering of the Arch Crystal. But had it?

"I am sorry," the prince said. "But did you say that the king was standing right here?"

"Yes," Traveris said, looking at him earnestly. "Your mother has named you the successor."

"But what about my brothers?" Sigismund asked in a frantic voice. "Certainly, they are older and more qualified than I. Jax is the eldest. Thaddeus is the wisest in military matters. And Killian—he is braver than I! How in the world could I become the king? I am just a young man!"

"All of that may very well be true, although I know damn well it isn't," the knight said. His eyes were red from the smoke in the air. "But they have been captured by the pirate king, the one called Darius Blackblade. He came from the Jeweled Islands with an immaculate fleet and a legion of raiders. At first, they demanded payment. Hypernea had been paying for fish and the fruits of the islands to be shipped to the kingdom ever since the tremendous blight began eighteen years ago. Alas, the last few years were nearly all on credit, which was not just on the king's personal credit, but that of the lords and ladies around Hypernea who took it upon themselves to help foot the massive bill. The interest built up, outsizing the king's ability to pay, never mind all of the other lords and ladies, and…well, you can see the results."

Traveris pointed upward. Then he bent over and coughed.

"Obviously, King Gerald could not afford to pay Darius Blackblade," he continued, "and so the king gathered the armies of the clans. Even the MacCallisters joined in, as well as the Forresters and the Smythes."

"The MacCallisters…" the prince said with trepidation. "Does that mean…"

"Yes, I am afraid so," Traveris said with a slight grimace. "They seized our friend Princess Melanie. The marauders carried her and your brothers away to the Jeweled Islands' staging point, the castle Stormkeep, on the coast of the Emerald Sea."

"Did we not fight back?" Sigismund asked, a hint of anger rising in his voice. "What good are our troops, anyway?"

"The seasoned warriors defeated our ragtag outfit of Hypernean soldiers, who truthfully were not ones for drilling or exercises," he replied. "I had warned them. But no one would listen to a lowly, disgraced castle guard."

"Oh, but I know the truth about that, Traveris," Sigismund said gently. "I know that you are a Knight of the Sacred Order of the Lion. One of your fellow knights, Gilead Highbloode, told us all about it and how you rescued my mother at the Battle of the Onyx Wastes! You should be recognized as a hero to this kingdom, and if I become king, one of the first things I will do is restore you to full knighthood and make you captain of the King's Guard."

Traveris Bane flushed bright red. "That name," he uttered through a slight gasp. "Gilead Highbloode. It is one I have not heard in ages. If anyone should be the captain of the King's Guard, let it be him."

Sigismund looked upon the Kindly Knight. He felt nothing but heartbreak for the loyal man before him. He did not want to be the one to tell him, but he owed him the truth. He also owed the great knight who gave his life in battle for the sake of the kingdom.

"Gilead Highbloode died a hero's death," he said to Traveris. "He died fighting the High Sorceress Morana."

The blood seemed to drain from the knight's face. His eyes bulged wide. A grim pallor passed across his expression.

"Take me to see the queen," Sigismund pronounced. "Only she can make me the king by royal decree, and it is up to me alone to bear this burden."

Sigismund's mind was overcome with a cascade of thoughts, which rained down upon him like a tempest. His return to Waverly Castle should have been triumphant. The prince was vindicated by the revelation that he was never cursed to begin with. Now that Waverly Castle lay in ruins, Sigismund realized the state of the world was even more precarious than when he was banished from the kingdom.

"What do you think, young Sigismund?" Manfred asked. "Do you believe yourself to be a king? Would you take me as your counselor?"

"Why wouldn't I want to become king, Manfred the Magnificent, powerful sorcerer whom I had only read about in storybooks just weeks ago?" Sigismund asked sardonically. "Why, we just met on a wild journey that included fairies, griffins, and of course, a moondrake, who, by the way, is waiting right outside those gates, unless he has eaten whatever livestock remained in this godforsaken land!"

The Kindly Knight's expression turned from one of sorrow to surprise. His eyebrows raised as he looked down upon the young man whose shoulders now carried the weight of the world.

"You might not want to hear this, Traveris Bane," Sigismund continued. "But a shadow dragon army led by the Dread Commander and the High Sorceress is poised to invade all of Hypernea. But let me go on.

"The Republic of Aeris has been captured by an army of shadow dragons under the command of Dracus Imprimus. The High Sorceress Morana, with her penchant for casual cruelty, has been wreaking havoc throughout their world. Unless, of course, Aenyx the griffin and Prospero, the White Druid, have somehow put an end to her maniacal reign of terror. And there is also the real possibility that she has killed them both, but I don't even want to dwell upon that.

"And all this is in addition to my castle lying in smoldering ruins and my brothers being captured by some crazy, money-hungry pirate king. And a gorgeous redheaded princess that I was instantly smitten with is now in the hands of island marauders who have an entire navy at their disposal!"

"Am I missing anything, wizard?" Sigismund said, looking up at the old mage.

"No, I think that about covers it," the wizard replied with a cocked eyebrow. Manfred put his firm hand upon the prince's shoulder.

"Before I do anything else, I need to see my mother," Sigismund said, glancing over to Traveris.

The Kindly Knight nodded his head and beckoned the prince to accompany him.

"I will accompany you as well," Manfred chimed in. "There are certain important affairs of state we must discuss if Aeris is to survive."

"Miranda, please inform our friend, the moondrake, of the reason for our lateness," the wizard remarked. And with that, the fairy flitted off to find Druix.

A truly daunting task was now set before them all. If they failed to act, it would mean the end of life as they knew it.

CHAPTER 36

HEAVY IS THE HEAD

Druix Coldshadow lay impatiently at the gate with his weary head propped on the stone walkway. His barbed tail flicked back and forth while his silvery eyes gleamed in the moonglow. His sleek neck was unwound and resting in front of his serpentine body, and his great wingspan was shamelessly outstretched upon the dewy grass outside the castle grounds. His companions were late.

Druix was painfully aware that the griffin and the druid could use his help right now. But the young moondrake also felt an oddly strong connection to this prince.

Druix wondered if the young man had lost a loved one in the castle attack. He wondered if he had lost someone like his own dad.

Meanwhile, Sigismund was traversing to the secret lair where his mother had taken refuge, pacing closely behind the Kindly Knight. Manfred the Magnificent paced a short distance behind them.

"Here it is, your majesty," Traveris said with a wry grin on his smoke-tarred face. They stopped in front of an unassuming stonemason's hovel that extended into the side of a hill. It looked like some place a peasant would live, if one actually had items of value to protect. Traveris put a hand on the young man's shoulder reassuringly. "You are ready for this. Do not doubt yourself."

Sigismund looked up at the kindly knight's war-worn face. Traveris looked as if he knew something of the dilemma he now faced and the tremendous weight of responsibility. Their gazes were steely and their expressions resolute, but something inside their eyes betrayed feelings of incredible weight. His duties as king would be immense.

"Mother?" Sigismund asked while knocking on the wooden door encased in steel reinforcements.

"Sigismund!" his mother's voice cried out from inside the building. It was the dead of night, but she must have been awake, awaiting word from Traveris.

The queen opened the door. Or at least, it must have been the queen. A figure in a dark-blue hood lingered in the doorway. Sigismund stood there before the hooded figure. His thin, chiseled face was smudged with dirt, and his hair was askew, hanging loosely over his crystal-blue eyes.

"Your eyes!" she cried out. "My boy, what happened to you?"

"It is a long story, Mom," he said. "I will tell you about it later. But first, I want to hear all about you."

He gazed into his mother's eyes, which now looked so much like his own. A hint of relief passed over her sorrowful face. The queen threw back her hood, revealing her smiling face. Sigismund smiled back at the beautiful, platinum-blonde woman who was both strong and dignified.

"You!" she exclaimed, turning toward Manfred. "You are the mage who appeared in our court so many years ago!"

Manfred the Magnificent gave a shallow bow, then rose with a smile on his face.

"I imagined for nights upon end what I would say to you if ever I were to meet you," she said with an apologetic air. "I am sorry that I treated you so derisively when you arrived at court that fateful day because, ultimately, your words were a spell of protection over my son. In some ways, if it were not for you, he would not be standing here with us."

"At your service, my queen," the wizard said with a bashful smile. The old mage tugged on his flowing white beard as if he were embarrassed by the queen's gratitude.

"And of course, my Kindly Knight," the queen said with a hospitable tone that was graceful and becoming of a woman of her stature. "What am I doing? All of you come in. This horrid night, I am sure, has exhausted you all. I will make some hibiscus tea. Sit down; please do sit down, all of you."

The trio entered the hovel and found their seats upon small wooden chairs arranged within the stony confines. A humble fire burned in the fireplace, its illuminating blaze throwing their shadows upon the wall. It was exceptionally cozy—for a last resort refuge from vicious marauders.

Queen Galadria returned with a tray of fragrant hot tea served in delicate white porcelain cups decorated with yellow chrysanthemums and tiny matching saucers. Even in the most extenuating of circumstances, the queen could be counted upon to show the finer touches of feminine grace.

She clasped both hands around her teacup and leaned forward in a rocking chair near the fire. Her face was smooth and as white as the porcelain cups. Her eyes danced in the firelight with a sense of urgency and worry. Her shocks of close-cropped platinum hair made her look boyish, as if to mask her identity from roving bandits.

"I am longing for information about you, my son," she began. "But I understand by the looks of it, you have journeyed a long way and want answers. So I shall give them to you."

The queen sighed deeply. Her thin, birdlike frame heaved while she mustered the energy to reveal the burdensome knowledge.

"Your father, King Gerald, is dead. As much as I loathe him for his wrong-headed plot to end your life, he died most honorably in combat while attempting to defend the realm."

Sigismund sat up straight and watched her closely. He was surprised by the revelation.

"Yes, it is true," she said, sensing his scrutiny. "The king tried to rally the soldiers to fight the pirates on a battlefield west of Waverly Castle.

His spies in Stormkeep had fled the coastal invaders and made their way to our castle, relaying the dreadful news. The king acted at once and decided to lead his men into battle."

"She is right, if I may," Traveris said.

He signaled his request to speak. The queen granted it with a slight nod of her chin and then took a sip of her tea.

"I fought beside him as the hordes of marauders, armed with curved blades and crossbows, invaded our land," Traveris said. "Our soldiers were overmatched, in part due to their poor training, and partly due to low morale. We hardly had the gold to pay our debts to Darius Blackblade, let alone raise an army to fight him. Your father…he had little choice but to engage in a desperate attempt to raise their spirits by riding out to meet the invaders on horseback. But after seeing his years of decadence at their expense, they were hardly moved by his rare act of leadership. His life ended with a crossbolt fired from one of the pillagers. I was told that it was fired by a slight but strapping man adorned with dark eyeshade, who was wearing black leather armor and a kerchief.

"I attempted to ride out to get revenge upon the assailants on behalf of the Hypernean kingdom, but we were overwhelmed by the marauders. My entire company fled for the hills. Sadly, my beloved horse, Moondancer, was struck in the neck by a raven-feathered arrow, killing her almost instantly. I was forced to retreat in a desperate bid to protect the kingdom. That is when I came to ensure the security of my queen, our Queen Galadria."

The Kindly Knight smoothed his long, dark-haired mane over his ear, then gritted his teeth before lowering his eyes to his teacup. Sigismund sensed the affection in the Kindly Knight's voice and was sure there was something more to it than mere knightly loyalty.

The queen averted her sparkling eyes and stared off into the fire while holding her teacup with both hands, seemingly lost in a daydream. Galadria spoke in the airiest of faraway voices while looking upon the crackling blaze. "Sigismund, how would you like to someday be king?"

The prince sat motionlessly, contemplating his mother's offer. Since his father was dead, she would decide who would become king. There was no obligation for her to choose the eldest, Jax, as indisposed as he may be while in the possession of the marauders. But Sigismund knew too much to believe the people's false assumption that becoming a king was some magnificent, desirable thing.

"Mother, I am so young," he said. "Becoming king is nothing I desire. It is in no way something that can bring me or the kingdom happiness. If I had my way, there would no longer be kings. Everyone would rule themselves and live with one another in happiness and harmony, only cooperating with one another and never seeking to rule another by force."

"My dear boy," she said and turned to him with a loving gaze. "I want the same thing. I am but a woman, and yet here I am, and people call me 'queen.' Any woman can be as good as I am, as patient as I am, as wise as I am, and yet not be called a queen, except, perhaps, by her own husband."

As soon as she finished speaking, the Kindly Knight and the gentle wizard burst out in a much-needed laugh. They looked with admiration upon the marvelous woman. Her refreshing display of humility only further cemented their loyalty.

Sigismund considered her words and looked upon the weathered faces of Traveris Bane and Manfred the Magnificent. If he was going to live his own life, he might as well emulate the men beside him. They were strong and noble but totally dedicated to serving the needs of others. If his own life were to have meaning, he would need to devote it to some worthy cause. And he could think of no better cause than protecting the people of Hypernea, but he was uncertain that he was up to the great task. In his heart, he doubted that he was strong enough. He feared his weakness would only make the tragic situation worse.

"Mother," Sigismund told her, "I have nothing but the utmost love and respect for you. But I am unsure, in all honesty, that I am fit to be a king. Before I can accept this offer to become king under your stewardship, I need to think. I need some time to be alone with my thoughts."

Queen Galadria stared into his newly blue eyes, searching for goodness in his soul. She deemed it to be there, but he was understandably confused and needed some time to himself. It had all been a blur.

"Of course, my son," she said. "Go for a walk and clear your head. But be careful and come back within the hour, or Traveris will go searching for you."

Prince Sigismund smiled at his mother, recognizing that she loved him and had faith in him. As he stood and walked toward the door, he knew that this may be the last time that he would be a mere prince. The true burden of wearing the crown could lie ahead in his future. As he walked by, the Kindly Knight peered up at him.

"Be safe, young prince," he said reassuringly.

The prince nodded and continued toward the door. As he opened it, he felt the chill night air rush upon his face. The castle grounds were perfectly still.

He closed the door softly behind him and, seeking Druix, he strode on the dirt path toward the castle gates. The path weaved through the silent nearby hillsides.

He finally saw the moondrake, who was lying wearily in front of the iron gates. Druix raised his head and looked at Sigismund with his beautiful, silvery eyes. He blinked twice, as if communicating that he was glad to see the prince.

The dragon growled a kind of greeting toward him, which the young man could not comprehend. But then he remembered. He reached into his pocket and grasped the crystal shard his mother had given him.

"It is nice to see you," the moondrake said. He saw that the prince had grabbed the magic object that facilitated their mutual understanding.

"Druix!" he said. "Do you hear the words I am saying? I thought it was only the druid's spell that gave us the ability to talk to each other."

"Of course, I understand you," Druix replied. "I am not a stupid dragon, after all."

"Right, right," he replied and chuckled.

"So, I am wondering, young prince," Druix said. "Did your family survive this catastrophic attack? It appears to have lain waste to this castle, which still smolders within from the flames."

"Thank you, kind moondrake," Sigismund replied. "But I am afraid that the king died in the attack. He was my father, although he did not act much like one."

"I see," he replied. "Or at least, I believe I do. What do you mean he did not act like your father?"

"He wanted me dead," Sigismund said with sadness.

Sigismund walked over to Druix's side, sat down next to him, and leaned his head upon the dragon's scaly chest. The moon was high in the sky, but it could barely be seen through the dark, gray wisps of smoke drifting by in the night breeze.

"I am sorry, young prince," the moondrake remarked. He looked airily upon the castle. He did not understand the affairs of mankind, but he did know something about fathers. "My dad was the greatest moondrake who ever lived. He fought off a shadow dragon to protect me, and he sacrificed his heroic life for it. He was the only moondrake in my life who loved me. My mother had died in a great battle, and all the other moondrakes of Lunastria rejected me due to my once-black eyes, which they believed to be part of a widespread curse."

The prince detected a sniff from the moondrake. Could dragons sniff? Was the creature crying?

Sigismund stood and walked toward the head of the creature, who had returned to rest upon the ground. Sigismund strode up to his crown and reached over with his long, slender arm and began stroking his head. It seemed to give the creature comfort.

"There, there, good moondrake," Sigismund said. "I accept you. I can be your friend. As long as you stay with me, you will always have a home."

The moondrake lifted his head. He felt a surge of energy flooding into his serpent bones.

"I will be your friend too!" he exclaimed. "We will make a fearsome pair!"

The moondrake was roused by the prince's offer. He began to prance around the castle grounds. His freedom from the evil moondrakes of Lunastria was now complete. He stretched his wings in the night and felt like flying.

"Why don't you patrol around the castle for trouble, Druix?" Sigismund said with a smile. "If you see anything alarming, come back to these gates and give us a loud screech three times in rapid succession. Repeat it a number of times. I believe Manfred will understand."

"Yes, of course, Prince!"

The moondrake ran from the gate and leapt into the air. His wings flapped as he took flight into the night, even stopping to twirl in front of the early spring moon.

The young man felt truly glad that he could help liberate this creature from the immense burden he must have felt. He had to feel completely alone; one of his kind in a strange, faraway land.

Sigismund realized that he had forgotten about his own problems. Seeing this creature's joyful reaction to his simple act of kindness was a kind of magic that rivaled even that of the wizards.

He walked through the gates and stood on the stone walkway. He could barely make out the rows of carnelian roses, which were the symbolic flowers of the Waverly House. He wanted to see a vision of its future before stepping in line to become king. He needed to behold a ray of hope before dedicating his life to defending and preserving the kingdom.

The prince took the crystal out of its velvet black cloth. He peered up at a sliver of moonlight that peeked its way through the clouds of smoke. Then, he thrust the crystal shard in front of him.

Instead of a glorious spectacle of life abounding, what he saw sucked his breath away. He beheld a mound of charred, black rubble, smoldering in an ashen heap, surrounded by a desolate wasteland. No flowers lined the walkway, only scorched earth. It crushed Sigismund's soul to see it.

The crystal no longer projected light and beauty, Sigismund realized, but death and destruction. It was horrifying.

As he put his left eye closer to the crystal shard with terrified curiosity, he saw that shadows were swirling within. Shadows in the shape of dragons.

He jerked away in horror. The black vision of death and annihilation was not the vision of hope that he had expected of the crystal shard.

The prince knew his answer. He fled to the underground hovel where his mother was hidden away. His feet flew down the pathway until he reached the door. Out of breath, he pounded on it with his fists.

"It is Sigismund, open up!" the prince shouted.

"Yes, I'll be right there," the Kindly Knight said as he unlatched the door. "What is it?"

"I have seen the most terrible vision," he exclaimed as he burst into the room. He was out of breath.

Siggie removed the green cloak from his shoulders and sat down next to the fire. The young man was shuddering and clasping his hands while rocking back and forth from fright.

"What did you see?" Manfred asked while standing in front of him.

The prince peered up at the old wizard. Sigismund's face was pale and drained from the fright.

"I agree," he finally said with a tremor in his voice. "I must become the king."

CHAPTER 37

ANNIHILATION'S APPROACH

he great serpent Gigantus lay in an immense, uncoiled mass on the forest floor. The black blood spilling from its gargantuan throat smelled as bad as the dead creature looked.

Aenyx looked in bewilderment at the empty air where the high sorceress had stood only moments ago. Dracus Imprimus had undoubtedly absconded with their enemy once the odds began to turn against the sorceress. He hated this Dread Commander already.

"Come on, druid," the griffin said to Prospero. "This dragon isn't getting any deader. We should scramble to Laketown to see if the villagers have organized any kind of resistance—although I don't have a lot of confidence in that. Then you may accompany me to Mount Rhaemor to settle an old score."

"Well, it seems that your mind is quite made up," Prospero said.

"Quite," the griffin said. "Hop on. This should be…interesting."

The White Druid climbed upon the griffin after stashing his bronze staff in a sling on his back. Aenyx bounded a few times and then leapt into the evening skies. He flapped hard to get high enough to soar with a full-grown man clinging to his back. He was neither as large as Druix nor particularly well-suited to acting as a courier for old men. Yet there he was, carrying a druid over the fetid swamps of Aborea and the eastern edges of the Solistrian Forest. What a day.

Aenyx looked into the darkening sky and spotted the constellation Synthesis, the goddess of fate. The pattern of stars looked like a seated woman balancing a sword in her hand. The constellation was far to the north this time of year. Synthesis's eye was the star Glynerian, and it was precisely due north, in the direction of the Obsidian Fortress. He used it to gain his bearings and flew northeast toward Laketown.

He was uncomfortable shuffling around to all of these godforsaken exotic locales just to encounter hostile enemies. Journeying to the Illusory Fortress only to meet the unbelievably combative sorceress with a shadow dragon about twice the size of an average dragon, which was already plenty impressive, was not exactly Aenyx's idea of an escape from his already near-insurmountable troubles back in Aeris.

The griffin flapped his feathery wings and soared upon the gusting winds. He could see nothing of the forest below except dark green blotches passing below. The moon above was ghostly and faint.

"What do you think, wizard?" he asked. "Can we make it to Laketown by morning?"

"I'm not a wizard any more than you are a donkey," Prospero replied. "And yes, we should arrive by dawn at this rate."

"If you aren't a wizard, then why do you carry a wizard's staff?" he asked.

"It focuses my natural powers, especially my healing abilities," he replied. "Druids are akin to rangers in that we are intimate with nature and all life within it. But we are also like priests in that we possess arcane powers to navigate the eternal conflict between life and death."

"Oh," Aenyx replied. "Is that it?"

"I wish it were more, believe me," Prospero responded.

Aenyx flew until his wings were about to give out. To the east, the first incarnadine rays of the sun sliced through the morning air to meet Aenyx's deep brown eyes.

He did not like what he saw. A pinkish haze rose into the air in the direction of the Mirrhenian Lake. It was eerie.

"Umm, Prospero," the griffin said. The White Druid was asleep as he clung to his back. His ridiculously deep, seemingly interminable old-man snoring had been a nuisance throughout the earliest morning hours. It was also a warning for him to keep right and not turn too sharply. And gods forbid he should do a barrel roll—that would just be cruel.

The White Druid awoke.

"Huh? Huh?" he asked. "Where are we, my good griffin? Oh, we should be by Laketown. We should most certainly be near…"

Prospero could not utter a single word further. The vision before them sent chills down his spine.

"Aenyx," he said. "Do you realize what you see? Or maybe, more accurately, what you don't see?"

The griffin looked ahead and saw Mirrhenian Lake, which now had what looked like a beach.

"I don't remember there being a beach," he mumbled in astonishment.

"That is because there wasn't one there."

As they flew closer to Mirrhenian Lake, Prospero became increasingly sure of what they were looking at.

"A shadow dragon attack annihilated Laketown completely," he said, aghast. "And by completely, I mean *completely*. These white ashes were created by flames so hot they burned everything nearly instantaneously. There was nothing left to burn, and so, there were almost no flames. That is why the skies are not still filled with smoke."

The druid looked down upon Laketown and tapped on the shoulder of the griffin twice so he would land on a field near the desolate site. Aenyx disliked the signal, but he did as the druid wanted. He landed on the field, then walked a few steps before bowing for the druid to dismount.

The old man pulled out his slender staff so that he could walk around and survey the terrain in the early morning light. It was hard to fathom as he looked out at the lake, which was thinly coated with ghostly vapor. Mounds of white ashes had replaced the entire fishing village.

"The dragons that Dracus Imprimus has unleashed upon Solarius must be among the most fearsome that Solarius has ever encountered," he remarked breathlessly. "Even shadow dragons are not supposed to be able to do *this*."

"We griffins know a thing or two about shadow dragons," Aenyx said. "I can assure you that the dragons I have witnessed recently are more powerful, fearsome, and deadly than any we have been prepared to fight. What those creatures did to this village is horrific."

"Truly, truly," Prospero said. "I believe the villagers would have known better than to stay and fight after the first terrifying blasts of flame rained down. Hopefully, the elder Timor Longbranch took the people to a safe haven in the woods."

"We were lucky I ripped Gigantus's throat out," Aenyx added. "I was able to seize the initiative and catch the beast off guard, thanks to the heroic actions of the knight Gilead. But even if we had a hundred knights like him, our army would be no match for a fleet of those ferocious serpents."

"Come, Aenyx," Prospero said. "Time is of the essence. We must look for Timor Longbranch and any survivors."

The White Druid again climbed upon the griffin, who deigned to carry him to the secluded destination where he hoped to find the village elder. The place lay beyond the Fields of Silence, an ancient battleground considered hallowed ground by the Laketown people, in the hills near the eastern woods of the Solistrian Forest.

They flew into the sunlight until Prospero directed Aenyx to land at a stonework shelter in the middle of a valley near gently flowing streams. The griffin landed in the middle of a stream, making a splash that got the old druid's legs wet.

"Hey, you wily birdcat!" the druid exclaimed.

"Aren't you thirsty?" the griffin remarked. "I am parched. So in that case, I recommend you fill up your canteen and stop complaining. We have arrived, anyway."

The White Druid looked up at the slopes surrounding the valley and the serene, idyllic bit of wilderness surrounding them. It was teeming with wildlife—he spotted a great blue heron spearing a flounder downstream.

The griffin plodded and splashed to the edge of the stream. The druid dismounted into the water and began to fill his canteen. Then he heard a voice.

"Prospero!"

The White Druid looked up the hill. A large, strapping old man was barreling downhill like a boy on the last day of school; his mighty arms were outstretched in order to give his old friend a hug.

It was Timor Longbranch.

The bear of a man collided with Prospero, sending him directly into the water. As he sat there and looked up at Timor, he squeezed his long, grayish beard like a dirty dishrag.

"Why, that's one way to tell an old man he is all right," he remarked dryly. "Next time, a simple *hello* will do."

Prospero pulled himself out of the water and rang out his long white robe, which was now speckled and soiled with river mud. He picked up his canteen, which was floating on the water, and strode with minor difficulty to get out of the stream.

"I hope you have a fire going, Timor," he remarked as they walked uphill toward the shelter. He put his wrinkled left hand on the man's broad shoulder and with his right hand, he used his bronze staff as a walking stick.

Aenyx stayed behind to fish the stream. Prospero looked back to see the griffin snag a rainbow trout, which he devoured gratefully.

"Tell me what happened, Timor," Prospero said, turning back toward the elder. "Although, sadly, I can already guess."

"It was already night, my friend," the village elder began. "The shadow dragons came out of the east, spouting flame, and began raining fire upon the settlement. The boats moored at the docks were the first to be set ablaze, and I immediately rang the alarm bells for everyone to flee. After what happened to Aeris, we had a contingency plan in place.

This saved many lives, and so we thank you for having your messenger, Miranda Sunray, forewarn us."

"How many do you believe perished in the attack?" Prospero asked.

"We believe that we lost four good men," he said. "A real blow to our settlement, but it could have been much worse. The women and children had already begun the evacuation after the fairy's warning."

Prospero nodded and tugged on his beard. His mind raced with disparate thoughts as he looked upon the humble shelter. There were stacks of wood outside and tools lying about. He saw men working in a patch of woodland away from the shelter, cutting and gathering wood, while women gathered herbs and berries in baskets from the suddenly bursting forest. But nothing suggested that the Laketown survivors could raise an army.

"There appears to be bounty here, but nature is still unbalanced," Prospero remarked. "This is an unusual effect from the shattering of the Arch Crystal. I am not sure how long this will last before nature corrects itself and the seasons realign. I don't like it. I don't like it at all."

"True, true, Druid," Timor agreed. "We can take advantage of it for a month, perhaps two, as the forest appears to be releasing the built-up energy that was somehow stifled by the Arch Crystal. But this settlement is not a long-term solution.

"Especially not with those," Timor added with a hush, "*creatures* flying about."

Prospero thought hard about the Laketown refugees' plight.

"My advice to you, Timor," the druid counseled, "is to take the survivors here and trek west through the Solistrian Forest toward Waverly Castle. Speak to King Gerald and tell him of your plight. Put yourself and your people at his service. He will almost certainly take you in and afford you the ability to settle. Let the strongest join his army, which I assume he is raising at the behest of my friend, Manfred the Magnificent, whom you may know as Talus Nightspell."

"Ahh, yes, Talus Nightspell," Timor remarked. "I know that wizard well. A good man, but a little secretive. Not like you, Prospero."

The man laughed and slapped Prospero on the back—a bit too hard. The druid stumbled forward and regained his balance with his bronze staff.

"You are too strong for your own good, Timor," he remarked and chuckled. "Leave tomorrow at morning light," Prospero said with finality. "Take as many nuts and berries as you can find locally, as well as stores of water. The marsh water surrounding the fetid swamp is not fit to drink and can cause a high fever and nausea. I am sure you will be happy in your new homeland, so take heart. There is even the Emerald Sea on the western side of Hypernea, should you desire to lead the fisherman's life again."

"Thank you, my friend," Timor replied. "I will do just that."

"Farewell," he said, and then turned to see that the griffin had caught up to them. He was lying on his back, apparently stuffed from eating fish. He had never seen a griffin on his back before. It was a most unusual sight.

"If you are quite finished gorging yourself with fish," he said to Aenyx upon his approach, "I believe there are griffins for us to rescue."

CHAPTER 38

A NIGHT RAID TO REMEMBER

Aenyx rolled over onto his claws and paws. He looked up at the druid sheepishly. The griffin was so thoroughly delighted to hear the old man agree to rescue his friends; he simply could not contain his enthusiasm.

He belched. Loudly. Then he did an exuberant dance in the stream nearby. He splashed the water all over, spraying the stoic druid, who stood on the banks with an unmoved expression. His scraggly wet hair dripped onto his drawn cheeks.

"Are you quite finished?" the White Druid asked in an unamused tone.

"Not quite," the griffin replied.

Aenyx slapped his lion's tail on the water's edge with all his might, sending a jet of water straight at the druid. Prospero was stone-faced, calmly observing the creature as it had its fun.

"Now I am done," Aenyx replied. "As for rescuing my friends, that may prove to be tricky. I believe we may have to conduct a night raid. Let me lie upon the edge of the stream and rest while you think of a brilliant plan. We should put that big brain of yours to use, somehow."

And just like that, the griffin lay down in the morning sun and enjoyed a cozy nap.

The hours of the day whiled away until midafternoon. Prospero, who had congregated plenty with the Laketown villagers, interrogating them on the events of the night and their future plans, finally couldn't stand it anymore. He marched down to the brook to nudge the griffin awake with his staff. Repeatedly.

"Come back here, you damn dragon…" Aenyx mumbled.

Prospero whapped him on his thigh.

"Hey!" the griffin said as he jumped up. "I was in the middle of a dream, if you don't mind. What is it?"

"If we are going to be in position by nightfall, we'd best depart now," the druid remarked. "I hope you have mustered enough energy and are ready to go to Mount Rhaemor."

"Oh, I am ready to go all right," he said. "Those shadow dragon goons won't know what hit them. As for Tyrex Goldeneyrie, I have a special surprise in store for that traitor."

Prospero didn't want to know. But he did know that without the griffins aiding the war effort against Dracus Imprimus and the High Sorceress, the situation would be even more dire. "That's wonderful, Aenyx," he remarked. "Can we leave now?"

"Nope," Aenyx said and looked toward the sun descending into the western skies. He stuck a talon in the air as if to test the wind. "Yep," he remarked. "Now, we can leave."

"Good gods, here we go," the White Druid said. He stepped upon the griffin's back. With his bronze staff slung over his shoulder, Prospero grasped the feathery scruff on the griffin's back.

"Hey, easy on the mane," Aenyx cracked.

After a few impressive bounds, the griffin leapt into the air. The Laketown refugees around the secluded shelter waved and cheered them on as they ascended high above their safe haven in the green valley, which was not meant to last.

Aenyx shuttled the druid for hours, well past the early signs of evening, until they were in the southern Mountains of Mordrath. The air was crisper and cooler.

The griffin looked forward to the day when he no longer had to carry old men around from realm to realm. He imagined a day when he could return to the freedom of a secure Republic of Aeris. And now that he wasn't a Redmark, the sky was the limit.

"We should arrive within striking distance of Mount Rhaemor shortly after sundown," Aenyx remarked. The White Druid concurred with an old-man grunt. "The burden of men is nearly as tiresome as the burden of perpetually staving off the great serpent army," he continued. "If only we could end the threat of dragons once and for all…"

"But would that not make us as evil as the great serpents?" the druid replied.

Aenyx thought of the vision he had perceived in the Arch Crystal. While the world he saw was free from division between the griffins, and accepted even moondrakes, there was no place for dragons in this world.

"Perhaps, druid. Perhaps," he grumbled.

"Then we must focus on the real enemy," Prospero said. "The orchestrator behind the scenes who drives dragons to hatred and acts of evil. Maybe they are not intrinsically evil but are taught to act that way."

"Let me remind you, druid," Aenyx said, "that my two friends are being guarded by shadow dragons. And I might have to clash with them tonight. So I would save the philosophy for a more convenient time."

"Ahh, but it is in times of tribulation that philosophy is needed most, good Aenyx," the druid replied. "But if these particular dragons are holding your friends hostage, then by all means, free them however you can."

"The griffin way," Aenyx said with satisfaction. Steely-eyed determination shone in his brown eyes.

As the day faded into dusk, the violet skies slowly melted away into a black, velvety cloak. Mountains threw themselves into relief upon the burdensome heavens. Their jagged peaks seemed to defy the weight of the universe itself.

This was Aenyx's homeland. This was Aeris. And he was intent on freeing it from the Dread Commander's grasp.

The griffin landed near a mighty white oak tree that had planted its roots near the peak of a mountaintop within sight of Mount Rhaemor. They stood and gazed upon the broad mountain with three distinct peaks. It looked like a crown from afar—befitting the capital of the griffin's realm, in Aenyx's opinion.

"We are now upon Mount Kildare," Aenyx said to the druid while scratching the rock with his talons. "This is an ideal staging ground for us to execute our attack."

"An attack?" the druid scoffed. "You really have lost it, griffin."

"Do you have a better idea?"

"Yes, how about using our brains?" Prospero retorted.

"Novel idea," Aenyx said thoughtfully. "I like it."

"What we need is a diversion," Prospero said after mulling it over for a moment. "Yes, yes, I have an idea."

"Well, I am all ears, conjurer," Aenyx said impatiently.

"Just be ready when I give the signal," he responded. "You will know it when you see it."

Evening became night. They departed into the mountain air and soared toward Mount Rhaemor.

"Do you see any guards?" Prospero asked the griffin.

"There are two shadow dragons perched upon the terrace where the Guardians once lived. I can see them through the colonnades. And… wait, their two masters are there as well. I believe they are the lieutenants who had accompanied the sorceress."

"That must be where your friends are being held, at the palace of the Guardians," Prospero remarked.

Aenyx spread his wings wide and banked right toward the far edge of the main arena. It was completely dark—stripped of the life that had once filled the griffin realm.

"Take me down and set me outside the outer walls," the druid said.

They landed on the outskirts of the main arena. The griffin climbed upon the outer wall to get a better view.

"Tell me what you see, Aenyx," Prospero said quietly.

His griffin eyes, well-attuned to seeing in the darkness, beheld an infuriating vision. His two friends had been chained, one on each side of the main door to the Guardians' palace. They were being humiliated, chained up like pets of the Nocteran dragon soldiers. Torches burned on either side of the palace door, illuminating them and the dark lieutenants. He saw the distinctive black armor of General Nemysis Drake, who held his wicked barbed spear.

"So, about that plan..." Aenyx remarked.

"Yes, I am working on it," the druid replied.

"Working on it?" the griffin said with disbelief.

"Pay no attention to me," he answered with a disturbingly even tone. "I am going into a deep trance and will not be able to talk to you further until you return—if you return."

Aenyx did not like the sound of that, but he decided that the druid's plan, whatever it was, was better than no plan.

The White Druid sat cross-legged on the rocky ground beside a few shrubs. His eyes turned white as they rolled back into his ancient head. His upturned arms started shaking, and his whole body vibrated. He began to hum. It seemed like he was trying to channel the forces of nature through his very being.

Aenyx was not in a position to question the druid. He wondered where this diversion was that he was talking about. And then he saw *it*. Or rather—them.

It began as a scattered array of tiny pinpoints of light in the blackness of the forests below.

The faint yellow pulses slowly began coming together and forming clouds of blinking lights. After a while, the glimmering clouds started moving up the mountainside. As the flickering lights crept up the slopes from all directions, he realized what he was looking at.

Fireflies. Thousands upon thousands of fireflies.

They were forming a gigantic swarm that was both dazzling in its beauty and ominous in its strangeness. It was like one hive mind controlled the tiny flying blips as they flew in unison toward him.

Aenyx wasn't about to stick around to find out what it was like being in the middle of a swarm of fireflies. The griffin stretched his wings and flew toward the shadow dragons guarding his friends.

The fireflies overtook the main arena with a light show that was stupefying in its splendor. It was like the heavens had been called down to illuminate Mount Rhaemor in a glorious golden glow. It was impossible to ignore. The Dark Lieutenants stood in awe of the spectacle. They watched from the palace walkway beside their sleeping dragons.

"Of all the damn things…" Captain Saevius Thornwood said to his superior. "The Dread Commander promised us a vision of glory like we would never imagine, but I never thought this would be it."

"We need to identify this sorcery," General Drake told the captain. "Something unnatural is stirring on this mountain."

Captain Thornwood nodded and started to walk down the stairs toward the walkway of griffin heroes that led away from the Guardians' palace. His black steel sword was drawn in front of him as he investigated the spectacular sight.

"Wait, soldier," General Drake called while snatching his long spear from its rack. "I want to see this for myself. Something isn't right here, and those griffins aren't going anywhere, not with two shadow dragons ready to tear them to bits if they should so much as breathe wrong.

The soldiers went toward the main arena to look into the source of the unwelcome light show. Aenyx's gaze followed their every footstep until he felt he could brave an attempt to get beyond the dragons.

The griffin flew high into the air to avoid the Nocteran soldiers' line of sight. He hovered in the air and waited as the soldiers moved past the statues of Aeris lore. When they had cleared the walkway, he dove for the marble colonnades at the palace gate, sweeping in without a single flap of his wings. As he swiftly flew past the marble colonnades over the sleeping dragons' heads and landed right in front of the palace door, Raven Whitecrest gasped.

The shadow dragon in front of her snorted, then moved its claws across the terrace. The long, curved talons, each as sharp and deadly as a scimitar, scraped the floor, producing a bone-chilling sound.

Aenyx landed on the terrace as gently as his paws were capable. The torchlight illuminated his dark brown eyes. He looked admiringly at Raven Whitecrest, then turned his gaze to Phoenix Stormguard, holding up a single talon.

"Shhh," he warned.

Aenyx strode to the main door and winked at his captive friends. He pushed open the oaken steel-buttressed door, and it yielded with a subtle creak. It was time to confront a tyrant.

CHAPTER 39

THE TYRANT'S NEST

Aenyx entered the Palace of the Guardians and sought out the traitorous wretch who was responsible for the captivity of a fellow Guardian and the friend who saved his life at the Griffin Trials. Tyrex Goldeneyrie would pay.

The griffin strode in like a lion on the prowl. His talons gently scratched the marble floor as he made his way toward the throne room. Torches flickered in their sconces upon the columns that flanked him to his left and right. In his mind burned one goal: Revenge.

Down the corridor, he found a set of massive swinging doors. They were bright red with bronze ornamentation. Each door bore the symbols of the five Prides: the Bluetips' print of a lionesque paw, the Stormguards' lightning bolt on a shield, the Whitecrests' jagged white crown above a moon, the Pridewatchers' golden egg flanked by griffins stretching a wing above it, and the Goldeneyries' gilded crown above a branch of olive leaves.

All the symbols of the Prides were scratched out—except for the Goldeneyries'.

Aenyx stood on his hind legs and bolted through the door. It gave way more easily than he would have thought. But with no griffins left upon Mount Rhaemor and shadow dragons guarding your palace, why would anyone bother to lock the doors? Of course, they didn't count on Aenyx Stormguard's return to Mount Rhaemor.

"Tyrex Goldeneyrie!" he shouted upon entering the Great Griffin Hall.

His voice echoed throughout the hall. It was a massive, dark room with only a hint of light thrown from the ensconced torches, which were burning low. There were no Nocteran guards; they had quartered for the night. It was just Aenyx and Tyrex Goldeneyrie.

The former Guardian and low lord under the reign of Dracus Imprimus was crouched on all fours on the central throne, a marble pedestal ornamented with gold leaves and the symbol of the Goldeneyrie Pride engraved upon its face. The bronze-maned tyrant peered at him with hateful eyes and a broken demeanor. There was a kind of poison in the air: Tyrex Goldeneyrie's self-loathing and contempt for anyone who reminded him of his treason against the Republic of Aeris. The griffin sat there silently.

"You are a foul traitor, nothing more!" Aenyx shouted. "All of this, for what? You could have warned us about the invasion, but instead you aided the Dread Commander—our sworn enemy! Why?"

Silence. Finally, a low cackle emanated from the griffin on the pedestal. "This…is the beginning of a new world, Aenyx Stormguard!" Tyrex roared. "You were never a Guardian, so you would not understand, but the republic was mired in stasis! There was no vision, only the incessant power struggle for the direction of Aeris. The other Guardian council members were indecisive fools. Aeris needed real leadership. The Dread Commander offered a solution: The destruction of the old order to make way for a glorious future!"

The griffin huffed a crazed laugh, and his eyes shone maniacally. On the walls, the fresco paintings of the republic's past had been defaced; the legendary griffins who had shaped the realm from its very origins appeared to look on, aghast at this craven griffin's power lust.

"So, you have Aeris all to yourself!" Aenyx replied while approaching the griffin seated on his lonely throne. "Are you truly happy? Where is your kingdom, pretender? All of the republic has fled from Mount Rhaemor. And you undoubtedly played a role in the murder of a Guardian, the death of another, and the kidnapping of the greatest one of all. That is why I have come—to deliver justice."

"Oh, but you are wrong about that, Aenyx Stormguard," he replied sardonically. "I did not just play a role in the murder of one Guardian, but in three. While you had witnessed the death of Captius Whitecrest, that was not an accident, but part of my arrangement with the High Sorceress. As for Sophia Pridewatcher, I had paid Gabriel Goldeneyrie to kill her with a poisoned attack and to make it look like an accident—your death would have merely been a fortunate side development. As for the last Guardian I murdered—Savagiras Bluetip. He was a tough one to put down, undoubtedly, but our dragons burned him to a crisp in front of our chained pets, your poor little friend Raven, and of course, Phoenix Stormguard. It was our little way of inspiring them to talk."

"Liar!" Aenyx retorted. "You are a traitor and a murderer, unworthy of even a mention in our republic's history, let alone a page. Your story ends tonight."

His lion's heart was thumping like a hammer in his chest. His blood pumped with white-hot fury. It took all of his restraint to keep from ripping Tyrex Goldeneyrie apart then and there.

"You are quite fanciful," the griffin replied. "Bold, but fanciful. Your delusions of vengeance will only lead you to certain death. Outside, two shadow dragons have undoubtedly awakened, and you will not escape with your life. Well, what are you waiting for?"

Tyrex Goldeneyrie stood on the marble throne and stretched his wings. The shadows of the griffin danced on the wall behind him. He appeared to be some great monster. Aenyx ignored the illusion and marched headlong at the creature with a fiery determination.

The griffins tangled in mid-air and then crashed to the ground in a heap. While Tyrex Goldeneyrie attempted to viciously bite Aenyx in the throat, Aenyx defended himself and grasped his attacker's throat with his talon. Aenyx squeezed as hard as he could and felt his claws dig into his enemy's throat. But while he had him in a death grip, he reached for the keys hanging from a necklace around his neck.

Aenyx released Tyrex Goldeneyrie's throat, and in one motion, snatched the necklace, keys and all. He backed away from the self-imagined lord, who grasped his throat in pain.

"Why?" Tyrex Goldeneyrie asked in a raspy voice. "Why didn't you just kill me?"

"Because you aren't worth it," he replied with a scornful air.

Aenyx walked toward the doors of the great hall. As he exited the chamber, he heard the griffin cough, along with the faint sound of blood gurgling in his throat. Aenyx did not look back.

He lunged for the palace door. Now that he had the keys, he could escape with his friends unscathed.

Aenyx pushed open the main door to the palace. The two shadow dragons were staring at him, their gaze deadlocked on his every move. They could burn him to a crisp then and there. He froze.

Then he realized something—the Nocteran guards were still away investigating Prospero's otherworldly diversion. Aenyx waved his talon up and down to test the dragons' response.

The shadow dragons snarled as if they would attack, but something was holding them back. Aenyx suddenly understood. They weren't ordered to attack anyone leaving the palace, only those trying to enter. They could not tell if he was an enemy or an ally.

"Kind dragons," Aenyx choked out. "I am your friend. Pay no attention, for I am doing the Dread Commander's will, and I am releasing these fine griffins. We are on your side, trust me!"

The dragons, who were utterly confused, glanced at one another for reassurance.

"That's right," he went on. "Go back to sleep! Good dragons—I mean, evil dragons! That's right."

The great serpents backed away, still watching them with hate-filled eyes that gleamed in the torchlight. Aenyx scrambled to free Raven.

"Aenyx!" The hushed voice conveyed emotion. Her light brown eyes shone with adoration for her griffin friend who dared not abandon them.

The griffin fidgeted and found the largest key. He inserted it into the lock that was snapped on the cuff over her hind paw. Grasping the key firmly with the inner webbing of his claw, he quickly turned his wrist. The lock opened. Raven was free.

She strode over to him and nudged her beak against his with gratitude. Then, he made his way over to Phoenix Stormguard, whose white feathery mane was disheveled. His eyes were tired—so tired. It looked like he had lived through a nightmare.

"Thank you, son," Phoenix said weakly as his lock was unlatched.

Aenyx looked up at the Guardian—the only true one left in the realm—and a sudden realization flashed in his dark brown eyes. He couldn't be—could he?

"Yes, Aenyx," Phoenix said with a tone of reassurance that required no further elaboration. A surge of emotion poured into Aenyx's brain as a swell of joy and immense dread filled his heart.

"We have to get you out of here before the Nocteran guards return!" Aenyx replied.

"Too late!" a thunderous voice snarled from behind them.

It was Captain Thornwood. The scruffy-bearded man's face was cracked and hardened through his years of servitude to evil. His expression displayed both unyielding grit and unrelenting hatred. The Nocteran warrior held a torch aloft in his left hand and a black steel longsword in his right.

"Stand down, Captain; I've got this," another voice barked. The captain stood aside to let the commanding officer approach. General Drake possessed an ominous presence that could only belong to someone whose life had been dedicated to unfeeling destruction.

The man paced the marble terrace, his heavy, leather boots clacking on the floor. His barbed spear sat in his gloved right hand, and his body jostled with the metallic sound of steel armor. Leather straps around his waist and across his chest bore various instruments of death. He was the living embodiment of war.

The shadow dragons raised their necks upward as if at full attention. They stirred like rabid dogs held in a cage, their talons scraping the polished marble floor. Their heads lingered oppressively just below the roof of the portico, restrained but eager to strike. They were prepared to unleash stygian fury at the mere utterance of a word.

The three griffins at the palace door were eager to make an escape. They watched in torpefying dread as the field general walked steadily but resolutely up the walkway. He knew his enemies were trapped.

"Nemysis Drake!" declared Phoenix Stormguard. "Your foul presence stains the sanctity of our fine palace. Take your dragons and flee from Aeris, or you will come to know the meaning of ruin. We have powerful allies organizing a counterattack. Now!"

"Save your breath, Phoenix Stormguard," the fearsome soldier said with a raspy voice. "You are no longer even a Guardian."

"Lies!" Aenyx shouted and broke to attack him. Phoenix grasped him by the shoulder and held him back.

"A feisty one, eh, General?" Captain Thornwood said with a grin, revealing many missing teeth.

The pale-skinned warrior lifted the spiked helmet he was carrying under his arm to place it upon his dark-maned head. The captain's dead eyes flickered in the torchlight with vicious delight. The behemoth dragons leered at the griffins while flashing their lethal, ivory fangs.

"This mangy griffin is itching for a fight," Drake said. "We will not need the dragons for this, Captain Thornwood. We will handle this ourselves. After all, I could use the exercise. And killing, I am told, is good exercise."

"Right, General," Thornwood obediently replied. He turned to his dragon. "Morta! Stand down."

The shadow dragon carefully retracted its massive serpent head to watch the battle about to unfold. The creature seemed to be disappointed.

Captain Thornwood lunged with his Nocteran battle sword pointed at Raven's throat. Startled by the suddenness and the violence of the attack, she dodged from sheer instinct but was gashed upon her feathery wing. She soon was dripping blood on the marble floor of the palace entranceway.

Aenyx was outraged and lashed out with unbridled ferocity. His sharp black talons struck the Nocteran captain's arm and sent the black sword flying to the ground.

Captain Thornwood backed away in horror. The griffin was in a position to make a deadly strike.

Aenyx leaped on top of the Nocteran warrior, ready to tear his armor off and finish him right then and there.

Morta reared its gargantuan head and watched the griffin pounce on its vulnerable master. The massive winged serpent lashed out with its ferocious claws. The shadow dragon struck Aenyx with a terrifying blow that sent him careening through the air, only to smash into the great palace door with a sickening thud that reverberated throughout the entranceway.

Aenyx lay on the ground in agony grasping his head as the columns supporting the entranceway to the palace began to waver. The dragon's tail had smashed two of the columns, yielding massive cracks that destabilized the entire portico. The fractured colonnades teetered as if about to collapse. The combatants froze, realizing what the dragon had wrought.

"Pathetic!" General Drake shouted. "I will do this myself."

The Nocteran field general hoisted his barbed spear to his shoulder, bouncing it and regrasping it to judge its balance. As he cocked it back to fling a mortal blow at Aenyx, the last true Guardian of Aeris rushed to the young griffin's aid.

Drake hurled the great spear at Aenyx with all his might. While the dire weapon sailed through the air, Phoenix Stormguard threw his body in front of his son. The dark blade pierced the griffin's body, shattering his formidable frame and sending him reeling into the wall.

"No!" Aenyx shouted in horror.

Aenyx dragged himself to where his father lay dying. He motioned to pull the spear from the wounded griffin's body.

"It's all right, son," Phoenix said with a sorrowful look. "Leave me here to be buried with my ancestors...our ancestors."

"I won't leave you here to die," Aenyx said with rage-filled tears. "I cannot!"

"The most important thing is that you make it out of here alive," Phoenix said. "Let your vengeance go for now; that is how you will defeat Nemysis, and perhaps, even Dracus Imprimus himself."

Aenyx trusted this griffin more than anyone he had ever trusted in the Republic of Aeris. He did not fully understand what his father was telling him, but if he wanted him to let go and escape with his life, then he would honor the Guardian's last command.

"Yes, Father," Aenyx said while fighting back his disconsolate heartache. "I will honor your memory; rest well among the legendary griffins of Aeris."

Phoenix Stormguard closed his darkening eyes. Aenyx would make sure that Aeris would rise again.

A contemptuous voice spoke up from behind him. "If I might interrupt this father-son reunion," General Drake said. "Oh-so-touching, by the way. Bravo! You are about to join each other in the unending beyond. I will gut you while your friend watches." The Nocteran field general produced two curved blades from his armor. He held them out at his sides and approached down the central corridor like an angel of death.

Suddenly, it looked to Aenyx like the whole world was leaning to the right. It wasn't his imagination. The cracked marble columns were collapsing—and if they fell, the tumbling portico might pull the entire edifice down with it.

"It's coming down!" Aenyx shouted and yanked Raven by the claw.

The limestone roof of the structure was pressing down upon the dragons. The impost blocks cracked at the seams and broke away from the support columns. Both Nemysis Drake and Saevius Thornwood knew what this meant—the great serpents' lives were now at stake. They were all in mortal danger of being crushed under the disintegrating entablature above them. Countless tons of marble and limestone would mark their tombs if they did not hurry.

While the Nocteran warriors began to coax their dragons to flee, the griffins seized the moment and made a break for it. They scrambled down the far-left row of colonnades.

General Drake leapt onto his mount and directed the dragons to whip around and fly out of the collapsing structure. Captain Thornwood, unable to move, watched in terror as the field general's desperate maneuver sealed his fate. When the dragons turned their massive bodies to escape, they knocked down what little support the fluted marble columns had offered.

Aenyx and Raven fled. They were already flying high into the night as crumbling limestone blocks and marble colonnades rained down around the captain's head.

Captain Thornwood watched as his field general abandoned him to die in the falling building. Saevius heard Phoenix laugh.

"And thus to tyrants," the Guardian gasped as the life flowed out of his body.

Inside the palace, the pretender Tyrex Goldeneyrie was muttering to himself in the last light of the torches lining the great hall. When the palace's edifice was pulled down, and the cataclysmic collapse inevitably came, the feigned prince cursed his fate and died an ignominious death.

CHAPTER 40

A KING'S RANSOM

Sigismund was unable to sleep. He stood in the tawny light of early morning. An ethereal wind gently stirred the leaves of the roses that lined the stone walkway. The Waverly Castle courtyard was otherwise in ruins.

As the sun rose reluctantly in the wan skies, the prince-who-would-soon-be-king reflected upon his journey. He had been a lonely child locked away in a tower, and an entire kingdom had believed him to be cursed. The Hypernean legends that lined his walls were a semblance of refuge, but their tales of heroism and beauty paled with his experience of real life. His eyes had been opened, cleared of false pretenses of easily won victory or beauty beyond the reach of despoliation.

It was not he who had been cursed all along, but it had been a kingdom wrought with superstition and tyranny. Somehow, nature's refusal to flourish within such a kingdom had been a blessing in disguise. The black eyes many believed were the source of a curse were eyes best suited to behold the people's injustice.

The rustling sound of the rose bushes before him had a calming effect that nonetheless reflected the disquiet he felt in his soul. As the flower blossoms bent upon their lithe stems in the morning breeze, he felt a special communion with them. The forces at work surrounding the Hypernean kingdom were beyond his comprehension, let alone his control. For some reason, he felt the best way to fight the gathering evil was to bend gently in the breeze and regrow his kingdom with life and beauty. But like the trampled castle grounds surrounding the rose bushes voicelessly testified, there was no way to cultivate a garden without protecting it. This was the foremost task of any king.

He had to come to terms with a harsh reality. Waverly Castle's gates had been breached, and Hypernea's enemies had mercilessly destroyed the castle from within. There was no lonely tower of refuge, no more fairy tales to believe in, and no more hope without a bold course of action.

He reached into his pocket and again touched the crystal shard his mother had given him. He realized now what his mother's gift really was—it was not a magic tool to solve all of his problems, but one that allowed for wisdom and foresight, as well as a vision of the potential of the world. It was useless without his action, which had to come from his own free will.

"Prince Sigismund," Manfred said from behind him.

"I have been thinking, mage," the prince said. "We must assemble a rescue party and journey to Stormkeep to free my brothers, Princess Melanie, and any others held captive."

He turned toward the mage, who was beaming with an inner strength and pride that he was only now beginning to fathom. It occurred to him that he would be unable to accomplish anything without the terrific friends he'd made on his journey. He would be powerless to reintroduce justice without them.

"Your mother is of the same mind," Manfred replied. "I have already dispatched messengers to find and gather our allies around the kingdom of Hypernea and beyond."

"Good," Sigismund said, reflecting upon the situation. "If there were some way of making the marauders of the Jeweled Islands our allies, some way of convincing the pirate king…"

"Yes, you are already beginning to think like a king," the mage replied. "The siege of Waverly Castle is nothing compared to the Dread Commander's winged army of great serpents."

Sigismund furled his brows and tried to digest the mage's every word.

"There is another reason that Blackblade's forces stormed Waverly Castle, took your brothers and other nobles hostage, and absconded with other sundries," Manfred continued. "Blackblade's kingdom is itself afflicted with a miserable scourge, and his own daughters have contracted a terrible disease. It has spread throughout the Jeweled Islands, and they do not have any semblance of a cure. This fact only added to the pirate king's desperation."

"But why would that compel him to destroy Waverly Castle?" Sigismund inquired.

"While Blackblade is a ruthless king, he is also a patient one," Manfred replied. "While his kleptocratic regime is best at looting and plundering, he will engage in whatever lucrative enterprise he deems fit. So long as the Hypernean kingdom is strong and vigilant, he cannot loot the coastal towns with impunity. It is quite simple. He wanted to drain the kingdom of resources over the years and then be the master of both the islands and the coasts."

"A good strategy, sadly," Prince Sigismund replied.

"Indeed, but the traders under his command grew desperate to be repaid for their years of providing fresh fruit and fish to Hypernea. When the kingdom's treasury ran dry and the credit proved unreliable, they deduced that this was the time to strike. They invaded Hypernea and seized whatever gold they could find, and Blackblade is not above taking slaves.

"I am afraid your tyrannical father's weak rule only encouraged the marauders," Manfred added with a sigh. "His desperation to make a deal with the pirate king instead of putting his own house in order only encouraged Blackblade and his marauders to wait for the right time to strike."

The prince and the mage surveyed the ruined castle grounds in silence. While the smoke had ceased unfurling from the towers, the acrid stench lingered in the air. If they were going to survive the coming dragon invasion, they would need a more solid keep than this devastated fortress.

Sigismund turned to the wizard. "Let us prepare for our march on Stormkeep."

CHAPTER 41

THE EMERALD SEA AND BEYOND

Queen Galadria asked Traveris Bane to arrange a covered wagon and two horses to haul their train to Stormkeep. The Kindly Knight was also instructed to have a group of villagers pack their remaining grain stores and vessels of wine into supply wagons. Separate horse-drawn wagons guarded by trusted men would carry the precious items the queen was able to save before the siege. Traveris also freed the bloodhounds in the guard's service to accompany them on their trip.

The company prepared to evacuate Waverly Castle for three days. Messengers alerted the surrounding villages that the fortress had been destroyed and that all able-bodied men were to form an army to defend Hypernea. The principalities to the north, particularly those who had fled to the Forrester, Smythe, and MacCallister castles, were notified through messengers that a dangerous winged army would soon invade from the east, and an ominous power would reawaken far to the north. The MacCallisters were most willing to quell their ancient feud with the Waverlys in the interest of freeing the captured princess.

On the third day of preparations, Timor Longbranch arrived with the Laketown refugees. Prince Sigismund immediately set the elder to work gathering supplies and assembling a volunteer army. The armory was reopened and the few remaining weapons, and those reclaimed from the fallen soldiers, were distributed among the volunteers.

It was a glorious sight when Aenyx returned. Mighty Prospero on his back and his friend Raven by his side, the griffin swooped in upon the remnants of Castle Waverly. He was flanked by dozens of griffin survivors from the siege, whom the trio had gathered with great urgency in the aftermath of Aeris' ruin. There were mighty Bluetips, veteran Stormguards, revered Pridewatchers, loyal Whitecrests, and sage Goldeneyries. Exactly the kind of reinforcements that Hypernea would need.

A battle plan was devised. Manfred the Magnificent, the White Druid Prospero, Queen Galadria, Traveris Bane, Timor Longbranch, Aenyx Stormguard, Druix Coldshadow, and Prince Sigismund formed a war council for the defense of Solarius.

In the evening, the allies gathered outside the queen's shelter, seated at two large tables arranged end to end. The torches burned around the tables. Draught ale and port wine were brought, as well as cheese wheels and roasted venison.

Druix and Aenyx preferred to have their meals raw and alive, much to the amazement and disgust of any who happened to be watching. After all were rested and of sound constitution, the war council officially convened.

"It is decided then," Manfred announced on the third day of deliberations. "We will dispatch the griffins in the first wave as forward scouts. They will survey the area and seek weaknesses in Stormkeep's defenses, particularly from above. It has been generations since their region has been visited by griffins, let alone moondrakes, so the element of surprise and abject fear are on our side."

"Right," Traveris Bane added. "If I know these marauders, they are allied to Darius Blackblade for two reasons only: money and fear. If we can strike enough fear into these curs, they may seek to abandon the fortress and flee with their own hides."

"Don't forget our moondrake," Prince Sigismund said. "Druix has the keenest vision of all, and he would certainly put the most fear into any marauder out there. I believe we should be out in front of the griffin pack. We may be able to strike fear into the invaders and end the battle before it even begins—the best kind of victory."

"I agree," Timor Longbranch said and nodded. "Fear and surprise are our greatest allies."

"Then we must delay no longer," Queen Galadria remarked with finality. "We will dispatch for Stormkeep at dawn, and we will not look back. Only when our enemy is vanquished can we hope to return."

"Well said, my queen," Prospero told her. "We must put away hope that this will be easy, but we must never put aside hope entirely."

The war council adjourned to make the final preparations. Sigismund's head was swimming from the realization he would be abandoning his childhood home, and things would never be the same. But as he knew well, along with disaster came the promise of change. Whether it was change for the common good or change resulting in shared misery was very much yet to be determined.

As he lay upon a makeshift bed in his mother's quarters, Prince Sigismund felt tempted to withdraw his crystal shard to see what the future might portend. But the last vision had terrified him so much that he did not dare look. He fumbled with the crystal shard as he lay in bed, falling asleep with it grasped in his hand.

The morning came suddenly. The world was already abuzz with activity outside the shelter's doors. Hypernea was on the move, and Sigismund needed to be at the front of its direction. He grasped his boots and slid them on, threw on his dark green cloak, fastened a dagger upon the leather belt around his waist, and went to join the others.

As he stepped out of the doorway, his thoughts turned to Druix, the wonderful moondrake risking his life on behalf of him and his kingdom. Of course, the fate of Lunastria might somehow be tied to Solarius' fate in a way that he could not yet foresee.

He tracked down Druix, who was grooming himself by the courtyard's gates. The moondrake's silvery eyes gleamed with anticipation. He was overjoyed to see the prince. The aural magic spell Prospero had cast upon them days ago still had effect, and there was no need to use the crystal to understand one another.

"Druix!" Sigismund said. "I am happy to see you too. We are on our way to have the most fantastic adventure ever. We are so lucky to have you with us!"

The moondrake nodded. It seemed words were not necessary between them. This was true regarding any creature he had met—perhaps including his father.

"Good Druix," Sigismund said, "would you be so kind as to allow me to ride you into battle?"

Druix gladly acquiesced. Sigismund mounted the moondrake, who turned and strode upon the castle grounds with a regal air. The drake's midnight-blue skin and silvery eyes were gorgeous to behold in the daylight, although the sun's glare was still difficult for the creature to endure.

"Well, look who it is," a wry voice said as they walked the castle grounds. "I hope you weren't thinking you could fly into battle without me."

It was Aenyx. He was wearing a brass chest plate and a strapped helmet with red-feathered plumage.

"Where did you get that armor?" Sigismund asked, clearly impressed.

"One of the other Stormguards was able to seize and haul a limited amount of armor from our stores upon Mount Rhaemor," Aenyx said.

"Well, I am sure you will put it to good use, noble Aenyx," Sigismund remarked. "If you would assemble the other griffins to depart to Stormkeep, due west of here, we are prepared for departure."

"Of course, Prince," Aenyx said. "This will be a battle to remember! I can't wait to see the look on those pirates' faces when we arrive. It will be phenomenal. I will tear them limb from limb!"

"It is my hope that we won't have a battle at all," Prince Sigismund said with a smile. "But I admire your courage and ferocity."

Aenyx gathered all of the griffin Prides and lined them up in formation in the castle courtyard. Manfred took his place upon the griffin's back while Prospero found the hearty Lieutenant Bart Bluetip for a mount. Aenyx had convinced him to be a commanding officer after they had squelched their feud from the Griffin Trials.

The war party set off for Stormkeep. It was a sight to behold: Dozens of griffins of various shapes and colors ascended high into the azure skies above the fallen castle.

"Could you ever imagine, dear Sigismund," the queen said to her son with a tear in her eye, while seated in her draped, seated carriage, "that you would ever see such a day?"

"No, Mother," the prince said, looking up from the moondrake's back.

"And look at you, seated upon a winged serpent," she said with a dry laugh. "Strange days, indeed, my boy!"

"Yes," he replied and looked at her with love. "But I believe it is all for the better. We must believe that!"

"I agree, my dear," the queen replied with a soft sigh. "We must."

The queen smiled bittersweetly as she looked upon the castle ruins. Her boy was growing into a man in front of her eyes. Her heart was bursting with pride for her son. If it took a broken kingdom to build up one great man, then that was the price that must be paid.

"Farewell, Mother," he said and looked anxiously toward the west. "I am off to free our brothers and the rest of our people!"

"Goodbye, my noble Sigismund," she replied. "Return to me safely, and I will be the luckiest mother alive."

"Come on, Druix," Sigismund said. "Let us see what these marauders are made of!"

The unlikely pair set off into the open skies. The clouds became their armor and the sun their guide as they flew into the daylight.

The moondrake's eyes were soon bleary from the sun's intense light, but he could not hide from the shining orb any longer. He would fly into its burning rays, into the brightness that illuminated their world because he could not deny the brilliance it had revealed to him. He had been expelled from a realm of eternal night only to be faced with the brink of death, then thrust into even more hopelessness and peril. But he would not trade any of it for the world that he had once known. The kinship he had found in their just cause against the dragon army was enough to fill his heart. If he died tomorrow, it would be with the satisfaction that he knew what it was like to have truly lived.

Druix and the prince forged ahead as forests dissolved into tawny heaths and hilly dunes that stretched out like sandy, brown blankets before them. Only the heartiest shrubs dotted the scenery in quilt-work patches below. They flew into the badlands until they spotted one of Stormkeep's dark towers on the horizon.

Prince Sigismund guided the moondrake ahead to the fortress that rose ominously above the coast of the Emerald Sea. Behind the distant keep, he could almost see the sea's deep green waves undulating and shimmering. A foreboding haze rose from the mist of the crashing waves. The crimson sun's glare cut through the haze to form a blood-red cloud. Stormkeep rose above it all.

"There it is," Sigismund said, pointing to the castle. "We can end this here and now. Let us descend upon the castle and demand that our friends be released!"

As they flew beyond Stormkeep and saw the open waters of the Emerald Sea, the prince gasped in awe. This was beauty unlike any he had ever seen or even imagined. It was a world unto its own, a frontier that tugged upon his heartstrings.

Druix had never seen a vista like the one spread before him. The flaming red sun licked the waves of the sea, and its light glistened on the crests. Even Mirrhenian Lake paled in comparison to what he beheld.

The mystery of what lay beneath the waves enchanted the moondrake. The vibrant colors and fragrant salty air elevated his spirits. Druix could not only see the sea and smell it, but he could also *feel* the sea. It was so foreign to him—but scintillating to his senses. The moondrake swept a circular path, banking back toward Stormkeep's central tower.

On the highest tower of the fortress, a central tower appeared like a magnificent lighthouse. Guards were on the lookout. If they approached with utmost haste, they might be able to seize the initiative. Druix drove on as fast as he could.

The moondrake's heart raced faster and faster. Sigismund peered at the fortress in front of them. The exhilaration of this flight into this newly explored world filled him with an unyielding resolution: They must protect the beauty of this world.

"There is no time to waste," Sigismund said. "We must rise and land upon the castle walls. There, on the top!"

Druix soared upward. Sigismund held onto the creature's shoulders with all his might. His legs dug into the moondrake's scaly body as they ascended above the fortress. Druix flapped his wings to slow down for landing. They touched down on the castle walkway around the keep's outer walls.

The three guards on the castle wall wore black leather armor and tattered rags. They were rough-hewn men, sun-dried and gritty, but when they saw Druix open his gaping maw, their eyes grew wide with fright. They dropped their long bows and feathered arrows and ran for the bastion.

"Don't even think about it, boys," Sigismund said as the great beast beneath him moved upon the stone path. The sound of its talons was disturbing enough to make the mercenaries fall to their knees.

"Please don't kill us," a marauder with a wiry red beard pleaded. "We were only doing the bidding of Darius Blackblade."

"If you value your lives," the prince said. "You will do the wise thing and free my brothers forthwith. They are from House Waverly. Then, you'll free all the lords and ladies you've taken hostage, particularly the one known as Melanie MacCallister."

"But King Blackblade will kill us!" an older man with a grizzled beard cried. His eyes were glazed with fear, and he seemed to speak for all of them.

"Well, you might say I have the distinct advantage of being able to kill you sooner than Darius Blackblade can," Sigismund said. "If you think this moondrake is fearsome, just wait until you see my army of wild griffins."

"Griffins?" a clean-shaven man inquired. His head was covered with a black kerchief.

There was no argument from the marauders, who seemed to agree with the prince's impeccable reasoning.

"We would be happy to free those whom you seek, but you are too late for the Waverly princes," the marauder with the red beard said. "They have been packed up onto our slave ships and taken to the Jeweled Islands under the command of the slave master Zmaragdus."

"You lie!" Sigismund exclaimed.

"We do not lie," the oldest marauder replied. "We have no desire to be fed to that...thing you are riding there."

Druix opened his mouth and showed his fangs. His wings flapped twice and curled inward to make him look even more formidable than usual.

Then, one at a time, the griffins began filing in upon the castle wall. If the sight of the moondrake had been the least bit unconvincing to the marauders stationed on the castle walls, then the sight of these griffins, some of them in body armor, was enough to force their complete surrender.

"Am I late?" Aenyx asked as he strode up to Sigismund and Druix. "If I need to make an example of one of these men, just say the word."

"No, no, that will not be necessary," the man with the red beard said. "Fetch the hostages and bring them up here."

The marauder wearing the black kerchief hesitated.

"Now!" he barked.

"In the meantime, I want all of you to lay down your weapons," Sigismund said. "But I have no intention of doing to you what Blackblade would do to us if we surrendered. I want you to join us in a common cause against a dire enemy who threatens all of Solarius, including the Jeweled Islands. If he succeeds in his depraved designs, there will be nowhere to flee to—not even by pirate vessel."

The men looked at one another in confusion. They did not even know what to make of the offer.

"Dracus Imprimus has returned," Sigismund said flatly. He did not need to elaborate further.

"Your highness," the black-kerchiefed marauder said upon opening the bastion's steel-reinforced door. "I present to you, Princess Melanie."

The invader held open the door. Out walked the most intoxicating girl he had ever seen. She was a striking vision to the prince—her audacity and nobility cut like a knife. Her pale-skinned hands were bound with rope in front of her, yet her immaculately shaped face revealed defiance, even a haughty expression. Her titian-colored hair flowed down her back like screaming flames. The girl no longer wore an elegantly cut jade-green gown but was dressed in jodhpurs and high brown leather boots. She wore a white silk blouse that embraced her curves. Her olive-green eyes danced dangerously in the twilight.

"Unhand me, you foul beast!" she said, jerking her elbow away from the guard. "And cut these ropes off of me immediately!"

The clean-shaven marauder produced a slim blade. She thrust her arms in front of her, and he sliced through the threads of the rope. The princess cast them off as casually as the bandits' pretense of enslavement. She tossed away the loose strands with a quick flick of her wrists, which were reddened from the marks of the rope.

"Now, hand me the blade," she told the man with a fierce look. Not wishing to trifle with the princess, he handed it over, turning the handle toward her.

"Thank you," she said, securing the dagger on her leather belt. She then slapped the man right across the face with a tremendous *whap*! His face reddened instantly—both from the impact of her firm hand and the shame of being beaten in front of friends and foes alike by this brazen girl.

"Princess Melanie!" the prince shouted as he dismounted from Druix.

"Since when do you ride moondrakes?" she asked with a coy grin. She approached the prince and threw her arms around him, kissing his cheek twice and then a third time.

"I knew you would come for me," Melanie said and winked. "But don't you dare think I wouldn't have thought of a way to escape from here eventually."

"No, no, of course not," the prince responded with a subdued chuckle.

"And griffins too?" she said and looked out upon the winged army. "I am impressed. But the likes of these creatures haven't been seen in Hypernea since—time immemorial. What is going on?"

"You might not believe this," the prince replied, "but we are soon to be under assault by shadow dragons from the land of Noctera, and we are now on a desperate quest. We need allies from every corner of Solarius if we have any hope of defeating them.

"That brings us to Darius Blackblade," Sigismund continued. He turned toward the marauders. "If there is some way to convince him to release my brothers and to join forces with us against Dracus Imprimus, I am all ears."

The marauders exchanged worried glances and began whispering among themselves.

"You see, Prince," the oldest man said. "Darius Blackblade's most beloved children, the twins Sapphyria and Acquarian Lovebreeze, have fallen deathly ill. Many across the islands have caught this terrible plague. Those who catch this disease experience a raging fever and unending thirst for water that cannot be satisfied. Their eyes turn yellowish and acquire a thousand-mile stare. It is as if they become more dead than alive for weeks until they finally pass from this world into the Great Beyond."

"That sounds horrific!" Miranda Sunray exclaimed.

Prince Sigismund hadn't noticed that she was there until just then. He jumped a bit, startled.

"But it sounds very, very familiar to me," she continued. "If it is anything like the dreadful plague that struck the southern Hypernean villagers many years ago, there may be only one cure for it. It is an herb known as Angel's Breath, a wildflower that grows in an area so wild that no people live near it."

"Peace, child," Prospero said. "I believe you may be right. But these marauders have much to do before we turn over the herbal remedy for their plague. They must agree to take us to Darius Blackblade and the slavemaster Zmaragdus to free the princes in captivity."

"If we take these people to the pirate king," the red-bearded man said with cautious optimism to his fellow marauders, "he might actually give us a reward instead of sending his elite personal guard to chop off our heads."

"It is agreed," the oldest marauder said. "My name is Simeon. I am the senior guard on these walls. We shall prepare the ships to sail away from here with complete urgency. We've grown tired of this place, anyway."

"Excellent!" the prince replied as he studied the illumined faces of those he had assembled around him. The diverse company was staring contemplatively at the last sliver of the setting sun as it sank beneath the sea waves.

Manfred the Magnificent looked sternly out from the Stormkeep battlement toward the darkening horizon. If anyone could find a way to defeat the Dread Commander, it would surely be the enlightened wizard.

Brave Aenyx gazed with his deep brown eyes upon the wide-open sea. He was now the unquestioned leader of the griffins of Aeris, whose homeland had fallen under the merciless occupation of General Nemysis Drake and his legion of shadow dragons.

Druix had taken the most courageous leap into their world. Everything was upside down for him, but there was hope that things were now right side up. A part of Sigismund wondered if the other moondrakes of his kind were more misguided than evil, having been deceived by Dracus Imprimus. He wondered if his friend Druix could become part of their salvation, if the moondrakes of the bleak kingdom of Lunastria could someday become their unlikeliest of allies.

Miranda floated above the castle walls with a lovely glow that was like the soft light of a golden candle. The fairy had become used to being disposable in the world of The Could-Be, but her healing spirit might offer Solarius the best chance of truly uniting. If the fairy kingdom could be persuaded to cross over from The Could-Be into the natural realm, what enchantment might they offer in their war against the dragons?

Sigismund's finger traced along the crystal shard in his pocket. He wondered if he would be able to find a way.

And of course, there was Princess Melanie, whose unquenchable spirit was more luminous than any star he'd ever had the good fortune to behold. She was a puzzle to him that he had not yet pieced together, and he was not sure that he wanted to. It comforted him to look at her and simply know that such a daring soul existed. As far as he was concerned, life was magic beyond anything that the sorcerers could conjure up.

While he looked upon the relieved face of Princess Melanie, he realized that natural beauty was more than the flourishing life that had revisited Hypernea for the first time since he had been alive. Not only was the world of Solarius at stake in their battle against the Dread Commander, but also the many worlds inside each of them and all of the innocent creatures across the Solarian realms.

Even in the face of almost certain destruction, he felt his fear dissolving into the boundless sea. Hope for the future swelled in his heart as he looked upon his companions.

He was no longer a prisoner in his own castle. He was his own king.

There was, indeed, beauty in the world. And he no longer felt alone.

CHAPTER 42

THE DRAGONKING'S VENGEANCE

The High Sorceress stepped slowly through the portal. She wore thigh-high black leather boots that gave off a glossy sheen and were adorned with curving upturned blades that ran all the way up the sides. The green phantasmagorical flames surrounding the edges of the portal flickered for a moment. Their spectral gleam dimmed, and the green flames were extinguished.

The raven-haired woman stood tall and defiantly before her lord and husband within the confines of the Obsidian Fortress. Her eyes were flecked with thin lightning-streaks of blood that cried out for vengeance. The pallor of her smooth alabaster skin resembled that of a pale doll. Her mind turned to the future and the thousands of helpless human beings who would soon lie writhing in agony, screaming, and dripping in blood, in order to avenge her sweet, beloved Gigantus.

The Dread Commander stood before her silently. His dark eminence oozed inconceivable power and unfathomable loathing. A deep craving dwelled within the evil being, a lust for power like a soul-swallowing void that attracted Morana. The profound emptiness devoured everything it touched, including her heart. She wanted it to consume her soul right then and there, transforming it into some greater power that was untamable. Indestructible. Beyond the reach of space and time.

"Commander," Morana said defiantly. She would not show him the satisfaction of knowing her heartbreak over Gigantus.

Dracus Imprimus hovered in the air. The shadowy figure began to slowly move backward toward his throne; his feet were suspended above the wet obsidian rock. A sliver of moonlight cut through the dark hall and briefly cast a pale, ethereal outline around the ominous figure before he disappeared behind its obscuring light.

The High Sorceress followed, her boots clacking melodically on the rough obsidian walkway toward the Dread Throne. She whipped out her silvery orbed scepter, and with a quick flick downward from her gloved wrist, she ignited the spectral orb with a white glow that faintly illuminated the great hall.

The oppressive darkness nearly smothered the faint glow. No bats scattered, and no rats scrambled for the walls. No living beings dared live in the presence of the Dread Commander, save the shadow dragons who lay sleeping in the sundry corners and innumerable caverns of the Obsidian Fortress.

"My love..." Morana began.

"Do not speak of love with me!" his voice boomed.

The words cut her as they echoed throughout the hall. It was as if hundreds of voices were shouting his hateful message into her ears. Her knees wobbled, but she maintained her balance and a thin veneer of confidence as she approached her husband. She briefly wrestled with her instinct to pity him, but then shunned the fleeting thought.

"Gigantus is...dead," Morana said.

"Yes, of course," the dragonking's raspy voice hissed. "And so is Captain Thornwood. I felt his soul leaving his body and entering my cold universe. His reward will be remaining unloved throughout eternity among the other pitiful lieutenants who have failed me."

Morana shuddered at the thought. She had no love lost for Captain Saevius Thornwood, but the prospect of eternal suffering within a pitiless realm devised by the evil mind of Dracus Imprimus was a fate that not even the High Sorceress could conceive.

"I will not fail you, Commander," Morana intoned.

"You already have!" Dracus Imprimus exploded.

The hateful voices again crashed down from the bleak walls in waves of pain. She wavered and felt the urge to collapse upon her knees, but she plumbed the depths of her soul to withstand it. She found her courage and faced the dragonking's wrath. It was not the first time, nor would it be the last, the sorceress reminded herself.

"Hypernea," the dragonking said quietly.

And with a flourish of his iron-fisted hand, the Dread Commander dismissed her. It was his unmistakable command to mobilize the shadow dragon legions for a full-out assault on Hypernea that none would withstand.

The High Sorceress snapped her heels and turned away from her husband to seek out a dragon worthy of her command. She knew just the candidate—a young drake with special capabilities that were untapped and would strike fear into even the steeliest heart. The only thing left for her to do was to wait patiently in the shadows for his arrival. Then she would have her own sweet taste of vengeance.

CHAPTER 43

THE HEROES DEPART

As Sigismund stood tall upon the castle battlement, he stared out upon the rose-colored sun while it dipped beyond the dusky sea waves and imagined his journey forward. Just moments before, he had felt a deep contentment swelling within him. Now he was merely savoring the sweetness of having discovered true friends and allies. The prince realized that he had merely been swept up in the moment and had been unbelievably naïve and self-centered about the situation.

A nauseating fear rose within him, fears about the impending invasion. Trepidation for the lives of his brothers. Longing for the hand of Princess Melanie, who might someday help him rule the Waverly kingdom. He feared the disastrous fate of Waverly Castle might soon become that of Stormkeep or the other bastions scattered throughout Hypernea. There were at least a dozen.

On the horizon, Sigismund watched seagulls soaring above the Emerald Sea as purple wisps of clouds floated obliviously through the darkening sky. In his mind's eye, he imagined these harmless birds were the forms of distant shadow dragons scouring the world for their next prey. The fleeting thought filled him with dread, and he knew it was time to act.

"Manfred," Sigismund said as he turned toward the wizard. "I believe the time for enjoying this taste of victory has passed all too soon. We must convene a war council at once. As we feast on the best of what Blackblade's men have to offer, we must strategize a bold course of action."

"I believe that would be most prudent, Sigismund," Manfred said with approval.

Sigismund turned toward Traveris Bane, who stood in front of a fully armored griffin wearing brass armor and a red-and-white riding blanket emblazoned with the Stormguards' white lightning sigil. The Kindly Knight wore a devil-may-care smile, and his brown hair fell to his shoulders. His eyes gleamed in the last light of dusk, and it almost seemed to Sigismund there was a hint of tears on the surface of his eyes.

"Traveris," Sigismund said. "I am going to need your trust and your loyalty more than ever. You have shown such honor and bravery on behalf of my mother, and if she consents, I would be best served if you accompany me on a most important quest. I will need your sword and your battle-hardened senses."

Traveris replied, "I am no counselor, not like the wizard Manfred here. But it is true enough that I have gotten into enough tight jams in my day to know a bad deal when I see one, and I have a knack for avoiding traps. If Queen Galadria releases me from my sworn duty to protect her, then I would be most honored to become your faithful bodyguard."

"More than a bodyguard," Sigismund replied. "You will be the captain of the King's Guard. At least, when there is a king to guard, that is. But that is the main object of our mission. We must compel Simeon, the senior guard of Blackblade's marauders, to take us to meet the pirate king himself."

"Ooh! Can I come?" Princess Melanie chimed in with a beam of excitement on her exuberant face. She wiped her brow, shaking her curly red tresses. "I have always loved the tales of pirate swashbucklers and the exotic climes of the Jeweled Islands—the hidden coves and secret waterfalls teeming with treasure! I've heard you can practically bathe among the rubies and emeralds and sapphires. And of course, I would love to help you liberate your brothers, who most certainly deserve such a magnanimous sacrifice on your part."

She winked and produced an infectious grin that Sigismund could barely resist.

He rolled his eyes facetiously and shrugged.

"Of course, Princess Melanie, you can come."

"One more request—stop calling me 'princess'!" she exclaimed. "From now on, just call me Melanie. I don't need a fancy title to define who I am. I can easily do that myself."

The cadre that had gathered on Stormkeep's rooftop looked upon her with surprise and admiration. There was more to this vivacious young lady than met the eye.

"Rest assured," Sigismund replied while looking into her beautiful green eyes, "we will honor your request."

"So, Manfred, that leaves you," Sigismund continued after a pause to admire the young woman's spunk. "What do you advise us to do now?"

"Your highness, I recommend that we leave any more preparations of strategy to the war council meeting," the wizard tersely replied. "It grows late and we have much planning to do."

"Aenyx," Manfred said as he waved his white, oaken staff toward the west. "Your griffin cadres are released to sleep upon the battlement of Stormkeep or on the fields west of the castle between us and the Emerald Sea. You stay with us, so that we may plan the liberation of Aeris."

"Very well, wizard," Aenyx retorted with a spark of ferocity in his eyes.

"The rest of you, prepare for the war council," Manfred added, "but before the meeting convenes, I would like to talk with you privately, Prospero."

"Of course, comrade," Prospero replied. His hand was resting upon the head of Druix, who was eagerly listening with the aid of the druid's spell.

"Traveris," Sigismund said. "Dispatch to find Simeon, the senior guard, who should tell his fellow marauders to make preparations for our war council. Also, please ensure that our consultations are made with utmost secrecy."

The Kindly Knight nodded and set off down the stairs within the castle bastion to make the war council preparations.

Timor Longbranch looked incredulously at the incredible cast of characters gathered at Stormkeep. He signaled for the Laketown allies of Hypernea to mount their unlikely steeds. The griffins and their riders dispersed into the skies above Stormkeep and made camp west of the castle. Flags signifying the Prides flew boldly on the shores of the Emerald Sea, amid Hypernean tents and campfires dotting the plains for as far as the eye could see.

The Hypernean reinforcements arrived upon horseback as the advance forces settled in for the night. They made camp on the northeastern plains outside of Stormkeep, on the brushy steppe that extended along the coast to the southern reaches of the Onyx Wastes. Queen Galadria arrived in her covered carriage, a royal conveyance draped with golden and white striped canvas and adorned with gold-fringed tassels.

Druix rested his weary moondrake head upon the stone floor of the keep. Miranda Sunray hovered in the background with a dim glow as she awaited further instructions from Manfred. In the background, she could hear the quiet lapping of the frothy Emerald Sea along the rocky Hypernean coastline.

Elsewhere, in the deepening twilight, the winking stars were beginning to commune overhead, and the mages consulted upon the Stormkeep battlement. The gentle glow of Manfred's staff faintly illuminated their secretive discussion.

"Manfred," the White Druid began, "there is a highly important mission that I must undertake if we are to successfully oppose Dracus Imprimus." Prospero uttered the Dread Commander's name as if the terrible dragonking might be listening.

"Mm-hmm," Manfred replied, listening attentively.

"We are in desperate need of allies, as you well know, and it so happens that a representative from an unlikely realm has fallen, or one might say has *flown*, right into our hands," Prospero said, sneaking a quick glance at the snoozing moondrake.

"Why, of course, of course," Manfred said as his eyes lit up. "Do you sense that these creatures might be persuaded to come to our aid, even against the mighty shadow dragons gathering to invade our lands?"

"Yes, I certainly do, old friend," Prospero said with a gleam in his eye. "I ask, as a courtesy, to set off with the moondrake at once to make contact with the moondrakes of Lunastria. They have taken refuge upon the volcanic mountain known as Mount Kildrath."

"Indubitably!" Manfred said. "I don't feign to overrule your judgment on a matter pertaining to the business of the Mighty Three. Yet, I must first share a matter that has been weighing on my mind about the third member of our clan, Salustrius the Wise."

Manfred peered up at the evening sky, then nodded for Prospero to follow him to the edge of the battlement, so they could look upon the sea and further discuss the matter. The crashing waves of the sea before them drowned out their hushed speech. Only the tiny ears of Miranda Sunray could pick up the quiet vibrations of their voices.

"As you know, Salustrius the Wise has been tasked to investigate the disturbances of the Equine Kingdom in the southern land of Wysteria," Manfred said. "That land has not only been struck by civil war over scarce resources, but the Silverine Lake is drying up as tributaries running from the Crystalline Source to the Raging Rivers to the lake itself have slowed their waters to a trickle. The Wysterian plants draw nourishment from these waters. If they die, then the unicorns also die out, as their magic fades with these mystical plants.

"Thus," Manfred said, "the unicorns from the eastern region of Misericordia, being the more aggressive of the equine, have invaded and taken over eastern Wysteria as they desperately seek water and the life force that sustains their being. But it gets worse…"

Prospero scratched his chin and looked at the blue-cloaked wizard, who communicated the gravest expression he believed he had ever seen on Manfred's face. "How could it get worse?" the druid asked.

"A dark force is rising in the southern limits of the region," Manfred said with a whisper. "Something evil. Something never before seen."

Prospero's eyes grew wide as the wizard explained.

"When I first heard the accounts from fairies living in The Could-Be, I could scarcely believe them," the mage admitted. "Entire beings were disappearing without a trace, parents had no memory of children that had once lived, and tears in the fabric of space and time suggested matter was being *undone* along with the consequences of their existence."

"But...how could that be?" Prospero responded with uncharacteristic bewilderment.

"It appears to be fairly recent," Manfred said. "Most concerningly, it coincides with our recent destruction of the Arch Crystal. It appears that Dracus Imprimus may have discovered a way to invert the powers of The Could-Be. That is to say, he can reverse them into their polar opposite."

"The Never-Was," Prospero whispered with alarm.

Miranda Sunray gasped and flew to Manfred's side, hiding her head in her hands.

"I know, little one," Manfred said. "This is most disturbing news."

"What do you propose, Manfred?" Prospero asked after some thought.

The weathered wizard sighed as he gazed off into the distance, inhaling the salty sea air to clear his mind and set his resolve.

"We must dispatch Miranda to consult with our colleague, Salustrius the Wise," Manfred said. "He is steeped in the arcane lore around such magic and knows many from outside the western kingdoms who may assist us in thwarting the insidious designs of Dracus Imprimus. There is word that beyond the Diluvian Streams, eastern realms remain unaffected by the Dread Commander's curse, and they may be slow to rise against the coming storm of hellfire and deadly plague waiting on their doorstep."

"The Baldurian Dwarves," Prospero remarked. "They might be roused to our aid if they perceive it as being in their self-interest. They are a commercial people who are industrious and practical, and live upon the mountainous coast on the other side of the Terrastrian continent. It would take weeks to alert them and many more to move them."

"Salustrius the Wise is conversant with the fleet pegasus of Wysteria," the wizard pointed out. "He could find a worthy steed capable of reaching the easternmost realms within days."

"Yes," Prospero said, nodding. "And there's the Thorastrian Elves who live in the deep forests along the southern coast of the Tiberian Sea. That mysterious and reclusive folk is steeped in some of the most potent magic of the Presentient Period, when mammoth firedrakes, behemoth sea serpents, and treacherous chimeras roamed Solarius. It is whispered the elves could conjure a magical force that could recreate these fearsome beings to fight their fiercest enemies, but they are loath to use this arcane magic in all but the direst circumstances."

"Indeed," Manfred said. Then he put his hand upon Prospero's shoulder. "And we must not forget the sleeping rock trolls of the far north, in the land of Cyrrhenia. They have remained aloof from the affairs of this world for eons. Solarius has likely not heard the last from these miserable beings, but they are not completely devoid of reason and would not infallibly commit to the dragonking's allegiance, should the fate of all life and even the world's existence depend upon their decision."

"It is done, then," Manfred concluded. "Miranda, did you hear everything the good druid and I have been discussing?"

The fairy smiled and darted to the mage's side. She hovered eagerly in the air, suspended in the night air beyond the edge of the parapet.

"Good," he said, "For your task is threefold and critical to the survival of all Solarius. You must embark to deliver an urgent message to Salustrius the Wise in the easternmost reaches of Wysteria. Divulge all of our thoughts and concerns, particularly inquiring about the destructive nature of The Never-Was. Instruct him to alert the easternmost realms, where he must reach the Thorastrian Elves and Baldurian Dwarves with a warning about Dracus Imprimus's nefarious plans. And lastly, procure the herb known as Angel's Breath, especially taking care to take it by the root, so that we may replant it here in Hypernea. As you know, its essence contains a probable cure for the accursed plague that is now running rampant through the Jeweled Islands.

"Do you have all that, my friend?" Manfred asked.

Miranda nodded slowly. The fairy was unsure how the weight of the world could somehow be resting upon her tiny, gossamer wings.

"I believe in you," Manfred said. "Now, fly!"

And with that, the irrepressible being darted like a firefly into the deepening night, where she headed south from Stormkeep into the ancient forests and endless swamps extending to the florid, dreamlike equestrian realm of Wysteria, where no mere man dared enter lest he fall into a perilous, unawakenable sleep.

"As for me, Manfred," the druid remarked, watching the fairy's light fade into the darkness, "I shall now rouse my own steed to travel north across the Onyx and Sulfurous Wastes to Mount Kildrath with the most improbable aim of turning his brethren against the shadow dragons. Based on what Druix has told me, I believe there may be an unspoken enmity between the ferocious beasts that we could possibly use to our advantage."

Manfred paused and looked askance at Prospero, who had lines of crow's feet spreading around his eyes. He nodded his head in assent as the White Druid went to wake Druix. The druid mounted the sleepy creature and quietly informed him of the task at hand. The moondrake looked upon Manfred sadly, wordlessly, showing the wizard his deep reluctance to leave his newfound friends, especially the prince.

The old wizard looked at the beautiful serpent sympathetically. He smiled encouragingly to communicate that this was all for the best. In the moondrake's silvery eyes, he could detect the glistening impression of teardrops.

Prospero raised his metallic staff and flicked it to produce a ghostly light. The slow, hearty beats of the moondrake's wings thwacked the evening air, and the majestic midnight-blue serpent lifted them both into the air above Stormkeep. The moondrake paused for a moment, reluctant to leave the wizard and abruptly depart on a secretive mission possessing the highest unlikelihood of success.

Manfred the Magnificent looked up and squinted to behold the shadowy speck of the mage and his moondrake steed pass over the full moon. The shadow soon merged with the blackness of night and finally disappeared. The wizard became lost in thought for the briefest moment, then swiftly turned his back to the sea and headed for the bastion door to descend into the bowels of the fortress. There was a war council to arrange.

CHAPTER 44

THE MYSTERIOUS ENCOUNTER

The refreshingly salty breeze of the Emerald Sea shore receded into the night, and the rhythmic sound of the waves lapping the rocky Hypernean beaches faded into the distance behind Miranda Sunray as she fervently pressed ahead into the darkening, oppressively humid night. The scrub-laden steppe of southern Hypernea was incrementally replaced by stony tundra beneath her dainty dangling feet, as her gossamer wings beat faster and faster to forge ahead. The stony tundra soon became crisscrossed with antediluvian streams, treacherous and unnavigable to mere mortals with their reckless, untamable desire to overflow and flood the unsettled marsh plains.

The stars overhead had become enshrouded in a rising mist. The vaporous veneer cloaked the world around Miranda's bleary aquamarine eyes, which were as moist with worry for her friends as they were from the fog accumulating in the marshy wilderness. Mankind had long abandoned settling these wildlands, as they were known to the northerners. Still, she forged on into the unsettled lands, holding her mission close to her heart, inseparable from her warm regards for the prince, the lonely moondrake, and the irrepressible griffin. She clung to the intractable hope that everything would turn out all right.

The night enveloped her in a dreamlike state. Her mind became absorbed by the wracking guilt she knew she would feel if she somehow failed her fellow creatures of Solarius. Her attention turned to The Never-Was and the horrifying feeling that it was growing somewhere in the southern land of Wysteria. She imagined a world where The Never-Was grew with furious abandon, engorging all that was swept into its ravenous path. The children who would be un-born, the fairies who would be un-spawned, the endless possibilities that would be un-done, the words that would be un-spoken—the infinite ways that the world would fade into nothingness. The soul-obliterating ramifications of the powers of The Never-Was began to torment her conscience. All of the consciousness of the planet would be emptied and devoid of meaning. It would truly have been all for nothing.

She scarcely knew how to even communicate these fears to Salustrius the Wise, should she find the elusive mage before it was too late. Surely, the vaunted wizard would have the answers! Surely, his sagacious mind would know what to do! At least, that was her desperate hope.

At last, the sovereign sun slowly raised the velvety purple curtain of night, and the limitless contours of space melted into the rose-colored haze, evolving into a golden mellowing light that spread across the horizon. Miranda rose straight up into the air above the wildlands to see her progress. Her tiny frame rose magnificently as she surveyed the panorama.

What she saw would have taken her breath away—if she had any. She was in the midst of an immense marshland that stretched beyond her imagination. Yet, in the furthest limits of her vision, she could barely detect what she had been searching for. An unbelievably bright swathe of abundant azure and magenta flora burst across the horizon's edge. It lay ahead like a crown of laurels interspersed with gorgeous exotic flowers. The bright, shining aura was surreal in its stark contrast with the unbearably dull expanse of decaying reeds and fetid swamp water that had been her sole environ for hours while she had pressed ahead at breakneck speed through the lifeless wetlands. But now—she knew what it all was for.

Ahead was Wysteria.

The fairy squealed with delight. This was a land untouched by mankind! It was pristine and wonderful and everything her heart had imagined. There was no way a dark, menacing force like The Never-Was could lay waste to the heart of this abounding natural paradise. There was no chance that the creatures of this world, the innocent pegasi and the majestic unicorns, could ever want for anything! This magical oasis could never be rent by civil war or plagued by famine or struck down by death! What if all of the rumors were wrong?

Miranda's spirits were positively rekindled. Her androgynous frame twirled twice in midair, then darted back toward the ground below. She zipped ahead with the wind tickling her boyish, feathery hair. Her tiny heart beat tributarily in her curvaceous chest. She could not help but let forth a primal *squeee*!

Her delicate wings flapped more furiously than ever, and she forged ahead into the mysterious unknown. She drove herself even faster, despite the headwind of a gentle, warm zephyr emanating from the legendary forests ahead of her.

The desolate marshes with their dead reeds and musty cattails yielded to an astounding pristine expanse of wetland. The murky brownish-green swamp water that had passed below her for countless leagues began to dissipate into bright, clean blue-green waters. Beyond the distant water's edge, she beheld a prairie dotted with purple larkspur and loosestrife flowers, powder-blue scorpion grasses, and golden amaranths. The unforgettable landscape seemed to forewarn of prophecy and danger.

Miranda knew that once she crossed the border into Wysteria, there could be no turning back. She hovered in the morning light as the shimmering rays of the golden sun enraptured her. She took a quick peek over her shoulder before boldly plunging ahead into the forgotten forests of Wysteria.

She found herself enveloped in a sleepy haze where she could not divine the line between fantasy and reality. It all blurred together in the most haunting fashion. Even though she had been fashioned by an enchantress to be a mystical helper, possessing the superficial traits of humankind, she found the place to be both bewildering and intoxicating. The famous wisteria vines that enveloped all trees in gorgeous turquoise and lavender vines exuded a sweet, musky scent that was both pungent and heady. The wonderfully bright sights and exotic floral perfumes bombarded her senses until they defamiliarized her sense of reality. Wysteria even began to blur the line between her sense of self and the florid, exotic environment.

Nonetheless, she raced on, knowing that the fate of Hypernea, indeed, all of Solarius could be in her tiniest of hands. As the vivid pastels streaked by, Miranda Sunray suddenly felt a surge of energy that was unfamiliar to her, as if she were being supercharged by the potential of The Could-Be. Her gossamer wings came to an abrupt halt in the midst of the floral forest, and she absorbed what she saw.

A trickling brook snaked through the heart of the Wysterian forest. The faint babble of its dark green waters was the only sound she heard. Its gurgling stream was so shallow, it barely passed over the mossy stones and dark blue shale. She looked around at the ubiquitous trees enwrapped in lavender and turquoise vines with their dangling tendrils of translucent-colored petals, illuminated by the iridescent rays of the midmorning sun. The deep swath of secluded woodlands was cast in an otherworldly glow of multihued light. The forest floor was steeped in the delicate perfumed petals of floral vines. It beckoned the viewer like a pleasant dream.

Despite its dazzling facade, a deep sense of sadness permeated the grove, an all-encompassing serenity that was humbling and awe-inspiring. Miranda had the feeling that something *unusual* was in her midst. Something that she could not put her finger on.

Then she saw *it*.

It was seemingly oblivious to her mystical presence, for it did not stir, but merely continued to imbibe the refreshing waters of the forest stream. It was a creature of such indescribable magnificence.

The beast's sleek frame was the vision of consummate grace. Its shimmering neck of deep, velvety black was arched over the gentle-flowing waters of the brook. On its back were two immense wings covered with large ravenlike feathers. Adorning its head was a pearly, lustrous horn nearly half the height of a man. The entire length of it shone with a pale white glow that contrasted with its black physique.

The fairy rubbed her aquamarine eyes, as if to ensure she was not imagining the entire thing. This must be the legendary pegacorn.

She squealed with delight. Miranda did not know where the effervescent display of glee arose from within her, but nonetheless, it was too late.

The beast raised its wide, wild eyes to behold the intruder. Her muscular frame triggered the inclination to bolt, and a sudden ripple of indecision radiated throughout her equine frame. She snorted twice.

Miranda Sunray knew this was her chance to make an extremely powerful friend. She was aware that she had to be cautious not to spook her before she bolted into the Wysterian forest, never to be seen or heard from again. "You are beautiful!" the fairy boldly declared, not knowing if the words would calm or confuse the creature.

The pegacorn squinted at the tiny fairy, who was flying in the near distance. "Thank you?" She snorted.

Miranda was ecstatic that her aural magic still worked within the mystical confines of Wysteria. She had been apprehensive that the forest's magic might overwhelm her own. "Look at you!" Miranda continued. "Those gorgeous dark blue eyes, and your wings—magnificent!"

The pegacorn was enthralled by the sudden praise. The fantastical creature unfurled its feathery wings and pranced lightly upon the mossy shale along the brook's embankment. Its majesty was evident to Miranda.

"And last but not least, that wondrous horn!" the fairy went on. "Why, I have not seen anything as marvelous as that in all my wanderings throughout Solarius!"

The pegacorn snorted and halted its high-kneed prancing. "You—you kn-kn-know Equinian!" She whinnied excitedly. "Wh-what brings you to Misericordia? We are a land besieged by w-w-war and far w-w-worse dangers! Reveal to me wh-wh-who—and wh-wh-what—you are, tiny being!"

"Oh, I'm Miranda Sunray," the fairy declared proudly. "I am on a most urgent quest to find a powerful sorcerer named Salustrius the Wise. He is said to be somewhere in the lands of Wysteria..."

"The w-w-wizard!" the pegacorn exclaimed. "Wh-why, he is my special friend! You see, I am an outcast in these divided lands of W-W-Wysteria. As you can plainly see, I am neither a pegasus, the w-winged equine who has fled to the once-raging rivers east of here, nor a unicorn, wh-who live here in the w-w-western lands of W-W-Wysteria known as M-M-Misericordia."

"You know Salustrius?" the fairy replied in disbelief, clapping her tiny hands with enthusiasm as she flew closer to the pegacorn. "We must go to him urgently and tell him all I know about the great evil stirring in the north! A Dread Commander and a strange force are believed to be brewing in southern Wysteria. It might even threaten Solarius itself!"

The pegacorn lowered her head and snorted softly. Her eyes grew big and wide. They were as dark and lustrous as her jet-black mane and reflected the fairy's gentle light.

"You know about..." She paused and looked around nervously. "The N-N-Never-W-W-Was?"

Miranda Sunray looked at the beautiful creature with sadness in her eyes. The rumors must be true then. She sighed. "That is why we must reach Salustrius," she told the pegacorn. "He will know all about this Never-Was and what we can do to fight it."

"Oh, yes." The pegacorn brayed. "We must go to the w-w-wizard at once!"

"But first, kind pegacorn," the fairy said, just as the equine creature began to turn away toward the Wysterian forest. "I never got your name."

"My n-n-name?" she replied with a slight grin. "It is Silvestria."

CHAPTER 45

A PIRATE'S LIFE FOR ME

Sigismund, the Hypernean regent, presided over an immense gathering of disparate parties on the western fields lying between Stormkeep and the foamy Emerald Sea. The salty waters were as dark as colored glass beneath the limitless expanse of late-night skies but murmured with a sonorous voice in the distant background.

The ghosts of previous invasions appeared to congregate upon the ancient battlefield as well, silent witnesses to the grave talks of war that had brought such a menagerie of warriors to their final resting places. Their eerie presence could faintly be felt among the still-living, including the human soldiers from the sundry Hypernean clans. These were the fearsome Forresters, the sturdy Smythes, and the mighty MacCallisters, along with the remnants of the proud Waverly clan, whose ranks were shattered by the pirate king's strike at the heart of Hypernea. At the head of the Laketown contingent was the strapping elder Timor Longbranch, whose tremendous voice was regaling the male and female warriors with epic songs of victory and woe.

Their multicolored tents stretched for miles along the shore, erected from the war wagons that had been driven west from the now-desolate

Waverly Castle. Bright banners of both man and griffin rapped proudly in the sea breeze. The brutish sounds of the war camp filled the air: Men clinking brass mugs and sloshing down honeyed mead and dark ale, raucous talk of war and raunchy talk of women, and the occasional short outbursts of fighting, which typically accompanied such nervous mortal energy.

On the outskirts of the camp, Aenyx Stormguard tilted his bronze-helmeted head to gaze at the starlight and pondered what this could mean for the liberation of his homeland of Aeris. The red feathers on his helmet wavered gently in the wind, and the feathers of his golden wings rustled subtly. He thrust his chest out, its plumage puffed up and proudly displayed upon the war leader's powerful chest.

Other griffins were feasting on live goats and sheep in a field east of the camp. The gory sight of griffins ripping flesh and the disconsolate sounds of animals wailing disturbed even the seasoned warriors. Bart Bluetip had already devoured three of the poor beasts in a single savage sitting. But Aenyx was not hungry.

"What's the matter, Aenyx?" asked Princess Melanie, who had clearly taken a fascination with the hybrid creatures. She had been wandering around the war camp, taking in the sights and sounds of Hypernea's new guests.

Aenyx looked back at her with his big brown eyes flickering in the torchlight. His brow was cast in deep shadow as he contemplated a response. He recalled that the wizard's aural magic had not been cast on the girl, and thus he bowed his head in a sign of respect and returned to stargazing.

"It will be okay, dear Aenyx," she said, realizing that the griffin was preoccupied with concern for his besieged homeland. "Sigismund told me all about the griffins' plight. If there is anything I can do to help, please know I shall do it for you magnificent creatures, and I am so grateful you have befriended Hypernea. I am personally indebted to you for your contributions to my freedom and safety."

She walked up to Aenyx and put her soft hand upon his mane, then gave him a peck on the cheek. As Melanie walked away toward the camp, the griffin marveled at these human creatures. For all of their stupidity and aggravation, he was growing increasingly fond of them.

Suddenly, a ram's horn blared in the night. It was the clarion call for the clan leaders and war chieftains to assemble for the council meeting. Aenyx jaunted toward the camp; his bronze armor jostled and lightly clanged, and the torchlight beamed with a golden aura off his gleaming battle gear.

"Gather around, fine warriors!" Sigismund declared. The regent stood at the head of a series of tables strung together in the camp. The blond-haired teenager was tall and gaunt but bore an august demeanor that was both resolute and battle-hardened. Robes flowed from his wiry frame, and a platinum crown sat loosely upon his head. His pale blue eyes were weary with concern for the kingdom but twinkled with their own inner spark. With a thin smile on his blood-red lips, which were wet with a robust wine, he greeted those who were gathering now for the war council. Silver chalices and plates lined the burgundy tablecloth. Adorned with gold fringe, it stretched from the regent to the table's foot. Vintage bottles of red wine and serving trays bursting with roasted lamb and spring greens were interspersed between the two dozen or so chairs that comprised the war chiefs' seats at the table. The feast was both a recognition of their imminent threat and the potential for renewed life.

"Hail, hail, good Sigismund!" Manfred cried as he pulled up a chair to the right of Sigismund and across from Queen Galadria. Traveris Bane remained seated beside the wizard as he lifted his overflowing goblet in a deft salutation.

"And you are a vision of splendor in these most difficult of times, my lady," Manfred added with a deferential nod to the queen.

"Quite difficult times, fair wizard," she replied. "And I thank you for lending your wisest counsel to this war council."

"Indeed," Manfred said as he studied the war chieftains gathering. Timor Longbranch entered with his retinue, including his bodyguards, Hans Lightfoot and Baron Broadcraft, and they were seated in the middle of the table. The griffin contingency, led by Aenyx Stormguard, Raven

Whitecrest, and Bart Bluetip, gathered at the far end of the table. Princess Melanie was seated beside Queen Galadria, and next to her, her father, the anxious Lord Alistair MacCallister, whose wispy, balding head was glistening with sweat and was tipped down toward his half-filled chalice.

Among those present were the highest lords and ladies of the Forrester and Smythe clans, as well as lesser nobles whose estates could be found on the fringes of Hypernea. The Forresters were valuable allies due to the rare prevalence of wild game in their extensive northern lands, namely mountain goats, and the sheep that survived by grazing upon the sparse vegetation of the steppe. Their lands also possessed iron ore deposits, and their blacksmiths were considered the best in the realm. Their warriors were stout and sure-handed, but not a very literate bunch. The rugged soldiers' preferred weapons were hatchets and hand axes, which possessed their own utility beyond merely cutting down adversaries.

The Smythes' lands included villages in the northern reaches of the Solistrian forest and near the western shores of Mirrhenian Lake, and they could readily supply smoked and salted fish, as well as various waterfowl such as duck and geese, to the army's food stores. Their ashen bows and birch arrows were renowned as some of the best in all of Solarius. Most importantly, the Smythes were exceptional archers and numbered nearly two hundred warriors among their ranks.

"We gather here tonight in defense—not just of Hypernea, not just of the griffin homeland of Aeris, not just of all Solarius," Sigismund began, "but in defense of freedom, dignity, and the right to lead our own lives as we deem fit."

The humans banged the table with their chalices in agreement, sloshing wine upon the burgundy tablecloth. Timor held up a leg of lamb in concurrence. "Hear, hear!" he shouted, then dropped his muscled arm before ripping more flesh from his chunk of meat.

Sigismund smiled thinly and continued with his address.

"And in order to secure the mutual defense of our lands, we must enact a unified strategy," he continued. "Soon, the shadow dragons of Dracus Imprimus shall be unleashed upon Hypernea, just as they were unleashed upon the Republic of Aeris. Unfortunately, the pirate king has made their dastardly efforts to conquer our kingdom easier by laying waste to Waverly Castle. That is why we find ourselves here, on the shores of the Emerald Sea, with Stormkeep as our new base of operations. From here, we have access to coastal transport and imports, but first, we must persuade Darius Blackblade to cease his piracy and join us in our effort to rid Solarius of the scourge of the Dread Commander."

The gathered host's raucous shouting came to a halt, and the warriors ceased stuffing their faces long enough to contemplate the young man's words.

"That is why we need complete commitment to our cause," Sigismund said, and then looked directly at Lord MacCallister. "Complete commitment—which means no more internal plotting against the Waverly crown, lest you'd enjoy joining the sheep outside the camp as griffin food."

Sigismund gave a wink toward the foot of the table to Aenyx, who winked back at him.

Lord MacCallister stood on his wobbly legs and addressed Sigismund. "I can assure you, my liege, there shall be no more plotting against you," Alistair said meekly. "I can see now that I misjudged you. The curse upon this land was undoubtedly not your fault, and it was as much a curse upon you as upon the land of Hypernea. Perhaps even more. I am eternally indebted to you for the release of my daughter, my dearest Melanie, and her safe return to us. I humbly extend my unyielding gratitude and the MacCallisters' loyalty to you."

Sigismund looked intently at Alistair, studying him up and down. After searching within the man's eyes, he found his apology to be sincere. "I accept!" he said, then slammed his chalice down.

The MacCallisters cheered, and they were joined by the Waverly soldiers gathered on the outskirts of the war council. The men slapped each other on the shoulders and clinked goblets, showing that they were ready to overlook their clans' historic rivalry. The Forresters and Smythes were likewise relieved that their small part in the plot against the crown would be forgiven and their fate would not be to wind up as table scraps for the strange, ferocious creatures the regent had brought to their lands.

"And that is why I am asking you, good people of Hypernea, to here and now defend Stormkeep with all your might," Sigismund said with a satisfied expression. "As for the griffins, we find the best course of action to strike back at the shadow dragons remaining in Aeris while the terrible creatures are scattered on the winds and Dracus Imprimus' reinforcements are undoubtedly still being gathered. Aenyx Stormguard shall lead a strike force against the shadow dragons occupying Aeris. Aenyx shall... claw-pick the most suitable griffins to accompany him."

Aenyx threw his talons on the table, rattling it and nearly tipping it over. "I am ready to tear those infernal serpents to bits!" the griffin exclaimed.

Bart Bluetip belted out a terrifying war screech that shook the human warriors to the core. The griffins burst out in laughter, which was made intelligible to the human hosts due to the wizard's spell.

"Easy, Bart," Raven Whitecrest said with a smirk. "We don't want these humans to rethink what they've gotten themselves into."

"Sorry!" Bart replied sheepishly.

"Nothing to forgive, my friend," Aenyx said. "We will need that kind of enthusiasm against the shadow dragons, for you shall be on my right flank."

"You know I won't let one of those bastards touch you!" Bart replied with a stern glare in his gray eyes.

"And you know I will be there for you too, Aenyx," Raven added. "I can watch your back with the best of them. No one knows you better than I!"

"Indeed, Raven," Aenyx replied. "Thank you."

"And as for me," Sigismund declared, "I am going on a mission to free my brothers and procure the alliance of Blackblade. It won't be easy, but we have a bargain in mind that the pirate king will be loath to turn down. Accompanying me on my voyage shall be the sailors and guides captured at Stormkeep, as well as Captain Traveris Bane, Manfred the Magnificent as high councilor, and at her request, Princess Melanie MacCallister."

Alistair looked at Sigismund in shock. The lords and ladies of the MacCallister, Forrester, and Smythe clans began to furiously whisper among themselves. Their chatter was noticeable among the war council.

Eve MacCallister, the lady of her clan, stood indignantly and addressed the regent directly. "I must object, your highness," she stated. "Melanie is but a girl! She cannot be traipsing around the Emerald Sea with a boy and those…pirates!" she exclaimed.

Princess Melanie stood with a fierce expression in her olive-green eyes. "That is quite enough, Mother!" she retorted. "Hasn't your scheming and plotting done enough? We are talking about the fate of Hypernea! Am I to sit idly by and quilt while the future of our people is at stake? And who would go with Sigismund? You? Father? I am not like you, Mother. I have no desire to be a prim and proper 'lady,' if that means standing by in the face of real danger. I am joining them, and you can't stop me. You might as well consent, and that will be the end of it."

"It is not the end of it!' Lady MacCallister exploded. "Alistair?" she asked and shot her husband a look, imploring him to *do* something.

"I am afraid she is right," Alistair responded as gently as he could. "I pledged my unyielding loyalty to Sigismund, and as much as I am afraid to lose my daughter again, it is her life to live and not our own. We have to let her go on this quest, which is more important than our parental fears. Sigismund, I hold you alone accountable for her safety. Go, Melanie, godspeed and return to us safe, I pray!"

"Do not fear, Lord MacCallister," Sigismund said. "You and the lady should remain confident that I shall do my utmost to defend the honor of your lovely daughter."

"And don't forget. I can handle myself," Melanie said with a smirk, drawing a dagger from inside her corset. This drew laughs from the warriors gathered around.

"I know, I know!" Sigismund said with a chortle. "Then it is decided. We shall depart upon a ship that I shall call *The Phoenix*, in honor of our fallen griffin comrade." Sigismund paused and looked at Aenyx, only to behold a glistening tear of acknowledgment.

"Thank you, friend," he said from across the tables.

The war council was dismissed, and the parties dispersed to their night quarters. The battle plan had been formed, and Sigismund and his comrades prepared to embark upon the Emerald Sea.

The wan morning sun arose and stretched its tawny golden arms across the calm, rippling waves of the glistening Emerald Sea. The day-star's spiraling tendrils reached into the royal tent where Sigismund had been dozing soundly.

The young man pried his heavy eyes open and stretched his lengthy arms on his feather bed, which had been overlain with luxurious lavender silk bedspreads that were faintly scented with jasmine. The sea air wafted through the tent flaps, rustling them gently and rhythmically; it was slightly salty and reinvigorating. His mind was completely clear.

The serene view of the seashore was such a stark contrast to the gray stone walls that had been his dull, familiar prison for eighteen years. The juxtaposition jolted him into recalling the shadow dragon that had haunted his bedroom the night before he had been forced to set off on this adventure. It was seemingly so long ago, yet it had only been a matter of weeks prior. He had told himself that the vision must have been some kind of illusion in order to comfort himself. But he realized now that he had suppressed its direst implications, for he couldn't shake the belief that it had been a warning from the Dragonking himself. If so, was the Dread Commander seeking him out personally?

The thought made him shudder. But instead of letting the fear overwhelm him, he thought about the vision of the Arch Crystal. There was another way. There was another possibility for the world. There was another Could-Be.

Sigismund lightly touched the crystal shard in his pajama pocket. He contemplated removing it from its velvety cloth to hold up in the morning sun's rays. *No,* he thought, *this is not a trifle or a toy. There are bigger things in store for my mother's greatest gift.*

It was early March, and there would finally be a real spring in Hypernea. The old curse had been lifted, and nature appeared to be returning to his homeland. But if Manfred's disturbing words about The Never-Was were indeed right—and he had never had a reason to doubt the wizard—there was an even darker curse brewing in the furthest southern reaches of Solarius. Something evil was brewing in Wysteria.

Sigismund rose and slipped on his slippers. He walked to the tent flaps and stood in the opening, stretching his arms as he admired the view.

"Come, Master Sigismund!" he heard Manfred shout from his right. The wizard approached with staff in hand, accompanied by Traveris Bane and Princess Melanie. She was dressed in a tight leather corset that hugged her curves. Her red tresses bounced as she approached, as light and airy as the way that she carried all of her burdens. She smiled a friendly devilish grin. They were all carrying leather rucksacks, and Traveris was pulling a chest of supplies on a sled.

"Darius Blackblade has gotten wind of the siege and loss of Stormkeep," Manfred said. "He is reportedly dispatching his elite corps, the Merciless Marauders, to intercept us and bring us to Blackblade for swift justice. We must set off at once and avoid a violent confrontation with these nefarious cutthroats. They are a dangerous lot, and we seek a more genial introduction to the Pirate King."

Sigismund nodded thoughtfully. "I will gather my things, and we will depart upon the *Phoenix* at once," he replied. "I trust the food stores are aboard the ship, as well as any other supplies we shall require."

"The orlop deck is fully stocked," Traveris replied. "You will need to familiarize yourself with sailing terms if you want a chance to gain respect from these pirates."

"Add that to the list," Sigismund said. "I will meet you at the dock shortly. I need to change into something more…suitable."

Melanie smiled warmly at Sigismund, causing his heart to pound a few strong thumps in his chest. His arms suddenly felt lighter than air.

She glanced at the wizard and the Kindly Knight. "Manfred, Traveris, I will stay behind and walk with Sigismund to the ship," she said, plunking her leather rucksack on the beach. "I will sit and watch this gorgeous sunrise as he gets ready."

"Very well, Princess," Traveris replied and continued down the beach.

"I said not to call me that!" she shouted while the old wizard and soldier sauntered down the beach. The Kindly Knight shrugged and continued to drag his sled behind him.

Sigismund shot Melanie a meager smile. Then he quickly ducked into his tent. A moment later, his pale hand reached outside, unfastened the flaps, and pulled them closed.

Melanie grinned wryly, then plopped down on her rucksack. She sat calmly with her back to the tent while the sun rose in the sky, and she stared out at the golden waves rippling on the emeraldine sea. "Don't worry, Sigismund," Melanie said sardonically. "I won't look—that is, unless you want me to!"

She giggled to herself before grasping a smooth, flat rock. She whipped her arm and skipped the rock across the surface of the sea. It hopped several times on the gleaming liquid surface before disappearing into the watery void.

Meanwhile, Sigismund was hastily emptying his chest of clothes into a leather sack that had been provided by his mother's retinue.

"Do you need any help in there?" Melanie shouted as she skipped another rock upon the sea. She was nearly as good at skipping rocks as she was at tormenting the young man with her mischievous remarks.

"You're not helping!" Sigismund shouted back as he pulled on his leather leggings. They were a bit too tight and a bit short for his long legs. No time. He pulled on his black leather boots and buttoned up his white silk shirt, tucking it in with the tail hanging out in the back. He threw on his velvet jacket and stuffed a kerchief in his pocket. It slumped over upon his breast, hanging there sadly as if it were ashamed to be a part of this overdressed attire.

He walked to the tent's opening, threw open the flaps, and stood there with outstretched arms. "Ta-da!" he exclaimed.

Melanie turned around and gathered an eyeful of the budding prince, who was now a regent in line to become the king of Hypernea. He looked ridiculous.

She stood and curtsied sarcastically before walking over to the young man. "My, how handsome!" she said with a sardonic grin. "Here, let's fix you up."

She tried to grasp his collar, but Sigismund flinched. Melanie shot him a stern look.

"Come now, you can't be afraid of a woman," she said. "How will you handle being face-to-face with the pirate king, or gods forbid, Dracus Imprimus himself? I have no intention of harming you, good Sigismund. Now, let me work my womanly charms."

The young lady gave a quick tug at Sigismund's collar, pulling the silk shirt smooth and crisp upon his tight chest. She stepped back and then suddenly reached forward to yank the edges of his jacket downward. Then, she reached inside his jacket and slid her delicate hands around to his backside, ever-so-deftly tucking his shirt in before he had time to object. Sigismund was squirming a bit, but he forced himself to relax. Lastly, she pushed down the white kerchief so that only the tip peeked out of his breast pocket.

"Now, this is the vision of a man the pirate king will respect," she said. "For it is you who ultimately must talk some sense into this Darius Blackblade."

Sigismund nodded firmly in agreement, then gathered the rest of his clothes and stuffed them into his leather rucksack before drawing the strings closed. He checked his inside pocket to be sure he had stashed his crystal shard. He then strung on a leather belt and touched the dagger hilt to be sure it was ensconced within its sheath.

Sigismund and Melanie walked along the seashore. Before them, a pier extended from the edge of the jetty. At the end was a massive three-masted ship, its white square sails furled upon their yardarms. The sailors were readying the ship. At the ship's stern was a winged figure.

The majestic beast spread its wings wide and flapped them twice in a greeting. The sun shone on his bronze helmet adorned with brilliant tufts of red. A wave of relief washed over Sigismund's face. It was Aenyx!

The creature took to the sky and dove toward the couple on the beach. When Aenyx reached them, the sound of the griffin's feathery wings was the most reassuring thing he could imagine.

"Aenyx!" Sigismund exclaimed. "I thought you were leading the war party's assault upon Aeris!"

"I had a change of heart," the griffin related as his claws clutched the sand. "I delegated Lieutenant Raven Whitecrest to lead the strike. Her team will find and retrieve any griffin eggs from the Golden Hatchery and carry them to a safe location that only we know of."

"But why are you coming with us?" Sigismund asked, scratching his head in disbelief. There was an irresistible awe-struck smile on his face.

"Because the fate of Solarius is more important than merely the fate of Aeris," Aenyx replied. "I pray only that the Golden Hatchery is safe beneath the rubble on Mount Rhaemor. As for the bulk of my comrades, they shall remain here in Hypernea to help our allies defend Stormkeep, should the shadow dragon army come for us. We are a stronger adversary together, and when I return after seeing our visit to the pirate king, who I am sure shall be most persuaded by my mighty claws, then I shall return with haste to lead the joint armies and strike the shadow dragon army itself. For now, my primary interest is to ensure your safety, Sigismund. After all we've been through together and the joint visions we shared at the Arch Crystal, it is our sacred duty to see that better world together."

Sigismund was so touched by the griffin's words that tears welled up in the deep pools of his ice-blue eyes.

"My dear friend, Aenyx," he replied. "That is a sacrifice beyond what anyone is calling for. Aren't you concerned about your homeland?"

"My homeland?" Aenyx responded thoughtfully. "My homeland is wherever my friends are. I learned that harsh lesson when I was betrayed by the Guardians, save for my mentor, Phoenix Stormguard. When you renamed the ship *Phoenix*, I realized that my destiny is to remain by your side and see this mission through. We shall liberate Aeris's ancestral home in due time. For now, Aeris is wherever we griffins call home."

Aenyx flapped his wings again, demonstrating their power. Sigismund had grown to love that sound.

"I am so relieved," Sigismund said. "If only Druix were here. I wonder where he is now…"

Aenyx bent his head and lay flat on the beach while Sigismund and Melanie mounted him, their rucksacks slung across their backs. The griffin rose into the clear blue sky, pausing only momentarily to adjust to their weight, and then he bore them carefully to the pier. Traveris and

Manfred were waiting there, standing on the wooden planks while the sailors carried their belongings on board.

Once Sigismund and Melanie arrived upon Aenyx, they climbed off his back and threw their sacks on the pier.

"Prince Sigismund, I believe you have the honors," Manfred said and handed him a bottle of fine red wine.

"Everyone off the ship!" Sigismund shouted to the sailors, who looked at him quizzically before they clambered down onto the pier. Roughly three dozen sailors lined the dock all the way to the shore.

Sigismund looked at Manfred, who nodded the go-ahead sign.

"In honor of our allies from Aeris and our fallen comrade Phoenix Stormguard, I dub the *Phoenix*!" he yelled and then struck the wine bottle with all his might on a metal knob on the ship's stern. It shattered and exploded blood-red wine upon the hull, and it slowly dripped from its wooden planks onto the waterline.

"Hurray!" Melanie exclaimed.

Aenyx's eyes shone with pride.

"A damn waste of fine wine, if you ask me," Traveris remarked ruefully. Melanie rapped him on the arm.

"We must dispense with the formalities," Manfred said after reflection. "Blackblade's finest marauders must be hot on our trail, and it is now up to us and the *Phoenix* to reach the pirate king before we risk a fatal naval encounter with those killers."

"Agreed, counselor," Sigismund said. "Men and women, secure our belongings below deck!"

The sailors filed by one by one, and a bearded man with leathery skin glared at him condescendingly before boarding the ship with a shockingly nimble leap onto the rope ladder and a quick climb to the deck. Sigismund turned and gave a sarcastic bow.

The file of sailors on the pier was a most unexpected sight. One of the pirates was shorter than the rest and remarkably curvaceous. Sigismund thought the buccaneer possessed the broadest chest he had ever seen. She was dressed in a black leather outfit with a V-shaped collar. The pirate wore a black captain's hat, and a cutlass hung from a thick black belt loosely fastened around her waist.

As the bedeviling figure approached, a set of deep blue crystalline eyes—bluer than any waters he had ever beheld—twinkled and locked upon his own eyes. The sparkle within her irises was even more magnificent than the sunlight dancing upon the rippling ocean waves at first morning light. They shimmered with a defiant gleam that bewildered him.

"Best get your sea legs beneath you, Prince," she caustically remarked as she passed him by. "You won't find life at sea nearly as comfortable as that feather bed where you snooze the morning away."

"Wait!" Sigismund shouted as he watched the shipmate walk away. Her voluptuous hips displayed a hypnotizing gait altogether unexpected for a pirate, let alone a pirate so presumptuous as to address him with such dismissive tones.

"Who are you to talk to me that way?" he exclaimed. "And what do you know of my royal quarters?"

She turned briskly and removed her leather cap, shaking free a mane of black hair that splashed wildly upon her shoulders like roaring waterfalls. Her skin was a cinnamon color, toasted from her long days at sea, where the sun's rays beamed down upon shipbound wanderers with relentless ferocity. Her face was taut and her body well-toned; her flashing eyes displayed an intense readiness, perhaps even a capacity for sudden violence, which he was unaccustomed to seeing in a woman.

"I am Dawn Stryker," she said with a fierce grin. "And I am the captain of this ship. It is my responsibility to know the proclivities of all those who board my vessel, even royalty like yourself, who deigns to rename a captured ship. You are most fortunate that I find your designation… well-chosen."

The captain's accent was lyrical and mesmerizing.

"One more thing, your royal highness," she added. "All of your fortunes and all of your titles won't save you from the sea, which knows no master. There is only one thing between you and her capricious nature, which dazzles you with beauty one day and drowns you mercilessly in its fathomless depths the next: Me. Luckily for you, I know how to massage her and sweet-talk her and cajole her into doing our bidding. So climb aboard—if you dare."

She smiled smugly to herself, then returned her leather cap and gave a tug at its rim. Captain Stryker turned on her heels sharply and darted up the rope ladder to board the *Phoenix*.

"A female captain?" Melanie remarked loudly enough for all to hear. "Just when I thought I had seen it all. I must get to know her at once!"

Melanie enthusiastically bolted toward the ship, where Traveris Bane was standing by. He held his hand out and helped her cross over onto the rope ladder. She carefully climbed aboard.

"Women," Traveris dryly remarked as Sigismund approached. "Welcome to their world."

Sigismund shot Traveris a consternated expression, then abruptly sprang onto the rope ladder. He scrambled up the hull onto the ship's deck. The prince regent was followed by Manfred, who gratefully accepted the help of the Kindly Knight. Traveris was the last to board the *Phoenix*.

All on board, the crew prepared to embark upon their treacherous voyage. The sailors began to work their magic, climbing the rigging, unfurling the square sails, and drawing the anchor. Standing upon the prow, the company felt the roiling waves of the deep green sea gently toss the ship to and fro, merely a subtle hint of the watery forces the sea could conjure up. Sigismund stood by Melanie, while Manfred was positioned near the front of the prow, his wizard staff planted firmly on the deck. Aenyx flew upon the outstretched stem and spread his wings like a figurehead that had come to life. They gazed ahead at the limitless unknown.

A sudden jolt buckled their legs. They were now at sea.

CHAPTER 46

SALUSTRIUS THE WISE

Silvestria bolted forward into the Wysterian forest. The pegacorn jumped over fallen branches and leapt over trickling brooks as she led the fairy deeper and deeper into the great unknown. Occasionally, she bounded particularly high and would stretch her wings out as wide as possible to catch flight and glide playfully. Miranda Sunray trailed eagerly behind and marveled at the creature's elegance with great amazement.

They continued apace for the remainder of the day, pausing only for the pegacorn to drink from a stream or to nibble on the local vegetation. As the hours wore on and the light darkened within the forest, the once-vivid colors of the Wysterian groves began to fade to pale pastels. It started to grow grayer and sadder, and Miranda felt an ominous feeling welling up. The shadows stretched longer, and the multihued colors of the forests grew increasingly muted along with them. Before she knew it, the trees were devoid of colorful vines, and the tree branches hung sparse and barren. A chill wind gusted through the trees, and she knew that something was amiss in this mystical land.

Just as the sun sank to the horizon, shining with a final burst of orange-crimson light, Silvestria and Miranda reached the edge of the forest. Before them was a wide and empty field leading onward without reprieve for an unknown distance. The grass was no longer green, but it was gray—literally *gray*. Miranda Sunray grew weak with horror at the sight. It was like the mass natural death that she had witnessed in Hypernea—except worse. Much worse.

"Silvestria!" Miranda bellowed. "What—what happened here?" She could scarcely believe her eyes. It was terrifying to behold.

"There is a m-m-menacing force on the other side of this field," she replied sadly. "It is m-m-much farther to the south, but it has been growing for years, and it has been poisoning our lands. It m-m-may even have pitted m-my naturally kind-hearted brethren against one another. But one thing I kn-know for sure—the one being w-who knows the m-most about it is in a cottage east of here. The w-w-wizard Salustrius."

"Finally!" she said. "We must go find him at once!"

They raced against the dying light and over the ghastly field until they spotted a tiny gray fleck. Not another structure could be seen across the nondescript panorama. It had to be the wizard's cottage.

"There!" Miranda shouted. "Let us fly!"

The newfound allies sped with all their might to reach the wizard's cottage. The fading light receded as the glowing orb sank to the very edge of the world, its last efforts to resist its nightly fate futile. The sun was beneath the horizon. Twilight spread to conquer the open skies. As violent rays unfolded across the horizon, the green, ghostly fingers of the southern aurora could be seen twirling in the sky. They seemed like skeletal hands reaching upward to the crystalline stars, coldly watching like aloof sovereigns on their distant thrones, waiting to grasp them in their ravenous clutches and drag them down into the starving earth to swallow them. It was a surreal and disconcerting sight.

At last, the fairy and the pegacorn reached the wizard's little abode. Its stone chimney was puffing out ethereal tufts of smoke. As the two stood for a moment and looked upon the cottage, the smoke unfurled to write a message to the visitors: W-E-L-C-O-M-E.

"Oh, this has to be it!" Miranda exclaimed.

"W-w-why yes," Silvestria replied. "This is the home of Salustrius the W-W-Wise."

As the two approached, the door opened by itself. A golden glow spilled out upon the gray, shadowy terrain.

"Come, friends; do not be afraid!" a voice emanated from the doorway.

The pegacorn led the way to the cottage. The winged unicorn halted suddenly and stood by the doorway. She turned back and motioned her spiraling horn toward the entranceway twice to nudge the fairy to enter first. Miranda looked at her nervously and proceeded into the wizard's home.

As she crossed over the threshold into the cottage, the heavy oak door shut behind her of its own accord, slamming with an abrupt thud. Miranda zipped back toward the door with sudden fear.

"Have no worries, dear Miranda," an elderly wizard with a pale gray cloak said in a reassuring voice. "We have no room in here for our friend Silvestria, whose marvelous wings could knock over my numerous potions and tinctures. Some of them are quite…irreplaceable."

The wizard smiled at Miranda, who noticed that the elderly gentleman had a genial face. His fuzzy gray eyebrows had grown like furry caterpillars, and they raised slightly upon his brow to give him a bemused expression. His eyes were cloudy white with two black dots like eclipsed moons. The inordinately tall man motioned with a crooked finger toward the many shelves that lined the walls. They were lined with bottles of every imaginable size—flasks with frothy brews of dark purple, bright maroon, and iridescent blue. There were tiny glass jars with moldy green herbs and clumpy black mushrooms. Oversized tomes with leathery red and brown covers and golden-fringed pages abounded. Some were slumped on shelves and others lay open on the many stools and tables. Their pages were covered with cursive writing in foreign languages, sketches of various fauna, sundry flora, and elaborate contraptions, as well as handwritten notes and scribbled markings. It seemed that this wizard was a collector, a scholar, a curator, and an investigator of many fascinating and obscure objects, both natural and arcane.

"But I have left the window open for her to grace our presence," he said reassuringly. "This is not the first time that Silvestria has been my guest."

"Hellllooo," Silvestria said as she poked her head through the open window.

"Hello," Salustrius replied with a mirthful laugh. Miranda wanted to join in the pleasantries, but it was all too odd for her to know how to react. She looked upon them curiously and decided to merely listen to what the wizard had to say.

The wizard was slightly too tall for his humble cottage, and his floppy gray cap scraped the rafters. He plopped down upon an old rocking chair that seemed to be rickety and worn from numerous years of constant use. Salustrius looked upon Miranda with a kind, inviting expression.

"Now, I know you have a very important message for me because you are in the employ of my colleague, Manfred the Magnificent, who is an esteemed member of the Mighty Three," he began. "Furthermore, you have many questions for me, which I am quite prepared to answer."

Miranda nodded slowly. She was not sure if the wizard's knowing salutation was due to his omniscience or merely a pretense so she gulped and looked upon him attentively.

"Go on…" he coaxed and then rolled his hands to gesture that she was free to speak.

"Hypernea…is under siege," she began in a quavering voice. "Aeris has already fallen. The shadow dragons have been unleashed upon the northern lands by the Dread Commander. And worst of all, we have heard ominous rumors of an unspeakable force growing in these southern lands. We do not know what to make of these whisperings, but we have come to call it The Never-Was.'

"Mm-hmm," the wizard said and screwed up his eyes, leaning back in his rocking chair. "Mm-hmm."

Salustrius reached inside his cloak and produced a puzzling little red pouch, which Miranda imagined must contain a magical powder or sacred charm that he would bestow upon them to ensure their safe journey. The mage then patted the other side of his cloak with his left hand until he found what he was seeking.

"A-ha!" he said in a gravelly voice.

What secrets must this wizard keep? Miranda wondered to herself.

At last, he produced the item and fumbled it in his long, aged fingers before finally twirling it forward. It was a tobacco pipe. "You must forgive me, kind guests. Smoking helps me conjure up the most distant thoughts that lie in the deepest, darkest recesses of this ancient mind," he said and tapped the pipe on his noggin. "When speaking about the most arcane and powerful magics, I find it is best to choose my words…carefully."

The wizard reclined in his rocking chair, and his eyes tilted toward the ceiling. Without looking down, he stuffed a few tobacco leaves into his pipe with his brown-tipped fingers. Miranda coughed at the sweet, acrid smell. The mage brought the tobacco pipe to his lips, then snapped his fingers to summon little orange-red flames on his fingertips. He inserted one into the tobacco bowl and puffed a few times. Smoke began pouring from the pipe, and, obviously satisfied, he snapped the fires off as deftly as he had brought them into being.

"Yes, most carefully," he repeated. Salustrius rocked the chair gently. His eyes were upturned toward the ceiling, as if lost in thought. Miranda studied the wizard's face and noticed that his eyes had suddenly rolled back into his head, exposing only the white sclera.

The smoke from the tobacco pipe gathered like a cloud above the wizard's head. It grew darker and thicker against the room's candlelight. Slowly, so slowly that Miranda thought she was imagining things, it began to take shape above him. It began to furl and roil into the shape of a long, snaking serpent and sprouted two bat-like wings. She watched the vision in utter amazement, too afraid to speak.

The wizard continued to meditate in his entranced state. The shadowy dragon figure then transformed into the shape of an ominous, leering, dragon-shaped helmet, so wicked and evil-looking that Miranda Sunray began to look away but found that she could not. She was too entranced by the shapes forming above the mage's head. Lastly, the smoke formed into the shape of the Arch Crystal. And with a sudden *poof*, the smoke instantaneously dissipated and vaporized into the night air.

The wizard's eyes rolled back into proper orbit. He leaned forward, shook his head from side to side, and then looked at Miranda and then at Silvestria.

"Where…was I?" he asked. His guests were speechless.

"Right!" he exclaimed. "I have traced your destiny, Miranda Sunray, and know all that might befall us should things continue upon this path. I hope you will forgive me for being so nosy, for I find these matters are too grave to waste time with idle chatter. We must get right to the heart of it. I know how to help you and your company, but it requires an urgent course of action."

He stood slowly, his legs straining considerably to lift the tall mage from his rocking chair. Salustrius set down his tobacco pipe, which was no longer belching smoke. The mage walked over to the shelf on his left, and he began searching his archive of potions and potables. He clinked a few glass bottles and moved a few long-necked flasks, mumbling to himself about where he might have put it.

"Eureka!" the wizard finally exclaimed.

Salustrius walked back to his guests, bottle in hand. He held it up in the candlelight, so Miranda could see it was a small green plant with roots suspended in clear liquid.

"This, my dear," the wizard said with a gleam in his eye, "is Angel's Breath."

She gasped with excitement. "How did you know?"

"Lovely Miranda, it is my job to know," he replied. "I am a wizard, after all. Now, take this back to Hypernea at once with our friend the pegacorn, who possesses a remarkable magic that even the Dread Commander himself fears. It is her destiny to change the course of Solarius's history, but it is vital that we take action now, should Dracus Imprimus nullify that with his own powerful sorcery."

The wizard walked over to a small chest near the wall and opened the lock with a wave of his hand. It opened and revealed leather bags, belts, and pouches. He looked quickly through it and found the riding bag and harness he was looking for. He walked over to Silvestria and patted her on the snout before placing the contraption upon her neck and securing it. He then held the bottle up one last time.

"You are not to open this bottle until you have reached Hypernea and are able to plant it," he said with a stern expression of warning. "This is one of the last specimens of Angel's Breath in all of Wysteria, for it became endangered when the Diluvian Streams and Raging Rivers ran dry. It is in a state of suspended animation until the bottle is opened. You could say I literally put time in a bottle."

He smiled wryly to himself and then placed the bottle in the leather bag around Silvestria's neck.

"As for The Never-Was," he said and paused thoughtfully. "It is imperative that we confront this destructive force together. I believe that there is one among you in the north who possesses a mystical object—a crystal shard from the Arch Crystal, which is capable of harnessing The Could-Be."

"Prince Sigismund!" Miranda exclaimed.

"Yes, that is the young man," he said and nodded thoughtfully. "That is the prince who will be king. When you return, you must tell Manfred that he must bring him here, for I live on the very outskirts of The Never-Was," Salustrius pointed southward out the window.

"The Never-Was is not merely destructive, it is a force that quite literally undoes the existence of all it touches. It unravels the fabric of space and time itself—not that I expect you to quite understand all of that—turning nature inside-out and running time backward. It is thus forming a gaping, unquenchable void in our midst that is swallowing everything in its domain. It *is* growing and it *is* spreading—and its insidious influence is being felt quite imperceptibly to all of the wildlife here, which are losing their children, and just as tragically, their parents. If they wander into its path, their children vanish instantly. It is quite a horrifying phenomenon, and I have never seen anything like it in all my wanderings. The only thing I expect you to fully grasp about it is that it must be stopped. And to do that, we must defeat the originator and author of this monstrous force: Dracus Imprimus."

The fairy was trembling uncontrollably, and Silvestria's eyes were wide, as if she had been spooked by a field mouse but was too terrified to move.

"We must gather allies, my darling Miranda; do not be afraid, for we will do just that," the wizard said reassuringly. His kind eyes sparkled in the candlelight. "Rest here 'til morn, my child, with our good pegacorn friend here, whose magic is quite potent enough to assist us in our quest. At the break of day, you and Silvestria must fly like never before to Hypernea to deliver the Angel's Breath that shall be most useful to fighting the plague upon the Jeweled Islands. Dry and powder the leaves and add one spoon to every hundred drops of clear water. Then take the tincture to the pirate king and exchange it for his aid and any reward he sees fit to bestow on our righteous cause."

Miranda swallowed hard and nodded her tiny head up and down to reassure the wizard that she understood everything. Silvestria whinnied nervously.

"But what about you?" she asked. "Can you come with us?"

"Oh, I would love to," Salustrius replied, "but I must secure allies to the far east who would be most troubled at the developments afflicting our world. It is of utmost importance to inform the ancient and secretive order of Thorastrian Elves of these ill tidings. They reside near the Tiberian Sea. The Baldurian Dwarves might be more stubborn to move, for they are a greedy lot, but not so greedy that they cannot understand certain death on their doorstep. If I can move them to sail east across the Tiberian Sea to carry out a joint assault on Noctera, that might prove to be a decisive blow against the Dread Commander. And we can be assured that the rock trolls of Cyrrhenia shall inevitably awaken, just as they did the last time our world was thrust into a raging war, the likes of which wiped out nearly all life on Solarius. We have only just begun to recover from that terrible calamity, and I am afraid we must bravely face this sad prospect again."

Miranda was struggling to follow the monumental impact of all these tidings, but she was grateful that the wizard was able to anticipate her instructions from Manfred. They had known each other so long that it seemed they could read each other's thoughts.

"But…but how will you get there, oh wise Salustrius?" she asked inquisitively.

The old mage cracked a smile that covered his entire face with wrinkled lines. His face was like an old, leathery map crisscrossed with rivers and tributaries, which led to two shining pools reflecting the wizard's sage and genial thoughts.

"As you may have heard, I have at my beck and call the swiftest pegasus this planet has ever seen—Philemonia the Fleet!" he exclaimed. "Why, in a matter of days I will have flown across the continent of Terrastria and will be consulting with beings who have never dreamt of Wysteria, Hypernea, Aeris, or the like. It will take quite the feat of diplomacy to persuade them to join us in our cause, but I find that when pressed, I can be quite…persuasive."

Miranda Sunray had no doubt about that. She yawned. It was growing late, and she was exhausted from her journey. The wizard was a kind enough host, but his vast knowledge and keen insight into the workings of their threatened world were a bit much to follow.

She fluttered over to a darkened corner and soon fell into the deepest sleep. The fairy's golden light flickered and then winked out.

CHAPTER 47

THE DARKEST RECKONING

Druix soared high into the midnight sky over the northern Hypernean wilderness. The full moon radiated a milky, white glow that coated his serpentine frame with a ghostly silhouette. The ethereal light traced a thin line along his barbed tail all the way around his gliding wings and up to his horned moondrake head. Prospero clung to the midnight-blue serpent. The wizard's white robes fluttered behind him in the breeze as the moondrake pressed toward the farthest reaches of Noctera.

Noctera was a land of utter darkness. It was a land of smoldering heaths and heaping mounds of black coal, of crystalline onyx and slabs of obsidian, of absolute desperation and complete desolation. The infernal wilderness that sprawled endlessly and ruinously over the northern wastes for unknown distances was far too dangerous for mankind to tread upon. If one had ever mustered the temerity to cross the godforsaken land, the unfortunate traveler would have faced certain death from above in the guise of countless shadow dragons and death from below in the form of boiling geysers and sulfurous pits. The stygian tundra was brimming with bubbling pools of sulfuric acid, overlaying a swirling subterranean cauldron of molten-hot lava. It was hell—or as close to hell as ever had been realized upon the planet of Solarius.

Dracus Imprimus was hellbent on making things worse—far worse—for the curse-afflicted inhabitants of the war-torn planet. Noctera was an idyllic paradise compared to the fate the Dread Commander had devised in its twisted mind. What the being desperately sought in its hateful soul wasn't simply for there to be nothing, but for there to be *absolute nothing.* Even…*less than nothing.* Life undone and never having existed.

Prospero pressed the moondrake to fly ever onward, northward into this unceasingly bleak vision of oblivion, which was chilling even his serpentine bones. As the moon receded into the orb-swallowing void of the horizon, Druix began to question the wizard's bearings.

Surely, the mage knows the route to Lunastria? he thought, feeling something was not quite right.

"Prospero," Druix finally grumbled aloud, "do you know where we are going?"

"Have no fear, my loyal steed!" the White Druid replied. "First, we must visit a trusted friend. Only then shall we proceed upon our journey to Lunastria to visit our future moondrake allies."

"You have…friends here?" Druix replied nervously.

"Ahh, yes," Prospero replied. "You shall meet my associate soon. And then you shall learn."

Druix disliked the sound of the druid's words, but he knew him to be a noble sage, even a member of the reputed Mighty Three! If a wizard like Manfred the Magnificent trusted the White Druid, then he was in no position to judge. Besides, he needed the druid to persuade his fellow moondrakes to join him in the life-or-death struggle against Dracus Imprimus. That was a daunting task he was simply not ready to face alone.

"Do not worry, Druix," the White Druid finally said after a period of silence. "We are almost there. And then tonight's flight shall be over."

"There—there it is!" he shouted a moment later. "There is the Obsidian Fortress!"

Druix blinked his silvery eyes and peered into the unfathomable blackness of Noctera spread out around him. A distant cliffside on the horizon overlooked a shadowy valley that appeared to have no bottom. Above it all, an ominous structure loomed over the devastated wasteland. Two jagged towers of uneven length projected defiantly into the sky like two daggers ripping into the belly of the night. This dark fortress intended to birth a world of unending misery.

The moondrake reared back in a sudden fit of unrelenting terror as if to turn away, but the druid was ready. Prospero held his wizard's staff aloft and locked the moondrake's head in place. The moondrake's mind was soon flooded with a white blankness that poured throughout his thoughts and momentarily wiped them as clean as a slate. His will was suddenly not entirely his own, for he felt the irresistible urge to do whatever the White Druid commanded. His wings were drained of their own strength to keep going, but he nonetheless felt them beating of their own accord. It was a mortifying feeling—being led against one's will toward a catastrophic fate.

"That's right, Druix," Prospero whispered into the captive drake's ear while clinging to his elongated neck. "Soon you—and all of your moondrake friends—shall swear their unquestioning loyalty to the Dread Commander, and thus you shall become the rightful property of your new overlord. And let me forewarn you, my sweet moondrake, the Dread Commander does *not* suffer treachery. You shall learn that lesson firsthand."

Tears began to well up in the moondrake's silvery eyes as he felt himself being led into a deep crevasse in the cliffs below the Obsidian Fortress. His heart thumped wildly in his chest as he became cloaked in shadows. Druix contemplated the terrible fate Dracus Imprimus must have in store for him.

Druix came to the agonizing realization of why he had been summoned. The dragonking had discovered his father's warning! It was the terrible truth, and yet he was murdered for it. His own escape and his flight from Mount Kildrath must have been something the Dread Commander had not anticipated. Worst of all, his being was wracked by the total, hopeless desperation that came from knowing he was now powerless to warn the others that the White Druid Prospero was a traitor.

The fear overwhelmed him. Druix knew no hope was left for him in this merciless world, and he was ready to succumb to his fate.

The moondrake landed within the hollowed-out heart of the Obsidian Fortress. His claws splashed in wet puddles of sulfuric acid. His upbringing upon Mount Kildrath had made his dragonesque scales resistant to the caustic, odorous brew. The pungent scent was familiar to him, and it opened his flared nostrils. Prospero clung to his back, not yet daring to set foot upon the cavern floor. They slowly approached; the drake walked catlike down an exceedingly dark corridor so pitch black that it challenged even his incomparable night vision to see ahead within it.

Druix's halting footsteps squelched on the floor of the wet cavern. Each step in the acrid puddles echoed down the corridor, frightening him tremendously. There seemed to be no other life around at first, but then he suddenly felt like dozens of eyes were all around him. He could detect fuming hot breath. It didn't smell like sulfur. The fumes were smoky—like dragon's breath.

When they came at last to the end of the tunnel, Druix paused to absorb the immense hall stretched out before him. In the distance, he beheld a faintly glinting presence that possessed two red pinpoints for eyes surveying its domain.

The Dread Commander.

Druix's knees wobbled as he was coaxed to forge onward into the very pit of evil. The White Druid's spell had bound the creature strongly, but the moondrake's will was more formidable than he had counted on. The moondrake was refusing obeisance to this embodiment of pure hatred. The druid would have to break him completely.

"Onward!" the White Druid shouted.

His terrifying voice cast off all appearances of kindness and patience that the druid had wielded craftily for years—decades even—to gain the misplaced trust of his friends and allies.

I will not break, I will not break.... Druix thought to himself, repeating this mantra in his mind as he pushed forward into the Dread Commander's chamber against the strongest will that he could muster.

"You shall break, my young Druix. Oh yes, you shall break," Prospero whispered into his ear.

"Enough!"

The Dread Commander's all-encompassing voice rang out in a cacophonous roar of voices that seemed to emanate from the walls of the Obsidian Fortress itself. They came crashing down upon his ears like black rain, penetrating Druix's consciousness, causing him to momentarily lose his bearings. As his body began to collapse to the floor, the seated Dread Commander lifted forth its iron-fisted hand as if to catch him. Druix was captured within the spectral grasp of the dragonking. Its grip was so omnipotent that he instantly lost all pretense of freeing himself.

His will melted away, and his serpentine body went limp. The moondrake was now at the complete mercy of the Dread Commander. And as countless beings had discovered before, the Dread Commander had no mercy.

"This must be the moondrake," its voice hissed.

Out of the utter blackness of the great hall, the reflective eyes of innumerable shadow dragons slowly came forward to surround Druix. The formidable great serpents encircled him in an unbreakable ring that promised fire and fury should he attempt to escape. Yet they knew that even the mere hope of escape was beyond anyone who had made it all the way to the throne room of the dragonking.

"Why, you are not quite typical, though, are you, Druix?" it continued. "Your hide—it is midnight blue. And if I am not mistaken, your eyes had once been black, but now they are silver. Do you know why that must be, Druix?"

The Dread Commander paused momentarily, savoring the suspense.

"Because you destroyed the Arch Crystal!" the dragonking roared. "It drained you of my poison, the poison that I had put there to lead you to the Arch Crystal and to destroy it for me!"

"Lies," the moondrake whispered.

"Lies?!" the voices again rang out within the great hall. Their reverberating intensity inflicted the severest pain upon his mind. But if he was going to die, he was going to die for speaking the truth, just as his father did.

"My eyes," Druix said weakly. "They are *my own*. They have always been my own. And the future I saw within the Arch Crystal…it is *glorious*, and you cannot stop it."

The Dread Commander was speechless. The dragonking sat quietly for a moment, immersed in deep thought, pondering the moondrake's intrepid response, seething in fury upon the obsidian throne. It was apparent that the creature had something that was invaluable even for it: A hidden knowledge of the Arch Crystal. It was maddening for the dragonking to consider that the moondrake possessed a secret that was impossible for it to behold.

Dracus Imprimus could not restrain his contempt for this impetuous creature who dared speak to him in such equivocating tones. He twisted his iron-fisted glove sideways and tightened his grip upon the beast's throat. He squeezed harder and harder, crushing the life out of the crumpling moondrake, and the White Druid slid from the serpent's back onto the obsidian floor.

"You…shall tell me all!" Dracus Imprimus shouted, its speech manifesting in a multitude of voices that was tormenting the moondrake's soul.

The dragonking lifted the moondrake with one hand from afar. Druix rose higher into the air until he was suspended in the midst of the chamber. The moondrake's body contorted into the most torturous of poses. It was pure anguish.

"No," Druix faintly whispered. He knew this word would seal his fate. He would choose death before service to evil.

"Very well," the Dread Commander replied, quite content to extinguish the creature's lifeforce in as agonizing a fashion as he could imagine, until there was nothing left but an empty husk of a pitiful being limply begging to spill its guts.

"You saw a vision…" the Dread Commander finally said. "And it was destroyed when the Arch Crystal was destroyed, was it not? Every shard of the crystal was vaporized from its release of energy, obliterating all potential of creating that world that you beheld."

"Not every shard," a voice said coolly in the pitch-black darkness.

Morana stepped out of the shadows in a draping black gown and glossy black boots that were licked by the faintest glimmer of light.

"That's right, my dearest Dracus," she said with an airy voice. "One of the two remaining shards of the Arch Crystal hangs here upon my neck."

The High Sorceress abruptly tore open the black corset strapped across her chest, breaking apart the leathery threads that tethered it together. Between her white breasts was a silver chain bearing one brilliant shard of crystal. Its white light beamed across the great hall, blinding the eyes of the Dread Commander with a vision too radiant for the evil being to behold. The spell upon Druix relented, and he fell to the ground with a sickening thud.

"Morana!" the White Druid shouted. "You traitorous wretch! How dare you assail our dark lord in such a manner! We shall feed you to the shadow dragons!"

"Betrayal is something you know all too well, Prospero," the High Sorceress spat contemptuously.

While the Dread Commander lay incapacitated on his throne, stunned by the unadulterated vision of The Could-Be, Prospero raised his staff to strike the sorceress. But at the last moment, she held up her orbed scepter to block the blow.

Morana backed away toward the slumped-over body of Druix, who lay senseless in a curled heap upon the floor. As she backed into his shattered frame, her hand lightly grazed his crown, which awakened him. Her scepter glowed with an eerie light, and she held it aloft before the White Druid and the shadow dragon audience. The great serpents were hesitant to act, seeing that the Dread Commander was still upon his knees near the throne. Morana was nearly as formidable a commander as the dragonking himself. They knew the hefty price for crossing the High Sorceress.

Morana swung her legs over the back of the midnight-blue moondrake, who was slowly regaining consciousness. The black gown that had barely obscured her semi-naked frame trailed airily behind her and draped upon the moondrake's back.

"Rise, Druix," she whispered encouragingly, still holding her orbed scepter aloft.

"Morana—what are you doing?" Prospero implored.

"Something I should have done a long time ago," she tersely snapped. "I let you take advantage of me for far too long, wicked Prospero. While I was still a young lady studying under your care, you corrupted me with your self-serving lies, and you took my innocence—by *force*! I was too vulnerable to resist, too hungry for my own power to fight back. I *needed* you—and that is what I hated most! I was weak…far too weak. And that is why I fled into the clutches of one far more powerful than even you!"

The White Druid looked in astonishment upon Morana; she sat astride Druix, who was now rousing his body upon all four of his claws.

"And I cannot let you do to this most special of moondrakes, what you have done to me," she continued. "You seek to corrupt him. Torment him. Break him and use him up. Dispose of him as if he were nothing more than a plaything—an instrument of your own wicked ends."

Prospero hung his head in complete shame. All he could do was listen. His heart was in too weak a state to fight her harsh truth.

"Look at me now, Prospero," she continued. "And mark my words: I *used* you. And this may shock you even more: I used our fine dragonking here. He is about to discover that I *too* can be a betrayer. For although you broke my heart in different ways, you never broke my will. I bided my time for years, tolerating the heartache and the pain, hiding my true nature, veiling my true designs, not only because I was nurturing and growing my vengeance, but also because I was protecting my greatest creations."

Prospero remained silent. The woman's words had completely disarmed him. He was too stunned to contemplate what Morana was revealing to him.

She flashed a thin blood-red crease of a smile upon her contemptuous lips.

"I am not the High Sorceress!" Morana shouted.

Her voice was so loud, it reverberated off every wall. It shook the druid to his core, and he fell upon his knees. The echoes were ungodly.

Prospero had never stopped loving Morana, or so he believed. More accurately, he had clung to his own twisted conception of love. He believed that he worshipped her, when, in actuality, all the druid had ever wanted was to enslave her.

And with that, Morana flung her glowing scepter upon the uncompromising earth. Its spectral orb shattered into a million pieces, unleashing a flood of ghastly green light. Trapped souls whose life-force had been imprisoned in the orb poured out into the great hall of the Obsidian Fortress. The wraiths shrieked with unimaginably heartrending voices as they devoured their first taste of sweet liberation. They then turned their vengeance upon the shadow dragons.

"That is right, my dear Prospero!" she yelled victoriously. "That is right, my dearest Dracus Imprimus! I am *not* the High Sorceress, as you have been led to believe for all of these long, arduous years."

"Behold my true form!" she shouted. "For *I* am the Fairy Enchantress! I am the one that they call 'M'!"

Suddenly, the enchantress lifted the necklace from her neck. She held up its crystal shard, which pulsed with a bright white flash of light so intense that it instantly blinded all the foul creatures within the dark heart of the Obsidian Fortress.

Before their eyes, the black leather garb of the High Sorceress melted away and was replaced by a glowing, ephemeral gown that was draped wispily upon her slight frame. On her head was a dainty crown of tiny red jewels. Around her feminine body, the gathering forms of fairies materialized like fireflies in a bell jar. They swirled around her, enveloping her and the moondrake in encircling spheres, whirling faster and faster around them, until there was finally one last blip of light.

And then they were gone.

Druix blinked once. He found himself upon a desolate plain outside of the Obsidian Fortress.

"Ready?" he heard a soothing female voice ask.

"What for?" the moondrake replied.

"We are going to discover your true hidden potential, Druix," M replied. "We shall return triumphantly to the land of Lunastria, the ancestral land of the moondrakes, where you shall become their greatest warrior."

"And what about my friends?" Druix asked. "Shouldn't we warn them?"

"Worry not, good Druix," the fairy enchantress replied gently. "All shall come to pass within The Could-Be."

The newfound allies flew into the deep night, fleeing with utmost alacrity from the Obsidian Fortress. They left behind an unspeakable past and forged onward toward a future as limitless as the midnight skies.

They knew the vengeful dragonking would rise again. But they pressed with great haste and boundless hope to the Onyx Wastes, the birthplace of the moondrake that would change the future of Solarius.

GLOSSARY

Aenyx: A griffin who is a key contender in the Griffin Trials, known for his black eyes and determination to become a Guardian.

Aeris: The Republic of Aeris, the homeland of the griffins.

Black Viper: A venomous snake that griffin recruits must capture and swallow whole during the snake-eagling competition.

Bluetips Pride: The clannish foot soldiers and scrappy working-class griffins.

Brandon: A Stormguard recruit and friend of Aenyx.

Captius Whitecrest: A Guardian and leader of the Whitecrest Pride.

Could-Be, The: A mysterious world of limitless potential that exists as an alternate dimension accessible to mystical fairies and unlocked by special beings possessing shards of the Arch Crystal.

Dread Commander, The: Another name for Dracus Imprimus.

Dracus Imprimus: The Dread Commander, a dark and powerful being who was once a man but is now possessed by an ancient evil.

Druix Coldshadow: A young moondrake who seeks revenge for his parents' deaths, an outcast because of his black eyes and midnight-blue scales.

Equine Kingdoms: The kingdoms of Wysteria and Misericordia, which are populated by rival equine beings of pegasi and unicorns, respectively, who are in a civil war over dwindling resources.

Felix Waverly: The second-oldest brother of Prince Sigismund.

Five Prides, The: The five main groups of griffins in Aeris: Stormguard, Goldeneyrie, Whitecrest, Bluetip, and Pridewatcher.

Forgotten Forest: A forest east of Waverly Castle.

Gabriel: A Goldeneyrie recruit and rival of Aenyx.

Giacquomo Spright: A jester who recites a prophecy about Prince Sigismund.

Golden Hatchery: The place where griffin eggs are kept and hatched.

Goldeneyrie: A secretive class of counselors and diplomats among the griffins.

Great Griffin Wars, The: The wars between the griffins and the moondrakes.

Griffin Elections, The: The elections to select new Guardians.

Griffin Grapple, The: A single combat event in the Griffin Trials.

Griffin Trials: A series of competitions that griffin recruits must pass to become full members of a Pride and potentially a Guardian.

Hall of Guardians: A mausoleum where Guardians are laid to rest.

High Council, The: The Guardian council members who decide on critical matters of state.

Hypernea: The cursed kingdom ruled by the Waverly House, suffering from a blight and famine for eighteen years.

***Hypernean Chronicles, The*:** A history book written by Manfred the Magnificent that is treasured by Prince Sigismund.

Jasper Stormguard: The Pridemaster of the Stormguard Pride.

Jax Waverly: The oldest brother of Prince Sigismund.

Killian Waverly: The youngest brother of Prince Sigismund.

King Gerald Waverly: The ruler of Hypernea who blames his son Sigismund for the kingdom's curse.

Laketown: A village near the Mountains of Mordrath.

Lofty Council, The: The ruling council of the Guardians.

Manfred the Magnificent: A wizard and archivist whose tales are treasured by Prince Sigismund, and a member of the Mighty Three.

Mighty Three, The: The wizards who contained the curse of Dracus Imprimus by binding it with the vast potential of the Arch Crystal: Manfred the Magnificent, Salustrius the Wise, and the White Druid Prospero.

Mirrhenian Lake: The lake to the north of Laketown.
Misericordia: The dying lands of the unicorns, located to the east of Wysteria.
Moondrakes: Dragon-like creatures that live on Mount Kildrath and are enemies of the griffins.
Moonchasing: Griffin term for hunting moondrakes at night.
Mount Kildrath: The home of the moondrakes.
Mount Rhaemor: The tri-peaked mountain that is the home of the griffins and the location of the Griffin Trials.
Mountains of Mordrath: A mountain range near the northern border of Aeris.
Never-Was, The: An ominous force that swallows existence itself. It undoes space and time and vanquishes the history of those that fall into its grasp.
Night-stalking: Griffin term for patrolling the night skies for the enemies of Aeris.
Obsidian Fortress: The dark fortress of Dracus Imprimus, located deep in the heart of Noctera.
Onyx Wastes: The southern plains where the Great Griffin Wars took place.
Pegasus: A winged horse that possesses the ability to fly throughout Solarius.
Phoenix Stormguard: A Guardian and leader of the Stormguard Pride.
Pridewatchers: The caregivers of the griffin young and watchers of the Golden Hatchery.
Prince Sigismund: The youngest prince of Waverly House, who is believed to be the source of the kingdom's curse.
Princess Melanie: A MacCallister princess who warns Prince Sigismund of danger.
Queen Galadria Waverly: The graceful and loving mother of Prince Sigismund.
Raven Whitecrest: A Whitecrest recruit and friend of Aenyx.
Reginald: The old tutor of Prince Sigismund.
Republic of Aeris, The: The homeland of the griffins.
Rhapsodia: The mother of Druix Coldshadow.

Ronax: A Stormguard recruit and friend of Aenyx.

Salustrius the Wise: A sage wizard and one of the Mighty Three.

Seraphinus: The father of Druix Coldshadow, a moondrake who fought in the Great Griffin Wars.

Shadow Dragons: Dark and powerful dragons allied with Dracus Imprimus.

Snake-Eagling: A race to capture and swallow a Black Viper as part of the Griffin Trials.

Solarius: The world of the Fallen Empires.

Sophia Pridewatcher: A Guardian and leader of the Pridewatchers.

Stormguard: One of the Prides of griffins, known for their fierce warriors.

Sulfurous Wastes: A desolate area south of Mount Kildrath.

Talus Nightspell: A wizard who prophesied the curse on the kingdom and the fate of Prince Sigismund.

Taryn Waverly: The scrappiest and most daring of the Waverly brothers.

Thaddeus Waverly: The cleverest of the Waverly brothers.

Traveris Bane: A castle guard also known as the "Kindly Knight."

Tyrex Goldeneyrie: A Guardian and leader of the Goldeneyrie Pride.

Unicorns: Mystical equine creatures possessing a magic pearly horn. Feared by the moondrakes.

Waverly House: The ruling family of the Kingdom of Hypernea.

White Druid Prospero, The: A druid who is a member of the Mighty Three.

Whitecrest Pride: The wise stewards among the griffins.

Wysteria: The lands of the pegasi, which are abundant and located to the west of Misericordia.

ACKNOWLEDGMENTS

I would like to acknowledge the contributions of my wife Irina, who made this book possible. She always encouraged me to pursue my dreams and believed in my ability. I would also like to thank my children Ethan, Alexander, and Daniel for being a constant source of amusement and inspiration. I want to thank my wonderful mother Nancy for her lifelong encouragement, and my brothers Shane and Kevin, as well as my sister Emily, for the valuable memories that we've shared throughout the years.

I would like to thank all of the great editors and publishers at Permuted Press for their diligent work to get this novel to press. This includes the publisher Anthony Ziccardi for believing in the work, the publishing director Aleigha Koss for her invaluable insights, and editor Taylor Graham for helping to finalize the copy.

ABOUT THE AUTHOR

Kyle Becker is a prolific writer and successful podcaster whose highly engaging content reaches tens of millions of people each year. Previously, he was a senior managing editor and director of viral media for a top news publication, as well as a writer and producer for the leading cable news show on television. Prolific on social media, he is followed by some of the most powerful figures and influential media personalities in the United States.

He has a Master's degree in International Studies from the University of Iowa, where he focused on Russian language and literature. When he was studying for his graduate degree, he conducted socio-anthropological research in Russia, while he worked full-time as an economic news journalist. Following this adventure, he pursued a doctorate degree in political science with an emphasis in international relations and comparative politics, but departed the field after being offered an attractive position in new media. A storyteller at heart, he strives to engage readers with thought-provoking content that sparks the imagination and inspires them to seek the truth.